Lilly Cullen
HELENA, MONTANA 1894

ANN CULLEN

BOOK MONTANA   •   HELENA

This is a work of fiction. The major events, most names, and many details are real: The setting and characterizations are intended to represent typical persons and lifestyles in Helena, Montana during the 1890s.

ISBN 0-9670759-0-4

Manufactured in the United States of America

Book Montana: First Edition

Foreword

The following story is a fictional account based on the people, places, and events found in the records of:

City of Helena, Recording Office
Forestvale Cemetery
Lewis & Clark Public Library
Montana State Historical Society Library
Montana State Historical Society Photographic Archives
"The Occasional Magpie", D. McCahon

In writing this story, no point of fact was intentionally negated or ignored. All people with last names are real. The two or three without are possible. The social events are actual, down to many of the details, i.e. the color of the ladies gowns, the flowers decorating the homes, and the food served. Characterizations and interaction were fabricated to facilitate the story line.

Chapter One

Katherine loved the deep corridor of stone and brick buildings. The noise of downtown Helena seemed to echo off the walls, intensifying the wonderful feeling of being alive. But being here again, driving through the din of the towering structures in a horse drawn buggy, well, the feeling had not diminished with time. It was still the most unequaled experience in Katherine's memory, an experience that just wasn't the same anywhere else.

Her father turned their horse at Sixth and Main Street, and proceeded on. Katherine smiled as she watched him. He was a candidate in the upcoming 1894 election, and it was thought he had a good chance of winning the senate seat for Granite County. Her father was well liked by everyone at home. Why shouldn't he be? He was their doctor.

"Katherine, I need to stop at the bank before we go on to Mrs. Osterhout's," Dr. Sligh commented to his nineteen year old daughter.

Mrs. Osterhout ran a boarding house on the stylish west side where Katherine's married sister, Bessie, lived with her small family. The Slighs had often stayed there throughout the seven years since they had moved to Montana. It was much more personable than a hotel, and it had family.

Katherine's father guided their horse down past Edwards Street, and over to the side. Then he turned to his daughter. "Katie, are you coming in?"

His daughter's eyes rose to the granite building before them. Montana National Bank towered over them, higher than its neighbors, it's upper floors bathed in sunshine. "Yes," she replied quickly. She needed to stretch her legs.

Montana National was crowded inside. Katherine and her father stopped briefly at the counter, and then joined the second line to the cashiers. It was the shortest, only six deep

Katherine surveyed the people. Everyone was preoccupied with their own affairs...all except three children. Their mother was holding the infant in her left arm as her middle child clung to her skirt. The oldest was being instructed to take his pull toy to the end of the counter where he could play away from the people but still within a few feet of her. After several minutes this was accomplished. Katherine moved forward with her father as both lines tightened. A short man now stood to her left as her eyes again drifted to the little boy and his toy.

The child hid himself tightly against the near side of the counter as he slowly and carefully pulled his toy horse toward him. Katherine could almost imagine the story of ambush running through the boy's mind, when suddenly her attention was diverted up and behind the child. A bank employee was coming around the end of the counter, his vision obstructed by the load of journals he was carrying. Katherine glanced quickly at the floor. The long cord of the toy lay directly in his path.

"Excuse me, daddy," Katherine responded quickly as she darted out of line.

People slowed her progress, and before she could intervene, the inevitable happened. Katherine watched the pull toy ensnare around the banker's foot as the child suddenly emerged from his hiding place with a cry. Startled and losing his balance, the man began falling as he desperately tried to prevent landing on the boy. Journals were abandoned in mid air as the bank clerk grabbed for the counter wall, catching himself before worse could happen.

The boy screamed as the journals landed on him, and began to cry pitilessly as he turned to kick at the books. His mother was instantly at his side, pulling her son into her free arm as she glared angrily at the banker, demanding an apology.

Katherine's attention shifted to the journals scattered across the shiny floor. One had burst its binding and pages upon pages lay scattered as far as the door. Incoming customers were trying to step across or around them. Then a heavy set man came through the door and planted a dusty foot directly in the middle of one. Without stopping, he continued on his way unaware.

Katherine hastened to the far reaches of the journal pages, and quickly began picking them up before more damage was done. Within moments she had cleared the doors, and then slowed down, checking the page numbers. Now methodically adding to her stack, she retraced the progress of the mess.

"I believe those belong to me."

Katherine picked up the one remaining page, and rose. The bank clerk now stood before her. His journals were again encircled by his white sleeves, all except hers. He was not in the best mood.

"I tried to keep them in order," she offered, "but I'm afraid a couple got walked on."

"Thank you," he responded as she handed over her stack.

Without another word, he disappeared. Katherine returned to her father. He was now second in line.

"Where have you been," he asked.

Katherine glanced at the line beside them. The short man was gone. She couldn't even see the end of the counter where the mishap had occurred. "There was a little accident," she offered in explanation. "A little boy tripped someone with his toy."

Her father's attention sharpened. "That was what all the crying was about?"

Katherine nodded.

"I thought a little one was cranky because it had missed its nap," her father noted. "Was anyone hurt?"

"No," Katherine replied.

Within minutes Katherine's father finished at the bank, and the two emerged out into the fall afternoon. They leisurely strolled the short distance to the buggy.

"I wonder how your mother likes running Mrs. Osterhout's boarding house by now," Dr. Sligh commented with a smile. "She's been after me to ask Mrs. Titus if she plans on retiring any time soon. Now that we don't work for the mining company in Granite and you kids are almost grown, a boarding house in Philipsburg just might keep your mother busy, and give me a chance to develop a medical practice there." He helped his daughter into the buggy, and climbed in beside her. "Mrs. Osterhout's been gone, what, about a month now?"

"Pretty close," Katherine replied as her father directed the horse back out into the street.

Mrs. Sligh had come to Helena on Labor Day weekend to settle in before Mrs. Osterhout left on her trip to New York, and to get her brother, Charles, enrolled in school. Dr. Sligh and Katherine had stayed behind in Granite, taking care of some unfinished business with the Granite Mountain Mining Company, packing up their belongings, and helping the new doctor take over the work there. With her father running for senator, he would hardly be available for medical emergencies.

Dr. Sligh turned on Benton Avenue as the sun declined in the sky. Within moments he pulled to a stop in front of a rather large two story house. Various members of their family abruptly emerged as excited greetings were exchanged. Mrs. Sligh then ushered everyone back inside.

"How was the trip up?" Bessie inquired as her four year old daughter kept trying to hide behind her skirt.

Katherine's brother wrinkled his nose at little Margaret as the family members sat down. A smile invaded his small niece's expression.

"Just fine," Dr. Sligh replied as he suddenly dug into his pocket. Pulling out a small toy, he offered it to his granddaughter.

Margaret suddenly climbed into her grandfather's lap, taking the brightly painted wooden elephant, and turning it over and over in delight.

"Thank your grandpa," Bessie coaxed.

Little Margaret did, and planted a big kiss on his cheek. Everyone laughed with amusement as they became lost in conversation.

"Blast it all," Dr. Sligh fumed as he foraged through his luggage the following morning. His head lifted. "Katie, do you know where your mother put my ties? She can't leave anything alone, and now she's clear downstairs, and I'm running late."

"I think they're in the closet," Katherine replied.

"In the closet, I looked in the closet," Dr. Sligh retorted anxiously.

Katherine reached in, and pulled a garment away from the wall. There Dr. Sligh's ties hung in perfect order.

"Thank you," he gratefully responded as he whipped one out and flung it around his neck. He retreated to the paperwork he had spent hours reviewing the night before as he tied the knot. Then he reached for his suit coat, and shuffled the papers back into order.

"Oh shoot," he exclaimed as he picked up a bank statement, "I forgot about this." He turned to Katherine. "I told the clerk I would get this back to Mr. Smith first thing this morning."

"It goes to Montana National?" Katherine asked.

"Yes, Mr. Smith," he repeated. "He has a desk in back. Could you run it down? I'll barely make my meeting as it is."

"Yes, daddy, I'll take it down," Katherine replied.

Dr. Sligh handed her the statement, and gave her quick kiss. "You're an angel. This hasn't been my morning."

Katherine smiled. She had to agree, but then spending half the night reviewing legislation under a kerosene lamp, and oversleeping his morning call couldn't have helped. Her father hastened downstairs. She heard the front door slam.

It was a beautiful fall day when Katherine emerged from Mrs. Osterhout's. The air was crisp and cool, and leaves scattered around her feet in brilliant colors. Katherine walked briskly downtown. It was only a matter of a few blocks until she reached bustling Main Street, and then she walked the distance to Montana National Bank.

She found Mr. Smith's desk in the rear of the lobby as her father had said, but the man was not present. Katherine lingered undecided as she wondered if she should just leave the statement. The bank clerk from the preceding afternoon emerged from the office behind. He was again in shirt sleeves and garters. Recognition entered his expression.

"You're the one from yesterday, aren't you?" the man inquired.

"Yes," Katherine replied. "I was looking for Mr. Smith. Is he here?"

"He had an errand to run. May I help?"

"My father wanted me to drop this by," Katherine replied as she offered the statement.

The clerk's eyes dropped briefly to the sheet of paper, and then returned to her. "Your father is Dr. Sligh?"

"Yes, he was running late for a campaign meeting this morning, otherwise he would have brought it by personally."

"Ah, one of the legislative hopefuls," the man replied. "What position is your father running for?"

"The senate seat of Granite County," Katherine answered.

"And if he gets it?"

"Then I imagine we'll be staying the winter," Katherine replied with a smile.

"I hope he wins," the bank clerk responded pleasantly. "So your family has suitable lodgings in the mean time? The city is so over-run with people, I understand there isn't a hotel room to be found anywhere."

"Yes, we're staying at Mrs. Osterhout's," Katherine answered as she found herself studying the man before her. The clerk was ten years her senior with dark hair and sad eyes. He shifted uncomfortably.

"Were your journal pages all right," Katherine asked quickly.

"The pages were in perfect order. Thank you. ...and the one binding had already seen much better days, even before it was given that swift kick. It was due for some repair work."

"I'm glad," Katherine replied.

The banker's dark eyes were now resting on her as he made no attempt to leave. "I'd like to apologize for the unfortunate incident yesterday," he began now slowly. "I was too curt with you."

"It is true, you didn't waste words," Katherine agreed cheerfully, "but you didn't see the little boy, and I don't imagine toys are an everyday occurrence on the bank's polished floors."

"No," he responded as he relaxed a little, "they aren't -- and I had just returned from a week's vacation, and had a lot of catching up to do. Toys were the last thing on my mind."

"Well it was very nice seeing you again," Katherine offered as a faint whiff of the man's shaving soap reached her nose. "I'd better be going."

"My name is Tom Marlow," he suddenly stated, "and yours..."

"Katherine Sligh," she responded. She offered her hand as propriety dictated.

He took it gently as their eyes met. "I am very pleased to make your acquaintance," he replied, "and I hope your family will be able to stay the winter. Maybe then I'll be able to find a way to repay yesterday's kindness." He smiled.

"That isn't necessary," Katherine replied as her hand slid from his. Her heart pounded within her as she took her leave. The man was so blunt, yet nice...lonely too, she decided as she thought about his sad, dark eyes. "I wonder where he went on vacation?" The thought went unanswered as she left the bank.

Dr. Sligh's position in the upcoming election had its advantages. Katherine and her mother were invited to a large reception the following afternoon given by former Governor Carpenter at his beautiful home on Madison Avenue.

"Mother, hurry up. We'll be late," Katherine complained nervously as she fidgeted with her wrap.

"Katherine, relax," Mrs. Sligh responded with an indulgent smile as she crossed the room. "We don't want to be the first ones there."

"But we've only got five minutes," Katherine retorted. "The horse would have to gallop the whole way to make it there that fast."

"Katherine, dear," Mrs. Sligh explained patiently, "it wouldn't be proper for us to get there in any less than fifteen minutes."

"What?"

"It's true," Mrs. Sligh explained. "In society the proper course of action is to arrive at a function between ten and twenty minutes after the announced time, particularly if one doesn't know the hostess well. Her friends may arrive earlier because perhaps they will help, or at least offer to, but no hostess wants her lesser acquaintances to arrive too early and perhaps catch her not quite ready to receive her guests."

"That's why you were habitually late back home?" Katherine gasped. "It wasn't slowness?"

Her mother broke into an understanding laugh. "No dear, it wasn't slowness. I often had to invent delays to keep your father from taking us places a half hour ahead of time."

"But he had patients he was going to see afterwards," Katherine remarked.

"None of them were emergencies," Mrs. Sligh responded, "though you'd never have known it by your father's temper."

Twenty minutes later Mrs. Sligh directed their horse alongside a parked carriage, and set the brake. Her eyes lingered on the quality of the vehicle.

"Mother, look at all the women. Their gowns are beautiful," Katherine gasped.

"It does look like a grand affair," Mrs. Sligh replied as she now got out. Together mother and daughter walked past the many carriages to the open gate where a throng of elaborately dressed ladies milled in the yard, on the porch, and essentially obstructed entrance into the handsome house.

"There must be over a hundred people here," Katherine whispered to her mother.

"More, I think," Mrs. Sligh responded quietly. "Do you see Bessie? Or maybe her mother-in-law?"

Katherine searched the crowd, looking for her sister.

"Sarah, dear, there you are," a matronly voice responded as she made her way through the throng of women. "I've been looking for you."

"Rachael, how lovely to see you," Katherine's mother replied in relief. It was wonderful to finally set eyes on someone she knew. "Katherine, you remember Bessie's mother-in-law."

"Yes, it's good to see you again, Mrs. Davenport," Katherine responded politely. The woman was not terribly tall though she probably gained another inch or two by the way she pulled her hair elaborately up on her head. Her demeanor, as always, held a rigid air of correctness. She was richly dressed, and every movement of her body was conducted with the disciplined appearance of dignity. "Is Bessie here?" Katherine asked.

"Elizabeth is inside assisting Miss Carpenter and Mrs. Hunt in the dining room. They were quite beside themselves when they realized the refreshments were placed far too close to the pyramid of roses, and couldn't be attended to properly."

"Oh dear," Katherine responded automatically, too automatically. Her response drew a critical look from Bessie's in-law. "Perhaps I can help," Katherine decided quickly as she withdrew from her present company.

"Yes dear, do try," her mother instantly encouraged. Then turning to Mrs. Davenport she commented, "Katherine is such an exceptionally clever girl. I'm sure she can be of assistance."

Katherine suspected that it wasn't her place to interfere in the dining room, but she had never gotten on well with her sister's mother-in-law. For some unexplainable reason, every time she was in Mrs. Davenport's presence she said or did something wrong. It was like all the dormant mischief within her suddenly exploded into life, screaming to be let loose. It was all she could do to remain civil.

Katherine worked her way through the crowd to the front door, and peered in around the ladies. The entry, under other circumstances, would have been ample and handsome. Dark woodwork defined its walls and encompassed the hall fireplace now shrouded in a mass of palms. The hostess was receiving her guests in the drawing room aided by four or five ladies. The parlor lay on the other side of the hall, and beyond was the dining room. Katherine directed her steps toward the latter.

"Katie, you're here," Bessie greeted as she hastened to her. "Come, I'll introduce you to my friends."

"This is my sister, Katherine," Bessie announced as she drew her sister into her group. A broad smile rested on her lips. "Katie, you know Violet from Mrs. Osterhout's, and this is her sister, Grace Cullen, and her friend, Wilder Broadwater."

"Broadwater..." Katherine repeated. The name was familiar.

"Yes, dear Kate, Wilder's father built the Broadwater Hotel -- you know the one mother continually talks about."

"Oh yes," Katherine responded. "It's outside of town, isn't it?"

"Yes, on Ten Mile Creek," Wilder agreed. "We have a hot spring out there, and people come from all over to bath in our pool. You'll have to come out some time."

"I'd like that," Katherine responded politely. "It's very nice to meet you."

"Daddy also knows Judge Cullen," Bessie continued as she diplomatically guided the conversation back to her other friends. "They've met on numerous occasions concerning the mining in Granite County."

"And I know absolutely nothing about any of that, and I hope you're not interested," Grace laughed as she warmly placed her hand on Katherine's arm.

"I'm afraid I don't, and I'm not," Katherine responded lightly.

"Good, then we can become great friends," Grace replied. "Wilder, why don't we smuggle Katherine some goodies, and then find someplace less crowded...and less married," she suggested with a devilish grin. "All married ladies want to talk about are babies and their in-laws."

Wilder promptly handed a plate to Katherine, and both girls began filling it. Then taking the offered drink from Miss Carpenter, Grace and Wilder headed for the back of the house, pulling their new friend along with them.

"Where are we going?" Katherine asked.

Chapter Two

"The cellar," Grace replied as she led the way. "We always escape down here, don't we, Wilder?"

"Regular as rain," Wilder agreed.

"But why?" Katherine asked. "It's so beautiful upstairs."

"Beautiful?" Wilder broke into a giggle.

"What's the matter," Katherine demanded.

"You really are from the sticks," Wilder snickered as she looked knowingly at Grace.

"Grass green," her friend agreed.

"Why, because I think the house and ladies look wonderful?" Katherine asked, perplexed.

Grace giggled.

"I don't understand," Katherine stammered uncomfortably.

"That's it exactly," Wilder laughed. "But you mustn't think we're being unkind, Katherine, we're just amused. You see it's not that the Carpenters haven't thrown a dazzling afternoon, it's that you are so impressed."

"Wilder and I have been to so many of these things that we couldn't begin to count them," Grace continued.

"We go because it's expected," Wilder explained.

"And because we want Mrs. Power and Mrs. Word and Mrs. Kleinschmidt to encourage their sons, nephews, or any other male relatives to attend the parties we go to, and if we're lucky, to encourage them to escort us."

"So you do it for the boys," Katherine surmised.

"Precisely," Wilder laughed. "I don't want to end up an old maid."

"Me either," Grace agreed, "though I'm probably less picky than Wilder...but then she has all those fellows that stay at the hotel to choose from." She laughed.

"The trouble with all those fellows at the hotel is that you don't know them from Adam," Wilder retorted. "I've had married men flirt with me, and poor ones too -- all pretending to be what they're not. It ruins everything. I don't know who I can trust and who I can't." She scowled. "No, Grace, I'd settle for a home town boy any day...like your brother."

"Ernest?" Grace gasped in surprise. "You're kidding."

"I'm not kidding," Wilder replied. "He's nice."

"And he has ears that stick out two miles on either side," Grace choked. Her eyes were wide with disbelief. "He's not like your brother. Charles is handsome and refined. Ernest, on the other hand, is as dull as...as, oh I don't know, but he's boring."

"I don't think he's dull, just a bit on the quiet side," Wilder replied. "I wish he'd talk to me."

Grace rolled her eyes.

"Maybe you could get him to talk to Wilder," Katherine suggested softly to Grace. "Who knows, they might be perfect together, and if they were...well, I would have loved to have picked out my in laws."

Grace's attention swung to Katherine as she pondered her words. They made sense. "Okay," she decided as her face brightened. "If Ernest is what you want, Wilder, we'll just see if we can't snag him for you." She smiled.

Wilder was obviously pleased as she now peered down at the watch pinned to her chest. "Oh gees, you two, we've been down here for ages. We'd better go back up top side, or we'll be discovered for sure."

The three young women scrambled from their refuge, emerging back into the world above. Violet was instantly at her sister's elbow.

"Wilder had better find her mother," Violet advised quietly. "Mrs. Broadwater is about ready to form a search party."

Grace grabbed her friend's arm, and whispered the urgent warning. Wilder glanced up with alarmed eyes, and without a word hurried away.

Katherine wandered over to the refreshment table, helping herself to the last few crumbs of the nut dish. Miss Carpenter no longer manned her post, and most of the guests were gone. Finally now in leisure, she turned to enjoy the tasteful room. She loved all the roses and sweet peas decorating the table, the sideboard, and the fireplace mantel. She loved the warm rose tone that predominated in the room. This was the kind of house she wanted some day; not a huge mansion or a castle, but a nice handsome house that was large enough not to be cramped, and with fireplaces in every room that she could afford to keep lit all winter long.

"Katherine, this is my mother, Mrs. William Cullen," Grace introduced as she brought the woman to her new friend's side.

"I'm very pleased to meet you," Katherine responded automatically.

"And I you," Mrs. Cullen responded warmly. "I talked with your mother earlier. She seems very nice."

"I understand my father knows your husband," Katherine stated now, not knowing what else to say.

"Yes, Dr. Sligh has provided much medical expertise to the negotiations of the mining interests in your area."

"Mother, don't bore her to death," Grace complained, "or she will never agree to dinner." The young woman's attention shifted to her new friend. "We were wondering if you would come have supper with us. We'll see that you get home afterwards."

"I'd like that," Katherine responded, "but I'll have to find my mother."

"I believe she's talking with Mrs. Carpenter out on the front steps," Mrs. Cullen offered.

Arrangements were made, and Katherine found herself riding away in the Cullen carriage with Grace and her sister, Violet. The two began to relate all the particulars of their recent trip to Chicago. Katherine listened to her new friends with interest.

The carriage pulled up in front of a handsome brick house across the street from an even bigger brick mansion. Mrs. Cullen, Grace, and Katherine alighted, while the former gave instructions to the driver to take her married daughter on to her rooms at Mrs. Osterhout's. Within moments Katherine was being led inside as Mrs. Cullen laid aside her things and picked up the mail, thumbing through the many letters and invitations.

"How many brothers and sisters do you have?" Katherine asked as she followed her friend into the parlor. Grace collapsed comfortably onto the couch.

"Besides Violet, three," she answered. "Ernest should be home any time with father, and I have two other sisters, Lilly and Puss."

"Puss," Katherine repeated, "that's an odd name."

"Oh, it's not her real name. Her real name is Mary, but everyone calls her Puss or Miss Puss." Suddenly Grace jumped to her feet. "Come on, I'll show you why."

Katherine followed her friend from the room, and out through the kitchen to the back porch. There nestled on the floor was a young lady of twelve or thirteen. In her lap two kittens wrestled with each other in play.

"Grace, you're home," the girl greeted. "How was the party?"

"The usual," her sister replied. "Puss, this is Katherine. Her father is running in the election; and if he wins, she'll be living in Helena."

"Hi," Puss greeted as her attention shifted to Katherine. "Do you like cats?"

"Yes," Katherine answered, "we had one down in Granite before we moved, but we couldn't bring him with." She reached down for the black and white kitten Puss was handing up to her. Within moments it was purring in her arms.

Puss smiled, and then her head turned as she heard a door slam. "Daddy's home," she announced as she quickly replaced the kittens in their box. She led the way back through the house.

"Daddy, you're home," Puss greeted as she threw herself into his arms.

"Yes, my darling girl," he laughed as he embraced his daughter. Then his eyes shifted to Katherine. "And who might this be?"

"Katherine Sligh," Grace answered.

"Doctor Sligh's little girl?" he asked with a smile as he disengaged himself from Puss, and placed a hand on each of Katherine's arms, surveying her from head to foot.

"Yes sir," Katherine responded as she noted the young man lingering at his side.

"Yes, you are," Judge Cullen acknowledged. "I can see your father in your face. Welcome."

"Thank you, sir," Katherine responded.

The judge now turned to his son. "Ernest, this is Doctor Sligh's daughter."

"Pleased to meet you," the young man responded automatically as his father wandered on into the dining room.

"Ernest, for heaven's sake," Grace exploded, "it's no wonder you haven't got a girl friend. You don't even try to be friendly."

An expression of annoyance crossed the young man's face as Katherine noted his ears. They did stick out a little, but not near as far as she thought they would. Grace evidently was prone to exaggeration, at least in her brother's regard.

Ernest came over to Katherine. "I'm sorry if I appeared disinterested. Welcome."

Katherine smiled. "I understand that you habitually break girls' hearts."

"Me?" he retorted in surprise.

"Yes you," she responded kindly. "They would give anything if you would only talk to them more."

"But we've never even met until now," he stammered, embarrassed. "How could you know anything about me?"

Katherine glanced at Grace as a wave of timidity suddenly swept her. Grace smiled, and nodded her head in encouragement.

"I've just come from the Carpenter's reception," Katherine stated as her attention returned to Ernest Cullen, "and one would have to be blind, deaf, and dumb not to see it."

Ernest just stared at her.

"If you ever need help, just say the word," Katherine offered as she boldly dared to take his arm, following the judge into the dining room.

Grace hid her face, stifling her laughter. Her brother was suddenly so complacent, readily walking with her new friend to the dinner table. Katherine was definitely a good addition to her circle of friends. Grace could only hope that Dr. Sligh would win the election, and stay in Helena.

"Where's Lilly?" Judge Cullen demanded as everyone congregated around the table.

"You have to ask?" his wife responded as she stepped out into the hall. Calling upstairs, it was only moments before the last member of the family appeared.

"Sorry, I'm late," Lilly responded as she quickly sat down with the others.

"Lilly, this is Katherine Sligh," her mother introduced as she indicated the new face at the table. "We met her at the Carpenters this afternoon."

"Katherine Sligh," Lilly repeated, "isn't your father a doctor in Granite?"

"Yes."

"Then I've met him," Lilly responded with a smile. "He showed me his surgery."

"He did," Katherine replied in mild surprise. "You were in Granite?"

"Yes." Lilly's eyes shifted to her father. "Wasn't it about two years ago? You were stung by a bee."

"Two years ago, August," he agreed. "We weren't there long."

"I was very impressed," Lilly offered. "Your father's surgery was so orderly."

"So tell me, Katherine," Judge Cullen continued, "what do you think of your father running for election?"

"I like the idea," she responded, "though I worry about his patients. The doctor replacing him isn't that experienced in mining injuries."

"But your father's experience is the very reason we need Dr. Sligh in Helena," Judge Cullen replied with a smile. "It's his expertise on the subject that will help us improve mining legislation. Isn't that right, Ernest?"

The young man looked up from his food as his eyes darted to Katherine. She obviously agreed with his father. "Yes," he responded as he pondered the young woman. She had a beautiful symmetry to her face. He rather enjoyed looking at it.

Katherine smiled, and looked back to his father. "It's a shame we can't be in two places at once."

"Here, here," Judge Cullen agreed enthusiastically.

"I'd like that," Puss piped up. "I hate leaving my kittens home, but they won't allow them at school."

A chuckle escaped Katherine as everyone smiled indulgently. The youngest member of the Cullen family had found an opportunity to enter into the serious discussion.

By the time Katherine got home to Mrs. Osterhout's, it was nearly nine o'clock. It had been a full day, and fatigue was bringing to nag at her. Her brother, Charles, sat on the porch steps, staring into the darkness.

"Hi," she greeted softly. "What are you doing out here?"

"Getting some privacy," he answered. "It's too crowded in there."

"Crowded is a family of seven in a small company house," Katherine retorted with an indulgent grin. "Mrs. Osterhaut's house is huge by comparison."

"But that was family," he replied with a frown. "These are strangers, and there are a lot more than seven."

"They won't be strangers for long," Katherine replied as she hesitated at the door. "Are you coming? You have school tomorrow."

The following morning Katherine was up early helping her mother make breakfast for all the boarders, and seeing that her brother got off on time. Then after the dishes were done, Mrs. Sligh sent her daughter on an errand. Katherine was to deliver the household bills to Mrs. Osterhout's book keeper downtown in the Power Block.

Katherine set out on foot. Scattered clouds covered the sky, shifting endlessly in the autumn wind, threatening rain. She hurried onward until finally she entered the shadows of the tall city buildings. She turned the corner on Main Street, and promptly entered the Power Building. The office she was looking for was on the fourth floor, and she trudged up the steps. She didn't get far when she felt a small pebble biting into her foot. She sat down, and removed her shoe as voices echoed down the stairs from above. She quickly finished her task, and was about to resume her climb when five businessmen were suddenly upon her, filtering past on their way downstairs. The last one stopped.

"Miss Sligh," he greeted pleasantly.

"Mr...." Katherine had forgotten the name of the bank clerk.

"Marlow," he finished for her with a smile. "Can I help you find an office?"

"I'm looking for..." Katherine showed Mr. Marlow the piece of paper with the name of Mrs. Osterhout's book keeper written on it.

"Fourth floor," he responded. "His office is down at the very end of the hall."

"Thank you," she replied.

Marlow's friends suddenly realized he was missing, but the banker waved them on their way.

"Miss Sligh," Tom Marlow began again, "I'm glad I ran into you. I was wondering if you would care to have dinner with me sometime? We could go out to the Broadwater Hotel. They usually have an orchestra and dancing."

"Sir, I don't know you," Katherine retorted in surprise. Then she blushed. "I mean..." Her voice fell off in embarrassment.

"That you don't know me," Tom Marlow agreed with a smile, "but maybe you know my aunt and cousin. Did you by any chance attend the Carpenter reception yesterday afternoon?"

"Well, yes," Katherine responded.

"Did you meet Mrs. Broadwater?"

"I met Wilder," Katherine responded with a smile. "She's really related to you?"

"My cousin," he confirmed.

"I liked her," Katherine replied.

Thomas Marlow smiled. "She's quite pretty, but she can be a little spitfire if crossed."

"And have you crossed her?" Katherine asked now, in growing intrigue.

"Not intentionally," Thomas Marlow laughed, "never intentionally."

Katherine smiled.

"Miss Sligh, will you consent to dinner?" he pressed.

"Would we be going with Wilder?" Katherine asked.

"No." Tom Marlow's expression fell.

"Perhaps we would be dining with Mrs. Broadwater then?" Katherine asked politely.

Tom Marlow's attention focused back on Katherine. She was interested in having dinner with him. Only propriety stood in the way. "Have we any other mutual friends?" he asked.

"Oh," she gasped as she realized his dilemma. Their mutual friends were the Broadwaters. "Wilder won't keep company with you?" she asked now. "You actually did cross her?"

"Her mother asked a favor of me about three months ago," Tom Marlow explained, "and well, it went astray. Wilder has barely spoken to me since."

"It doesn't sound like it was your fault," Katherine responded.

"That depends on who is the judge," he replied with a indulgent smile. "As far as Wilder is concerned, I was entirely at fault."

"So your cousin won't keep company with us," Katherine responded.

"I think it's safe to say she would rather be on her hands and knees scrubbing bar room floors," he replied with a chagrined expression.

"Oh," Katherine responded in dismay. Then her countenance brightened. "Wait. Maybe she will go."

"Wilder?" he repeated.

"Maybe. If I can manage to convince a particular young man to go too. Maybe there's a chance."

"Katherine," Tom Marlow responded in sudden exasperation, "that is exactly how I got into the mess with Wilder in the first place. I arranged an escort for her."

"As a favor to her mother?"

"Yes."

"Then why did it go wrong?" Katherine asked.

"Wilder found out that it wasn't the young man's idea, that I paid the expenses. She was outraged."

"Well, then, I'll simply tell Wilder the truth to begin with," Katherine stated.

"She won't do it," Tom Marlow warned.

"I don't know. She might," Katherine replied.

"Isn't there any other way?" he asked helplessly.

"I can't think of any," Katherine confessed, "not unless you'd like to take one of my parents with. They're very particular about propriety." Then she smiled. "I found out a little something about Wilder that might help. Let me talk to her."

"It won't do any good," he sighed in disappointment.

Katherine smiled. "I'll probably see Wilder tomorrow afternoon at the women's gathering. How late will you be at the bank?"

"As long as you need," he responded. He hadn't much confidence in his cousin's forgiveness, but at least he could look forward to seeing Katherine again.

"I'll try to get by then before you close for the evening," Katherine responded. "Okay?"

"Okay," he agreed. He watched momentarily as Katherine now headed up the stairs.

The following day Katherine accompanied her mother as she talked to one woman after another. They were at the women's headquarters downtown in the Bailey Block, working for the promotion of Helena as the capitol city of the state. No one wanted Anaconda to reclaim the title. The air literally buzzed with excitement as Mrs. Sligh finally turned back to her daughter.

"Your father and I need to return to Granite for a few days," she explained. "Being so close to Anaconda, we have to remind the voters why Helena makes a better capitol city." She hardly paused. "I've already talked to Mrs. Cullen, and she has invited you to stay with them while we're gone. Bessie and Violet are going to look after the boarding house in our absence."

"Is Grace here?" Katherine asked as her eyes swept the crowd.

"Yes, somewhere," her mother answered. "When we get home, you'll need to pack a bag. We'll drop you off at the Cullens on our way out of town tomorrow morning."

"Okay," Katherine responded. Her mind was on finding Grace. She hadn't seen her or Wilder. Katherine's attention shifted to Mrs. Cullen who was sitting at a desk two aisles over. She went over. There was a line up of women waiting to talk with the judge's wife. Katherine slipped up the side, and waited until Mrs. Cullen reached for a handful of leaflets from a box behind her desk. "Where can I find Grace?" she asked quickly.

Mrs. Cullen's face turned upward. "Oh Katherine, hi," she responded with a smile. "I think she's over by the podium."

"Thank you," Katherine replied, and hurried off.

She found Grace sitting at a table with two other young women. They were giving away "Helena for Capitol" badges by the dozen.

"Grace," Katherine greeted, "can I help?"

"Sure," Grace responded as she reached behind her for a box and an extra chair. Then she handed Katherine a spool of string. "Can you bundle some of these badges up in groups of twelve?" she asked.

Katherine sat down, and began counting and straightening the badges. "Have you seen Wilder?" she asked.

Chapter Three

"Wilder? No, not yet. But she'll be here. She said she was coming," Grace answered.

Katherine tied a bundle of badges securing together. "Does your brother ever invite girls out?" she asked now.

"Occasionally," she replied, "very occasionally. Usually just when his friends want to round out their group for some outing."

"Could you talk him into it, do you think?"

Grace turned to her friend. "If you want Ernest to ask Wilder out, you'd better do it yourself, Katherine," she responded. "Didn't you see the way he literally melted when you called him a heart-breaker?"

Katherine's attention shifted to the door. "There's Wilder," she suddenly exclaimed. "Excuse me a moment, will you Grace?" she demanded as she hastened to her feet. Katherine caught Wilder as she was depositing her wrap in the cloak room. No one else was present.

"Hi," Wilder greeted.

"Hi," Katherine responded. "How serious were you about Ernest Cullen? Do you want to go out with him?"

Wilder stopped. "Where did all this come from?"

"Do you?" Katherine pressed.

"Sure, I guess," Wilder answered.

"Even if I have to talk him into it?" Katherine asked.

"Katherine, Grace told me how you seem to have a way with Ernest, but good gosh girl, I didn't expect you to arrange our marriage." She grinned.

Katherine suddenly relaxed. "I guess I was being a little pushy."

"A little?" A broad smile rested on Wilder's face. "So what's up? Why all the zeal? Is Ernest getting interested in someone else?"

"No, I don't think so. It's just that sometimes a guy needs a little prodding, and I wondered if you would mind."

"You wondered if I would mind what? Are you talking about dropping a subtle hint or two, or going out and hog tying the poor guy? You know that no one in their right mind likes to be trapped. They run at the first opportunity."

"I also know when people find themselves someplace unexpected, they often enjoy it," Katherine rebutted.

"So where is this all leading?" Wilder asked. "You want me to go out with Ernest?"

"Yes."

"And you'll arrange the whole thing?" Wilder asked.

"Maybe," Katherine replied hesitantly.

"So who are we going with, you?"

"Maybe," Katherine answered.

Wilder leaned back against the door frame. "Someone's asked you out, and you need another couple to go along, right?"

"Yes."

A smile crept over Wilder's face. "I wondered how long it would be, a pretty face like yours. Who is he?"

"A bank clerk," Katherine answered.

"A bank clerk? Katherine, you must really like him," Wilder commented with a certain amount of admiration. "They hardly make any money."

"He's not quite as destitute as all that," Katherine retorted with a smile, "and he has at least one thing to his merit. He's your cousin."

"My cousin? I don't have a cousin who's a bank clerk," she responded. "It's not possible. What's his name?"

"If I told you that, you would think he finagled the whole thing," Katherine replied quietly.

Wilder's clear eyes became clouded with thought.

"You like Ernest, right?" Katherine asserted quickly. "...and you were about to agree to the whole thing, weren't you?"

Wilder's eyes settled on her friend. "Tom Marlow has asked you out, hasn't he?"

"Yes," Katherine answered.

"Then why did you call him a bank clerk?"

"Because he is."

"That's what he told you?" Wilder demanded.

"No, I just assumed... I met him at the bank. He was in his shirt sleeves with a stack of books..." Katherine's voice fell off as bewilderment engulfed her.

"Well let me tell you," Wilder began now, "Tom Marlow is no bank clerk."

"Then what?" Katherine asked.

"He's the gal darned president of my father's bank," she retorted.

"The president," Katherine gasped.

"And financial advisor to my mother," Wilder added. "The man thinks he can do anything, but he's no gentleman, not really."

"Because he arranged for an escort to take you to some big deal?" Katherine retorted.

"He told you?" Wilder cried.

"He warned me," Katherine corrected, "he warned me that you wouldn't agree to go with us, especially if it involved matching you up with someone. But I wouldn't believe him, not after what you said about Ernest. But maybe he's right." She paused. "You know, the escort wasn't his idea. It was your mother's. He just arranged it."

"My mother's?" Wilder repeated.

"And this one is essentially yours, at least it was at first," Katherine went on. "You said you wished Ernest would talk to you more, but you have to have opportunity, like spending an evening together. And as far as your cousin is concerned, he feels really bad about what happened. He does." She fell silent.

"All right," Wilder stated.

"All right?" Katherine responded as a small fragment of hope kindled within her. They had just had words, and she was not all too sure how their new friendship was surviving it all.

"All right, I'll go – only you can't corner Ernest into it. He has to want to go willingly. And Tom can't pay our way. This time it has to be done right."

A relieved smile emerged in Katherine face. "Thank you, Wilder."

A reluctant grin gradually made it's way to Wilder's pretty oval face. "So when is this fateful evening to take place?" she asked.

"I don't know," Katherine replied. "There was so much concern whether or not it was even possible." She paused momentarily. "I was planning to drop by Montana National before they close tonight, and let Mr. Marlow know whether you agreed or not."

"Which wrap is yours?" Wilder suddenly demanded as she reclaimed her shawl.

"That one, why?" Katherine answered.

Wilder handed Katherine her cloak, and then grabbed her hand. "Come on, let's get this thing settled."

"Wait," Katherine objected as she resisted her friend's momentum, "what about the rally?"

"They won't even miss us," Wilder exclaimed. "The bank isn't far. We'll be gone and back in no time."

"But I was helping Grace," Katherine objected.

"And now Miss Emmeline Green is helping her," Wilder replied as she pointed.

"Wasn't she at the Carpenter's the other day," Katherine asked as she now followed Wilder from the building.

"Yes she was, did you meet her?" Wilder asked.

"No, not yet," Katherine responded as they hurried along the city streets. It wasn't long before the two entered Montana National. "This place is always busy," Katherine noted.

"That's because it's Friday afternoon," Wilder explained. She made her way through the people, and back to where the offices were. She drew to a stop at Mr. Smith's desk.

"Miss Broadwater, it's been a long time since you've paid us a visit," he greeted with a smile.

"Mr. Smith, we would like to see my cousin please," she requested.

"I'm afraid he is with someone at present," Mr. Smith replied.

Wilder glanced at the closed door of her cousin's office. Then she handed Mr. Smith her calling card. "If you would be so kind as to give this to him, I'll wait."

Mr. Smith took the card as he reluctantly glanced at the closed door. It was obvious he did not want to disturb his superior. But as his eyes fell back on Wilder, his expression took on resolve. He went over to Mr. Marlow's door, knocked softly, and went in. Within moments, he returned.

Wilder went over to the row of chairs lining the wall, and sat down. Katherine followed suit. But they had hardly settled themselves, when Mr. Marlow's door opened. He and another gentleman emerged. Within moments Thomas Marlow disengaged himself, and turned to Wilder. "Come in," he greeted as he indicated his office. He ushered both young women through the door, and closed it.

"May I assume, Wilder, that you are speaking to me again," he asked as he sat down on the front edge of his desk.

"Yes," she answered simply. "I believe you know my companion," Wilder offered as she turned in her seat to Katherine.

"Yes, I do," he answered. "It's good to see you again, Miss Sligh."

"It is primarily on Miss Sligh's behalf that I am here," Wilder continued. "You see, Tom, a bank clerk has asked her out for an evening of entertainment." She stopped as mischief grew in her eyes.

"A bank clerk, you say," Mr. Marlow repeated in confusion. He had thought Wilder was there on his account.

"Yes, and his lack of money doesn't even seem to phase my new friend's interest in the man. Do you suppose you can help us?"

"Help you, how?" Tom Marlow asked. "Where does this bank clerk work?"

"Oh, he works here," Wilder retorted.

Tension tightened Marlow's expression. His eyes narrowed. "What is his name?"

"Oh, his name," Wilder laughed, "of course you would want to know that." She turned to Katherine. "What did you say his name was?"

Katherine felt a hot flush rise to engulf her neck as Thomas Marlow's attention settled on her. She floundered momentarily, embarrassed by Wilder's game. Then taking a deep breath, she met Tom's eyes. "Wilder is making fun of me," she answered quietly. "I didn't know you were the president of Montana National."

"She thought you were a lowly bank clerk," Wilder interjected quickly and jubilantly so her cousin would not misunderstand the situation. A devilish grin emerged on her lips.

Thomas Marlow's attention returned to his cousin. "You're enjoying yourself, aren't you?"

"Yes, I am," Wilder admitted openly. "How does it feel, cousin, to be at the mercy of someone else's game?"

"Not good," he replied. "So Wilder is there a purpose in all this, or is it just for your personal sport?"

"Oh, of course, there's a purpose," she retorted. "Katherine has asked me to join you two for dinner one night, and I just wanted to make sure that this time you would not go out and hire an escort for me." She glared momentarily at Marlow.

"I wouldn't think of it," he responded quietly.

"Good, then if that's settled," she continued, "we need to know which night you had in mind."

"I've been forgiven for past wrongs?" Tom Marlow asked.

"Yes," Wilder replied.

"How about a week from tonight?" he offered quietly.

"We'll see if it can be arranged," Wilder responded. She rose to her feet, and offered her hand. "Thank you, Tom."

"My pleasure," he responded automatically.

Then Tom Marlow turned to Katherine. "I'm sorry if this has caused you any embarrassment."

"No apology is necessary," she responded quietly. She offered her hand in turn, and then she and Wilder walked out of his office.

Wilder glanced over her shoulder as they reached the bank's door. "Wow, he's got it bad for you, Katherine," she exclaimed.

"What do you mean," she asked as she turned momentarily back.

Mr. Marlow was still standing in view as he talked to Mr. Smith. His hand rose in farewell.

Katherine returned the gesture, and then stepped outside.

"See what I mean," Wilder laughed. "Tom is in love. There is no doubt about it."

Katherine flushed once again. "Wilder, you have the nerve of a pole cat. How could you treat him like that?"

"I didn't do anything he didn't deserve," she responded.

"Then how about me?" Katherine demanded. "Did I deserve all that?"

Wilder stopped as she turned to her new friend. Her face visually softened as she suddenly realized what she had done. "Katherine, I'm sorry. I didn't even think…"

"Maybe I did deserve it," Katherine decided slowly. "I did get a bit pushy with you." A wane smile emerged on her lips. "At least it worked out all right."

"Do you think Ernest will come around?" Wilder asked as they walked.

"I don't know," Katherine answered truthfully. "I guess we'll just have to wait and see."

"You'll have to find a way to talk to him some time before next Friday," Wilder noted. "Do you think you can manage it?"

"Fate has already intervened, Wilder my dear," Katherine responded in an easy tone. A large smile rested in her face.

"What do you mean?"

"Mrs. Cullen has invited me to stay with them until Tuesday. My parents are going back to Granite County to do some campaigning."

"You're staying with the Cullens?" Wilder gasped. "You're kidding! When are you going over?"

"First thing in the morning," Katherine answered as they turned in at the Bailey Block.

Katherine was let off at the Cullens at seven thirty the following morning.
"Have you had breakfast yet," Mrs. Cullen asked as she set Katherine's
things at the bottom of the stairs.
"Just a cup of coffee," she replied. She could smell the bacon and eggs,
and her mouth watered.
"Then you'll have to join us, or rather what's left of us," she continued.
"I'm afraid the judge has already left for the office, and Puss is out on the
porch feeding her cats the cold pancakes." They entered the dining room.
"Here, sit next to Grace," she offered as she took a plate from the china closet
and set it before her. Silverware followed.
"Thank you," Katherine responded as the woman now left the room.
"Hi," Grace greeted with a smile. "Guess what!"
"What?" Katherine asked as she helped herself to the scrambled eggs.
"Mother's invited some of my friends over this morning to help make new
buntings for the election. You'll get to meet everyone."
"How many is 'some'?" Katherine asked between bites.
"Oh just a few," she answered with a smile. "Don't worry."

By nine o'clock Grace's guests began to arrive; and amid happy greetings
and furious conversation, her mother managed to get the young women started
on the buntings. Katherine found herself hemming edges opposite Miss
Carpenter. They chatted about the reception, the upcoming election, and their
fathers
Katherine glanced at Grace. She still hadn't had an opportunity to ask
where Ernest was.
Katherine finished the hem she was working on. She had finished two
buntings in the time it took everyone else to finish only one side. She rose to
her feet, placed the finished article neatly on the table, and wandered out into
the hall.
Lilly was sitting on the stairs tucked behind the banister, reading her
book. She looked up.
"I've finished my bunting," Katherine stated lamely.
Lilly smiled. "Do you like sewing?"
Katherine wandered over to the steps. "It's okay, I guess."
"I hate it," Lilly declared. "No, that's not true. It's not the sewing I
hate."
"What then?" Katherine asked Grace's sister.
"I hate the idle conversation," Lilly stated in a quieter voice. "It's boring.
What does it matter which dress I where, or whether or not I even go to Mrs.
so-and-so's little afternoon gathering. It won't affect the state of Montana. It
won't even affect my life, except by making it more tedious."
"But the buntings are for a good cause," Katherine replied with a smile.
"The election is a good cause," Lilly replied. "The buntings are
extraneous details."

"But they make things seem so much more festive and fun."

"There are a lot of people who enjoy creating 'fun'. I'm just not one of them," Lilly declared.

"So what do you enjoy?" Katherine asked.

"Knowledge," Lilly responded eagerly. "I like to understand how and why things happen." She held up her book. "I love logic, and how everything relates to it."

"Like how come it takes everyone so long to hem such a short piece of fabric," Katherine stated quietly as she glanced behind her down the hall.

"Oh you noticed that," Lilly laughed.

"Yes, I noticed that. How could I not? I hemmed four sides to their every one."

"That's because they didn't come here to sew," Lilly explained with a chuckle. "They came here to talk and be a part of the great fun of the election. And if a little work gets done along the way, well that's their contribution to the bigger picture."

Katherine contemplated Grace's sister. She was old enough to be a part of the proceedings downstairs. She should even have had her Coming Out Party by now, especially in a city like Helena. But here she sat with a book.

"How old are you?" Katherine asked suddenly.

"Sixteen, why?"

"Are you still in school?"

"Absolutely," Lilly exclaimed. "I go to St. Vincent's."

"Why?" Katherine asked, and then quickly added, "I mean, what are you going to do with your extra education?"

"I don't know," Lilly responded, "maybe I'll teach."

"You don't want a husband and family?" Katherine retorted.

"I'm not opposed to a husband and family," Lilly replied, "there's just a lot I want to do before I settle down."

"Like what?" Katherine asked.

"Like travel," Lilly responded.

"Teachers can't afford to travel," Katherine stated bluntly. "You need a rich husband for that."

"Well maybe I'll find one; I don't know," Lilly laughed. "But in the meantime, I have my books and my dreams."

"My mother would kill me if I wasted so much time on books," Katherine confessed, "and my father would be quick to point out all the suffering in the world."

"The human species has suffered since the fall of Adam and Eve," Lilly stated. "Problems of such magnitude cannot be solved by a sudden burst of compassion. It takes careful long years of study if we are to have even a hope of a solution lasting more than a few days."

"You've really thought about this," Katherine gasped.

"For hours and hours," Lilly admitted, "but there's one major problem I can't seem to get around."

"What's that?"

"Human nature," she answered with chagrin. "Choice is our sacred gift from God, but choice is also what gets us into trouble."

"I can't imagine," Katherine exclaimed, "how you can possibly spend so much time on such utterly wretched subjects."

"Perhaps you'd rather talk about boys," Lilly offered with a subtle smile.

The door knob turned, and Ernest walked in.

A warm flush broke out across Katherine's cheeks as she recognized Lilly's older brother. "How did you know it was him?" she demanded in a whisper.

Chapter Four

"I heard him on the porch, and it's time," Lilly laughed. "If you want to see something really funny," she continued with a grin, "come sit with me and watch the girls."

Katherine sat down on the steps next to Lilly. They had a perfect view of the hall through the spindles of the stair rail. Ernest had hardly shut the front door when two of Grace's friends emerged, fawning over him. He politely kept them at bay as he retreated. Two more girls appeared, and he took to his heels, leaving them behind.

His pace halted at the stairs. Ernest visibly relaxed as he now stared at Katherine. "What are you doing back here? Has Lilly kidnapped you?" he asked.

Katherine smiled. "Oh no, we were just talking."

"About you," Lilly interjected with a chuckle.

"What about me?" Ernest asked in surprise.

"She wanted to know where you've been?"

"At the Pancake Feed. Didn't you tell her, Lilly?" he demanded.

"She didn't have a chance," Katherine replied as she threw Lilly a look of consternation.

"Yes, Grace has kept her quite busy with all her friends," Lilly explained calmly.

"Yes, her friends," Ernest repeated with a disgruntled glance back over his shoulder. Then his attention returned to Katherine. "You were looking for me?"

"I was wondering if you had given any more thought to what we talked about the other day," she began uneasily. Here was her chance to ask him about Wilder, but the opportunity had come so unexpectedly, so sudden. She wasn't prepared.

"You mean about talking to girls more," he replied. "Yes I have, but there is a time and place for everything, and now is not one of them."

A grin emerged on Katherine's lips. She had to agree with him.

Ernest unbuttoned his coat.

"I was thinking of something where the odds would be a bit more fair," Katherine offered. "You know Wilder Broadwater?"

"Of course," he responded.

"Do you like her?" Katherine asked.

Lilly stifled a grin.

Ernest noticed, and then turned back to Katherine. "Sure, but what has that got to do with anything?"

"She's a girl, Ernest. You don't talk to her," Katherine replied.

"I don't?" he responded with a look of bewilderment.

"You don't," Katherine confirmed, "and she's one of the prettiest young ladies I've met in Helena. She absolutely beautiful, like a porcelain doll."

"Probably as frigid and boring as one too," Ernest retorted.

"Not Wilder," Lilly objected. "She's got a mind of her own."

Ernest noted his sister's comment. "So I don't talk to Wilder," he stated. "What's the big deal?"

"She likes you, bonehead," Lilly laughed, "and you ought to like her. You have more in common with her than any other girl in the whole valley."

"I do?" he replied. "Like what?"

"Like everything," Lilly answered. "She loves the out of doors, but nothing goes on in this city she doesn't know something about. She's a real kick." Lilly grinned.

Katherine stared at her young friend. She thought it was going to be hard to convince Ernest to escort Wilder, but she hadn't counted on Lilly.

"So you want me to talk to her," Ernest stated softly.

"Yes," his sister responded.

"When?"

Lilly turned to her companion.

"How about next Friday?" Katherine asked. "We could go to dinner at the Broadwater, and maybe dance a little afterwards."

"Can't next Friday," Ernest responded. "I'm leaving Thursday night for Seely Lake with the Holter boys."

"That's right," Lilly acknowledged. "You won't be back until Tuesday."

"I guess it will have to be another time," Ernest noted as his eyes lingered on Katherine. "You aren't mad, are you?"

"Mad? Of course not," she responded as disappointment set in. "You didn't know what we had in mind."

"Good," he replied with a smile. "You let me know when we can get together then, okay?"

"Sure," Katherine replied softly as Ernest now headed on up the stairs.

"So you still need another couple for Friday, and Wilder is out," Lilly noted quietly.

Katherine's eyes darted to her. "How do you know that?"

"Your disappointment."

"My disappointment, what disappointment? Your brother just had other plans, that's all," Katherine responded miserably.

"Don't worry," Lilly bolstered, "it can't be that hard to find a few people to go out to the Broadwater Friday night." She rose to her feet. "I think mother is serving lunch."

Katherine followed Lilly downstairs in utter silence. The chatter around her seemed excessively superficial as she pondered her recent companion. Lilly seemed to sense things, to understand things, things that were never said. The propriety needs for Friday evening were just as obvious to Lilly as all the things Wilder and Ernest had in common. This sixteen year old girl might spend excessive time with her nose stuck in books, but she didn't miss anything about the people around her. Her understanding was automatic.

Katherine sat down next to Grace. Miss Greene sat in the chair beyond. Lilly had disappeared into the kitchen, and was helping her mother serve the sandwiches, egg salad, crab croquette, chocolate, tea, and coffee. Ice cream followed.

Lilly whispered something in her sister's ear. Grace smiled. Within moments, Grace had Emma Greene's attention, and then the whole table. By the time the conversation reached Katherine, she could only listen to it in surprise. Everyone at the table had decided that they would go out to the Broadwater Friday night to hear the new Weber Orchestra.

"And bring anyone you want," Grace encouraged, "especially your brothers."

Katherine glanced at the kitchen door. Lilly lingered there silently observing.

Within the hour, Grace's friends bid her good bye, laughing and chattering gaily about the outing Friday evening. Katherine found Lilly in the kitchen.

"You're coming too on Friday?" Katherine asked.

"Of course, I wouldn't miss it," she replied with a smile.

"Good." Katherine paused. "Thank you."

Lilly's smile broadened, but she said nothing. Katherine glanced at Mrs. Cullen.

"I think there will be a big turn out," she offered. "Everyone is very curious to see how the new orchestra will fill their predecessor's shoes. Did you know that our former Professor Sharpe was offered a position at the Music Conservatory in Victoria, British Columbia?"

"No, I didn't," Katherine replied.

"We're going to miss him, but change is good too. The new orchestra will probably play more popular tunes."

"I hope so," Grace interjected as she joined them.

"Everyone is gone?" her mother asked.

"Yes." Her eyes surveyed the kitchen. "It looks like the dishes are done."

"Yes," she agreed. "Did you count the buntings?"

"They're all done except three, and they're at least started."

"I guess that isn't too bad," Mrs. Cullen responded, "though we may have a little tear-out to do. Elizabeth can't sew worth a darn."

"Oh we don't need to worry about hers," Grace chuckled. "I gave her scraps to work on. She didn't know the difference."

"She didn't," her mother gasped, "oh well, as long as her feelings weren't hurt. It will certainly save us some time."

Katherine attended church the following morning with the Cullens. St. Peter's Episcopal sat on Warren Street across Last Chance Gulch from their house. It was a nice church with the sanctuary a comfortable half dozen steps up off the street and the Sunday school and meeting rooms below. Katherine loved the beautiful rosette window above the foyer.

Judge Cullen led his family to their customary pew. They were on the early side, and slowly more families entered the sanctuary. The judge nodded greetings. He knew almost everyone. Even Reverend Love hesitated on his way past, taking a moment to exchange a few brief words with the judge and his wife.

"They're cousins," Grace whispered to Katherine. "Grandma was a Love before she married."

Katherine grinned. She couldn't help it. "I bet your grandfather thought so too," she whispered back.

Grace broke into a chuckle as she caught the play of words.

Puss leaned over to her sister. "What's so funny?"

Grace whispered into her ear. Again laughter broke out, and immediately drew a scowl from the judge. The girls quieted down.

Katherine's eyes rose as her heart skipped a beat. Tom Marlow was escorting the Broadwaters into the pew on the opposite side of the aisle. She seemed to run into the man everywhere she went. He caught her eye, and smiled.

"Old man Marlow smiled?" Puss exclaimed. "Did you see that!"

"Old man Marlow?" Katherine whispered quietly back to Puss. "Why do you call him that? He's not so old."

"He acts like he is," Puss exclaimed. "Nobody likes him. He's always grumpy and vile."

"I don't understand," Katherine whispered. "Is he a member of this church?"

"Of course," Puss responded, "and he gets after us kids all the time for being too loud. He says we're to be seen and not heard."

"And are you loud?" Katherine asked.

Puss scowled at her. "Not that loud, we aren't shouting or anything."

"And he never smiles, never?" Katherine asked further.

"Well almost never," Puss replied. "I guess maybe he smiles some when they thank him for helping. They're always doing that."

"What does he help with," Katherine asked, knowing that she should let the conversation drop, that the service was about to begin. But she couldn't help herself.

"He helps arrange things for the poor," she whispered back. Her eyes glanced momentarily at her father, and she fell silent.

Reverend Love appeared before them in his long black robe. His voice rang clear and strong as he invited his congregation to open the service with a hymn. The liturgy that followed was the same as Katherine was used to from their church in Granite. She didn't need to look at the hymnal. Her responses were automatic.

Katherine's eyes wandered across to the Broadwaters. Wilder sat with her mother and brother, but her attention was on the Cullen pew. Her eyes shifted from Ernest to Katherine. It was obvious she was wondering about Friday night. Katherine shook her head "no", and Wilder's expression fell. The young woman turned her attention back to Reverend Love.

Katherine followed suit. Another hymn was sung, and then Reverend Love took the pulpit. He read his text from the Bible, and then took a moment to scan his congregation. But unlike Katherine's pastor in Granite, he did not let out a torrent of words, designed to capture the attention of everyone present and put the fear of God into them. Reverend Love, this morning at least, began a systematic discussion of his text. It was more like a Bible study. Katherine relaxed, and sat back to listen.

By the time Reverend Love said "amen", Katherine had learned that contradictions in the Bible did not exist, despite what everyone said. If two passages seemed to contradict each other, it was only because they had application in different situations. Each biblical principle had a position in a system of priorities, and only one had preeminence in any given circumstance.

Katherine glanced at Lilly. She was busy looking up something in her Bible.

Another hymn was sung, and the benediction was given as the service closed. The congregation spilled into the aisle way as Puss and Grace disappeared into the crowd. Katherine stepped from the pew, backing up against its end. Here she waited as the judge and his wife passed, and then Ernest. He winked at her, and made his way over to the Broadwater pew.

"Wilder," he greeted with a smile, "I'm sorry that I'm going to be out of town Friday night. Maybe we can get together another time, all right?"

"I'd like that," she exclaimed in surprise.

Ernest bowed slightly, and left.

Wilder watched him momentarily stunned, and then her eyes darted back to Katherine. Thomas Marlow was blocking her view.

"So Friday night is off?" Tom Marlow asked Katherine as the others shuffled slowly down the aisle. He had seen Wilder's change of mood.

"Actually no," Katherine answered. "It seems that quite a number of my friends will be going to the Broadwater Friday evening."

"Really," he exclaimed, "I thought it depended on Wilder's friend."

"I thought so too," Katherine explained. "But when it turned out he already had plans, Lilly came to the rescue."

"Lilly? Judge Cullen's daughter?" Marlow asked.

"It was really amazing," Katherine continued. "She seemed to know everything without anyone telling her anything; and when she realized it all revolved around Friday night, she took care of it."

"She took care of it?" Tom Marlow responded. "How?"

"Grace had a small party of her friends over; and before I knew what was happening, everyone was talking about going to the Broadwater Friday night to hear the new orchestra. It was Lilly's idea."

A chuckle erupted from Marlow's lips, and he began to laugh openly and happily.

"What's going on?" Wilder asked as she joined them.

"Everyone's going out to the Broadwater Friday night to hear Weber's Orchestra," Marlow explained. "You can come with or without your young man."

"Everyone?" she asked as her attention shifted to Katherine.

"It seems that way," she answered. "The plan is to catch the seven o'clock streetcar."

"Then Grace is going?"

"And Lilly and all the others," Katherine added with a smile. "By the way, why weren't you at Grace's party Saturday? I understand you were invited."

"Oh mother and I were up at St. Vincent's. The Sisters asked us sometime ago to be on their planning committee."

"Oh, I see," Katherine responded.

"I've got to find Grace," Wilder exclaimed. "Excuse me."

Katherine's attention returned to Thomas Marlow. He was gazing at the Cullen pew. Lilly was still there, absorbed in her reading. He walked over, and she looked up.

"I understand, Miss Cullen, that I owe you a thank you," he stated pleasantly.

"Me?" she exclaimed in surprise. "What have I done, Mr. Marlow?" She stared at him, unable to imagine what he was talking about.

"Did you not instigated the plans for Friday evening at the Broadwater?" he asked with a smile.

"I'm afraid I still don't..." Her voice fell off as Katherine joined them. Then her attention returned to Marlow. "You," she exclaimed, "you're the one she wanted to spend the evening with?"

A twinkle rose in his eye. "Miss Sligh was worried?"

Lilly's hands rose to cover her mouth. Her eyes danced with delight. "I never dreamed it was you," she exclaimed finally as the initial surprise wore off. "I thought it might be some gold-lined pocket, but never you."

"I'm assuming you approve?" Marlow asked uneasily.

"Oh gosh, yes," Lilly exclaimed. "Katherine is going to spend an evening with someone who has a mind capable of thought, real thought." A smile ran rampant over her face. "This is simply grand."

"Well, I'm happy you approve," Thomas Marlow responded as he relaxed. "You'll be coming on Friday too?"

"Wild horses couldn't keep me away," she laughed.

"Katherine, Katherine," Grace called as she hastened back down the aisle with Mrs. Murphy at her heels. "Katherine, Mrs. Murphy needs one more to help with her Butterfly Tea Thursday night. Are you free?"

"Thursday night, yes," Katherine replied.

"Oh my dear, I am so relieved," Mrs. Murphy responded. "We have so many people coming, and there is so much to do. We'll need you in the morning too."

"Excuse me," Thomas Marlow stated as he disengaged himself from the group. He smiled briefly at Katherine.

By ten o'clock Thursday, Katherine found herself at the Murphy home. She and nearly twenty other girls decorated the drawing room and the parlor with nets and butterflies. There were four hundred of the winged creatures to distribute throughout the two rooms, and the girls actively created worthy settings for them. Mrs. Murphy had hired a family of Chinese to make the butterflies, and they were truly a work of art. Made out of crepe and gauze and tinted paper, the creatures fluttered their wings with the least hint of breeze.

The drawing room was divided in two by a great blinding light that illuminated throngs of imprisoned creatures in a net suspended from the ceiling. One side of the room was decorated with yellow butterflies caught in nets against the walls and in front of windows; great fellows with spotted wings, or tiny ones whose gauzy flutterings could be heard with anyone's passing. The other side was decorated in pink, and possessed the tables of refreshments and toilet accessories. All was designed to tempt the eye and the pocket book.

Across the hall in the parlor, a room of Oriental richness was the home of black and gold nets holding gorgeous butterflies of deep tones. Even Mrs. Murphy gasped at the results of their labor. Here as elsewhere, tables were placed for tea. All proceeds would benefit the Mandolin Club and its musicals.

"If we make a lot of money," Grace whispered to Katherine, "Mrs. Murphy has promised to throw a party for us."

"For us, when?" Katherine responded.

"I don't know just when," she answered, "but there are going to be boys."

"Now ladies," Mrs. Murphy called as she gathered them together for last minute instructions, "it is important that you dress in the gowns we talked about, because your color must correspond to the room you work in. Grace, dear, we decided on your yellow crepe, didn't we?"

"Yes ma'am," she replied.

Mrs. Murphy looked down at her notes, and corrected an entry. "Addie, you're in pink, and Katherine..." Her voice faded momentarily. "Katherine, you said you had a white gown, didn't you?"

"Yes ma'am," she replied.

"I thought so. We'll put you in the parlor. All right, ladies, we are through for now, but I need you back here at four thirty. We have a lot of last minute things to take care of."

The young women gathered their wraps and headed home for an early supper.

"You look beautiful," Katherine's mother commented as she pinned the last of her daughter's hair in place, "absolutely beautiful."

"Are you and daddy coming tonight," Katherine asked.

"Oh yes, we'll be there. But we've been invited to dinner with the Curtins, so we'll be by later."

Katherine rose, gave her mother a quick embrace, and picked up her cloak. Her father dropped her off at the Murphy residence as numerous other young ladies also arrived. The rustle of skirts glided over the already frozen ground. Inside, the young women pinned butterflies in their hair and attached larger ones to their shoulders in last minute preparation for the tea.

When the first guests arrived at the door, expressions of amazement dropped from everyone's lips at the sight of the butterflies, an incident that only became much more frequent and profuse as the evening wore on. The refreshments and the butterflies sold readily, so much so, that orders for duplicates were taken for the handsomest of the winged creatures. The evening proved to be an artistic, social, and financial success.

"Mother, you bought one of the great yellow fellows," Katherine exclaimed as she walked with her parents out to their buggy.

"I couldn't resist," Mrs. Sligh laughed. "I want to send him to my aunt. She's so poorly these days. I thought he might cheer her up. She's going to love his spots."

Chapter Five

All of Helena was buzzing with news of Mrs. Murphy's Butterfly Tea the following day, and especially over the fancy work occupying the guests of Mrs. Floweree. Katherine sat across from Grace, and next to her sister. Bessie's sister-in-law, Miss Davenport, sat on her other side. Three of them had helped the evening before, but Pearl Davenport wanted to hear every detail of what went on outside her pink room. Katherine left most of the description to Grace. Her mind was elsewhere.

Thomas Marlow occupied Katherine's thoughts. She didn't know why she was so attracted by him. She didn't even know him very well. But there was something about the man. Maybe it was his age. Maybe it was his eyes. Maybe...it was the paradox of the man. He seemed so strong and capable, yet at the same time his eyes could look so vulnerable. It made her heart ache.

"Katherine, which room did you work in?" Bessie asked.

"The Oriental one," she answered as her train of thought was broken.

"I wish I'd gone," she lamented, "but poor little Margaret was so croupish, I didn't dare leave her."

"How is she now," Katherine asked.

"Better. Violet is taking care of her." Bessie's eyes shifted to Grace. "You worked in the Yellow Room, didn't you?"

"Yes," Grace answered. "You should have seen the men, Bessie. They were more enthralled with the butterflies than their wives. We sold a big one to Mr. Carpenter. He said he was going to send it to Mrs. Astor to show her that Montana also did things in a big way. But his wife thought the ideas was nuts, as if the Astors didn't already have plenty of everything. If he was going to give it to anyone, it should be her."

"I had two women fighting over a pretty pink butterfly we had," Pearl Davenport laughed as she added her observations. "Mrs. Hauser and Mrs. Clarke both wanted it. Mrs. Hauser wanted to send it to a friend in Chicago, and Mrs. Clarke wanted it to go in a flower arrangement she is planning for tonight's reception she's giving for the Women's Christian Temperance Union. Mrs. Clarke was very insistent that she have it, but Mrs. Hauser told her if her flowers weren't showy enough without a butterfly she had better find a new florist."

Katherine's mind wandered back to the Broadwater Hotel as she continued to crochet the fine lace she was working on. She had never been to the Broadwater, but her mother had talked about it for months. At last she was going to see it, and she wanted to wear the dress she had worn the evening before. Back in Granite, she had hand stitched hundreds of small pearls onto the satin to make her plain white gown more fashionable and eloquent. With the added chiffon, the alteration had been a success.

The afternoon drug to a close as Grace and Katherine found themselves finalizing the arrangements for the evening. Mrs. Cullen would drop Grace and Lilly off at Katherine's on her way to Mrs. Word's whist party. Katherine had seen Mrs. Word's house the Sunday before when her father had taken the scenic route home from church. It sat on Madison Avenue, a gorgeous place set on a raised yard. The house had a stone foundation with walls towering up in brick, and finished off in the chateau style roof, complete with spire. It was like something from the fairy tales of Europe.

Katherine's thoughts returned to the evening before her as she headed home. Once Grace and Lilly arrived, Tom Marlow would escort all of them to the train station where they would catch the streetcar for the Broadwater Hotel. She couldn't wait.

Katherine entered the Osterhout house, and climbed the stairs to the second floor. Her father sat at his desk, absorbed in his work as she entered their rooms. Her brother was in his bedroom, doing school work. Dr. Sligh looked up.

"Hi," he greeted, "how was the party?"

"Okay, I guess. What are you doing home?"

"Oh just working on a couple of speeches I've got to give."

Katherine wandered over, and looked momentarily over his shoulder. "So where are you giving them," she asked.

"In every town from Garnet to Philipsburg, I'm afraid," he answered. "It's going to take me a couple of weeks."

"A couple of weeks," she repeated. "We're going home? What about the boarding house?"

"Mrs. Osterhout will be home in a week or so, and Bessie is going to run things until then, and look after your brother. He can't miss school. We're leaving Sunday. Didn't your mother tell you?"

"No," Katherine responded in dismay.

"Well you have been a little busy of late." He smiled through the dark hair of his beard as his eyes twinkled affectionately under a high brow. "You're going out tonight as well, aren't you?"

"To the Broadwater," she answered.

"Well you'd better get ready. I don't think your mother will be home for quite a while yet."

Katherine went to her room, and took off her dress. She had just two hours before Grace and Lilly would arrive, and she would need every minute if she planned to do her hair over again.

"Katherine, your friends are here," her father announced from their open door.

Katherine quickly fastened her mother's pearls around her neck, glanced a final time in the mirror, and reached for her cloak. She said good bye to her father as she headed downstairs with Grace and Lilly.

They greeted Tom Marlow as he came through the front door.

"I have a cab waiting outside," he offered as his attention settled on Katherine. "You look lovely, Miss Sligh." He helped her on with her wrap, and then all four went out. Within minutes they were enroute to the train station.

"Wilder is meeting us at the depot," Katherine stated.

"Oh good," Grace responded. "I heard she might be coming."

"Wild horses couldn't keep her away," Lilly noted quietly.

"Why is that?" Grace asked. "Ernest isn't going to be there."

Tom Marlow's attention shifted to Lilly. Their eyes met. The statement was a warning.

"Because," Lilly began now in a lighter tone, "she heard that tonight was your idea." She smiled sweetly.

Within moments the cab pulled up in front of the station, and everyone got out. The streetcar stood waiting as a crowd of passengers boarded.

"Grace, Katherine," a feminine voice called, "over here."

They found several young women from Grace's Saturday party in the rear of the car. They were in a group of about twelve.

Excited greetings were exchanged as Tom Marlow silently found empty seats conveniently close to the others, and guided Katherine there. Grace disappeared among her friends. Lilly sat down on the other side of Katherine.

"Katherine, there you are," Wilder exclaimed as she finally broke through the commotion. "How was Mrs. Floweree's? I really wanted to go; but with school, I just wasn't able to get there."

"It was fine," Katherine answered.

"But she has such a wonderful house," Wilder responded. "She must have served something really special."

"No, just ice cream," Katherine answered. She couldn't believe she was answering in such a nonchalant tone. Before she came to Helena, she would have considered ice cream very special. But now, she couldn't even count how many times she had had it.

Katherine glanced out the window. They were moving through the darkness. She noted the hour. It seemed funny that it was growing dark so soon. Somewhere in the last couple of weeks, the season had definitely turned into autumn. Summer was lingering no longer.

Wilder talked incessantly with Lilly as Katherine now ventured a glance at Tom Marlow. He smiled, but said nothing. Suddenly Lilly's earlier comment struck home as Katherine's eyes turned to Wilder. She knew that Katherine was out with her older cousin. Was that why she was sticking so close when there were so many others to talk to?

By the time the streetcar reached the Broadwater, the passengers were so worked up that they essentially poured off, eager for dancing and a good time. Katherine and Tom followed at a slower pace. Lilly was ahead, lingering one moment and crowding Wilder the next as if she were herding the young lady onward.

"I've made arrangements for a quiet dinner," Tom Marlow offered as he and Katherine walked. "We can join the others later."

Katherine smiled as his arm slipped through hers.

The last of Grace's party of friends disappeared inside as Tom Marlow took a turn toward the dining room. As he did, he waved at Lilly. She waved back, and disappeared into the ballroom where the orchestra was already setting up.

"I believe Miss Cullen has turned into our guardian angel," Tom Marlow mused to Katherine. "She seems bent on keeping my cousin at bay."

"I don't understand Wilder," Katherine commented as they entered the dining room. She fell silent as they were ushered to a window table in the corner, and informed of the house's specialties. The waiter left.

"I believe Wilder is just a little curious," Tom Marlow offered now. "My little cousin has always kept her eye on me. You see, I came from the east, and for what ever reason her father took to me. So here I was a stranger, a relative, and someone who her father told things to that he didn't tell either her or her brother. It's a curious relationship really."

"I suppose so," Katherine agreed as Tom Marlow flagged their waiter, and asked for a bottle of port.

"So where are you from Katherine Sligh," he asked with an intent smile. "Have you always lived in Granite County?"

"I was born in Grand Rapids, Michigan," she answered, "and I've spent some time outside Chicago in the little town of Sycamore. Have you heard of it?"

"Yes, but I don't believe I've ever been there," Tom Marlow answered.

"We moved to Montana about seven years ago. Daddy got a job with the mining company as their doctor." She paused. "Where exactly are you from?"

"I was born in Missouri, but my family moved back to Maryland. That's where I really grew up," he answered. "But my life didn't really start until I came west. It's a whole different world out here. You can't imagine."

"I've heard the east is a bit stuffy," Katherine responded.

"To say the least," Tom Marlow chuckled.

"You've certainly done well," she responded, "bank president, wow."

The port arrived, and Marlow had two glasses poured. Then he ordered dinner. As the waiter again disappeared, Tom Marlow's attention returned to the young woman across the table.

"So Katherine Sligh, what are your dreams and hopes?"

"Right now, I'd settle for my father getting elected," she laughed. "I like Helena."

"And then..." he asked.

"And then we'll see," she answered with a smile. "As a city, Helena has a lot more to offer than Granite, and it looks like she might even become the capitol of Montana."

"Very probably," Tom Marlow agreed. "After stealing everything out from under Anaconda in the middle of the night under an armed guard, I don't really think there's any question that Helena will do almost anything to keep the capitol city here."

Katherine chuckled. "Boy, was Anaconda mad. Granite still tells the story."

The two were served dinner as they continued getting to know each other. Before they knew it, the dining room was closing for the evening. Tom Marlow escorted Katherine toward the strains of music drifting down the hall.

As they entered the ballroom, Tom pointed out Lilly as she talked to a young man neither knew. Then he glanced around for his cousin. Wilder was nearby, dancing with another young lady as most of them were since the girls far outnumbered the boys in the group.

"Would you care to dance?" Tom Marlow asked.

"I would love to," Katherine responded.

He took her in his arms, and swept her onto the dance floor amid the other dancing couples. Their conversation fell off as Katherine fell under Tom Marlow's spell. They were touching. His one hand was in hers, the other on her hip, and they were waltzing to music, wonderful music. The moment was hypnotic.

The music drifted from one piece to another, each time slower and more romantic. Katherine was dancing closer to Tom now, the soft vanilla scent of his cologne wafting in her senses. His moves were so graceful, so smooth. He seemed like a different person, no longer articulated by bluntness.

Katherine looked into his eyes. They were warm and happy. A smile grew on his lips.

"Would you like something to drink," he asked as the song closed.

"No thank you," she answered, "but could we go for a walk?"

"The room is a bit stuffy," he agreed. He pulled out his pocket watch. "Yes, we have time for a short one before the car leaves."

The two walked hand in hand toward the door as Katherine recognized several faces from Grace's party. Then she spotted Wilder. She had almost forgotten about her. Wilder was heading in their direction when suddenly Lilly crossed her path. Taking Wilder by the hand, she urgently requested something. Katherine couldn't quite hear what it was. She didn't care. She and Tom Marlow walked out into the hall, retrieved their wraps, and wandered out into the crisp moonlight night.

"It's so beautiful," Katherine commented as she looked up into the midnight blue sky. The stars twinkled in their brilliance.

"Yes, it is," Tom agreed. His arm was now around her shoulder, and she snuggled against him.

They walked in silence under the young trees, down the paved walks.

"When can I see you again," Tom Marlow asked.

Katherine stopped, turning to him.

"What is it?" he asked.

"We're returning to Granite County on Sunday. My father has some campaigning to do."

"Sunday? For how long," Tom asked.

"Two weeks," she groaned. "What will I do if daddy doesn't get elected? I don't want to go back to Granite, not to live."

"He will win," Tom consoled. "His competition is weak. I don't think you have to worry."

"But Anaconda doesn't want Helena to be the capitol, and there are people throughout Granite County that don't want it either. Helena is farther away."

"Shh," Tom consoled as he put his arms around her, "your father is going to win, regardless of the capitol city debate. He knows the right people. They won't let him loose."

Katherine's eyes rested on his. "Who does he know?"

Tom smiled. "I can't say for certain, but the indicators are there. Your father will win. Just be patient, and help him wherever you can. Looks are important."

Katherine stared at Tom Marlow, pondering his confidence.

"I will miss you while you're away," he stated softly. "But it's only for two weeks, and then you and your family will be back. There will really be parties then." He smiled.

"I don't care about the parties," Katherine replied miserably.

"I know," Tom responded, "but parties provide opportunity. Maybe I'll get invited to one." He smiled.

They began walking now in the direction of the streetcar.

"I probably won't see you until Sunday services after you get back," Tom noted now as more and more people emerged from the hotel. "Okay?"

Katherine nodded silently. They were at the car now. She dreaded going in.

"Wilder is already aboard," Tom noted, "and Lillian. You've become good friends with the judge's daughter, haven't you?"

"Yes, I guess I have," Katherine agreed, "though I don't know that much about her."

"What's there to know," Tom Marlow asked. "She's a fine Christian young lady who knows a bit of decorum when it's needed."

"She knows an awful lot for being only sixteen," Katherine commented.

"Well I understand she's studying at St. Vincent's," Tom Marlow offered. "Maybe she's taking advanced courses."

"No I don't mean that," Katherine replied. "She has a sense about things, things that aren't obvious to most."

"Well maybe that comes from being a judge's daughter. Her father has to be aware of everything in his line of work. Maybe he's passed it on."

"Maybe," Katherine agreed.

Lilly looked up as they walked down the aisle to two empty seats. She smiled, a knowing smile, a pleased smile. But she said nothing. She did not leave her seat. She left them alone.

Tom Marlow saw Grace and Lilly safely home, and then walked Katherine to the door at Mrs. Osterhout's. Warm inviting lights shone from the windows, but no one seemed to realize anyone was outside. Tom drew to a stop as his eyes focused on Katherine. "I really enjoyed tonight."

"I did too."

His forefinger rose to tenderly trace the outlines of her face, his eyes drinking in the pleasure of her company. Then he touched her lips, smiled softly, and said good night.

Katherine watched as he returned to the cab, and then went in.

That night Katherine dreamed of Tom Marlow, and in the morning thoughts of him lingered with her in everything she did. Her mother swept her off after breakfast to the dressmakers. Each of them was scheduled for a dress fitting, but it wasn't certain whether the gowns would be finished by election time. The dressmaker, however, did promise to try.

The final arrangements seemed to take forever. Katherine was ready to explode. She wanted to talk about the previous night, about Tom Marlow. But her mother was hardly aware of her existence right now, let alone her heart's desires, she was so preoccupied with the campaign.

Katherine's thoughts turned to Lilly. It was Lilly who had made the evening possible. It was Lilly who had guarded her time with Tom Marlow. It was Lilly who Katherine craved to talk to.

By the time Katherine and her mother finished at the dressmaker's, there were a hundred other things to be done. Katherine watched with alarm as the day ticked away. They were leaving tomorrow morning, early.

"I'd like to say good bye to a few people," Katherine now told her mother.

"Now? Haven't you done that already?" she demanded impatiently.

"I only learned about the trip last night," Katherine replied quietly.

A frown seized her mother. "You have to pack."

"Yes," Katherine agreed.

"And I don't want you leaving it until after supper. You get packed, and if there's any time left maybe you can say good bye to a friend or two. But you won't have the buggy, your father and Charles are taking it just as soon as we get back."

"All right, mother," Katherine responded.

They headed home. In near panic Katherine pulled out her trunk, and began filling it, trying to make everything fit as it once had. But she had acquired a few more things since her arrival. In desperation, she stared at the pile on her bed that refused to be included within the trunk's straps.

"Katherine, you don't need to take everything," her mother offered as she came into her daughter's room. "We'll be back. Just take what you need for two weeks."

Relief swept Katherine as she quickly assessed what she could leave behind. "There that should do it," she announced.

"You're done?" her mother gasped.

"All except the last minute items," she replied as she closed the lid of her trunk.

Her mother suddenly smiled. "All right then, go say good bye to your friends. But be back in time for supper, I'll need your help."

"Okay," Katherine agreed as she reached for her coat, and swept from the room. Within minutes she heading up Benton Avenue on foot. She couldn't remember Lilly's exact address; but she knew if she turned left on Gilbert, she would find the Cullen house.

Ten minutes later, Katherine reached her destination. She was winded as she paused at the front door. She took a moment to catch her breath, and knocked. She heard footsteps inside, and Puss opened the door.

"Hi Katherine," she greeted with a smile.

"Is Lilly home?" Katherine asked.

Chapter Six

"No, Lilly's still at Belle's surprise birthday party."

"Belle?" Katherine repeated. This was not a name she recognized.

"Belle Murta. Lilly knows her from school," Puss responded. "Do you want to come in?"

Katherine stepped inside.

"Grace is gone too," Lilly's younger sister informed her. "It's just me and mother. Would you like to see the kittens?"

"Sure," Katherine agreed.

"Katherine, how lovely to see you," Mrs. Cullen greeted as she appeared from the parlor with an election bunting in hand.

"Mrs. Cullen, hi," Katherine greeted. "I came by to see Lilly, but Puss tells me she's at a birthday party. Will she be gone long?"

Mrs. Cullen glanced at the hall clock. "It's nearly three. No, I should think she'll be home within the hour."

"Did all the buntings get finished?" Katherine inquired now, looking for an excuse to stay longer.

"No dear, I was just working on one. Would you like to help?"

"I'd love to," Katherine accepted eagerly. Then her eyes swung to Puss. "Can I see your kittens afterwards?"

"Puss, why don't you bring a couple into the parlor," her mother suggested. She led Katherine through to where two buntings lay unfinished on the table.

Katherine quickly removed her coat, and set to work. Within minutes the kittens arrived, and then cups of tea. Katherine was enjoying herself when Lilly returned home. She finished her last bunting, and followed Lilly up to her room.

"So how was last night?" Lilly demanded as she pulled Katherine through the door, and shut it. Her eyes sparkled. Her face glowed.

"It was wonderful," Katherine exclaimed.

"So when do you see Mr. Marlow again?" Lilly asked.

"Well, that's the problem," Katherine replied as her enthusiasm faded. "My family leaves first thing in the morning for Granite County. Daddy has some campaigning to do. We'll be gone for two weeks."

"So soon?" Lilly asked. "My father doesn't have to be in Lima until the twentieth."

Katherine frowned as she sat down on the bed. "What if my father doesn't get elected? How will I ever see Thomas Marlow again?" she asked.

"Oh I wouldn't worry about that," Lilly chuckled. "The way you two were last night -- he'll find a way to see you."

"You really think so?" Katherine asked.

Lilly smiled. "Two weeks, that's not such a long time. Besides, absence makes the heart grow fonder, you know."

"I wish I could believe it," Katherine replied.

"Believe it. By the time you get back, Mr. Marlow won't be able to wait to see you."

Katherine remained silent.

"What is it?" Lilly asked gently.

"With all the pretty girls in town, why would he wait around for me?" Katherine asked quietly.

"Maybe because he likes you."

"No, I'm serious," Katherine responded.

"So am I," Lilly replied. "Maybe...you're the first one to touch his heart."

"What do you mean," Katherine asked.

"Mr. Marlow is not an easy man to get to know. He doesn't attend many social functions."

"Why not?" Katherine asked.

"Well, for one thing, he is not a gold-lined pocket. He works for a living."

"So does my father," Katherine responded.

"Yes, but your father is a doctor, and running for the state legislature. There's a difference."

"But there are plenty of other girls," Katherine insisted.

"Of course there are, but it's not the same. Mr. Marlow has impeccable taste. You can see it in his clothes, the way he does things. He's not the type of man to settle for just anyone."

"So why me?" Katherine demanded.

"I told you," Lilly smiled. "You're attractive, bright, and... How did you meet?"

"He tripped over a child's toy at the bank, and his books went everywhere. I helped pick them up."

"Ah, there you are," Lilly replied. "You're attractive, bright, and have a kind heart. What man can resist that?"

"Plenty," Katherine retorted.

"But not Mr. Marlow," Lilly responded. "He needs someone like you."

"He does have sad eyes," Katherine commented.

Lilly smiled. "They weren't sad last night."

"No, they weren't," Katherine agreed as a cautious smile rose slowly in her face. "Do you think he really likes me?"

"Yes," Lilly answered, "and two weeks will disappear before you know it."

While everyone in Helena was busy talking the capital question, the candidates, like Dr. Sligh, were busy canvassing their own interests, mostly out of town as they looked after their country constituency.

What Katherine found fascinating was the role her mother assumed with so many other women, writing letters, forming clubs, speaking, making badges, and essentially working without money or salary with only the great object in view, that of doing all that women could do to aid in their battle for justice, right and truth. On the surface it appeared that such efforts produced only meager results, but Katherine, her mother, and all women involved met with such tremendous encouragement and success, they each knew for themselves that the results were far from meager. November 6th would prove much credit was due to mothers, wives, and daughters when Helena was claimed as the state's capitol by a large majority.

The two weeks flew by for Katherine as she participated in her father's election, and in the choice of the state's capitol. These were issues she could help with despite the fact that women had no vote. Yet they had influence, and this they nurtured and encouraged in all women that they might influence those around them who did have the vote. This was their voice.

It was dark when Dr. Sligh pulled up in front of Mrs. Osterhout's. Rain poured from the sky, and washed down the streets. He couldn't step from the buggy without standing in a full inch of water. He helped his wife and daughter out as they ran for the porch. Mrs. Osterhout met them inside with a hot pot of tea.

"What a beastly night," Dr. Sligh complained as he shook the water from his coat, and hung it over the stair rail. He sneezed.

"Oh dear, you aren't catching cold, are you?" his wife asked with concern.

He sneezed again, and pulled out his handkerchief. "I hope not, but I did get a bit wet." He now reached for a cup of tea.

"I'll help you with the trunks," his son offered.

Dr. Sligh looked at Charles. "Is your homework done?"

"Bessie made me do it before supper," the boy answered, "and I have my coat right here."

Dr. Sligh took another drink of hot tea, and set it aside. "Let's get it over with then. I'd like to change into something dry, and go to bed."

Church bells woke Katherine the next morning, but she rolled over too exhausted to care. Then suddenly she realized she was in Helena, and she sat up like a shot. This was Sunday, and the two weeks of campaigning were over. She had to go to church. Thomas Marlow would be there.

Katherine scrambled from bed. Her folks were still sound asleep, and she tiptoed into her brother's room. "Charles, Charles are you going to church?" she called softly as she shook his shoulder.

"Leave me alone," he cried groggily as his pillow rose to cover his face, and he buried himself deeper in his covers. Katherine quietly left, returning to her own room to dress. She glanced at their clock on her way out. It was early yet. She must have heard the bells from Catholic Hill.

Outside the sun was shining on the freshly washed world. Katherine paused momentarily, and then set out down Benton. She would turn on

Lawrence. The walk would be a fairly long one. She had to cross Last Chance Gulch to reach Warren Street and church.

When she approached St. Peters, buggies and carriages were tied everywhere, and she realized it had taken longer to walk the distance than she thought. She hastily climbed the steps, and went in as the congregation rose for the opening hymn. Katherine slid into a back pew, and reached for the hymnal. As she began singing, she now scanned for the Broadwaters and the Cullens. But with so many people in front of her, only the back of Ernest's coat was visible. At least, she thought it was probably Ernest. She wondered if he would talk to Wilder. Katherine unbuttoned her coat. She was suddenly feeling awfully warm.

Reverend Love was speaking from the pulpit as Katherine removed her coat. The air was suddenly so stuffy and warm. She longed for a breath of the cool October air outside, but no one would be rude enough to leave in the middle of the pastor's sermon. Katherine shifted her position uncomfortably as Reverend Love finally closed. She was feeling strange now, almost weak. She didn't rise as he gave the benediction. She hardly heard it. Then as singing filled the air around her, she mustered enough strength to gain her feet with the rest of the congregation, steadying herself against the pew in front of her. The hymn closed, and as the people began to disperse into the aisle ways, she was finally free to claim some October air. She took two hasty steps as her vision clouded, and then went black.

"Oh," a woman cried, "catch her." The woman's husband broke Katherine's fall as he slid her back into the pew.

People crowded around, curious and concerned. "Does anyone know her?" the man asked.

"It's Katherine Sligh," Puss piped up. She had squirmed her way through the commotion for a look.

Down the aisle way, Thomas Marlow heard Puss's voice. He hastened to her as Katherine began to come to. He now handed his handkerchief to Puss. "Find some water and get it wet," he instructed. Puss disappeared.

Katherine's eyes opened, and landed on Tom Marlow. She instantly sat up as her head spun. She fell limp.

"What's wrong with her," Reverend Love demanded as he made his way to the scene.

"She swooned," a young boy answered. "Twice."

Puss reappeared and handed Tom Marlow the wet handkerchief.

"Is she okay," Reverend Love asked as he now directed his attention to Marlow.

"I think she's just fainted," he answered, and laid the wet handkerchief across her brow.

Katherine again came to. This time, however, Thomas Marlow held light pressure against her shoulder so she would not sit up. Her insides felt queasy, and she turned to the side as she doubled over. Her stomach felt like it was rising into her throat. Then slowly the awful sensation eased, and was gone.

Stunned and a little shaken, Katherine was now struck by a wave of embarrassment as she realized everyone had gathered around her.

"How are you feeling," Tom Marlow asked gently.

"Better," she replied.

"Have you had anything to eat?" Reverend Love asked.

"There wasn't time," Katherine answered.

"Where is your family?" the reverend asked.

"Home. We've been gone, and we got in late last night," Katherine answered quietly. The crowd around her began to disperse until only the Broadwaters and the Cullens remained.

"Is there anything we can do," Mrs. Cullen offered.

Thomas Marlow glanced at her family. He noted the judge's absence, and Ernest's presence. "I wonder if you would have room for my cousins in your carriage. I'd like to take Miss Sligh home to her father. He's a doctor."

"You'll have room, mother, if I go with Katherine," Lilly offered as she suddenly appeared. Grace's attention was on Charles Broadwater.

"Yes, we would," Mrs. Cullen agreed, "but how will you get home?"

"I can walk," Lilly offered.

"I'll return her safely to you," Mr. Marlow offered now. He was helping Katherine to her feet.

"All right," Mrs. Cullen agreed as she turned to the others. She motioned for Charles and Wilder to join her family. Grace took the opportunity to walk alongside of Wilder's brother as she made small talk. Ernest walked out with Wilder.

"Lillian, would you stay with Katherine while I bring the carriage around?" Thomas Marlow requested.

"It's already in front of the church," Lilly offered.

"How..." Thomas Marlow's voice fell off as he offered his support to Katherine, and the three walked out together. He found the Broadwater carriage exactly where Lilly had said. Once Katherine and Lilly were settled inside, Thomas Marlow drove it directly to Mrs. Osterhout's.

"I can walk. I'm feeling fine," Katherine protested as Tom Marlow helped her out.

"You weren't earlier," he objected.

"I'm fine. Everyone is making too much fuss," Katherine retorted. She walked toward the house, and up the porch stairs. Tom opened the door for her, and escorted her to the couch.

Mrs. Osterhout appeared from the kitchen. "What's wrong," she exclaimed.

"She fainted in church. Is Dr. Sligh in?" Tom demanded.

Mrs. Osterhout hastened upstairs. Within minutes, Dr. Sligh and his wife were both bending over their daughter in concern.

"Katherine fainted?" Dr. Sligh repeated as he turned to Tom Marlow. "I didn't even know she'd gone to church." His attention shifted back to his daughter as he wiped his nose. "How do you feel, honey?"

"Kind of tired and heavy," she replied. "I'm sorry. I didn't mean to cause so much trouble."

"Nonsense," her father responded. "Did you walk to St. Peters?"

"Yes," his daughter answered quietly.

"On an empty stomach?"

"Yes."

"And the church was warm?"

"Very warm," Lilly answered. "They had the stove on."

"Is your daughter all right," Thomas Marlow asked now.

Dr. Sligh turned. "Yes, I think so. She just over did it a bit, particularly with all the traveling we've done these past couple of weeks." He looked closer at Marlow. "Don't I know you?"

"Montana National," Thomas Marlow answered, "you bank there."

"Oh yes," Dr. Sligh agreed, "yes, of course." His attention returned to his daughter. "You need something to eat, and then a lot rest, Katie."

"I was just about to start lunch," Mrs. Osterhout offered.

"Then perhaps we should leave," Tom Marlow decided as he glanced at Lilly.

"No," Katherine objected, "don't go yet."

"Yes, stay for lunch," Mrs. Osterhout encouraged. "We can't have you running off so soon, not after you brought Katherine home and everything."

"Will it be all right with your mother, Lillian?" Tom Marlow asked as he turned to her.

"She'll understand," Lilly replied.

Forty-five minutes later, Mrs. Osterhout and Mrs. Sligh served lunch. Katherine tried to maintain minimum conversation during this time, but the morning had taken its toll, and she fell asleep on the couch. Nobody woke her until the table was set, and the food was dished up.

As everyone sat down to eat, conversation flowed freely, and the boarders asked about the Sligh's experiences over the last couple of weeks. Then the conversation turned to Mrs. Osterhout's trip east.

Only Katherine said little. Her eyes were often on Tom Marlow as he listened and compared stories with the others. Even Mrs. Sligh had antidotes to tell, and it wasn't until the meal was nearly finished that Thomas Marlow swung the conversation around to that morning's church service, and to her.

"Miss Sligh, I don't suppose you heard Reverend Love mention the social at St. Peters Thursday night, did you?"

"No," she answered softly.

"Mrs. Babcock is supposed to give a solo, and there will be other music, and I think, a recitation. Would you like to go?"

Lilly nearly dropped her fork. Her eyes shot to Katherine's father and mother. Thomas Marlow had just asked Katherine for a date in front of everyone, including the boarders.

"It sounds like a lovely evening," Mrs. Sligh responded. "Katherine dear, Mr. Marlow has been so kind, I don't see how you can possibly refuse him."

A smile crept into her daughter's face. "I would love to go," she stated as her eyes lingered on Tom Marlow.

"You'll see that she doesn't get overheated, though, won't you?" Dr. Sligh asked quickly.

"You can count on it," Tom Marlow responded. He then rose from his chair, and turned to Mrs. Osterhout. "Thank you for the delicious meal," he stated now, "but I think I'd better get Lilly home before her mother wonders what has become of her."

Dr. Sligh walked Tom Marlow and Lilly to the door. "Thank you for bringing Katherine home."

"You're welcome," Marlow replied. His attention shifted to Lilly. "Shall we go?"

The two walked out together.

"That was some way to ask Katherine out," Lilly commented as Mr. Marlow helped her into the carriage.

"It was, wasn't it," he agreed as he climbed in beside her. They headed down Benton. "Lilly, Katherine is invited a lot of places," Tom Marlow noted after a few moments. He paused. "What are her ties?"

"Ties?" Lilly repeated. "What do you mean?"

A frank expression took command of his face. "Miss Cullen, you know Dr. Sligh is running for office. There isn't much about his life that isn't public knowledge, but Katherine...she's running with society, but she comes from Granite. What are her ties?"

"You mean, who is she?"

"Yes," he agreed, "there are a lot of 'would be' office holders whose daughters sit at home while Helena's elite party."

Lilly hesitated to answer as she pondered his motives. Questions like this shouldn't matter if he really liked her.

"Ah, I see you don't approve of my question," Thomas Marlow responded quietly as they crossed the intersection. "Yes, you're quite right. It shouldn't matter."

"What am I, an open book?" Lilly retorted.

Mr. Marlow smiled. "Katherine thinks the world of you. She says you understand things others miss."

"Flattery will get you far," Lilly replied quietly.

"This is not flattery," Thomas Marlow responded in abrupt distaste. "It's fact. Your father does the same thing."

"And you?"

"I try," he answered as he brought the horse around a corner. "I try to understand circumstances, motives behind actions, just like you and your father. Business demands it. Life demands it. You're demanding it now." He paused. "You hesitate to give me information which can help me understand the situation, information that all of Helena's right families already know." He fell momentarily silent. "I like Katherine. I like Katherine a lot, but..." He looked Lilly square in the eye. "Is she intended for someone else?"

Chapter Seven

"Not that I know of," Lilly answered honestly.

"But someone is making sure she's invited to all the right functions," he replied. "Is it your mother?"

Lilly became momentarily lost in thought as they traveled down Dearborn street. "You met Don Davenport today at lunch?" she offered quietly.

"Yes," he replied.

"He's married to Katherine's sister, Bessie."

"Is he Major Davenport's son?" Thomas Marlow asked.

"Yes," Lilly answered.

Thomas Marlow said nothing for several moments. "Is Bessie happy?"

"She appears to be," Lilly responded quietly. "I think she loves her husband."

"But..." Marlow waited for more.

"Major Davenport is kind man," Lilly offered now more slowly, "but there seems to be some tension from the mother. I understand Bessie goes into quite a tizzy every time her mother-in-law visits. Everything has to be 'just so'."

Thomas Marlow pulled his horse to a stop in front of Lilly's house. "They're hoping Katherine will marry well," he stated quietly.

"Mrs. Sligh is hoping she will marry well," Lilly offered. "It would help secure their position in the city, but," Lilly continued, "Katherine doesn't seem to socialize in her sister's circle any more than she has to. She seems to prefer my sister, Grace, and her friends."

A smile broke across his face. "Thank you, Lillian. You're honesty means a lot."

"You're falling in love with Katherine, aren't you?"

"Yes," he answered softly.

"I thought so," Lilly responded with a subtle smile.

Lilly was right, Katherine decided as she retreated upstairs to her room. Tom Marlow's heart had grown fonder of her. She smiled to herself. It was rather bold of him to ask her to the social Thursday night in front of everyone.

Then her face flushed again at the thought of the morning's fiasco. How could she faint like that? Embarrassed and weak, she thought she would die when she discovered all those people staring at her. Only Tom Marlow had made it bearable. He was so gentle and kind. Her thoughts drifted into sleep.

For the remainder of the day, as well as the following one, Katherine took it easy. Her parents did the same, exhausted from the campaigning. But as Tuesday arrived, so did Katherine's restless spirit. She looked forward to the evening's entertainment. She was invited to the Wallaces. It was to be a night of Spillikin, whatever that was. But Katherine didn't care, a little mystery was always fun.

Seven o'clock arrived, and Katherine stepped into her father's buggy. Her mother had arranged for the livery boy to drive her to the Wallace house.

"Katherine, you're back in town. I was hoping you would be able to make it," Mrs. Wallace greeted.

"Thank you for inviting me," Katherine responded as she entered the house.

"How are you feeling?" Charles Broadwater asked.

"Fine, thank you." Katherine couldn't quite remember who he was, but Grace's attention was definitely on the young man.

"You gave us all quite a scare Sunday," Ernest Cullen noted as he joined them. He reached over and whispered in her ear. "Grace is very grateful to you, even if she isn't showing it at the moment. She's totally lost on Charles, and she was overjoyed when we had to give him and Wilder a ride home from church."

"Charles?" Katherine's attention shifted back to the young man who had inquired after her health. "Oh Charles Broadwater," she gasped as she suddenly realized who he was.

"Yes, that's me," Charles agreed with a smile. "Has anyone figured out what Spillikin is?"

"Jackstraws," Grace answered. She had gained his attention, and she wasn't going to loose it.

"See." Ernest spoke under his breath to Katherine. Then his attention shifted, and he wandered off.

"I think they want us to sit down," Virginia Atchison decided as she joined Katherine. "Did you get a card?"

"Yes, Mrs. Wallace gave me one," Katherine responded as she recognized the young woman from Mrs. Murphy's Butterfly Tea.

"Which table are you at?" Virginia asked.

"How do you tell?"

"Here," the Atchison girl pointed to the flower in the corner of the card. "You have white chrysanthemums. I have red roses. Our cards match with the center pieces."

"So are you any good at jackstraws," Katherine asked as they headed to sit down.

"Is anyone good?" she laughed. They parted company, and found seats at their respective tables.

"You've got chrysanthemums too, Katherine?" Grace asked as she and Charles joined her.

"Yes." Charles helped Grace with her chair as Ernest appeared and took the remaining place at the table.

Each of the young ladies was given a corsage to match the center piece, and the fellows a matching boutonniere. Then the game commenced.

Charles moved the centerpiece to the side as he dumped the bundle of sticks squarely in the middle of their table. Then each member of the table tried to pick up as many sticks as he or she could without moving any of the others. Katherine vied against Ernest as they deftly added more and more to each of their personal collections. Charles was all thumbs, and Katherine suspected that Grace was being clumsy on purpose, though she said nothing.

"Ah, there," Ernest claimed majestically. "Beat that, Katherine."

"How many did you get?" she cried.

"Seven," he announced.

"Seven, there aren't seven left," Katherine protested.

Ernest smiled.

The game was progressive; and Ernest having won, moved on to another table. Norman Holter claimed Ernest's chair. He was a very august young man, and instantly assumed the authority role as they played another round.

"So Miss Sligh, your father is running for office," Norman Holter stated. He picked up a stick, and tried for another as its neighbor wobbled.

"Yes," Katherine agreed as she now claimed three jackstraws. Grace claimed one, and this time Charles managed to pick up two in a row.

The conversation became superficial, and Katherine concentrated on her game. She wanted out of this group.

"Katherine, you did it," Grace exclaimed.

Katherine rose from her seat as refreshments were served. She wasn't particularly hungry, but the strawberry ice cream served in green spun candy was something she had never seen before. She had to try it. She sat down at the next table. Here her luck was also good, and she moved to the next table. Ernest hadn't done as well. He smiled as she joined their group. Then as luck would have it neither Katherine nor Ernest won any more rounds; and as eleven o'clock approached, Mrs. Wallace finally declared Miss Amy Rosenbaum, the ladies' winner, and Mr. Ferguson, the men's. They were awarded prizes, a shell hair pin and a silver nail file, respectively. Miss Cruse and Mr. Thompson were consoled for their lack of dexterity.

"Can we drive you home?" Grace asked Katherine as they were reclaiming their wraps. Charles had already left.

"Mother is sending the livery boy to pick me up," Katherine replied.

"So send him home. We'll drive you," Grace insisted.

"Okay. Are you and your mother going to Governor Rickards tomorrow afternoon?" Katherine asked as they walked out. Ernest joined them.

"Probably."

"Is your mother going?" Ernest asked.

"I don't think so," Katherine replied. "Daddy's come down with a terrible cold, and she's not much better. Both are worried they might loose their voice."

"That wouldn't be good with the election coming up," Ernest decided.

"So do you need a ride, Katherine?" Grace asked. "The governor lives clear across the gulch."

"Yes, that would help," she replied.

"We'll pick you up then," Grace responded with a smile.

"What about later? Do you have plans, Katherine?" Ernest asked. "It's Halloween, you know."

"Don't pay any attention to him," Grace scoffed. "Mother's making him chaperone Puss's party, and he's been trying to get out of it all week."

"That's not true," Ernest retorted. "I like Halloween, but mom's making me help with table arrangements and food and stuff -- and I'm no good at it. I just thought Katherine might be, and Puss needs someone to help."

"You're asking me...with all the women in your family?" Katherine responded.

"Mom and dad have been invited across the street to the Ashbys, and Grace will be at the Barnabys," he replied.

"What about Lilly?" Katherine asked.

"It's test week at St. V's, and she's probably going to have her nose stuck in some book."

"Okay, I'll come," Katherine agreed.

"Katherine, are you sure?" Grace responded.

"Sure, I like Puss," she replied, "and I haven't been invited anywhere else."

"Then you could come home directly from the Rickards with us," Grace slowly decided. "You could eat supper at our house."

"That would give us more time to get ready," Ernest agreed. "Puss will be overjoyed."

They walked out together; and having dismissed Katherine's buggy, Ernest drove them home.

"Grace, I don't see anyone I know," Katherine commented softly as she watched Mrs. Rickards greet her guests.

"I saw Pearl Davenport a second ago," Grace confided, "but yes, everyone seems older. Let's make our appearances, and then maybe we can leave early without being noticed."

Katherine followed her friend to the end of the receiving line. Flower bouquets were large and everywhere, their sweet scent mingling with the warmth of so many people and the strains of the Broadwater orchestra.

After about a fifteen minute wait, the receiving line brought them to Mrs. Rickards. They greeted the governor's wife, and said the expected things. Then the flow of the guests moved them to the dining room where the refreshments were, along with a profusion of white chrysanthemums. They saw Pearl Davenport across the room, and waved. The crowd was too dense to do more.

"All right, let's be wicked and get out of here," Grace suggested.

"What about your mother?" Katherine asked.

"She won't be ready to come home yet," Grace replied, "but she won't mind if we walk."

"Oh good, you're back," Puss greeted with a broad smile. "Hi Katherine. Ernest said you were coming." Her attention turned to Grace. "Lilly isn't home yet, and mother left a list of things to do, only I can't make any sense out of it."

"Let me see," Grace responded.

"No, I'll help her," Katherine offered as she took the list. "Grace you have a party to get ready for. Go change." She glanced at the clock. It was a quarter to five. "What time is supper, Puss?"

"Six," she answered.

"So we can't change the table cloth until after that," Katherine decided. She flipped over the list. On the opposite side she found more instructions. "Okay, Puss, here are the things we're supposed to do before supper."

The two set to work arranging cornstalks, spreading dry autumn leaves, and finally adding the pumpkins, some carved, some not.

"Ernest made this one," Puss laughed as she arranged the gruesome fellow by the door. "Now all we need are the spiders and bats."

"Weren't there some in the kitchen?" Katherine asked.

"I think so," Puss agreed.

Katherine retrieved the box. "The spiders are heavy," Katherine noted.

"Yeah, they're painted rocks with dyed pipe cleaners," Puss giggled. "Ernest and I made them."

"Then your brother really likes Halloween?" Katherine asked.

"Yeah. When he gets home, he's going to string up the cobwebs," Puss bragged.

"So how many of your friends are coming?"

"Practically the whole class," Puss declared. "Everyone was talking about it at school."

The front door opened, and Lilly came through. "This looks great," she declared.

"Can you help?" Puss begged. "We haven't even begun to get the games ready."

"All right," Lilly replied. "But if I help now, I won't be around later. I have a test in Logic tomorrow."

The three set to work stuffing gilded walnut shells with small strips of paper predicting futures. Then they hung apples, dished up nuts and candies, and prepared everything for the games. By the time Ernest and his father walked through the door, everything was ready except the refreshment table, and of course the cob webs. These things would have to wait until after supper.

Mrs. Cullen arrived within minutes. She greeted everyone, and then turned to her youngest. "Puss, everything looks great. How did you get so much done?"

"Katherine helped, and Lilly," she answered.

"Where's Grace?" she asked.

"Upstairs getting ready for her party," Katherine replied.

"Lilly, you'd better call your sister. It smells like dinner is getting too done, and we need to eat as soon as possible."

By the time Puss's guests began to arrive, Judge and Mrs. Cullen were across the street at the Ashbys, Grace was at her party, and Lilly was upstairs studying. Puss hosted her party as Katherine and Ernest worked behind the scenes, making sure everything ran smoothly.

By ten o'clock the party began to wind down. Games had been played, food eaten, and fortunes told. All of Puss's friends had a grand time.

As Puss saw the last of her friends out, Ernest turned to Katherine. "Thanks for helping. It wouldn't have been as much fun without you."

"My pleasure," Katherine replied as she stacked the dirty plates together.

"The decorations looked great too," he added, lingering beside her.

"The cob webs too," she commented as she worked. "Puss tells me you like Halloween."

"It's one of the best holidays of the year," he answered. "It's one night a person can really cut loose."

"You like cutting loose?" Katherine asked.

"That's what life is for, isn't it?" he responded with a grin. "Surely, we weren't put on this earth only for the drudgery."

"I hope not," Katherine chuckled, "but I never thought of Halloween quite like that. Maybe I cut loose differently."

"How?" Ernest demanded.

"Oh I don't know," she replied. "Maybe I cut loose at other kinds of parties, you know, dancing and talking." Her thoughts drifted to the Broadwater.

"One party is probably as good as another," Ernest agreed. "So which party is next?"

"I hope it's my father's victory party," Katherine laughed.

"Have you an escort yet?" Ernest asked.

"No. I don't even know that he'll win," Katherine replied.

"Well if he does, I expect to hear the news from you, okay?" he asked.

"Okay," Katherine agreed.

"Ernest, help," Puss suddenly cried. "Your grumpy pumpkin is turning black."

Her brother hastened out into the hall. Katherine glanced toward the kitchen. Lilly stood there leaning against the door frame.

"He's got a crush on you," Lilly stated quietly.

"Ernest? You must be mistaken," Katherine responded. "He's Wilder's."

"No one asked him who he likes," Lilly replied, "and I'm afraid it's you."

"No. It can't be," Katherine replied.

"Puss, it's just soot." Ernest's voice carried into the dining room.

Lilly grabbed Katherine's arm, and pulled her out onto the porch as she shoved a borrowed coat at her.

Chapter Eight

"He likes you. I saw it the day you two met," Lilly declared as she pulled the porch door closed. "I just didn't realize it until now."

"I never encouraged him," Katherine protested as both slipped into miscellaneous coats. "I never meant to..."

"I know," Lilly interrupted with a soft smile, "but now you have a choice between a banker and an attorney."

"What should I do?" Katherine asked in stunned tone.

"Consider your options," Lilly laughed. "There could be worse things."

"I know, but Ernest is your brother," Katherine responded miserably.

"And he has a profession that allows him to mix freely with Helena's elite. Bank employees don't have that. They aren't invited to all the things you've been going to. ...and Ernest is closer to your own age."

"That's true," Katherine admitted reluctantly. "But Ernest..." Her voice fell off. The young man was far from what she had imagined in a husband. True his ears did not stick out as far as Grace liked to imply, but his eyes were set rather close together. But setting his looks aside, Ernest simply was not the type of man Katherine was looking for. He lacked spirit. He lacked confidence in himself. So he mingled with all the right people, the fact would probably afford him a comfortable living. But what of Ernest himself? Would he ever become his own man? Consternation rose in Katherine's expression.

"I'd probably feel the same way," Lilly admitted softly. "I love my brother, but you're right. He will never be the man Thomas Marlow is."

Katherine focused sharply on Lilly. "You mean that?"

Lilly smiled. "Yes."

By Thursday Katherine's parents were feeling much better, and planning the last major push of her father's campaign. They would return once again to Granite County so Dr. Sligh could give his final speeches, and garner as many votes as possible for Tuesday's election. They would leave the following day for Drummond, Hall, Maxville, and Philipsburg. They would attend church at home, and then visit various mining camps. On this trip, however, both their children would remain in Helena.

"Bessie will look after you and Charles while we're gone," Mrs. Sligh informed Katherine, "and you can help her with refreshments on Sunday. She's having Don's parents over."

Katherine straightened from her ironing. "No thank you," she responded.

Mrs. Sligh stopped. "What's wrong with helping your sister?"

"I'd rather stay with friends like last time," Katherine stated firmly. "I don't have that much in common with Bessie any more. All she does is talk about married people and babies."

Her mother's expression softened. "That will all change soon enough, Katherine. But for now, she could really use your help on Sunday."

"No," Katherine decided, "I don't want to help."

"Katherine! What's gotten into you? Bessie is your sister."

"I didn't marry into that family. She did. Let her get her own refreshments on Sunday. I don't want to."

"Katherine!"

"Mother, you know very well that nothing Bessie can do will make things perfect enough. I don't know why she even tries."

"She tries for Don's sake," her mother stated firmly.

"Then let Don help her. He's used to his mother. Just don't ask me. I am terribly uncomfortable around Mrs. Davenport."

"Katherine, Rachel has been very good to us. Who do you think has been so instrumental in getting us invitations to everything? And she has been invaluable in advising us on etiquette. Helena is a lot different than Granite."

"Mother, I don't want to go," Katherine asserted. "Find an excuse."

Mrs. Sligh stared at her daughter. Katherine rarely resisted her, never with this much strength. Had something happened between her and Mrs. Rachel Davenport? She thought about the Rickards afternoon. Katherine had attended that affair without her.

"All right, Katherine," Mrs. Sligh conceded reluctantly, "maybe I'll call on Mrs. Cullen this afternoon. You wouldn't mind staying with them again?"

"No, I like the Cullens," Katherine replied quietly.

After lunch Mrs. Sligh paid a visit to Mrs. Cullen. She was readily received, and showered with nothing but praise for Katherine. Encouraged by the fact, Mrs. Sligh brought up her little dilemma. Mrs. Cullen instantly insisted that Katherine stay with them. With that problem solved, Mrs. Sligh returned to their rooms to find most of their packing completed. Katherine had been busy in her absence.

"Katherine, you can stay at the Cullens," her mother informed her. "They have nothing but good things to say about you." She smiled as she checked the time. "It's getting late, and we have to pick up Charles before we meet your father for dinner. You have the church social tonight."

Katherine gazed into the mirror as she fastened her pink beads around her neck. They matched perfectly with the pink sash of her dress. She straightened the rose quartz stone, and the dangling beads fell into place, setting off the lines of her neck. She rose as she heard the door open downstairs. Mr. Marlow had arrived for her.

Katherine's heart skipped a beat as she descended the stairs. Thomas Marlow had removed his hat. His great coat hung long over his lean body. He turned from her father, and a twinkle lit his eyes.

"You look lovely," he responded.

Katherine handed him her cloak, and he helped her on with it. Then Tom Marlow turned to her father. "We should be back by ten."

"Enjoy yourselves."

Katherine glanced at her mother. Mrs. Sligh had barely said a word since Mr. Marlow's arrival. She just stood on the stairs watching. Tom cordially acknowledged her as they went out.

Tom Marlow helped Katherine into the carriage, and climbed in beside her. "Mrs. Babcock is not one of my favorite singers," he admitted now as his eyes rested on Katherine, "but I thought it would be a way of seeing you."

Katherine smiled. "It's all right," she responded. "She has to be better than some I've heard at home."

"Oh, she's a good singer," Marlow replied, "just not my style...but that's not why I brought it up. Alexander Salvini is going to be at Ming's theater Monday night. His acting is superb. I wondered if you would care to go?"

"Alexander Salvini," Katherine responded, "I've read about him in the newspaper. Yes, I'd love to. Have you ever seen him before?"

"Back east, this last summer," Thomas Marlow replied. "He's quite good."

"Monday," Katherine mused. "Mother and father won't be back from their trip until late Tuesday."

"Are you going with them again," Marlow asked.

"No, I'm staying with Lilly and Grace," she replied.

"When are your folks leaving?" he asked.

"Tomorrow morning."

"Lilly could come with us," Tom Marlow offered.

"To Salvini? I think she would like that," Katherine decided.

"I'll come over tomorrow after work, and we'll see if she wants to go. Besides, it will give me an excuse to see you again." He smiled. "Your father won't mind if the three of us go, will he?"

"No, I don't think so, and I'll be staying with the Cullens anyway."

St. Peter's Episcopal Church was well attended for the vocal performances of Mrs. Babcock, Miss Stuart, and Miss Barnaby. The Foote girls played a violin and piano duet, and Miss Fisk gave a stirring recitation. These were the highlights among the various choir pieces sung. Afterwards, light refreshments were served.

Katherine and Thomas Marlow each placed a cookie and a small piece of cake on their plate, and then mingled with the crowd. However, they inevitably ended up alone as their attention was focused more on each other than anyone else. They didn't mind. Conversation was constant between them. Tom Marlow related some of his experiences in Big Sandy while Katherine listened, spellbound.

Marlow looked up. Less than a dozen people still lingered in the church basement. "We'd better be going," he decided as he pulled out his watch. He breathed a little easier.

"What time is it?" Katherine asked.

"Only nine thirty," he answered. "There's plenty of time to get you home." Within moments they were on their way.

"I enjoyed being with you tonight," Tom Marlow told Katherine as he helped her down from the carriage in front of Mrs. Osterhout's. The moon lit her face.

"Me too," she responded softly.

His eyes were on her now, and she felt their warmth. "Katherine," he began softly. "Katherine, I really like being with you," he repeated as the words floundered in his mouth. His hand rose, his fingers picking up the rose quartz stone that hung at her neck. Then his eyes shifted back to hers. "I'm falling for you, you know."

Time seemed to stand still. Every thought in Katherine's mind evaporated. All she knew was him, his touch, his smell, his presence.

Tom Marlow looked down. In his hand was his pocket watch. "You'd better go in," he noted softly. "You don't want to be late." In silence a wane smile rose to his lips. "Until tomorrow night," he whispered. Then he led her up the walk, and opened the door for her. Without a further word, he left.

"Where's Mr. Marlow?" Mrs. Sligh asked as she appeared from the parlor. "Isn't he coming in for a few minutes?"

"No mother," Katherine answered. Her thoughts were still with Tom as she wandered up to her room.

"That's strange," her mother remarked as she followed her daughter. "It isn't that late."

"He knows you and daddy are off early tomorrow."

"Katherine," she began now as they entered their rooms, "it was nice of Mr. Marlow to take you to church tonight, after your fainting spell and all, but I wouldn't take it all too seriously."

"What do you mean, mother," Katherine asked as she abruptly turned.

"There are bigger fish in the sea than Mr. Marlow," she responded, "much bigger."

"I like him," Charles stated as he looked up from his school book.

"You shouldn't listen in on other people's conversations, young man," his mother scolded.

"You mean there are wealthier men to snag, mother, wealthier and snootier," Katherine retorted.

"Katherine," her mother exclaimed, "I was just trying to point out..."

"Leave the girl alone," Dr. Sligh interrupted from his desk. "If she wants to keep company with a bank president, let her. She could do worse."

Katherine only felt relief when her parents left the following morning. Dropped off at the Cullens, Katherine could now look forward to an evening without her mother's watchful eye. She was in good spirits as she helped Mrs. Cullen and Grace with their various charity work. The weather, meanwhile, grew threatening and dark with the afternoon. Heavy clouds broke over the hills as hail dropped from the sky and pelted the earth.

Mrs. Cullen joined the girls at the window, staring out at the weather.

Grace abruptly turned to Katherine. "You have an invitation to the recital at the McConnells tonight, don't you?"

"No, I don't think so." Katherine's thoughts drifted to the last minute envelope her mother had handed to her. "Wait, maybe," she exclaimed as she ran upstairs.

Grace followed.

"Yes, this is the invitation," Katherine noted. "Things have been so busy over the last couple of days, I must have missed it."

"Good, we can all go together," Grace decided. "Wilder will be there."

"It's another music program," Katherine noted, thinking of the evening before. Her eyes darted to the time. Tom Marlow was supposed to stop by. Would he arrive before they had to leave?

A flash of lightening lit the room as both girls' attention was drawn back to the weather. Thunder followed.

"You can borrow one of my dresses," Grace decided as she retreated to her closet. "I think I'll wear this one, but you could use my yellow crepe." She pulled it out, and held it against Katherine. A smile rose to her lips. "I bet it fits perfectly."

Excitement bubbled in Grace as she helped Katherine change that evening. "Perfect," she declared. "You can borrow my glass beads to go with it." She pulled them from her dresser drawer. Suddenly she stopped. "No, with your dark hair, I think we should use the black ones...and I have a black sash we can use at the waist."

Katherine glanced down to where Grace's watch lay on the dresser. Tom Marlow should be off work by now. Grace finished with the sash, and Katherine instantly slipped away, heading down the hall to Lilly. She hadn't spoken to Grace's sister since she had gotten home from school.

Lilly looked up from her reading. "Hi," she greeted. "Is that Grace's yellow crepe?"

"Yes," Katherine answered. "Lilly, Tom Marlow is coming by tonight."

"Here?" Lilly asked.

"Yes. I didn't realize I'd been invited to the McConnells, and I wouldn't go, except I've made no excuse to them. Plus, Grace is counting on me. Oh Lilly, I'm afraid I'm going to miss Tom."

"Don't worry," Lilly reassured as she set aside her book. "When he comes I'll just explain things. It's not like Grace has given you much choice in the matter."

"I really want to see him," Katherine admitted miserably, "but he's actually coming by to see you."

"Me?" Lilly responded.

"Yes." Katherine's attention shifted back to the hall. Grace was calling her name.

"You do realize Ernest is going tonight too, don't you," Lilly volunteered.

Katherine's sense of propriety evaporated. "I can't go. I just can't go," she cried.

"But Wilder will be there," Lilly encouraged, "and the sooner you get those two matched, the sooner Ernest will be off your back. You saw the way he kept watching you at dinner."

"How could I help it," Katherine replied in exasperation.

"Exactly, so go to the recital, and I'll explain things to Mr. Marlow," Lilly stated.

"Katherine, we have to go," Grace called. "We're already late."

"You'd better get going," Lilly prodded as she walked her friend into the hall.

"Lilly! Lilly," Puss cried frantically up the stairs, "the kittens are gone."

"Katherine, come on," Grace called. "Ernest is waiting in the carriage."

Both Katherine and Lilly headed down, parting ways at the bottom. Lilly's mother intercepted her as Katherine followed Grace out the door.

"I'll help Puss with the kittens," Mrs. Cullen offered quickly. "You have a visitor in the library."

Lilly crossed the hall as the others disappeared through the back of the house. Mr. Marlow stood looking at one of their books while he waited. He turned as she entered the room.

"Mr. Marlow, I'm afraid you've missed Katherine. My sister has spirited her away to a recital," Lilly offered.

"I actually came by to see you," Tom Marlow responded calmly as they sat down, "and my friends call me Tom."

"You wanted to talk to me about something," Lilly asked.

"Yes. Katherine and I are planning to see Alexander Salvini Monday night. Would you like to come?"

"Alexander Salvini," Lilly gasped, "no one at St. V's can get tickets. All the reserved seating is sold out."

Tom Marlow smiled. "Yes, I know."

"Really? You're really inviting me?" Lilly cried.

"Yes."

"I'd love to go," Lilly exclaimed.

"There is one condition," Tom replied now. "I don't want you to feel like a third wheel. You need an escort."

"An escort?" Lilly responded as her expression fell. "Mr. Mar... Tom, I go to a girl's school. I don't know any fellows, except maybe my brother or Tom Hauser."

"Tom Hauser?"

"The Hausers have been family friends forever. Tom might as well be my brother," Lilly replied with a quiet smile.

"So in all of Helena, there is no one special?" Marlow pressed.

"Oh, I don't know about that," Lilly retorted. "I just don't know him."

"Then you might consider someone you don't know," Marlow asked carefully.

"Possibly."

"Let me see what I can do," Marlow replied.

"Wait a minute," Lilly suddenly giggled. "Are you setting me up on a blind date?"

"Would you object?" he asked.

"Well no, I guess not," she responded. She succumbed to a moment of confusion. "He would be gentleman, right?"

"A gentleman, definitely." Marlow smiled.

"All right," Lilly agreed, and she laughed nervously.

The weather still threatened rain as Ernest escorted Katherine and his sister into the McConnell house on Fifth Avenue. This was the first recital of the newly formed Medley Club to which several of Grace's friends belonged. Grace no sooner stepped inside than she was hailed by Wilder. The latter's face brightened further as Katherine and Ernest followed.

"Come sit with me," Wilder demanded.

Katherine followed Tom's cousin down the narrow row between the chairs with Ernest behind her. Grace trailed behind, talking to various friends. Wilder sat down, and suddenly Katherine realized she was between Wilder and Ernest.

Chapter Nine

"Wilder, let me trade places with you," Katherine decided. "I need to be closer to the wall. It's cooler there."

"Oh sure," Wilder agreed, "we don't want you to pass out again."

She promptly changed seats, and sat down next to Ernest. But her conversation returned to Katherine. "Do you faint easily?"

"No, the church was just very warm," Katherine replied. "Ernest took you home, didn't he?"

"Yes," Wilder responded with a big smile, "but we didn't go straight home, did we Ernest?"

"No, mom had some things she wanted to drop off at the Wallaces."

"The weather was beautiful, not like tonight," Wilder continued. Her eyes shifted to Ernest.

Katherine glanced at Grace's brother. He was looking at her. Katherine screwed up her mouth, and tilted her head in Wilder's direction, hinting for him to talk to Wilder. He reluctantly complied.

Within minutes the recital began, and Grace hastily took her seat next to her brother. The program was a mixture of vocal and instrumental pieces, spiced with an occasional whistling number. The unusual variety of talent was thoroughly enjoyed by the audience; but as it concluded, Katherine could only let out a sigh of relief. Her mind had not been on the performance. She felt guilty and disappointed for missing Tom Marlow, and she could only hope that Monday evening was still in the offing.

Ernest pulled his family's carriage up in front of their house, and helped his sister out, then Katherine. She was about to follow Grace in, when she realized Ernest had not let go of her hand.

"Wilder is nice, but she's not you," he commented softly to her. "Why do you push it?"

"You don't like Wilder?" Katherine asked.

"She's not you," he repeated.

"Maybe I'm not who you think I am," Katherine responded.

"What do you mean?" he asked, confused.

"My life has been very different from yours."

"I doubt it has been that different," he replied.

Katherine glanced at the house. Grace had already disappeared within. Her attention returned to the young man. "Ernest, you have always had so much. You don't know what it's like to want for anything."

"So…"

"So others have. Others understand what you can't."

"I know more than most about what goes on," Ernest countered.

"Certainly in the field of law, but not in life."

"I don't see the difference," he retorted.

Katherine smiled. "Yes, I know."

Ernest shifted uncomfortably. "Maybe we'd better to in," he decided.

Katherine gratefully acquiesced. She didn't want this talk in the first place.

"Katherine, you're home," Lilly exclaimed. "Come up to my room. We've got to talk."

Katherine heard the front door close carefully behind them. Ernest was observing them. Without a word, she followed Lilly up.

As Lilly closed the bedroom door behind them, her face glowed with excitement. "Guess what?"

"Tom Marlow was here," Katherine replied calmly.

"Yes. He was actually here before you left, only we didn't know it. Mother thought he only wanted to see me."

"Tom was here before I left?" Katherine repeated in disbelief. "Where?"

"In the library," she replied with a grin. "Do you know where he wants to take us?"

"To Alexander Salvini," Katherine answered. "Can you go?"

"Can I go?" Lilly exclaimed. A broad smile broke across her lips. "You bet I'm going. But that's not all."

"What else is there?" Katherine asked.

"Mr. Marlow is fixing me up with someone," Lilly exclaimed.

"Who?"

"I don't know," Lilly answered with a grin she couldn't keep away.

"You don't know? He's fixing you up with a blind date?"

"Yep."

Katherine gazed at her friend's jubilation. "You don't mind that Tom will be paying and arranging for everything? It won't be the fellow's idea at all," she cautioned.

"Of course it won't," Lilly responded. "I wouldn't expect it to be. It's just a chance to meet someone new, and see Salvini at the same time. What could be better?"

"Nothing, I guess," Katherine replied. "What are you going to wear?"

"I don't know. That's just it. I've been waiting hours for you to come home. Come have a look at my closet. What color does Mr. Marlow like?"

"Rose, a deep dusty rose," Katherine answered, "but that doesn't mean your fellow will."

"I know," Lilly giggled. "Are you wearing a rose gown then?"

"No, I don't have one," Katherine replied.

"Grace does," Lilly offered. "You're wearing her yellow crepe right now, aren't you?"

"Yes," Katherine answered as she suddenly remembered the fact.

"Well, we'll just have to talk her into letting you borrow the rose one. What color is the one you brought with?"

"White. It's the one I wore to the Broadwater."

"Oh I remember, the one with pearls," Lilly replied. "It's beautiful."

"If Grace lends me her rose one, would you like to try my white silk?"

"I'd love to," Lilly responded.

As Monday evening approached, the fervor of the house only grew. Lilly excitement remained undiminished, despite her attendance to Lulu Bach's card party Saturday afternoon, and the quantity of schoolwork she was accomplishing to insure that no complications occurred for Monday evening. Katherine, too, was looking forward to the performance. Church on Sunday had not allowed much more than a glimpse of Tom Marlow. He had waved and smiled, but Judge Cullen was in a hurry to get home. With the election so near, he and his wife had several meetings to attend. Grace, Katherine, and Ernest accompanied them.

"This is enjoyable," Ernest commented facetiously as he stood with Katherine and Grace, surveying their elders.

"It is boring," Grace readily agreed.

"But expected," Ernest retorted. "We aren't wanting for anything here, are we Katherine?"

His tone was bitter. Her mood was depressed. Katherine wasn't used to surviving such tedium, and she reacted against Ernest.

"Try listening to a man's screams after he's been crushed under a mountain of falling rock with air so full of dirt that you can't even see," Katherine replied.

"You were there?" Ernest asked.

"I was outside the mine when it happened," Katherine answered quietly. "My father could only help those that got out."

"What's eating you two?" Grace demanded.

Neither answered her.

Monday found Mrs. Cullen, Grace, and Katherine at the Women's Headquarters in the Bailey Block, manning the booths and handing out literature and buttons on the capitol issue. By the time Katherine got home, Lilly was waiting for her. Together they headed upstairs to get ready for the theater.

Thomas Marlow stepped from the cab and waited for his companion. Then together they walked up to the Cullen door. It was opened by the judge.

"Tom, good evening," Judge Cullen greeted as he invited them in. "The girls are expecting you."

"Judge, you know Ed Holter, don't you?" Tom Marlow introduced.

"Yes, Anton's son," Lilly's father confirmed. "How's college coming?"

"Good," Ed Holter replied. "Good."

"What are you doing home, Ed?" Judge Cullen asked as he led the way to the library. "Thanksgiving break can't have started yet."

"There was a death in the family," Ed Holter explained, "on my mother's side. So I've had almost a week off."

"Oh, I didn't realize," the judge responded. "Please convey our condolences." He reached for a couple of liqueur glasses. "Would you like a drink? Lilly and Katherine should be down soon."

Upstairs, Grace raced down the hall. "They're here," she announced. "You two are so lucky. I wish I had fainted in church."

"I would have traded places with you willingly," Katherine laughed. "It was so embarrassing."

"But look, now you both get to see Salvini. What could be better? I'd go with the devil himself to see Salvini," Grace exclaimed. She glanced at the watch pinned to her blouse. "Two more minutes, and then you can go down. That should be enough time." Her eyes swung to Lilly. "Remember, talk to the fellow, and nothing too bookish, okay?"

"Let's go," Katherine suggested.

As Katherine and Lilly descended the stairs, Judge Cullen emerged from the library with his two companions. His eyes settled on his daughter. "You look lovely, Lilly. Like a spring flower in the highlands."

"Oh daddy," she cried in pleasure, "you're too sentimental."

"Maybe," he responded, "but I doubt it." He smiled, and briefly complimented Katherine. Then he turned to the men. "I expect them home at a decent hour. Enjoy the theater." With that, he walked away and left the four to see themselves out.

"I understood, Lilly," Tom began now, "that you didn't know any young men, but Ed tells me the two of you know each other from church."

"He must want to see Salvini as much as me," she replied quietly.

"I do," Ed Holter agreed.

Tom's attention focused sharply on the two. "What's going on?"

"I used to tease her," Ed confessed quietly.

"And I used to insult him," Lilly added.

"So was this a mistake?" Tom Marlow asked.

"Not as far as I am concerned," Holter replied.

"Lilly?" Tom asked.

"I'd like to see Salvini," she replied as she handed Ed Holter her cloak. "Do you go to the theater often?"

"It really depends on what's playing," Ed Holter replied cordially as he helped Lilly with her wrap. Holter's manners held with no trace of his former mischief. Lilly pondered her old acquaintance. He had evidently changed a great deal since he'd gone away to college.

Tom Marlow opened the door for Lilly and Ed as he pondered their behavior. The two displayed impeccable manners as they went out. The evening could prove interesting. He and Katherine followed.

As the four took seats in the waiting cab, Tom turned to Lilly in an attempt to keep the conversation flowing. "I understand St. Vincent's has quite a good orchestra. Do you play an instrument?"

"I'm afraid that is not among my talents," she replied. "My sisters tell me I should, anything to get me away from my books. But I am content." She smiled.

"What do you read?" Ed Holter asked politely.

"Mostly the Roman writers," Lilly replied as she watched her companion warily, waiting for his fun making to start. "I can't read Greek, so that limits me to whatever I can find in Latin."

"Then you've read Livy?" Holter asked.

"Most of it," Lilly responded in surprise. Holter question was serious and academic. "Have you?"

"No, but I have read a translation of Herodotus," Ed Holter replied.

"You have," Lilly exclaimed. "Is this the same Ed Holter?" Her eyes turned in bewilderment to Tom Marlow.

"His family claims they can hardly get Ed to come home from college. I figured any two people who liked studying as much as you two must have something in common. I'm sorry I didn't know about your feud." A chagrined smile rose to Tom's lips. Then his attention turned to Katherine. "You haven't read Livy, have you?"

"Livy who," Katherine laughed. "I can hardly get my family to leave me alone long enough to read Mark Twain."

"Good, I wouldn't want my education to look like it was lacking," Tom responded with a small chuckle.

Katherine's attention shifted to her friend. Lilly was already in a discussion with Ed Holter; and as the cab passed under a street lamp, their growing interest in each other was obvious even in the dim light.

It wasn't long before the cab pulled up in front of the Ming Theater. Long lines of people led away from the ticket booths, but the Marlow party walked straight through to the inner doors, and presented their tickets. The usher led them immediately to their seats off the center aisle. Ed Holter took the inner most seat, followed by Lilly, Katherine, and Tom Marlow.

As they sat down, Lilly broke into a nervous giggle. "No one I knew could even get reserved tickets," she exclaimed, "and here we are in the best seats of the house."

"She's having a good time," Katherine whispered softly in Tom Marlow's ear.

"Yes," he replied as he took Katherine's hand in his own, "though I wasn't too sure at first."

"They say love and hate are two sides of the same coin," Katherine responded with a grin.

"So tell me you love me," he retorted. He instantly regretted his flippant remark, and flushed.

"I do," Katherine responded. "You're a good man."

"I wasn't serious," Tom floundered.

"I was." Katherine brought his hand briefly to her lips, and kissed it.

The lights of the theater dimmed, and slowly the heavy stage curtain was pulled back to reveal a painted terrace. Tom Marlow hardly noticed. His heart was beating wildly in his chest. Katherine loved him. She had said so. Never had he felt such euphoria. To be loved by such a beautiful, gentle creature was beyond his wildest imagination. Every moment in her presence was a piece of heaven, and she loved him. She actually loved him. Tom Marlow stared in front of him as joy ran rampant within him. Alexander Salvini was the farthest thing from his mind.

The performance at the Ming theater was a huge success as Salvini cast a spell over his audience convincing them that the heroics of his several characterizations were none too marvelous, their audacity none too daring, and their bluster none too ridiculous for belief. For despite the excitement, the speeches, and the gatherings elsewhere in the city, the performance drew such a crowd that the little boys who customarily haunted the gallery were displaced by well dressed adults. There was not even standing room left on the floor, and the enthusiastic crowd thunderously applauded the outstanding performance.

The house lights went on as the audience stood clapping after the final encore. Then the ladies and their gentlemen flowed into the aisle ways, and poured out of the warm theater into the November chill. Snow was lightly falling, dusting the cloaks of the many people in white. A festive spirit radiated from the crowd. They had enjoyed themselves, and the holidays promised even more wonderful things ahead.

Katherine settled comfortably into the cab next to Tom as her eyes shifted to Lilly. She and Ed Holter were again lost in conversation. Katherine smiled to herself, and then she turned to Tom.

"You know Ed Holter from church?" she asked.

"I know his brother, Norm," Tom Marlow replied. "We got talking at the trade meeting the other morning, and he told me his brother was in town for a few days. So I inquired whether he thought Ed would be interested in seeing Salvini."

"With Lilly?" Katherine asked.

"With Lilly," Tom answered. "Norm raised an eyebrow, but nothing was said about their little feud."

"Ed is going to find me a translation of Herodotus," Lilly exclaimed as she turned to Katherine.

"I borrowed the one I read," Ed Holter explained.

"How long are you staying in Helena, Ed?" Katherine asked.

"Just a day or two," Holter's eyes shifted out of the window as the cab pulled to a stop in front of the Cullen house.

"Would you like to come in," Lilly asked as the men walked them to the door.

"We'd love to, Lilly," Tom Marlow responded, "but I'm afraid I can't. I have to be up early in the morning." He smiled. "I hope you had a good time tonight."

"I did," she responded with a warm smile. "Thank you."

Tom Marlow turned to Katherine, and they walked a few paces away for their good bye.

Lilly turned to Ed Holter. "You've changed."

"So have you," he noted softly. "Your vocabulary isn't limited to insults any more." He smiled. "I'd like to see you again before I leave. Can I come by tomorrow?"

"I'd like that," Lilly answered, "but we'll be downtown most of the day. Tomorrow's the election."

"Maybe tomorrow evening then," he suggested.

"Tomorrow," she agreed.

Ed Holter retreated to the cab as Lilly went inside.

"Your folks will be back tomorrow?" Tom Marlow asked Katherine.

"Yes, my father wants to be here when the returns come in," she replied.

"When can I see you again?" Tom asked.

"Tomorrow," she replied cheerfully. "You can either help us celebrate, or console me."

"I'll come by to congratulate your father," Marlow responded with a smile. His words faded. His eyes became intent. "I love you too," he stated softly as his fingers reached to gently touch her cheek. Then he returned to the cab.

Katherine lingered in the November cold until the vehicle was out of sight. Her heart beat quickly, excitement pouring through her veins. Tom had actually spoken the words. He loved her.

Chapter Ten

"Gentlemen, I think that about wraps things up," Tom Marlow concluded as he surveyed the half dozen men at the conference table. He rose from his chair, and offered his hand to Mr. McNamara. "Thank you, C.J. for your presence. I appreciate it."

"Think nothing of it," Mr. McNamara replied. "You would do the same for me."

As the gentleman slowly dispersed from the room, Tom Marlow turned to C. J. McNamara. "How about some lunch? We could go over to the Montana Club."

"Maybe another time, Tom. I have a train to catch," McNamara replied as the two men left the room. Ed Holter waited outside.

"Ed, what can I do for you," Marlow greeted with a smile. His hand raised in a brief farewell to Mr. McNamara, and then he motioned for Holter to follow him into his office. "What's up?" he asked now.

"Lilly Cullen... Do you think she likes me?" Ed Holter asked abruptly. His eyes were intent on Tom Marlow.

"Yes, I think so," Tom replied pleasantly. "Why?"

"This isn't going to work," Ed Holter retorted. "She was such a kid when I left Helena, but now..."

"She's a lovely young lady," Tom finished for him.

"But I'm a whole continent away," Ed countered, "plus she's younger, a lot younger. Do you really think she likes me? You saw that grimace on her face when she discovered she was stuck with me for the whole evening. Heck, I honestly don't know if she could ever fit into my crowd. I like the east. It's not like here. You know what I mean, you lived there, right?"

"Yes, I did live there," Tom Marlow acknowledged as amusement rose within him. Ed Holter was rambling on like a smitten man. "The east isn't like Montana," Tom continued. "That's true, but I wouldn't sell Lilly short. She's more than just bright, a lot more."

"What do you mean?" Ed Holter asked.

"She's quick to pick up on things...like her father."

"You think Judge Cullen's daughter is a fair match then even for the east?"

"I think she's a fair match for anything she puts her mind to," Tom Marlow replied with a growing smile. "And if it's meant to be, you and Lilly will find a way. Why don't you go see her?"

"She's not home," Ed Holter responded. "Today's the election."

"She's probably just down the street then," Tom offered. "The women have their headquarters in the Bailey Block. Do you want to walk down? I have to vote yet anyway."

"Sure," Ed Holter responded. "You really think she's there?"

"We won't know without checking," Tom replied.

The two men walked out together. The Bailey Block was only a couple of blocks north, and swarmed with activity as Tom Marlow now excused himself to vote. Ed Holter wandered into the women's headquarters alone.

Ed Holter moved through the mass of people, scanning for Lilly. He made two full passes without success when he finally spotted Katherine. "Is Lilly here?" he asked as he paused before her table of literature.

"Oh hi," Katherine responded. "Yes, she's in the back getting more pamphlets." Katherine pointed to the partition spanning the rear section of the hall.

"Thanks," Ed Holter responded. He made his way through the crowd. At the partition opening, he drew to a stop, watching Lilly and Grace sort out several boxes.

"There," Grace exclaimed, "that's all of them. I can't believe we've given out five boxes of buttons in one day."

"Mrs. Carter is not going to be happy when we run out," Lilly noted. "She thought we would have lots left over."

"Isn't that the truth," Grace replied. "Come on, grab this box of pamphlets with me, Lilly. It's heavy."

"Let me help," Ed Holter responded.

Lilly looked up as a pleased smile emerged on her face. "What are you doing here?"

"Looking for you," he answered as he took the box from Grace. "Hi, remember me?"

"Ed," she responded as she quickly turned to Lilly. "Is he the one from last night?"

"Who would have guessed?" Holter chuckled as his eyes settled on Lilly. "Do you have a minute?"

"Just as soon as Mrs. Carter gets this box of pamphlets," Lilly grinned.

"Good. That one is Mrs. Carter, right?" he asked as he pointed.

"Yes." The two young women walked him to the opening. Then as he disappeared into the throng of people, Grace turned to her sister. "Ed was your date? How did you survive it?"

"He's grown up," Lilly replied thoughtfully.

"So you actually got through the evening without drawing blood?" Grace asked with a grin.

"Yes, we did," Lilly replied. "He actually turned out to be rather nice. It's too bad he's leaving."

"This is incredible," Grace exclaimed. "The two of you...what in the world did you talk about?"

"Books," Lilly replied in quiet triumph.

"Books! I guess he deserved it," Grace exclaimed. She just shook her head in disbelief and wandered off.

Ed Holter returned. "Lilly, I know you're busy, but I wanted to ask if you would write to me," he asked. "We hardly had a chance to get re-acquainted." He tentatively pulled a small paper from his pocket.

"I'd like that," Lilly responded as she reached for the address. For a split second their hands touched. It startled both of them, and the paper fell to the floor. Both instantly knelt to retrieve it. As Ed Holter picked it up, Lilly's hand withdrew. Their eyes met, and Ed Holter offered it again. Lilly took it from him as her face flushed. "Thank you," she muttered softly.

"My pleasure," he responded. They both rose again to their full height. "I won't be by your house later."

"I don't know what time I'd get back anyway," Lilly replied.

"Well, good bye then," Ed Holter stated.

"Good bye," she responded.

As the final ballots were deposited Tuesday, electricians from the Rocky Mountain Telephone company installed wires to receive the returns at the Women's Headquarters, as well as Mrs. Child's residence and the Auditorium. With the final votes coming in, all energy was now channeled into an intense interest in the returns received. Each time the phone rang, breathless silence was broken only by eager questions. Outside a sea of people thronged the night streets, all expectant, all eager as they watched the screens on which the returns were thrown.

"Mother, daddy," Katherine exclaimed as she spotted her parents making their way through the crowd toward her, "you're back."

"How's Granite County doing?" Dr. Sligh asked anxiously. "Are many of the returns in yet?"

"We're just waiting to hear from Drummond and Garnet," Katherine responded.

Her father noted the information. "How's my senate seat doing?"

Katherine repeated the last report she'd heard. "It looks good. The telephone operator has the tallies," she offered.

As her father headed for the table, her mother asked, "What about the capitol issue?"

"It was doing pretty well until an hour ago," Katherine responded. "Now it's touch and go."

"Katherine, Katherine, have you heard?" Thomas Marlow shouted as he made his way through the crowd. "Your father's won."

"Won?" Mrs. Sligh exclaimed. "I thought we were still waiting for two returns." She looked at her daughter.

Katherine turned to the telephone operator who was sitting behind her. He shrugged as he wrote down some incoming news.

"Katherine, your father has won," Tom Marlow repeated as he joined them. "Drummond couldn't get through on the lines, so they called the Auditorium. Garnet did the same. It's true, your father is the new senator of Granite County."

A squeal of delight escaped Katherine's mother, and she instantly rushed to her husband as the crowd yielded before her. James Sligh listened intently to his wife, and then a broad smile broke across his face as he embraced her. A cheer rose from the surrounding people.

"I told you so," Tom Marlow laughed as he embraced Katherine as well.

"Tom," she exclaimed softly, "not here."

"Too late," he responded as he let her loose. "It's just the election." His eyes twinkled. His face beamed. "Now you can stay in Helena."

Katherine smiled broadly. It was true.

Mrs. Cullen appeared. "Katherine, I just heard the news. Congratulations! Where are your parents?"

Katherine pointed.

Suddenly the telephone operator rose to his feet, and the hall quieted as he announced the election results of another county. Cheers filled the air, and moans. But with these results in, Helena barely maintained its narrow margin of votes. The location of Montana's capitol was becoming very uncertain.

"Katherine," Grace exclaimed as she emerged from the crowd, "you get to stay. Congratulations!"

"Thank you." The two young women embraced.

"Where's your sister," Tom Marlow asked Grace.

"Lilly's at home, Mr. Marlow. She has school tomorrow." Her attention returned to Katherine. "Everyone is going to be so pleased. Oh, there's Elizabeth. I've got to tell her," Grace exclaimed as she hastened off.

"Would you like to tell Lilly your father's news?" Tom Marlow asked. "I think we could slip out."

"Slip out where?" Ernest asked as he appeared out of nowhere. "Where are we going?" He looked at Marlow momentarily, and then back to Katherine.

"We wanted to tell Lilly my good news. I get to stay in Helena," Katherine responded with a smile. "Grace says she's at home."

"She's probably sleeping by now," Ernest agreed. "Sure, why not. Let's go wake her up."

The three left the hall, and made their way through the crowd outside.

"So Marlow, you and my sister seem to be keeping company quite a bit lately," Ernest commented as they walked the dark streets. "You're a number of years older than she, not that that is particularly unusual any more, but she is still in school."

"Your sister is a remarkable girl," Tom Marlow stated. "She's been a good friend to Katherine and me."

Ernest slowed to a stop. "Katherine and you?"

"Surely you know that Katherine and I have been seeing each other," Marlow replied.

Ernest turned to Katherine. "Is this true?"

"Yes," she answered softly.

"But he's never at any of the parties," Ernest exclaimed as he turned to glare at Marlow.

"I wasn't invited."

"But Katherine is," Ernest retorted. "Doesn't that tell you something?"

"No," Tom Marlow replied quietly.

"It should," Ernest retorted with angry eyes. He now turned to glare at Katherine. "Are you crazy? At least you could have picked someone with a family, someone I could at least be jealous of." His eyes flashed momentarily at Marlow, and then he turned and stalked off.

"This was a bad idea," Tom Marlow decided. "We'd better go back."

"No. I've got to talk to Lilly, especially now," Katherine responded. "Besides, we're closer to the Cullens than to headquarters."

Tom had to agree with this, and reluctantly walked on. Ten minutes brought them to Lilly's door. A light still shined from the drawing room as they knocked. Within moments, Lilly appeared.

"Katherine, Tom," she exclaimed. Her eyes immediately took on a knowingly look. "Your father won the senate seat, didn't he?"

"Yes," Katherine responded as they stepped inside.

Lilly joyously embraced her friend. Then her attention turned to Tom Marlow. "I bet you're happy."

"Yes," he replied.

She pondered him momentarily, and then her eyes shifted to Katherine. "Why are you both so reserved?"

"Ernest just found out Tom and I have been seeing each other," Katherine explained.

"Oh no," Lilly moaned. "Where is he?"

"He left us on Lawrence," Tom replied.

"You've just come from Women's Headquarters," Lilly asked as she grabbed her coat.

"Yes."

"Then let me go back with you. Daddy will know what to do about Ernest."

The three of them headed back downtown. As they made their way through the crowd at Women's Headquarters, Lilly spotted her father and left their company.

"Would you like some punch," Tom now asked Katherine.

"Yes, I could use something," she agreed.

"I'll be right back," he promised.

"Katie, I wondered what became of you," her father remarked as he joined his daughter. His eyes followed Tom Marlow. "You know, I rather think you've caught the eye of a certain bank president."

"We've been seeing each other, daddy," Katherine stated.

"I hardly think one church social classifies as dating," her father replied.

"I met Tom that day at the bank when the child was screaming. Since then we've gone to the Broadwater, and last night he took Lilly and me to see Alexander Salvini."

"You saw Salvini?" her father demanded.

"Yes."

Her father pondered her momentarily. "You are seeing Marlow."

"Yes."

"Your mother isn't going to be too pleased. She was hoping you would find a bank owner, not a bank president," he replied quietly.

"And what were you hoping for," Katherine asked.

"A doctor, of course," her father responded lightly. He smiled. "If you like Tom Marlow, that's fine by me. He's a good man. Did you know he pulled Montana National out of near bankruptcy last year?" His arm encircled his daughter's shoulders.

"No, I didn't," she replied.

"Well, he did. Marlow's smart," her father stated, "so if that mother of yours throws cold water on you, be a duck and let it slide off. She means well, but she doesn't understand business." His attention shifted. "Ah, it looks like your fellow is coming back."

It was late and rainy when the crowds began to disperse early Wednesday morning. The capitol issue was still unresolved. Slowly the exhausted populace left the streets, Mrs. Child's, Women's Headquarters, and the Auditorium making their way home. But Helena was merely catching up on a much needed night's sleep. By the time business closed down the following afternoon, a parade of people swept through the city's wet streets, ecstatic with the news of Helena's great victory.

"Oh look," Katherine chuckled to her father as her breath fogged in the chill air, "there's Mrs. Cruse, Mrs. Child, Mrs. Floweree, Mrs. Ashby..." She continued to name Helena's most august ladies who had put their better judgments aside, and joined the great sea of people, wearing celebration hats and tooting horns.

"There goes Helena's finest."

"Tom," Katherine exclaimed as she turned.

"Why aren't you two out there with them?" he asked.

"They couldn't find us," Dr. Sligh laughed. "Katherine and I was looking in on a patient."

"So you're planning to practice medicine along with your legislative duties?" Tom Marlow asked as he watched the parade.

"Oh no," Dr. Sligh replied. "This was just a favor to a friend."

The exuberance of the city was not to be denied. The parade was followed on Thursday night by a victory celebration at the Osterhoat's, on Monday evening at the Auditorium, and on Tuesday afternoon at the Cruse's. The Sands Brothers gave a Souvenir Sale in their silk, cloak, and fur departments in grateful recognition of the splendid services rendered by the ladies; and telegrams and letters poured in from all over the country expressing the joy of women everywhere over the Capitol Committee's happy result.

As a new state senator's wife, Mrs. Sligh was caught up in the excitement, and barely noticed the increased presence of Thomas Marlow in her daughter's life. When Katherine wasn't tending household duties or involved in some upcoming social event, she was to be seen in Mr. Marlow's company often at church, in her father's company, or at other public gatherings. During these times the two conversed extensively, getting to know each other better and in detail. It was no surprise to Katherine when Tom Marlow furnished her father with the only acceptable lead he was to receive for a suitable house over the winter. With the city so crowded with legislators, the new members and their families were lucky to find any lodging at all.

"Mrs. Easler's house will be available the week of Thanksgiving," Dr. Sligh informed his wife as he let out a sigh of relief. "She and her family will be joining her husband. He writes that the weather in Los Angeles is wonderfully warm."

"I would imagine most anywhere would be warmer than here," Mrs. Sligh laughed happily.

Mrs. Easler's house was a comfortable one, and Mrs. Sligh immediately set to work on the arrangements. She had an image to maintain now. But as she focused her attention on this new challenge, she suddenly realized just how much Mr. Marlow was becoming a part of their lives, and in particular her daughter's life. It was time Katherine visited her sister. The move would provide just the excuse.

Chapter Eleven

"No mother, I don't want Carrie to be alone for Thanksgiving," Katherine replied.

"Well your sister can't come here, we'll be in the middle of moving," Mrs. Sligh told her daughter. "There will be men and boxes everywhere. You and your sister will be better off in Deer Lodge. Besides, you enjoyed catching up on all Miss Bellenberg's news last week at the Carter's and the Kleinschmidt's. How long has it been since you've been to Deer Lodge?"

"Probably a year," Katherine answered. Miss Bellenberg invited Carrie and me over for an evening last fall when I visited."

"That's right, that was after her mother was feeling better. Your father knows his medicine." She smiled.

"So when do I leave?" Katherine asked reluctantly.

"Tomorrow on the afternoon train," her mother responded.

"Why so soon?" Katherine asked.

"Because, dear, the movers will be arriving first thing Monday morning, and everything will be very hectic. I want to spare you that."

The next morning at church, Katherine left her parents to sit with the Cullens. She knew her mother was not pleased about it, but she didn't care. Tom Marlow sat in his usual pew with his aunt and cousins Wilder was particularly quiet.

"She's just getting over the flu," Lilly offered quietly. "She was out of school most of last week."

"So what's new with Ernest?" Katherine whispered as the congregation rose to their feet.

"He's been eyeing the Clarke girl," Lilly replied, "so I think you're finally off the hook."

"Good," Katherine responded. "At least that's good news."

"Have you said good bye to Tom Marlow yet," Lilly asked as the congregation sat down again.

"I will after church," Katherine answered.

Lilly could see the misery in her friend's face. Her attention was finally drawn back to the front of the church. Reverend Love had claimed the pulpit for his sermon.

By the time church let out, everyone except Tom and Katherine left the pews. There behind everyone's back, they said good bye. Tears glistened in Katherine's eyes as he encouraged her to be strong, that they had been apart before.

Dr. and Mrs. Sligh took their daughter home, got a bite to eat, collected her luggage, and left for the train station. Placing Katherine on the two o'clock train to Deer Lodge, they said good-bye.

Katherine made her way through the Pullman car to a seat by the window. The train vibrated with energy as she waited for the last passengers to board. The whistle blew, and the doors shut. Slowly they began to move. The depot rolled gradually past the window as Katherine's eyes suddenly focused on a man. Tom Marlow stood alone alongside the tracks at the far end of the depot, his arm outstretched in farewell. Katherine raised her own hand, placing it against the cold glass of the window. Tears boiled in her eyes.

"Tom, did I miss her?" Lilly gasped as she hastened through the depot and spotted the banker walking toward her. She had planned to see Katherine off, but she had been unavoidably detained at home.

"Yes, I'm afraid so," he answered quietly. "Even her parents have already left."

"Oh," Lilly sighed with disappointment.

He smiled softly. "I'll tell Katherine you tried to get here."

"Then you're going to write her," Lilly responded on a brighter note.

"Write?" he repeated.

"Yes, like Ed Holter and me."

Tom Marlow's attention sharpened on her. "You and Holter write?"

"Once a week like clockwork." Lilly smiled.

"Well I'll be darned," Tom responded with an incredulous smile. "Is that right!"

"So what about you and Katherine?" Lilly pressed.

Tom Marlow smiled. "Do you have her address by any chance?"

"Of course."

The weather took on a definite chill by the 7th of December as Dr. Sligh waited for Katherine's train to return from Deer Lodge. The sky was a light gray, and small flakes of snow were falling.

A train whistle broke the din of noise that echoed within the station. Dr. Sligh's attention directed itself down the tracks. Katherine's train rounded the curve and was in sight. He breathed a sigh of relief. He hated waiting for trains.

"Daddy," Katherine exclaimed as she stepped off the Pullman car. She instantly wrapped her arms around him. "Where's mother? Where's Charles?"

"At the dressmaker's and at school," he answered in order. "Your mother is determined to have a new gown for Christmas, and her seamstress couldn't schedule a fitting for any other time. She sends her apologies."

"So are you in a hurry to get back to your senatorial duties," Katherine asked as she produced her luggage claim.

"I'm only in a hurry to get your luggage, and then we'll see," her father replied in good spirits.

Dr. Sligh retrieved Katherine's luggage, and then they headed out to the buggy, now turned sleigh. Ten minutes brought them to their new residence on Harrison Avenue. The two story Victorian sat neatly in the snow. Dr. Sligh led his daughter inside.

Katherine had seen the house before she left for Deer Lodge, before the Easlers had departed for California, but now even though the wallpaper and furniture were the same, the house felt different. Her mother had rearranged much of it, and added just enough of their own things to change the demeanor of the house.

"What do you think?" Dr. Sligh asked his daughter.

"It's home," Katherine replied with a smile.

"Your mother does have a way with houses," her father chuckled approvingly. "I think you'll like your room."

That night Katherine attended Mrs. Murphy's Thank You Party. It was an evening of games and music. The contests were challenging and varied as the young ladies found themselves paired up with Helena's best young men. Power, Word, Hirshfield, Holter, Cullen, Streator, and McPhee were among the names present, each taking a turn at entertaining Mrs. Murphy's young ladies. Katherine enjoyed herself, more because she was finally home than anything else. Once the games were over, Norman Holter asked her to dance.

Katherine looked up into the august masculine face. "I met your brother recently," she offered simply.

"Yes, I remember. Tom Marlow arranged a date for Lillian Cullen," Norm Holter responded.

"We saw Alexander Salvini perform," Katherine replied she wondered what she should say next. Why Norman Holter had asked her to dance was beyond her imagination. She didn't even know what to say to the man.

The music turned suddenly light and fun, and Katherine broke into laughter as her partner tried to loosen up. The song simply didn't match the man.

"Surely you aren't laughing at me," Norman Holter protested.

"No, I'm just enjoying myself," Katherine replied as she toned down her levity.

Holter smiled. He had been asked by Mrs. Murphy to see that Katherine had a good time. There was concern among certain ladies that she was spending far too much time in the wrong company. He didn't agree. Tom Marlow was his friend, and Katherine seemed nice. But if he could monopolize a little of Katherine's time, he could at least protect her from other male attention, and give himself the opportunity of getting to know Marlow's young lady better.

Mr. Power danced with Katherine next. But as he swept her along to the music, she noted the pallor of his otherwise strong countenance.

"Are you feeling all right," Katherine asked.

A wane smile rose to his lips. "Of course," he responded slowly, "I'm dancing with you."

"Mr. Power, please don't bother with flattery," she replied with concern. "You are ill."

"It's just a bad cold," he answered quietly.

Katherine fell momentarily silent. She knew a cold when she saw it. This was worse. "Mr. Power, I'm getting rather warm. Would you mind if we got something to drink?"

The man gratefully gave up dancing, and they walked over to the punch bowl. "Your father is a doctor, is he not?" Mr. Power commented to Katherine.

"Yes," Katherine answered.

"And do you sympathize with his work?"

Katherine turned to Mr. Power. His eyes were exhausted as he made small talk.

"I believe in what he does, Mr. Power," Katherine responded. "Shall we sit down?"

"Yes, I would like that," Mr. Power replied.

The two claimed nearby chairs, watching the others dance. Conversation was slow, but regular as Mr. Power claimed Katherine's company for the remainder of the evening. He was not up to a lot of dancing, and she seemed to understand and allow him a gracious alternative.

By eleven o'clock, Mr. Power was ready and willing to call it a night. "Miss Sligh can I drop you off at home?" he asked cordially.

"Yes, thank you," she accepted as she suddenly realized the stares of the other girls. Mr. Power had eluded all their attention.

Katherine was escorted to the man's coach, and helped inside. The ride home was a quiet one. Fatigue was catching up with Mr. Power, and Katherine was beginning to regret accepting the ride. She had little doubt Mr. Power would be asleep by the time he reached his own house. As the coach pulled up outside of Katherine's new residence, she quickly got out, thanking Mr. Power as she did. She had no desire for him to escort her to the door. Glancing at the driver, she flagged him on. She got no dispute. Even he realized Mr. Power was ill.

Saturday Katherine spent with her mother, shopping for Christmas gifts they would mail to relatives back east. Katherine enjoyed the day tremendously. There was so much more selection to pick from than at home. She loved Helena, especially when they shopped at the Sands Brothers. The people there were so nice, recognizing their contribution in the recent election…that, and they were just down the block from Montana National Bank.

Katherine was not, however, afforded any opportunity to talk with Tom Marlow. When they passed the bank, it was closed, and Tom was nowhere to be seen. Still, Katherine was not discouraged. Tomorrow was Sunday.

"Katherine, be sure to dress warm enough for church," her father advised as he paused on the way past her room. "La grippe is making its wicked rounds of the city. There were three cases reported this week."

"La grippe? Is that what it is," Katherine responded.

"Yes, do you know someone with it?"

"Friday night at Mrs. Murphy's, Mr. Power claimed to have a bad cold, but it was more than that. He was weak and his stomach bothered him. I know it did."

"Young Mr. Power?" Dr. Sligh asked.

"Yes."

"And did you dance with him, Katherine?"

"Just once. We spent the evening talking. It's the only way I could think of to keep him off his feet."

A wane smile rose to her father's lips. "I wish people would stay home when they are ill."

It was hard to stay perfectly warm on the short journey to church. The mercury simply refused to climb past the single digits of the thermometer before mid afternoon. Wool undergarments, wool dresses, and wool cloaks protected the ladies from the elements for the most part, but their fingers and toes still managed to grow numb and their cheeks briskly red from the intense cold.

Katherine gratefully followed her parents into church where the wood stove warmed the sanctuary. But this week, her father did not lead them to a miscellaneous pew in the midsection, but rather to the one directly behind the Broadwaters. Katherine held her breath as she sat down directly behind Tom Marlow. The Broadwaters turned and greeted them, inviting them out to the hotel to enjoy the ice skating. Katherine's heart pounded within her as Tom also turned, greeted her parents and then said hello to her. It was brief. Reverend Love was already announcing the first hymn.

By the time the service was over, Katherine was in no hurry to leave. As she lingered behind her parents, Tom Marlow did the same, allowing his aunt and cousins to disappear into the crowd.

"I loved your letters," Tom offered.

"Thank you for writing," Katherine responded.

"Lilly gave me your address," Tom stated softly, "but I told you that."

"Yes," Katherine responded.

"Are you coming out to the Broadwater this afternoon?" he asked. "The ice is perfect. You do skate?"

"I skate," Katherine responded as Lilly suddenly joined them.

"Then you have to come," Lilly encouraged. "We're all going out, well everyone except my brother. We can all walk down and catch the streetcar at the train depot."

"I'll check with my folks," Katherine responded. Then she turned to Lilly. "Thanks for giving Tom my address."

"My pleasure," she responded. "I've got to go. If you want to come with us, be at our house by two. Okay?"

"Okay," Katherine replied. Then she turned back to Tom. "I'll try and make it, but I can't promise." Her attention shifted to her father. He was gesturing for her to join them. "I've got to go."

At two o'clock Katherine was still half a block from the Cullen house, hurrying along as fast as she could over the frozen ground. Her mother had made other plans for the afternoon, and it took Katherine some time to disengage herself from them.

Lilly emerged from the front door, saw her, and waved. Within minutes the family was walking the three blocks to the train station.

"You're coming to the work party on Tuesday?" Grace asked Katherine as she made reference to one of Reverend Love's announcements for the upcoming week. "We have to get the stage ready for the shows."

"Of course," Katherine responded, "it sounds like a wonderful bazaar. St. Peter's should sell a lot of dolls."

"And no child should be without a Christmas doll at our prices," Mrs. Cullen replied with a smile. "Have you got a part yet in the skits, Katherine?"

"Mother, she just got back in town yesterday," Lilly cried.

"Oh, I didn't realize," Mrs. Cullen responded as they walked. "They'll probably assign you one on Tuesday then."

"I hope so," Katherine replied.

"I play a French miss," Grace offered.

"And I'm to be in the Garden of Flowers," Puss proudly added.

"And Lilly?" Katherine asked.

"Lilly's not anything," Grace scoffed. "She's too busy tutoring at school."

"And if she wasn't, her pupil might not pass her next exam," Judge Cullen asserted as he stepped back to let his family board the streetcar ahead of him. He smiled encouragingly at Lilly.

Katherine inwardly grimaced. She had spoken without thinking. She knew Lilly had different priorities than most.

The streetcar was packed. Everyone in Helena knew the ice was finally thick enough to skate on. The Cullen family split apart, finding vacant seats where they could. Katherine sat down next to Lilly as the car got underway.

"What subject are you tutoring?" Katherine asked quietly.

"Trigonometry," Lilly answered. "Lizzie is having a terrible time with it. She keeps inverting her number sequences."

"I didn't mean to imply…"

"I know," Lilly responded. "Don't worry about it. Grace is just sore because I won't let her wear my French perfume. I don't have much left." She smiled. "We're almost there."

The Broadwater Hotel was in view, and it was only minutes before everyone was pouring off the streetcar. The benches lining the banks of the frozen water were immediately full as everyone buckled on their skates.

Katherine surveyed the crowd, looking for Tom Marlow. Then suddenly somebody covered her eyes from behind. She instantly spun. "Tom?"

Chapter Twelve

"Here I am," Thomas Marlow replied with a smile.

"I was looking for you. I almost didn't get to come," Katherine responded. "Mother had the day all planned."

"Well you're here now. Let's get your skates on," he prodded.

Tom Marlow reached for the straps straddling Katherine's shoulder, and fastened them on her feet. Then she followed him onto the ice. The surface was hard and smooth as Tom drew her after him. He skated backwards, zigzagging left and then right, keeping an eye on the people behind. A smile rested on his lips as he now spun her around him. He caught her at exactly the right moment, and suddenly they were skating together with both arms linked.

"You're a good skater," he complimented her.

"You're not bad yourself," she replied as her eyes diverted momentarily, and she greeted someone she knew.

But skating was not the foremost thing on their minds, they were together again. Their hands were linked, their arms intertwined, their bodies close. Both hearts pounded within them as their consciousness centered on the fact, and on each other. The ice glided blissfully beneath them. The other skaters faded into the background, and they were alone, together, in the crowd of people.

Their speed picked up as their hearts raced, weaving in and around other skaters. Then it slowed into a leisurely pace as Tom and Katherine huddled closer together.

"Katherine, we're going in for some hot chocolate," Grace called as she skated past. "Are you coming?"

Katherine abruptly became conscious of the people around her again. Lilly was laughing with a girlfriend as they skated opposite one another, attempting to circle. The Judge and Mrs. Cullen were approaching, hand in hand. Fog was settling in at the foot of the hills around them. It was a beautiful winter afternoon.

"Would you like some cocoa," Tom Marlow asked.

"Sure," Katherine agreed.

They removed their skates, and joined the Cullens as they headed for the hotel. Lilly's father turned to Marlow. "Have you been up to Big Sandy lately?"

Tom shook his head. "No, I haven't."

"You still have interests up there, don't you?" The Judge stopped to open the hotel door.

"Yes," Tom Marlow replied as the two men waited for the ladies to pass, "but I've been rather preoccupied here of late. I've got the bank's annual report to get out."

"Yes, I see," Judge Cullen agreed as his eyes followed Katherine. "It is getting to be the end of the year."

The men followed the ladies inside to the dining room. The hot chocolate did much to warm them as they talked about the ice, weather, and upcoming holidays. Then Judge Cullen pulled out his pocket watch.

"Well, Mrs. Cullen," he began as he smiled at his wife, "if we want to get any more skating in this afternoon, we had better get back out there and enjoy it. The five o'clock car waits for no one."

He rose to his feet as did the rest of his family. Katherine and Tom followed more slowly. Katherine suddenly noticed Norman Holter. He was seated at the second table over, watching. He smiled, and Katherine diverted her attention to Tom. "Norman Holter has been to several parties lately," she commented softly.

"That doesn't surprise me," Tom Marlow answered. His eyes shifted to Mr. Holter's table, and they exchanged nods of acknowledgment.

"He seems very hard to talk to," Katherine added.

"Really?" Tom responded. "I never found that to be the case. He's always interested in anything that promotes Helena."

"Then maybe that's the key," Katherine decided. Her attention shifted out through the window. Fog was now obscuring the lake.

"Would you like to skate some more?" Tom asked.

"I'd rather walk," she replied. "I love the feel of fog. Everything is so quiet, and yet so loud at the same time."

Their steps retraced much the same ground they walked the first evening they shared at the Broadwater, but the fog made everything different. The voices of the skaters were muffled and distant, while their own footsteps crunched loudly in the snow.

"You're right," Tom Marlow agreed, "everything is quiet and loud at the same time."

Katherine smiled in response, and he slid his arm around her shoulders. Both were happy in each other's presence.

Thoughts of Sunday afternoon lingered with Katherine after she returned home on the streetcar, through the evening, and into the next day while she did the family's laundry and other household chores. Then starting on Tuesday, Katherine attended the work sessions for St. Peter's Doll Fair, practiced for the skits, and showed up on Friday to set up for the actual performance. Twice, Tom Marlow found time to look in on the progress. At these occurrences, Katherine's heart skipped a beat, and a pleased sensation warmed her despite the fact that they unable to exchange much more than a brief greeting.

With all the attention given to the church event, crowds of people flocked to the Auditorium for the afternoon and evening performances of the Doll Fair on both Friday and Saturday. In the center of the hall was a hexagonal pavilion with a surmounting dome, covered with evergreens that scented the air.   In the four corners of the pavilion were triangular booths containing saleswomen and displays of countless dolls of every variety and description. At the sides of the hall were more booths selling chrysanthemums, lemonade, and candy. The stage promised further pleasures.

During the afternoons, Mother Goose entertained with rhymes and jingles, accompanied by songs of the parish children (including Puss Cullen). These delighted everyone present.

In the evenings, Helena's elite was introduced to the Puppen Fee, an idea recently brought home from Germany by Miss Cora Sanders. Here Katherine, Grace, Wilder, and many others presented themselves as dolls, and were inspected and expected to perform as jointed, mechanical contrivances would. Some talked, some walked, some played – all in a limited, humorous way. Katherine would have walked straight off the stage in her delicate white dress if the watchful salesman had not caught her. Grace was equal to "papa" or "mama" if her string was pulled. Wilder proceeded to dance in a stiff-jointed manner when wound up, and delighted her critical buyers so that she was boxed up and sold for $99.99. Then a fairy appeared in a gauzy dress with a golden wand, and she touched the dolls, bringing them to life. All the dolls then danced until the curtain rang down.

The excited participants were all a flutter as they finished off their last show. The crowds had been enormous and appreciative, and the sales were expected to exceed their wildest expectations. Happy laughter accompanied Katherine as she and the others were congratulated by nearly everyone. She joined her parents as she spotted Tom Marlow. He was dressed in evening attire, and he smiled and waved his congratulations over the heads of the crowd. She waved back as her attention was diverted. Puss Cullen was smiling knowingly, her crepe paper costume now in her hands.

"I knew he would be here tonight," she commented.

"Katherine, put on your coat," her father instructed as they headed out.

A icy blast exploded through the door, and Katherine instantly obeyed. She was still warm from the performance, but she was cooling fast. Outside, she could see snow blowing sideways, and she knew the moist condition of her warmth could quickly turn to chill. She pulled up the hood of her wool cloak and wrapped the fabric tightly around her as the family headed home.

Sunday morning dawned clear and cold as Katherine turned restlessly in bed. An hour later she came to as church bells rang in the distance. She rolled over again, too fatigued to do more. Suddenly she realized it was time to get up, and she sat straight up as a groan escaped her lips. Katherine's head spun, and the equilibrium of her body revolted from the sudden movement.

"Are you okay?" her mother asked as she hesitated on her way past Katherine's door. Mrs. Sligh now entered the room, laying a concerned hand on her daughter's forehead.

"I'm not feeling too well," Katherine muttered.

"You are a little warm," Mrs. Sligh noted. She peered into Katherine's face. "Maybe last night was too much for you."

"I did get cold on the way home," Katherine admitted softly.

"We all got cold on the way home, dear," her mother noted. "It's hard not to when it's barely 5 above. I think I'll get your father."

Dr. Sligh appeared within moments. His demeanor was quiet as he looked over his daughter. "How's your stomach?" he asked finally.

"Fine," Katherine answered.

"No cramping?"

"No."

He looked down her throat. "It looks a bit red, but not bad. Is it sore?"

"Just a little when I swallow," she answered.

"Well I don't think it's la grippe," her father noted with relief, "but you will still need to be very careful, or you could get that wicked stuff on top of what you already have now, and that could be dangerous."

"You need bed rest and plenty of it," her mother instructed. "I'll fix you some chamomile tea."

Katherine's attention shifted to her father. "I wish it tasted better."

"Nothing tastes good when you're sick," he replied with a smile. "Mother is planning a roast chicken for dinner, so I'll have her fix you some broth later with extra thyme. That should help keep your fever in check."

Katherine's father pulled her blanket up under her chin. "No church today, young lady." He smiled, and then left her to sleep.

Katherine's eyes closed as she pondered missing church, and Tom Marlow. She hadn't been sick in months aside from her little fainting spell. She wished she could go to church; but the way she felt, she could easily pass out again, and that was the last thing she ever wanted to do again, particularly in public. Sleep closed in around her thoughts.

For three days Katherine's fever slowly rose, and then suddenly it broke, leaving her with the miserable symptoms of a bad cold. Her father kept a careful eye on her, forbidding her to leave the house, and insisting on plenty of rest.

By Saturday she was feeling much better, though more than a little dismayed to realize her plans for a week of Christmas shopping were shot to the winds. Her parents, of course, came to the rescue, purchasing a few needed gifts for her, but it wasn't the same. Katherine sat at the kitchen table wrapping a present for her sister, Carrie, as she lamented missing out on all the fun of shopping. This was the first year she had not made gifts, hoping to take full advantage of Helena's numerous stores.

Katherine busied herself with light household tasks as her father again forbid her to attend church the following morning. She was restless, but she also realized she tired easily. Carrie was arriving the following day to spend the holidays with them, and Katherine tediously made up the extra bed, and then added some Christmas evergreens to the room to make it more festive.

Her mother had a bucket of Douglas fir branches sitting just inside the back door.

"Katherine, are you doing too much?" her mother complained as they returned from church. She stomped heavily on the wipe rung, knocking the snow from her shoes.

"I don't think so," Katherine answered as she eyed the Christmas tree emerging through the front door behind Mrs. Sligh. It was huge.

"We got the tree," Charles announced as he guided the front end.

"The Bachs cut it last night," Dr. Sligh added as he emerged through the door as well. "I told them last week that I was looking for a ten foot tree, and they offered to cut one for us when they got theirs. I just didn't expect this fat of one." He smiled broadly as he turned to his wife. "So where do you want it, Sarah?"

"In the window," she answered, "but don't you need a stand?"

Charles held up a coffee can already mounted in a wood contrivance. "All dad has to do is nail it on," he exclaimed as Dr. Sligh now hauled the tree into the parlor. Here he raised it to its full height.

"Perfect," Dr. Sligh exclaimed. "Get me a hammer, will you Charles."

His son retrieved the tool, and impatiently danced from one foot to the other as Dr. Sligh attached the stand to the tree.

"Don't get pitch on your pants," his wife advised with concern. "That's your best suit."

"Oh fuss and nonsense," Dr. Sligh exclaimed as he triumphantly raised the tree, and placed it in the bay. "There."

"Oh, it's beautiful," Katherine exclaimed.

"Turn it a little to the right," her mother instructed.

"How's that?" her father asked.

"Perfect," Charles exclaimed.

"I think that will do," Mrs. Sligh agreed. "We'll decorate it tomorrow evening after Carrie gets here."

Katherine always looked forward to stringing pop corn and cranberries for the tree. It was their family's Christmas Eve tradition, and Carrie would be with them. Her mind wandered back through the years to when her two married sisters still lived with them. Now they had families of their own, one over on Benton Avenue, and one clear back in Newport, Rhode Island.

"Katherine, you were missed at church," her father commented. "The Cullen girls were asking for you." He smiled. "Does Puss have an actual name?"

"Mary," Katherine answered, "but no one calls her by it."

Her father's eyebrows raised in a fleeting look of bewilderment. Then his hand reached into his pocket, and emerged with a small wrapped box. "I was asked to give this to you."

"What's is it?" Katherine asked.

"I think the tag is self-explanatory." He smiled. "I was also asked about your health."

Katherine read the tag. The small package was from Tom Marlow. A warm feeling spread through Katherine, and a smile emerged on her lips. "What did you tell him," she asked.

"That you are doing well," her father answered, "maybe well enough to be back in church on Christmas Day."

"Oh daddy, thank you," Katherine exploded as she threw her arms around him in an instant embrace.

"You might want to open your gift in private, Katie. With all the Christmas 'to-do', and trying to schedule Christmas around the Davenports for Bessie, your mother's nerves are already a bit taunt. I'd hate for her to say something that you both might regret, if you understand my meaning."

Katherine slipped from the embrace. "Will she ever like Tom?" she asked quietly.

"Has she ever learned to like my aunt?" he asked with a smile.

"No," Katherine responded. "Is that how it's always to be?"

"Mother will learn to tolerate Tom, and to be cordially polite. Beyond that..." Then he smiled encouragingly "But I like him, doesn't that count for something?"

"Yes daddy," Katherine replied, "of course it does. It means a lot."

Carrie's train arrived in Helena the following day just past the noon hour amid a mob of holiday travelers. She was met by her sister Bessie, who took her to lunch, and then delivered her to their parents new home at four thirty. By that time Katherine and her mother had everything but the Christmas tree decorated for the holidays. Even festive treats were laid out, waiting to be consumed.

"Mother, Katie, Charles...it's so good to see you," Carrie exclaimed as she came through the front door and instantly embraced her mother and then her little brother. "You've grown, shrimp," she declared as she stepped back to examine Charles. "Are you as tall as dad yet?"

"Almost," he responded proudly.

Then Carrie turned to Katherine. "I'm told you've been under the weather. How are you feeling?"

"Better, much better," Katherine replied as Bessie's husband came through the door with Carrie's bags.

Her mother pointed to the stairs. "The second door on the right, Don," she instructed.

As he disappeared upstairs, Carrie again turned to her sister. "Oh, I do hope you didn't catch your illness from me when you were at Deer Lodge. We've had so much sickness among the children this fall, and I did come down with a nasty cold the evening you left. I was confined to bed for five straight days."

"I was too," Katherine replied.

"I'm certain Deer Lodge does not hold a monopoly on illness," their mother interjected as Bessie's husband returned.

"Thank you, Don," Carrie responded as she flashed him a grateful smile.

"You are more than welcome," he replied, and then his attention turned to Mrs. Sligh. "We're looking forward to tomorrow," he offered politely.

"We are too," she responded. "I hope your mother is not too distressed over putting her dinner off an extra hour."

"We will all survive," he replied with a smile. "I wouldn't worry." Then he turned to Carrie. "We'll see you tomorrow too."

"Tomorrow," Carrie agreed.

Don Davenport reached for the door knob, and went out.

"Let me show you our room," Katherine offered now. "I think you'll like it."

"I'm sure," Carrie responded. Then she turned momentarily to her mother. "When will daddy be home?"

"Any time," she answered. "He said he would be through with his meeting by four, but then he had to drop by Senator Folsom's office and leave off some information. I rather expected him home by now, but maybe he got talking to someone."

"All the important affairs of state," Carrie grinned. "It's really something to have a senator for a father." She followed Katherine upstairs. Charles followed them.

"Oh this is nice," Carrie noted as Katherine led her into their bedroom, "and it smells so good. Did you do the decorating, Katie?"

"Yes."

She turned to their brother. "Which room is yours?"

"I'll show you," Charles offered quickly. Carrie followed him down the hall as Katherine sat down on the bed, awaiting their return. She smiled as she heard their lively chatter. Charles always liked it when Carrie came home. He seemed to miss her more than their other sisters. She did too.

"So how is this fellow you like?" Carrie asked as she finally returned alone.

"Which fellow?" Katherine replied evasively.

"Oh, there's more than one?" Carrie retorted with a mischievous smile. "Maybe I should be living in Helena."

Katherine made no reply.

"I meant the fellow you were writing to," Carrie continued more seriously. "Are you still seeing him?"

"It's kind of hard when daddy won't let me out of the house until I'm well, and mother won't let him in," Katherine replied.

"You said mother didn't approve," Carrie noted. "That I can't understand. She loves daddy, and I can't understand why she won't let us marry for love. It's not like any of us have ever considered falling for a bum. What's it matter if the fellow is society or not? Mine certainly won't be, not if I have anything to say about it."

Katherine smiled. "So have you snagged a miner lately?"

Carrie laughed. "Wouldn't that just frost mother! We could get married in the mine, and have a lantern lit wedding."

"Oh gosh," Katherine burst as she nearly doubled with laughter. "She could hardly give me a bad time then."

"True," Carrie giggled. "Maybe I'll have to see what old flame I can dig up, the dirtier the better."

Katherine chuckled uncontrollably.

"And it wouldn't have to really be true," Carrie stated. "Mother could just think it was for a little while. You know, to gain perspective."

"She would be mortified," Katherine responded.

"Better that she was mortified temporarily than for you to be bound for life to someone you don't love," she replied. "Look at Bessie."

"Bessie loves Don," Katherine responded.

"Yes, Bessie probably does love Don, or at least she thinks she does," Carrie replied softly. "But look at her. She's not the same Bessie we grew up with. She's always fussing about one thing or another. Nothing is ever good enough anymore, and she's always apologizing for it. She's trying so hard to be something she's not."

"She was pretty impressed when our big sister married Asa Kennan from Newport, Rhode Island," Katherine noted.

"Wasn't she," Carrie agreed, "too much so, in my opinion." Carrie sighed. "I'd rather be an old maid than get caught in that trap."

Suddenly they heard the front door.

"Daddy's home," Katherine announced.

Chapter Thirteen

The Slighs spent Christmas Eve at home together, stringing cranberries and pop corn as Dr. Sligh fitted their traditional glass star on top of the tree. As the red cranberry garlands became complete, Mrs. Sligh draped them gracefully between the branches. The white popcorn garlands came next, overlapping the cranberries at the draped midpoint. At each supporting branch, the family hung a deep red tassel in the rise of the garland arch. The candles were fastened above this. Last came the new hand blown glass ornaments imported from Berlin. A certain quiet fell over the Slighs as they appreciated the beauty of the tree.

"Beautiful, simply beautiful," Dr. Sligh breathed at last. He slid his arm around his wife as Carrie crossed the room to where she had left a basket brimming with presents. These she now stashed under the tree, against the white sheet that hid the coffee can stand.

"And the picture is complete," Carrie noted with satisfaction.

"...until morning at least." Her father smiled.

"Yes, Christmas morning," his wife responded, "I'd better check if we have enough coffee."

Dr. Sligh placed a restraining hand on her shoulder. "If we don't, it's too late anyway. We can have hot cocoa." He gave her a squeeze. "Don't fuss like Bessie. We'll be fine."

That night sleep came too easily for Katherine. Worn out from all the excitement, she drifted off long before she had finished savoring the evening's moments. She enjoyed her time with Carrie. Her sister was strong and independent, and Katherine admired her for it. Carrie's chosen life style wasn't exactly what Katherine would pick, but she did prefer it over Bessie's. Her mind wandered to her sister, Lila, in Rhode Island as she wondered what her life was really like. All Lila's letters sounded impressive, but letters could leave out an awful lot.

Christmas morning dawned cloudy and gray. The house was quiet as Katherine climbed out of bed, and instantly reached for her heavy house coat. The air was cool as she opened her curtains. The world below was covered with a thick blanket of snow. Tiny flakes persisted in falling, though not in any mass, nor in any hurry.

Katherine reached into the pocket of her robe where she had placed Tom Marlow's gift. She turned it over and over in her hands, reluctant to open it, pleased merely with its presence. This was the first physical thing she had from him, other than the ticket stub from Alexander Salvini's performance, and she relished the object as evidence of his existence when he wasn't near. To open it would diminish it, it would take away a certain amount of the package's mystique. Yet Katherine hoped to see Tom later that morning at church, and she would need to thank him for whatever it was. She tore off the paper, and opened the box.

The light of the window reflected off the highly polished links of gold chain, and sparkled in the tiny garnet settings that joined the two different length strands. At the midpoint the longer one was drawn up to its mate at another garnet setting, but this one also held the beautifully engraved gold locket. Katherine took a deep breath as she appreciated its intricate, yet graceful design. She opened the locket. A small piece of paper slipped from the otherwise empty pendant.

Katherine picked it up. Tom had written but one line on the paper. He loved her. A smile of joy rose to Katherine's lips as she carefully replaced the tiny note within the locket, and closed it tightly.

Katherine stared dreamily out at the white yard below. Time slipped away unnoticed until the house came to life. Katherine fastened the locket around her neck, and tucked it inside her nightgown. Then she got ready for church.

Evergreens and candles decorated the sanctuary of St. Peter's Episcopal Church Christmas morning. Katherine hardly noticed as she searched for Tom Marlow. There were three services to be held that morning. Communion was already over, and Bishop Brewer wasn't speaking until the eleven o'clock service. That was the service they usually attended, but not this morning. Bessie's family was coming over for breakfast, and they had to be through in time to go to the Davenport's for dinner. Frustration grew in Katherine as it became obvious that Tom Marlow was not attending the nine-thirty service.

"Katherine, what are you doing here so early," Lilly greeted as she detained her friend momentarily.

"Bessie is coming to our house for breakfast, and has to be at her in-laws for dinner," she answered.

"That sounds familiar," Lilly noted, "two places on the same day. It's a regular juggling match."

"Yes," Katherine sighed, "and I think I'm going to miss Tom."

"He didn't know which service you were coming to?"

"No, I haven't seen him. I've been sick," Katherine lamented.

"But you will see him today," Lilly coaxed.

"I don't know," Katherine responded in frustration. "He sent a gift home to me with my father, but I haven't talked to him in ages. I couldn't even get out to get his Christmas present."

"Oh, you have been out of circulation," Lilly cried. "Are you all well now?"

"I think so," Katherine acknowledged.

"Good. Mother is planning a party on Friday. Did you get the invitation?"

"Yes, I did. Thank you."

"No, you goose," Lilly retorted, "don't thank me. I just want to know if you're coming. I tried to talk mother into inviting Tom, but she was concerned about your mother. She says Mrs. Sligh has made it known that she doesn't like you seeing so much of Mr. Marlow, and…"

"What," Katherine exclaimed, "my mother told your mother that?"

"Well, I don't know if she was actually talking to my mother at the time, or if mine was just in on the conversation."

"How dare she," Katherine fumed.

"But are you coming on Friday, Katherine?" Lilly pressed as she realized they were running out of time before the service. "Your sister is invited too."

Katherine stared silently at Lilly.

"Katherine, please don't be mad at us," Lilly entreated. "We did try."

"I'm not mad at you," Katherine responded quietly, "and Carrie and I would love to come on Friday."

"Oh good," Lilly sighed in relief. "I have to go. The service is about to start."

As Lilly hurried down the aisle to her family's pew, Katherine did the same, finding a seat next to her father. She was glad it was him. She didn't know if she could tolerate her mother at the moment.

"This is awfully good hot chocolate," Bessie exclaimed as Mrs. Sligh took her daughter's cloak. They hadn't been home from church for more than five minutes. "Did you add anything special?"

"Just a little honey," her mother answered as she hung up the wrap.

"I'll have to remember that," Bessie noted. "We always use sugar."

Dr. Sligh gave his wife an approving glance as they watched Don add their packages to the many already under the Christmas tree. Bessie's little daughter walked right past, stopping at the dining room table where two round coffee cakes, frosted with white icing and trimmed with holly, set at either end of the advent candles. Her mother took her by the hand, and led her back into the parlor.

"Do you remember, girls, when you used to sneak down at daybreak to shake packages before your father and I could join you?" Mrs. Sligh asked as she offered her granddaughter a small treat to help her wait for breakfast. She then took a seat next to her husband.

"I remember the Christmas when daddy was out delivering some miner's baby," Bessie recalled. "We waited and waited for him."

"Until one in the afternoon," Carrie added. "I thought that child would never be born."

"A boy, wasn't it," Mrs. Sligh asked, "and they moved right after that."

"Yes," Dr. Sligh smiled, "and the delivery was a slow one. I went over about nine o'clock the night before. His mother would be in labor one minute, and then it would just stop. It was the darnedest thing. I just about came home a half a dozen times."

"We wished you had," Bessie laughed.

"You're lucky your father wasn't a doctor, Don," Carrie offered.

"No, yes, I see what you mean," he floundered self consciously. "Actually my father missed Christmas twice when I was a child. His train got snowed in once, and the other time he was just too far from home to make it back in time."

Silence fell over the group.

Katherine picked up a present, and handed it to Don. "Merry Christmas."

"Oh thank you," he responded, pleased.

Katherine's eyes wandered to her mother. The woman had encouraged Bessie in her relationship with Don at every opportunity, and they had had some shaky times even in their courtship, but they had married.

Don held up a silver pen knife. "Thank you, Katherine."

"Oh let me see," Bessie exclaimed.

Katherine sat down next to Carrie. "We've been invited to a party Friday night. Did mother tell you?"

"No she didn't," Carrie responded. "Is it a dance?"

"I think so."

"And are all the right people going to be there?" Carrie asked as she turned to watch Katherine's expression.

"Probably all the right ones," Katherine answered, "but not the perfect ones."

Carrie turned away, satisfied with her answer.

Gifts were handed out now in great profusion as Margaret squealed in delight. Wrapping paper came off in a great hurry as the little girl exposed her new things. Katherine looked down at her lap. She had accumulated three packages. She thoughtfully began to unwrap one. It was from Carrie.

"Oh Carrie, scented English soap, how delicious," Katherine responded as she lifted them to her nose. A warm smile rose to her lips.

"I got you the big box," Carrie grinned. "I thought you would have lots of use for it living in Helena with all these fine city people."

Katherine thanked her sister, but she knew the thoughtfulness of the gift was not intended for Helena's population at large. It was intended particularly and only for Tom Marlow's benefit.

The clamor of the family ebbed and flowed as individuals opened their packages. Katherine had already opened her best gifts, and her enthusiasm drained as she none the less expressed the proper appreciation for each package. Then the family migrated into the dining room where her mother offered the best breakfast that would grace the table until at least Easter. Little Margaret was simply elated, and filled her plate far beyond the capacity of her small stomach.

Then suddenly the time had slipped away, and Bessie and her family were hustling into their wraps. As they hastened out through the wintry cold to the waiting sleigh, Dr. Sligh closed the door. His wife had already retreated to the dirty dishes in the dining room.

"You've been awfully quiet all morning," he commented to Katherine. "Tom wasn't at services, was he?"

"Not at the nine-thirty," she answered as they wandered together into his study.

"I'm sorry about that," her father apologized. "Perhaps I should have mentioned our holiday schedule."

"I didn't have a gift for him anyway," Katherine replied quietly. "It's probably just as well. Now I'll have a chance to pick up something."

"True," her father responded, "but that doesn't explain all of your mood, does it?"

"My mood?"

"Now Katie, don't look away," he admonished. "Tell me straight. What is it?"

"Mother has told her friends that I've been seeing too much of Tom," Katherine confessed slowly. "Mrs. Cullen would have invited him to her party Friday night, but for that."

"Katherine, no," her father responded.

"Yes," Katherine insisted. "Lilly Cullen told me herself."

Dr. Sligh walked away, pulling on his dark beard as he mulled over the news. "I shall have a talk with her," he decided. "I shall have to have a talk with her."

"I don't know what good it will do," Katherine replied quietly. "She can hardly tell the ladies she's changed her mind."

"I will have a talk with her," Dr. Sligh repeated, and left the room.

Katherine wandered out into the hall. Her hand rose to touch the locket beneath her blouse, and then she escaped upstairs to her room.

"Katie, are you in there," Carrie called as she knocked softly on the bedroom door.

Katherine hastily wiped her eyes. "Yes Carrie, come in," she responded.

Katherine's sister came quietly into the room, and shut the door behind her. "Mother and daddy are having one of their arguments," she noted softly. "What do you say we get out of here for a while. We could go for a walk, or something, maybe even go sledding."

"I'd love to but I'm not totally over my cold," Katherine replied.

"Your bloodshot eyes and drippy nose are from crying, aren't they?" Carrie asked bluntly as she sat down on the end of the bed. "You looked fine earlier."

"I'm still congested," Katherine replied, "and daddy doesn't want me to take any chances. There have been several cases of la grippe in town."

"But you were crying," Carrie repeated. "That's why mother and daddy are arguing, isn't it?"

"Mother told some of her friends that she didn't like me seeing so much of Tom," Katherine explained, "so Mrs. Cullen didn't invite him to the party Friday night."

"Good grief, Katie, mother didn't," Carrie exclaimed in shock.

"She did."

"What is the big deal?" Carrie exploded. "Bessie's Don is only the vice-president of his phonograph company. Tom is president of Montana National."

"But Don is a Davenport," Katherine sighed. "Tom is only the nephew of the Broadwaters, and rumor has it, a poor relation."

"He's hardly poor if he's a bank president," Carrie retorted. "I bet he makes more money than old Don, a lot more."

"Probably," Katherine agreed, "but you know mother. Looks are everything."

Carrie went over to the door, opening it cautiously, listening to the quiet below. After several moments she shut it again. "Well, it sounds like they've had their words," she noted softly. "This is turning out to be 'some' Christmas."

"I'm sorry," Katherine responded. "I didn't mean to ruin it for you."

"You didn't do anything," Carrie replied as she sat down next to her sister. "It isn't your fault you caught my cold and can't go sledding, and it surely isn't your fault that mother is the way she is." She patted her sister's arm. "You've got to give Daddy credit though, he doesn't mince words; and if something is wrong, he tries to fix it no matter what day of the year it is." She smiled encouragingly at Katherine. "It must be the doctor in him."

As soon as the shops opened the following day, Katherine and Carrie were on streets of Helena, looking for the prefect Christmas gift for Tom Marlow. The selection of course was considerably picked over, but the proprietors were more than willing to talk about the price of their goods with the exception of the Sands Brothers who were planning a massive clearance sale for the following week.

"I don't know, Carrie," Katherine sighed as she left the fifth shop they had searched that morning. "Tom's gift is far nicer than anything I can afford."

"But the necklace might not be solid gold," Carrie replied, "it might just be gold filled."

"It's eighteen carat," Katherine replied. "One of the links is stamped."

Carrie's pace slowed. "Quality, I should have guessed. So what are you going to do?"

"Just the best I can," Katherine replied quietly. "To do nothing wouldn't be right, and I can't do any more than I have money for. I just wish mother had been a little more frugal when she bought my other gifts for people. I really haven't much money left."

"I have a little extra," Carrie offered. "You can borrow it if you want."

Katherine smiled. "Thank you Carrie, but no. I don't know how, or when I could repay you, and you're on your own now. You need a little tucked away for the unexpected."

"This is unexpected," she replied. "Who would have thought you would get sick, and mother would end up doing your Christmas shopping?" Then she stopped. "Have you seen anything that has caught your eye?"

"Well the watch chain is too expensive even with the shop keeper's offer to take twenty percent off," Katherine lamented, "and I can't buy a gold filled one. Whatever I chose has to be quality."

"Katie, how can you buy quality on your budget? Even a watch fob is out of your range."

"Then it just can't be gold," she concluded.

"Well, I guess a warm neck scarf would be nice," Carrie decided.

"Or a tie, or socks," Katherine agreed in discouragement. "I wanted something different, something special."

"What about a shirt?" Carrie suggested. "From what you've told me, I don't think a hammer or a saw would be quite what you had in mind."

"We can look," Katherine agreed as they turned in at Babcock & Company's Clothing shop, "but it has to be nice."

The two young women were greeted by the clerk, and shown every possible shirt in the store. Still Katherine drug her feet. Somehow she wasn't impressed despite the quality of goods. She wandered over to the accessory counter, frustrated and discouraged as she played with the key rings.

"What am I going to do?" Katherine asked over her shoulder. "Nothing feels right." She dropped the leather fob down on the plate, and took another.

"I don't know," Carrie replied, "but you're going to have to decide on something, sometime. What about a wallet?"

"A wallet, that's an idea," Katherine responded. But as she looked, it was obvious that the styles were not Tom Marlow. "I think I saw his once," she commented now as she returned to fingering the key rings, "and you know, it was in perfect shape."

"Then how about a key ring," Carrie suggested. "You keep playing with them."

"It's not the rings. It's the dish," Katherine responded. She picked up the bone china piece, and examined it.

"It's called a valet plate," the clerk offered as he came over. "It's for a gentleman's watch, coins, and keys; those things that might scratch the wood of his dresser."

"It's not very masculine looking," Carrie noted.

"But it is nice, and I can afford it," Katherine responded with a smile.

"Do you think he would use such a thing?" Carrie asked.

"I don't know," Katherine replied, "but it's not pottery, nor tin, nor anything cheap."

"We have another that hasn't been out on display," the clerk offered.

"Is it the same color?" Katherine asked.

"Well, no," the clerk answered as he brought one out in a box. "It's less colorful, with just a gold rim around the natural china color."

"Oh I like it better," Katherine responded. "What do you think, Carrie?"

"You know him better than I do," she replied as she bit her lip in doubt.

"Well I can't afford a watch chain, and at least he won't have twenty of these already," Katherine decided.

"No, I doubt he has one at all," Carrie agreed.

"I can reduce the price by ten per cent if that would help," the clerk offered. He smiled. "It will be one less thing to inventory."

"All right," Katherine decided, "wrap it up."

"This is to be a gift then?" the clerk asked.

"Yes, a Christmas gift. I was ill last week, and unable to get out."

"I hope he likes it," Carrie offered doubtfully as she waited with her sister. "It's not something every man has," or wants, she continued to herself. Her attention shifted outside. "Katie, would you mind if I run across the street for a few minutes while you wait on your package. I'd like to pick up some candy for an old lady friend of mine."

"Go ahead," Katherine encouraged. "In fact if there is anything else you would like to do, I'd like to run this to Tom. The bank building is only a couple doors away."

"Okay, when I finish I'll go down to Butcher & Bradley's," Carrie replied. "I'm sure I can keep myself occupied there until you finish." A big grin encompassed her face.

"All right then," Katherine agreed. "I'll see you in a little bit."

Katherine waited patiently for the gift as excitement grew within her. All the disaster of the previous day faded from her mind as she anticipated seeing Tom again. It seemed like an eternity since she had talked to him.

"Here you go, Miss," the clerk finally stated as he presented Katherine's package.

"Thank you," Katherine replied. She hastened out of the store as she pulled on her gloves, careful not to loose hold of her package. Her eyes were on what she was doing when she nearly collided into a pedestrian.

Chapter Fourteen

"Miss Sligh, hello," Mr. Power greeted as he successfully dodged her.

"Oh, Mr. Power, I'm sorry. I didn't see you," Katherine cried. "How are you feeling?"

"Fine, just fine." He smiled. "You were right, though, I was getting sick that night."

"Oh Mr. Power, I am sorry," she responded.

"Don't be, I'm fine now," he replied with a gentle smile. "I heard through the grapevine that you haven't been too well yourself. Did you come down with la grippe?"

"No, just a fever cold," Katherine responded, "though my father treated me as if I had. He knew it was going around, and watched me like a hawk."

"A wise man, very wise," Mr. Power responded. "I'm afraid I'm not the only one in my house to have contracted la grippe. My mother is not feeling well."

"I'm sorry to hear that," Katherine replied.

"I'm afraid I may have passed it on to her," Mr. Power admitted with a certain amount of guilt. "I hope she doesn't have too hard a time of it."

"I hope not either," Katherine responded. "Wish her a speedy recovery for me, please."

"Thank you, I will," he responded. "By the way, I never got to thank you for the dance at Mrs. Murphy's. I really appreciated spending the evening with you."

"My pleasure, Mr. Power," Katherine responded.

"I would like to invite you over to our house some time," he began now. "Maybe after mother is feeling better, we'll have a dance or something."

"That sounds very enjoyable," Katherine replied.

"We'll send you an invitation then," he acknowledged with a slight nod.

Katherine responded with a smile, and Mr. Power proceeded down the street. Katherine headed to Montana National.

The bank was as quiet as Katherine had ever seen it. Only two people stood at the tellers' windows. Most employees were busy at their counters and desks. Katherine walked through the lobby, and came to a stop at Mr. Smith's desk. She handed him her calling card.

"One moment, Miss Sligh," Mr. Smith responded as he took the card in to Tom Marlow's office. The two men reappeared together.

"Katherine, it's good to see you," Tom greeted warmly. "Won't you come in?"

She walked through the office door, and Tom shut it quietly behind her.

"This is unexpected," he responded as he invited her to sit down.

"I needed to thank you for the Christmas present," she responded, "and I wanted to give you this." She pulled his gift from her shopping bag. "I'm afraid we missed each other at church. Mother rearranged our schedule so my sister could have Christmas breakfast with us, and Christmas dinner at her in-laws."

"I was afraid you were not feeling well enough to attend church," Tom confessed as he sat down on the edge of his desk.

"We were at the nine-thirty service."

Tom Marlow looked down at his Christmas present. "What's this?" he asked as he slowly began to open one end of it.

"Well it's not what you might expect," Katherine responded with a grin. "I had quite a time finding anything since this was the first and only chance I've had to shop for a full two weeks."

"You didn't need to get me anything," Tom responded as he pulled the paper free of the box, and set it on the desk.

"I wanted to," Katherine replied, "but it's nothing compared to the locket you gave me."

"You liked it then?" he asked as he paused before lifting the lid.

"I love it. I just didn't have the money to buy you something equally as nice. I'm sorry."

"Don't be," he replied. "It's always the thought that counts." He smiled as he now opened the box. His fingers instantly reached in. "It's china," he exclaimed in surprise.

"Yes," Katherine confessed as a wave of doubt suddenly rushed over her, "but it's not for women. It's a valet plate. You know, to put keys on so they don't scratch your dresser."

"I know what a valet dish is, Katherine," he retorted in good humor. "I've just never had one, not a bone china one at any rate."

"I didn't see any other kind. Maybe I should have looked harder," Katherine replied quietly.

"No, no, I like this," Tom responded with a smile. "I just never expected china. This is great."

"Then you like it?" she asked.

"Yes, of course," he laughed as he turned it over and over, admiring it.

Katherine watched, a bit perplexed. "You don't have to say you like it just to please me," she stated quietly.

Tom Marlow looked up. "Is that what you think?"

"China is not exactly a man's gift," she suddenly decided.

Tom Marlow stared intently at her for a moment. "Katherine, when I was a little boy, my mother always served our meals on enameled tin ware. It was easier to come by, and it didn't break, only dented or chipped. Plus it weighed less and therefore was easier to pack and carry. You see, we moved when I was just a year old...some eight hundred miles to Maryland, and then back to Missouri when I was ten. Five years later we moved across the river to Quincy, Illinois. The only time we ever ate off china is when we visited family in St. Louis." He smiled as he recalled a particular memory. "My grandmother loved her china. She used to serve me rice pudding in a glass dish set on one of her china saucers. I once asked her why she bothered with the plate since I was old enough not to spill, but she just gave me a hug and told me that's how proper people did it." He paused. "China is special. Don't ever apologize for giving bone china."

"Then you really like the valet dish?" Katherine asked in growing relief.

"I really like it," he confirmed with a warm smile, "probably more than you like your locket."

"That's impossible," she laughed.

He smiled. "I didn't have a picture small enough to put inside. I'll have to remedy that one day, but for now maybe you'd accept this." He offered her a manila envelope.

"What is it?" she asked.

He made no reply as she pulled out a photograph of him.

"Oh Tom, thank you," she responded as a brilliant smile lit her face. "I love it."

"It's not too egotistical of me?" he asked with a grin.

"Oh no," she cried.

"So are you well then?" he asked as he changed the subject.

"Pretty much," Katherine answered as she slipped the photo carefully back into its envelope, "though daddy still keeps his eye on me. There have been several cases of la grippe in town, and he's afraid I might catch it."

"We wouldn't want that," Tom responded. He paused momentarily. "Will you be strong enough by Friday to go skating? We could catch the seven o'clock streetcar to the Broadwater."

"I'm afraid I've already made plans for Friday evening," Katherine replied, "and I'm not sure daddy would approve of me spending the entire evening out in the cold. Perhaps an afternoon would work."

"Saturday then?" Tom asked. "It seems like an eternity since we've done anything together."

"Saturday should be fine," Katherine responded.

"And your friends from Friday night could come along," he suggested. "That should appease your mother."

"My mother?" Katherine repeated.

"It's hardly a secret that she doesn't like me," he replied with a wane smile.

"What has she done now?" Katherine demanded.

"Done?" He fell momentarily quiet. "Katherine, I don't run with the same crowd as you. It bothers her."

"It shouldn't," Katherine retorted.

"Maybe not, but it does."

"My mother is out of line," Katherine stated quietly.

"I love you, Katherine. She can't stop that," Tom offered softly.

"What are we going to do?"

"Give it time," Tom replied. "Maybe she'll mellow."

"She didn't with my father's aunt," Katherine grumbled.

A warm smile rose into Tom's expression. "She doesn't have to like me, just accept me."

"And if she doesn't?" Katherine asked.

"She will when we announce our engagement," he replied, "as long as we don't force things too fast. She does have an image to maintain, and if I prove to be less of a dog than she likes to think..." He smiled. "Give it time, Katherine."

"My sister is visiting from Deer Lodge," Katherine offered now. "You can meet her Saturday."

"Does she know about me?" he asked.

Katherine smiled. "Yes."

"Then I shall look forward to meeting her," he replied.

"I'd better go," Katherine decided as she rose from her chair.

"Katherine, does it bother you that I'm not invited to the parties?" Tom suddenly asked.

She stopped. "It would be more fun with you there," she replied.

"But do you like the parties?" he pressed.

"Most of them," she replied. "It's better than sitting home at night. ...and ones like the Butterfly Tea at Mrs. Murphy's actually raise money for one good cause or another. Why?"

"I just wondered," Tom answered as he walked her to the door. "I'll meet you outside the depot on Saturday," he stated as he reached for the door knob. His face passed incredibly close to Katherine's, and it drew to a stop in front of hers. "You wouldn't object to an engagement?" he asked softly.

"No, of course not," she breathed as her heart raced within her.

His face bent closer, his lips lightly brushing hers as they sought response. Katherine dared not move, afraid that in so doing her passion would escape all reason, all bounds.

Tom drew back. His eyes questioned her.

A wave of guilt rushed through Katherine. She wanted him. He wanted her. What was the sin of a little kiss? Without a further thought, she reached forward and kissed his cheek briefly, but passionately. Then she escaped the room, and Tom Marlow. He didn't follow.

Friday evening was cold and clear as Dr. Sligh dropped his daughters off at the Cullens. The house was glowing with activity as Katherine and Carrie hurried the short distance to the porch. Grace met them at the door.

"Katherine, where did you get that dress? It's absolutely stunning," Grace exclaimed as her friend removed her cloak.

"Mother had it made for me," Katherine replied.

"Well, it's a gorgeous blue," Grace declared. "Your mother has superb taste." Her eyes settled on Carrie.

"Grace, this is my sister, Carrie," Katherine introduced. "She lives in Deer Lodge."

"Then you must know Miss Bellenberg," Miss Hauser decided as she joined into the conversation.

"Yes," Carrie responded. "Do you know her? She visited the Kleinschmidts over Thanksgiving."

"No, I didn't actually meet her," Miss Hauser replied. "I was away at school."

"Carrie, this is Ellen Hauser," Grace introduced. Then she turned to Katherine. "You've met Ella before, haven't you?"

"No, I haven't," Katherine responded. She turned to Ellen Hauser. "It's nice to finally meet you. We're looking forward to your New Year's party."

"Yes, I'm afraid Mrs. Allen is going to out-do herself with the cotillion," Ellen laughed. "She's such a dear."

Katherine turned. Music was coming from the library, and she recognized the piece.

"It's Weber's orchestra," Lilly offered as she appeared at her elbow. She turned to Carrie. "You must be Carrie. Welcome. I'm Lilly Cullen."

"It's nice to meet you," Carrie responded. "Thank you for inviting us."

"We're glad you could both come," Lilly replied. She smiled as she noted Katherine's suspenseful mood.

"You must recognize the piece, Katie," Carrie commented.

"It's the same piece she danced to out at the Broadwater," Lilly explained with a smile.

"It must have been magical," Carrie laughed as the three of them walked into the drawing room.

"Miss Sligh, may I have the pleasure of this dance," a masculine voice interrupted.

Katherine turned, awakened from her dream world. Mr. Power was standing before her. "Of course, Mr. Power," she replied, disoriented. Excusing herself, she left the company of her sister and friend.

Mr. Power and Katherine joined the other dancing couples. "You seem a little off balance," Mr. Power observed. "Are you feeling all right, Miss Sligh?"

"Yes, Mr. Power, I'm fine. You just caught me in a daydream." She smiled.

"It must have been some dream," he retorted in good humor.

"I suppose it was," she laughed lightly. "How is your mother?"

"Not good. If she doesn't perk up soon, we shall have to call the doctor," he informed her.

"Well I hope that won't be necessary," Katherine responded. "Do wish her the best for me."

"Of course," Mr. Power responded. He was about to change the subject, when he received a tap on the shoulder.

"You mustn't hog Miss Sligh," Norman Holter warned with a mischievous smile, "not like you did at Mrs. Murphy's."

"Norm, you son of a gun, can't a fellow even finish out a dance with a young lady," Power retorted. With a frown, he ceded Katherine to his friend.

Katherine glanced quickly around for her sister. Carrie was talking to Ernest Cullen. She sighed with relief.

"You know, if I didn't know better, I would think you didn't like dancing with me," Norm Holter stated.

Katherine quickly looked up. "No, it's not that," she replied. "I was just checking on my sister. She visiting, and I didn't want her to feel left out."

"Is that her in the green dress," Holter asked.

"Yes."

"She looks pretty well occupied to me," he replied. Then he smiled. "You realize Power and Marlow are competitors, don't you?"

"Competitors?" Katherine responded. "No, I didn't realize."

"They are. Actually, I am too. The Powers, the Hausers, and my family all have interest in the First National Bank. It's the oldest bank in Helena. But old or not, we all took a big hit with the silver panic. It nearly shut us down. How Marlow managed to pull Montana National out of bankruptcy is still being speculated on, but he did, and you have to admire him for it."

"Why are you telling me this," Katherine asked.

Norm Holter shrugged, and grinned. "I just wanted you to know who you were dancing with." The song drew to a close, and they walked from the floor together. "Would you like something to drink?"

"Yes, please," she replied. "So what else do you think I should know?"

A smile crossed his face as he picked up two crystal cups of punch. "Do you think there's more?"

"Yes," she answered as they strolled over to a vacant part of the room.

"Maybe there is. Maybe there isn't." His attention shifted to Lilly. "My brother enjoyed Salvini when he was home. Did Lillian?" Norm Holter asked.

"Yes, she did," Katherine answered.

"Amazing," Holter responded. "They finally found one thing they agree on."

"I understand your brother likes college," Katherine offered.

"Hmm," Norm Holter concurred, "though I'm never quite sure if it's his studies or the glamour of the east that's caught his fancy. He hardly comes home more than once a year."

"Maybe he just needs a good reason to come back," Katherine reasoned.

"Like what?" Norm replied.

"A young lady," Katherine responded.

"Well if you have any suggestions, let me know," Norm chuckled. "Ladies have never been his strong suit."

"He and Lilly saw Salvini together."

"I believe the draw was Alexander Salvini, not each other," he responded with a smile.

"But Lilly would be a good match?" Katherine asked.

"You mean, would her family be acceptable?"

"Yes, would they?"

"Of course," Norm answered, "her father is a very successful attorney. But I wouldn't hold my breath over those two."

"What about Ella Hauser? Would she be a better match?" Katherine asked.

"Ella," he retorted in surprise.

"Ella Hauser," Katherine repeated. "You said her family had vested interest with the Powers."

"Oh, I see," Norm replied more quietly. "You want to know if I'm courting money."

"You?" Katherine responded, startled. "No, I meant in general."

"Of course you did," Norm replied as his attention shifted. "Excuse me, Katherine, will you?" He briskly walked away.

Katherine stared silently after him, stunned by his reaction. Was Norm courting Ella Hauser? Katherine had only just met the Hauser girl, and she certainly didn't intend to imply anything. She was simply trying to find out if Lilly had any rivals for Ed's attention.

Katherine knew there were always preferred families in a community, families who were thought to be the ultimate social and marriage partners. Her mother was very aware of it. Her father scoffed at it. What she hadn't counted on was the sensitivity of it all. The Holters evidently were not status quo with the Hausers, and she had just managed to commit a major error in etiquette. Katherine felt bad as she watched Norm Holter walk away. He approached Lilly, and asked her to dance. Lilly accepted.

Katherine now looked around for Carrie.

"Ella is jealous as heck that you've been occupying all of Norm Holter's time," Puss Cullen noted as the young girl came up alongside Katherine.

Katherine turned. "How would you know that?"

Puss turned, and pointed to the young woman. Ella immediately diverted her eyes.

"Don't point," Katherine quickly admonished as she too looked away, "especially when you're tattling on someone."

"It's true," Puss asserted.

"Maybe, but you don't want everyone to know you know."

"Why not?" she asked.

"Because some may not like it."

"Oh," replied Puss. "Was I wrong to tell you?"

"No, I appreciate it," Katherine replied with a smile. "Have you seen my sister, Carrie. She's wearing a green dress."

"Is that her, talking to Grace and Charles?" Puss asked.

"Yes, thank you," Katherine replied. "By the way," she began now as she took a moment with Puss. "How are your cats?"

"We gave them away."

"All of them?" Katherine asked.

"All except mama kitty," Puss answered.

"Does that make you sad?"

"I miss them, but there will be more." Puss smiled. "I think I'll go get some cake. Would you like some?"

"No, not right now," Katherine answered. She watched Puss disappear through the crowd. Then her eyes shifted to her sister. She had left the company of Grace and Charles Broadwater, and was approaching her.

"Hi," Carrie greeted softly. "You certainly have been popular."

"I would make mother proud," Katherine replied with a besmirched smile.

"So true," Carrie laughed.

"I'm sorry I deserted you," Katherine stated.

"Hey, I'm not some wall flower," Carrie boasted. "If I want to dance, I'll find someone."

"And did you?" Katherine asked.

Carrie smiled, and indicated the one. "He asked me."

"Mr. McPhee?" Katherine responded. "He was the telephone operator at Mrs. Child's the night daddy won the election."

"I knew he was a good soul," Carrie laughed.

"Have you seen Lilly?" Katherine asked as she again surveyed the couples around her.

Carrie discreetly pointed. "Is that her?"

"Yes."

Lilly had left Norm Holter, and was heading for the punch bowl alone. But before she could reached it, a younger man intercepted her.

"Who is that?" Carrie asked.

"Albert Holter, Norm's youngest brother," Katherine answered.

As the two disappeared into the dancers, Katherine and Carrie were each asked to join in as well. Mr. Murphy, Mr. Carpenter, Mr. Sanders, and Mr. McPhee each took a turn with Katherine on the dance floor as she added a few more names to her list of acquaintances. Her sister was not left out either. Carrie's new face attracted dance partners more and more as the evening wore on.

It wasn't until nearly eleven thirty that the party began to break up. Katherine joined Lilly as Kate and Addie Murphy departed.

"Katherine, hi," Lilly responded as she waved good bye. "Did you manage to have a good time, even without Tom?" she asked.

"Yes," Katherine responded with a soft smile, "but it would have been better with him."

"Of course," Lilly replied.

"I noticed that you danced with both the Holter brothers," Katherine commented. "Did they tell you when Ed will be coming home again?"

Chapter Fifteen

"They hope sometime this summer," Lilly answered pleasantly.

"Have you asked Ed yourself?"

"No."

"Why not?" Katherine asked.

"Because I don't think he really wants to come home," Lilly answered.

"You're joking," Katherine gasped.

"No."

"But he likes you. Why wouldn't he want to come back?"

"Because he likes what he's doing," Lilly answered. "Helena is not his cup of tea any more."

Katherine stared silently at Lilly. "Doesn't that bother you?"

"No, why should it," Lilly asked.

"I thought you liked him."

"I do," she replied.

"Then how..." Katherine's voice fell off.

"Katherine, Ed Holter is happy back east. He has all kinds of hopes and dreams. I can't compete with that. I don't want to. I have hopes and dreams of my own, and I wouldn't want to forget them because of someone else."

"But you'll never get together then," Katherine responded.

"You're wrong," Lilly laughed. "We're together every time we read each other's letters. It's great."

"Does that mean you would go east?" Katherine asked tentatively.

"Not right now," Lilly replied. "I have school. But who knows, maybe later some time. I do like to travel." She smiled. "Katherine, do you and Carrie have a ride home? The Corys are leaving. You could go with them in their sleigh. They live only about a block from you."

"Yes, we could use a ride," Katherine responded.

"Oh heck, Carrie," Katherine responded as she undressed for bed, "I forgot to tell Lilly about the skating tomorrow."

"Maybe she's going anyway," Carrie commented.

"I suppose it is possible."

"I overheard a lot of people talking about it at the party tonight," Carrie offered. "I think the McPhee fellow said he was going." Then she grinned. "I'll finally get to meet Mr. Thomas Marlow."

Carrie overheard correctly. Nearly everyone from the party was waiting for the one o'clock streetcar to take them out to the Broadwater. It was a beautiful day. The sky was crystal blue, the sun brilliant, and the ice hard as the skaters eagerly buckled on their skates and hurried over the frozen water amid shouts and yells and laughter.

"See you on the ice," Carrie called to her sister.

"Your sister is in a good mood," Tom Marlow noted as he and Katherine stepped onto the ice. They glided silently for several minutes, getting used to their blades again after a two week absence. "Did you enjoy yourself last night," Tom asked.

"Yes, it was very interesting," Katherine answered as her attention now shifted to him.

"The party was at the Cullens, right?" Tom asked.

"Yes." Katherine fell momentarily silent. "They were going to invite you, you know. They would have except for my mother."

Tom reached for her arm, and drew her alongside him. "Yes, I know," he responded quietly. "The judge came to see me."

"Judge Cullen?" Katherine retorted. "You're kidding."

"No," Tom replied in a soft tone. "I have the invitation in my pocket."

"But you didn't come," Katherine cried.

"I thought it would be better if I didn't."

"Because of my mother?"

"Because the judge told me some things I didn't know."

"Like what?" Katherine demanded.

Tom guided her to a vacant section of ice. Here he slowed to a stop, and bent down to check his skate. "My presence would have looked like Mrs. Cullen was insulting your mother, and your mother has been courting some pretty hefty political support since she's been in Helena." He rose now to his feet, smiled briefly, and then took Katherine's hand as they began skating again.

"Does it have something to do with the Powers and the Hausers?" Katherine asked in a quiet tone.

Tom slowed. "Why would you ask that?"

"Because Norm Holter made certain I knew they owned interest in First National Bank," she answered.

"So does Norm Holter," Tom replied.

"So do they have something to do with it?"

"No, I don't think so," Tom Marlow replied. "First National has been having a tough time since the panic, but I don't think the bank is involved where your mother is concerned."

"Then tell me about the Cullens," Katherine requested.

"The Cullens? What about them?"

"What is their status in this city?" Katherine asked.

"Lilly's father is a judge, Katherine, you know that."

"But he's not a Power or a Hauser," she replied.

Tom Marlow gazed as her silently for several long moments. "You had quite a talk with Norm," he commented finally.

"It was short, but informative," Katherine replied.

"I guess," Tom retorted. Then he became more serious. "Judge Cullen is one of the most able attorneys in his profession, Katherine, but his clients are mostly the railroads and the mine owners. This sometimes puts him in direct conflict with local interests; and though this is the way the adversary system is supposed to work to attain truth, it sometimes also creates opposition beyond just the court room."

"So he is not liked by some," Katherine replied.

"There are those that fear what he might be capable of, if circumstances should turn against them," Tom explained. "The judge is a good man, and he's good at what he does." He paused as a smile rose to this lips. "Any more questions?"

"Lilly," Katherine replied.

"What about her?"

"Do you think she's right for Ed Holter?"

"Do I think..." Tom's face puckered as laughter burst from his lips. "How should I know?" he cried.

"You know the Holters, don't you?"

"I know Norm, and Al a little. Katherine, I've only been in Helena for a couple years. I've maybe seen Ed two or three times at most, and then it was only at church. Ed's been away at school."

"So you don't know him, you don't know if he and Lilly fit."

"No."

Katherine skated away. Tom followed.

"Katherine, wait," he cried.

She slowed.

"What's the matter?" he asked.

"Lilly won't ask him to come home, but I think that's what Norm wants."

"Good for her," Tom responded.

"Why?" Katherine cried.

"Because sometimes its hard to live in a big brother's shadow," Tom replied. "I wouldn't want that for Ed or Lilly."

"But you're a big brother, aren't you?" Katherine asked.

"Yes, and sometimes it's just as hard to live in your father's shadow. I left Illinois to make my own life. That's what Ed Holter is doing." Tom Marlow smiled. "Come on, you're getting cold. Why don't we go get a cup of something hot."

Katherine followed him to a bench where they removed their skates. Carrie whizzed by, and made a sudden stop.

"You two aren't leaving, are you?" she cried breathlessly.

"No, we're just going in for something warm," Tom responded. "Want to come?"

"No thanks," she grinned as several people from the party pulled in around her. "You stay warm, Katherine," she admonished, and then took off skating again.

Tom Marlow re-buckled their skates and slung them over his shoulder. Then the two headed for the hotel.

"Is Norm Holter your friend?" Katherine asked now.

"Norm? Yes," Tom replied.

"Even though you're competitors?" she asked.

"Probably because of that," he replied. "We share a lot of common ground."

"You both want what is best for Helena," Katherine decided.

"Yes." Tom smiled. "So what do you think if I threw a party, would anyone come?"

"What kind of party?" Katherine asked as they gained the warmth of the hotel lobby.

"I don't know," he mused. They followed the smell of hot coffee. "What kind would you suggest?"

The following morning Dr. Sligh led his family down the aisle at St Peter's Episcopal Church to join the Broadwaters in their pew. Cordial nods of greeting were exchanged as Dr. Sligh took his seat next to Tom Marlow. Katherine's mother was next, and then the girls. There was room for everyone since Wilder was away for the remainder of the holidays.

After the service, Dr. Sligh took pains to engage in a brief conversation with Tom Marlow. Her father was doing his best to mend the discord his wife had caused, and Katherine could only feel gratitude. Her mother on the other hand was disgruntled at her husband's gesture, and displayed her ill humor all the way home.

"Mother, why do you hate Tom Marlow," Katherine demanded as they finally gained the inner recesses of their home. Dr. Sligh and Carrie had conveniently disappeared.

"I don't hate him," her mother replied quietly.

"Well you surely don't like him," Katherine retorted.

Her mother turned. "No, I don't like him. I don't like him turning my daughter's head. You could have any man in the city, Katherine, if you would just apply yourself. You are a lovely young lady, and second to none in looks. It could be the engagement of the season, perhaps of all time."

"So who do you recommend?" Katherine asked facetiously. "Mr. Power or Mr. Word?"

"Either would be a fine choice," Mrs. Sligh replied. "You would never lack for anything. You would have it all."

"All except what really counts," Katherine commented.

"You can choose who you want to love," her mother replied. "He doesn't have to be a nobody."

A new surge of emotion burst within Katherine. Tom Marlow wasn't a nobody, but she bit her tongue, and tried to follow her mother's logic.

"I can only love someone I respect," Katherine replied now.

"Then respect Mr. Power or Mr. Word," her mother advised.

"Mr. Power is second generation money," Katherine responded quietly. "I want first."

Mrs. Sligh stared at her daughter. "What's difference does it make?"

"First generation made the money themselves. If something happens, they can make more."

"And something usually does happen to first generation money," her mother retorted. "They often lose it all. Then what?"

"They make it back, because they know how."

Mrs. Sligh grew silent, pondering her daughter. Katherine had a stubborn streak, a stubborn streak that wasn't easily budged. Was there any sense to what her daughter was saying? "You think Mr. Marlow is more adept at making money than Mr. Power?" she asked.

"I think Mr. Marlow is making a better income than Don Davenport," Katherine responded, "and you were well satisfied with Bessie's engagement."

"But Bessie didn't have the opportunity that you do," her mother replied. "Here, you're rubbing shoulders with the very best young men all of Montana has to offer, Katherine. Why settle for less than a Mr. Power or a Mr. Word?"

"You would auction me off to the highest bidder then?" Katherine replied.

"Katherine, no," her mother cried.

"I love Tom Marlow," Katherine stated quietly. "I don't want Mr. Power or Mr. Word for a husband, and they don't want me."

"Katherine…"

"Mother, the men in this city are in no rush to get married, especially not the society boys, or haven't you noticed? They enjoy their parties. They enjoy their freedom. Why should they give it up, and get married?"

"Because they'll want families," Mrs. Sligh replied.

"Certainly when they are forty or so, but not now. Do you know how old I'll be when most of them reach forty? They won't look at me. They'll rob the cradle, and marry someone half my age."

"Mr. Marlow isn't exactly young," Mrs. Sligh commented.

"But he's not forty," Katherine responded. "And how many times does love knock at the door? Would you prefer me as an old maid?"

Mrs. Sligh fell silent. She felt somewhat helpless. The few times Katherine had chosen to be stubborn, Mrs. Sligh had never prevailed against her. It was as futile as asking Katherine to stay at Bessie's during the election. Her daughter had fallen in love with Marlow. Was there anything that could be done? She doubted it. Still, she didn't have to like it.

Mrs. Allen's cotillion for Ella Hauser on New Year's Day again drew Helena's very best young ladies and gentlemen. Mrs. Allen, assisted by Miss Hauser and her mother, received their guests in a charming gold and white reception room before they embarked into the large hall set aside for dancing. The old English woodwork, staircase, and paneled ceiling were in heavy oak, as was the fireplace complete with settles. The sideboard in the dining room offered cooling refreshment.

Katherine and Carrie joined the dancing, taking up the two-step or the waltz as required for the many intricate and varied figures, and were continuously subjected to changing partners. Ella Hauser and Norm Holter led them through the figures, often with favors of tiny fans and mandolins, brownie pins, celluloid pin trays and book marks, or crepe paper picture frames and bon bon boxes. Ernest Cullon was preoccupied with the large dice being shaken in fancy baskets when his partner, Miss Rosenbaum, was waltzed off with by Mr. Bach. Laughter exploded within the group, and Ernest was consoled with a doll.

Katherine suddenly found herself opposite Norm Holter. He wore a smile that suddenly diminished as he politely performed the routine. Then at the first opportunity, he escaped to the men's smoking room, an alcove of Japanese decor furnished with bamboo furniture, tobacco boxes, and a wide assortment of pipes (from the big Dutch to the stately meerschaum or the oriental hookah).

Katherine visited the sideboard, and found a cup of cool punch waiting. She was warm, and a little flushed as she pondered Norm Holter. She had insulted him. She hadn't intended to, but she had.

"Catching your breath," Mr. Power asked as he reached for a drink as well.

"Yes," Katherine answered. "How is your mother?"

"Not good," he confessed. "Her doctor has confined her to bed for the week. We're hoping it will help."

"Oh, I am sorry," Katherine responded. "Is there anything I can do?"

"Well now that you ask, I was wondering if your father could spare me a few minutes sometime tomorrow," Mr. Power replied. "Mother insists that her doctor is the ultimate authority on everything, but he doesn't talk to me – no doubt because my mother won't let him. In any case, it would be most helpful if I could discuss the situation with someone like your father. I'm sure her symptoms are far worse than she admits."

"Of course," Katherine smiled. "What about lunch at the Montana Club? I believe my father is planning to eat there tomorrow, right after he sees my sister off on the eleven-thirty train."

A relieved smile broke across Mr. Power's face. "That will be perfect," he responded. "You'll arrange it?"

"Yes."

"Thank you," Mr. Power responded. He took her empty cup and set it aside. "Would you care to do a little two-step?"

"Please."

The dancing did not cease until nearly midnight when Weber's Broadwater Orchestra finally quit. People in mass lingered as they enjoyed the refreshments, and cheered in the New Year. Carrie was among those thoroughly enjoying herself, having gotten better acquainted with many from their Saturday afternoon of skating.

Katherine watched Norm Holter. She wanted to make amends with him, but she wasn't sure how she should go about it. At the moment he was at Ella Hauser's side, telling a prolonged and evidentially fascinating story.

"You look bored."

Katherine turned. Ernest Cullen stood beside her. "I am," she admitted. "So which reality have you come to live in," he asked, "the one you once described, or mine?"

"Yours," she answered. Her concession cut the tension between them like a knife, and it vanished.

He smiled. "Friends?"

"Friends," Katherine replied. Her eyes settled on Grace who was also intently listening to Norm's story. She wore a dress of green velvet with pink satin contrasts. "What's Lilly doing tonight?" she asked Ernest.

"Probably sleeping by now," he replied. "She has school tomorrow."

"Does she talk to you much?" Katherine asked.

"About what?"

"Oh I don't know, school, boys, travel..." Katherine replied.

Ernest smiled. "She'll talk to anyone who will listen about the ancients. Boys, well no, not much. Grace is always riding her about being too bookish, that she'll never catch a husband. I think it makes Lilly a little self-conscious even though she tries not to let it. She just enjoys her books, and I think Grace should leave her alone. If she doesn't marry, what's so bad about that? Dad will always see that she is taken care of."

"What about travel?" Katherine asked.

"She does like that," Ernest replied. "We went to San Francisco once, and she loved it."

"So tell me Ernst, how long has Ella had her eye on Norm?"

"Probably forever," Ernest chuckled, "and Holter has known about it for just as long. Sometimes I think he tries to make her jealous, sometimes he just ignores her. Ella gets so mad. That's probably why she finally just up and went away to school. I think it was her way of trying to make him jealous, and by the looks of things, it may be working." Then he turned. "Why? Do you like Holter? I thought you and Marlow were an item."

"We are. I don't," Katherine answered.

"Hmm, you must be bored," Ernest mused. "Most girls don't know what to do around Norm Holter. He's too hard to talk to." Then he suddenly smirked. "Okay, okay, I get the point."

Katherine smiled. Ernest had just described himself. Her attention shifted. Norm Holter had finished his story, and was walking away. Katherine quickly excused herself, and intercepted him.

Norm drew to a stop as Katherine obstructed his path, his strong countenance defying her action.

"I'm sorry about the other night, Norm," Katherine stated quickly. "I didn't know about Ella. I'd only just met her, and I didn't mean to imply anything. I'm sorry," she repeated awkwardly. She could feel the heat rising off her flushed face, and she didn't wait for a response, but quickly escaped.

Chapter Sixteen

The following day Katherine and her mother said good bye to Carrie at the house, and then Dr. Sligh took their daughter down to the station. The weather was brisk and cold with light clouds hovering on the horizon.

Katherine retrieved the carpet broom from under the stairs as her mother took down the Christmas decorations and threw out the evergreens. Pine needles littered the floor, the furniture, and even the window sills.

"What a mess," Katherine groaned as she began to push the sweeper back and forth.

"It happens every year," her mother responded with a smile. She packed the ornaments away in a box.

"There's ice skating again tonight," Katherine commented. "I thought I would go, if it's all right."

"Bessie was talking about going out, but she has to help Don get ready for his trip to Omaha. He's leaving tomorrow."

"I think the Cullens are going skating," Katherine offered. "A lot of people from last night were talking about going out."

"Will Mr. Power be there," her mother asked.

"I don't know," Katherine replied.

"Well just be sure you dress warm, and don't get over heated," her mother replied.

"There's a straw ride tomorrow night," Katherine added. "They're going to pick everyone up."

That evening Katherine walked over to the Cullens on Dearborn Street, and after warming up, they continued together the three additional blocks down to the train station. Katherine looked for Tom, but she didn't see him. She had talked briefly with him on Sunday, but evidently his plans for skating had met with some obstacle or another. Katherine found a seat on the streetcar as it left.

"So he's not here," Ernest surmised quietly as he bent over her shoulder.

Katherine turned. "No."

"But I am," Earnest claimed as he wiggled his eyebrows up and down, "though of course, I don't count."

"Ernest, stop it," Lilly scolded.

"Why?" he asked as he sat down next to Katherine. "She's finally smiling, isn't she?"

"Am I that glum?" Katherine asked.

"Yes," Ernest retorted, "glum as an old...pickle."

Katherine's eyes lifted. "A pickle?"

"Sure, why not," Ernest laughed.

The streetcar pulled in at the Broadwater, and everyone got off as snow began falling once again. Katherine made her way down to the lake's edge and strapped on her skates. She stood up, waiting for Lilly to finish.

Gloves suddenly covered her eyes, and Katherine instantly spun. "Tom?" she cried. "Oh Norm," she responded as her joy turned to reserve.

"No, not Tom," Norm replied quietly. He glanced at Lilly who had now gained the ice.

"Catch up when you can, Katherine," Lilly called as she skated away.

Katherine waved. "I didn't even realize you were on the streetcar," Katherine offered as her attention returned to Norm Holter.

"I wasn't. I had dinner here with some friends," he replied. "Look Katherine, I guess I owe you an explanation. I didn't mean to be rude last night, but you threw me quite a corker the last time we talked, and I was afraid you might get into it again at the Allen's. That wouldn't have been prudent or wise, and frankly you had me a bit unbalanced."

"I'm sorry," Katherine responded.

Norm Holter smiled. "Where is Marlow anyway?"

"I don't know," Katherine answered.

"Something must have come up," Norm decided. "Do you have someone to skate with?" he asked. "I could rent some sk..."

"No need for that. Ella Hauser would only get jealous," Mr. Power interrupted as he skid to a stop beside them.

"Power, you son of a gun," Holter retorted, "you should talk. How is your fiancee anyway?"

"You're jumping ahead of the game, Holter," Charles Power replied. "I just came by to thank Miss Sligh for a kindness she did me." He smiled. "The least I can do in return is offer her some company while she skates. She would have to wait for you."

"Kindness, what kindness," Norm Holter demanded.

"Something to do with my mother, you bore," Power retorted.

"Oh, your mother. How is she?" Holter asked more politely.

Katherine glanced beyond them. Tom Marlow was walking over from the hotel. She could just make him out under the electric lights. She instantly removed her skates, and ran to meet him, leaving the bickering men behind.

"Katherine, I'm sorry I'm late," Tom greeted as he caught her in his arms.

"You're here, that's what counts," Katherine gasped happily. "I was afraid you weren't coming."

"Delayed," he replied, "just delayed." He looked over her shoulder. Holter and Power were staring at them. "What's going on?" he asked.

"They did notice I left," Katherine giggled. "They were plaguing each other so bad, I didn't think they would."

Tom's attention shifted back to Katherine. "St. Vincent's is having their Christmas Cantata Friday. Would you like to go? Lilly will be there, won't she?"

"We can ask her," Katherine replied. "There's a straw ride tomorrow night. Can you come?"

"Tomorrow, no," Tom answered. "I have a dinner to go to with an investor, and it will probably run late. Is Lilly out here?"

"Yes," Katherine replied. "There she is."

Ice skating and straw rides dominated the social calendar during January. Tom Marlow joined Katherine and Lilly when he could, and the three became solid friends. The three also attended the Cantata at St. Vincent's Academy on January 4th, the Masquerade at the Auditorium on the 10th, and the 25th Anniversary of the arrival of the Sisters of Charity to Helena at St. Vincent's on the 22nd.

February brought more straw rides, one of which ended up at the Cullen house on the 5th. Frozen to the bone, the young crowd thawed out with refreshments and dancing while Grace tried to monopolized Charles Broadwater's attention, and Wilder tried to catch Ernest's interest. Lilly watched all in amusement as Katherine lingered outside in the cold with Tom Marlow. Within minutes they said good bye for the below zero temperature prohibited more than a very short discussion. Tom still did not feel he could intrude on Mrs. Cullen's hospitality.

"We're throwing a grand ball," Tom told Katherine, "at the Electric Hall. It should be a huge success. Governor Rickards is coming."

"You and who else?" Katherine asked.

"The Board of Trade," Tom answered. "It's scheduled for the weekend of Washington's Birthday. The following week will be the last of the legislative season. You'll come with me?"

"Of course," Katherine responded with a smile.

"And maybe, just maybe it will impress your mother enough so we can figure out a way to keep seeing each other once your parents move back to Granite County," he responded hopefully as he rubbed his hands briskly together. "I'd better go. It's cold." He reached over and gave Katherine a quick kiss on her cheek. "I'll see you Thursday?"

She nodded. "I hope it warms up a little."

"If it doesn't, we can spend the time inside the hotel drinking hot chocolate instead of skating," he laughed. He reluctantly pulled his hand from hers, and headed home.

Dr. Sligh was called home to Granite on Thursday to attend a patient, and Katherine went skating that evening with Tom. On Friday, she was invited to the Powers. Her mother was very excited about this. It was to be a masquerade, and Katherine decided to go as Cleopatra when she ran into Katherine Carpenter at the costume shop. They were about the same height, and decided if they both went as the same thing they might cause some fun confusion at the Domino Dance Party.

Katherine Sligh arrived at the Power residence, and joined the various costumed guests at the door. She recognized no one as she entered the mansion. The sheer sumptuousness of the house made her feel suddenly shy and insignificant. After living in the small company domicile at Granite this residence reminded her more of a school than a home. Yet there were no children, and the grandeur of the furnishings far excelled any learning institution.

"Hi," Miss Carpenter greeted as she joined her mirror image. "Do you know anyone?"

"No one," Katherine answered quietly. "Wait, is that Charles Broadwater in the black?"

"It looks like it could be," Miss Carpenter replied. "He stands the same way."

"How about you? Do you know anyone?" Katherine asked.

"Just my brother," she answered as she pointed. "He's the one by the fireplace." Suddenly she gasped. "Oh gees, someone's coming this way. He's going to ask one of us to dance. Do you have any idea who it is?"

"No," Katherine replied. The knight proceeded to ask her companion to dance. Miss Carpenter rolled her eyes as she accepted.

A jester in the crazy quilt style now approached Katherine. "Would you care to dance?" he asked flatly.

Katherine accepted. She didn't recognize the voice, and the man's stature was too short for Norm Holter, and too thin for Mr. Power.

"Shall I call you Cleo?" Katherine's companion asked.

"If you wish," she replied.

"Do you enjoy reading about ancient Egypt, Cleo?" the jester asked.

"I like a few of the stories," Katherine replied.

"How about Greek or Roman stories?"

"No, not generally," Katherine responded. "What about you?"

"Love them," her companion replied, "especially Herodutus."

Katherine stared at the masked face. "I know someone like that," she responded slowly, "but she's not here tonight."

"I know," the voice replied.

"You do? So where is this person then?" Katherine inquired.

"Madison Avenue," the jester replied.

"Madison Av..." Katherine's voice faded. Lilly Cullen was at Tom Hauser's party that evening, and the Hausers lived on Madison Avenue. "How do you know that?" Katherine demanded.

The jester's smile showed despite his mask, and he was about to reply when a fellow dressed as a skeleton cut in. The jester acquiesced reluctantly.

"So who's the fool? It can't be Norm Holter."

"No, he's too short," Katherine replied with a grin as she instantly recognized Charles Power.

Her smile was not wasted on her companion. "I've given myself away already?" he asked.

"I'm afraid so," Katherine replied, "but how did you know it was me?"

"The host has certain privileges," the Power heir answered. "The invitations were marked."

"You cheater," Katherine retorted.

"Shh, not so loud," Charles Power objected. "I had to make sure you were here. I owed you a night of entertainment."

"And how is your mother feeling these days?" Katherine responded.

"Fine, never better," he replied. "She thinks highly of your mother."

"My mother," Katherine repeated, "how nice." She fell sullenly silent as she thought about the many times her mother had tried to encourage a relationship between Katherine and the Power heir.

"Ah oh," Mr. Power surmised, "you've had a difference of opinion with your mother."

"And what if I have," she asked.

"Then you and I are essentially in the same boat," he concluded simply. "My mother likes things her way."

"And you?"

"I like things my way." He smiled. "So does my father. It runs in the family."

"So who decides?" Katherine asked.

"It depends." He smiled again. "I wouldn't let it bother you. It usually works itself out in the end." The orchestra finished the waltz. "Would you like to see the house?"

Katherine followed her companion from the dance floor. The house was a mansion, a virtual palace, and she had never been in it before. Suddenly a man dressed as the German Bismarck fell across their path, spilling his drink all over their host.

"Oh I am sorry," he blurted in dumb tones as he picked himself up, and apologized again and again.

Mr. Power was not amused, and excused himself. Herr Bismarck took Katherine's arm. "Don't take the house tour," he admonished quietly. "It takes hours."

Katherine stared at her new companion. The man winked, and then excused himself. It was Norm Holter.

Katherine danced with one partner after another as everyone tried to guess who everyone else was, but Katherine's heart was not in it. Norm Holter had continuously intervened between Charles Power and herself, keeping her reputation safe for his friend. When Mr. Power did reappear, he did not return to her. The humiliation had been enough for him. He was more interested in the oaf who had spilled the drink.

"Cleo," a familiar voice greeted as a shorter, smaller Herr Bismarck now claimed Katherine as a dance partner. He pulled her discretely out of Charles Power's sight.

A smile broke over Katherine's face as she recognized her former jester. "What happened to your quilt costume?" she asked.

"Someone had more need of it," he replied as he nodded in Norm's direction. "I could use a favor."

"Anything," she responded.

"I need to look different, or I'll be tagged as the clumsy numskull that threw punch all over our host."

"I think I can help," Katherine decided quickly, "come on." She led the way out into the hall, and then to the small parlor where everyone's coats were. She pulled off her sash, and turned it inside out. Then draping it over one of her companion's shoulders, she pulled it across his torso and secured it at his waist, much like the costume of the Russian czar she had noticed at the costume shop. Then she re-arranged his medals. "There," she noted quietly.

"Clever," he responded, "but I won't need it for long. I'm leaving shortly. But what about you? You no longer match the other Cleopatra."

"So maybe Mr. Power will mistake Katherine Carpenter for the one he thought was me," she laughed. "What does it matter?"

Her companion smiled as he removed his mask. "I have one more favor to ask."

"Ed! I thought you were Albert. When did you get home?"

"Just tonight, and I leave tomorrow at noon, but I want to see Lilly. Can you help?"

"Just tell me what you want me to do," Katherine cried.

"I need an excuse to get Lilly out of the Hauser party. Maybe you can write a note or something," he suggested.

"I'll go get her myself," Katherine offered as she grabbed her coat.

"No wait," Ed Holter exclaimed. "People have been congregating around the front door all evening. You don't want to insult Power."

"Then lead the way," Katherine responded.

Ed Holter peered cautiously out of the room. "Come on," he urged as he led the way into the crowd, through a hall, down some stairs, and finally outside through a heavy door. Within moments they were running along the snowy street, undiscovered.

"What are you going to tell the Hausers?" Ed asked.

"Grace is home with a turned ankle. She slipped on the ice last night. It shouldn't be too hard to find an excuse to get Lilly out," Katherine answered.

Ed Holter suddenly stopped. "I can't go like this." He threw his coat onto a nearby tree, and began peeling off his costume. Katherine waited as she formulated her escape plan for Lilly. Within minutes both were heading down the street again.

Katherine slowed. "You wait here. I'll go around to the front of the house, and get Lilly."

Ed Holter stopped. "Are you going as Cleo?" he asked.

"I haven't much choice," Katherine grinned. Her hair was tucked under a wig, and her eyes were painted Egyptian style. She hastened over the low stone wall, and cut across to the front steps. She knocked on the massive wood door.

Ed Holter watched a light emerge at the front entrance. He could see someone talking to Katherine, the sound of their voices mingling with the music that was escaping the house. Katherine disappeared inside. The door shut, and the music faded. Ed Holter waited as his attention now shifted to the current of water tumbling down the street. The weather had warmed, and the snow was melting. The Hauser door opened again as two ladies emerged onto the porch, and hastened down the steps.

"Lilly, I fibbed," Katherine declared as she caught her friend's arm at the sidewalk. "Grace is fine. Ed is here."

"Ed," she exclaimed as she suddenly recognized him walking toward them. A soft squeal of delight broke from her as she rushed to him. "Ed, what are you doing here," she demanded. "Your family said they weren't expecting you home until summer."

"I'm on term break," he explained. "It's a short one. I have to leave again tomorrow at noon."

"It's so good to see you," Lilly responded.

"What do you say we go somewhere," Ed suggested. "We've got a lot to catch up on."

"We could go to my house," Lilly suggested. Then she stopped, "but we need Tom."

"So we stop by Marlow's place on the way," Ed Holter responded. "Where is it?"

"The Montana National building," Katherine answered. "It's the opposite direction from Lilly's."

"But it has warmed up, and the walk will be nice," Lilly encouraged.

"Let's go then," Ed decided.

Katherine did not refuse. As she fell in step with Lilly and Ed, her thoughts drifted to the end of the month. The legislative assembly would be over. Her parents would go back to Granite County; and she did not want to go with. What was she going to do? How was she going to stay in Helena?

The walk downtown was filled with chatter between Lilly and Ed. Within minutes the three were heading for the upper floors of Montana National. Tom Marlow answered the door as a look of pleased surprise fell across his expression.

"We're heading to Lilly's. Would you like to join us?" Ed asked.

"Sure," he responded. "Let me grab a coat." Within moments they were back outside, walking back up Main. "I didn't know you were in town, Ed," he commented.

"It's just a short trip. I leave tomorrow."

"That is a short one," Tom replied.

Their walk ended with hot chocolate in the Cullen kitchen. Lilly's mother was the only one home, and busy in the library writing letters to friends. It didn't take long before Lilly and Ed were deep in conversation.

"I take it your mother doesn't know you're here," Tom Marlow surmised as he pondered Katherine's costume over a steaming cup of cocoa. "Cleopatra, huh. Did anyone dress up as Mark Anthony?"

"Mother thinks I'm at the Power masquerade," Katherine responded, "and no, there weren't any Mark Anthonys at the party."

"Good," Tom retorted in good humor. "By the way, does Power like you?"

"Maybe, why?" Katherine asked.

"Norm Holter has been saying things, but not saying things, if you catch my drift."

"Norm Holter has been my guardian angel," Katherine laughed. "Every time Charles Power gets too close, Norm is suddenly there. My mother would kill him if she knew."

"I wondered," Tom replied. "I'll have to thank him."

Chapter Seventeen

"Is there any way you can stay in Helena once the legislative session closes?" Tom asked as he changed the subject.

"I don't know how," Katherine replied.

"Maybe you could stay with your sister," Tom suggested.

"I don't think I could stand living with Bessie," Katherine replied quietly.

"It wouldn't have to be forever," Tom responded. "Maybe you could get a job, and a place of your own."

"Over my mother's dead body," Katherine retorted. "I'd have to stay with someone. She wouldn't allow it otherwise."

"All right, I'll do some inquiring for you," Tom decided. Their conversation drifted into other topics.

As eleven o'clock approached, Ed pulled out his pocket watch. "We'd better be going," he decided reluctantly. "The parties should be just about over." He rose to his feet, and retrieved their coats.

Tom and Katherine left Ed at Lilly's door as the two headed down the walk, and across the street, arm in arm.

Katherine slowed as they passed the Ashby mansion. "It's a gorgeous place," Katherine commented.

"You want a mansion?" Tom asked.

She smiled. "I'd love one, but you aren't making that kind of money, are you?"

"No, not as bank president," he laughed. "But maybe someday..."

"Then someday I would love a house just like this one," she decided with a smile, "with a curved drive up to the side door, a magnificent entry, polished floors, fireplaces everywhere out of gorgeous wood, and gardens that don't stop."

"And what would you do in such a grand house," Tom asked in amusement.

"Why, give you a family, of course," she replied as they began walking again. "Think of all the fun we could have."

Tom pulled Katherine to the side of an ice patch she failed to see, crunching through the frozen old snow. Suddenly Katherine's foot slipped in the melt off.

"I've got you," Tom responded as he caught her.

She relaxed in the security of his arms. "Thank you," she breathed as her heart still pounded within her.

He smiled, his eyes resting on her as Katherine's inhibitions melted within her. His lips closed on hers. His touch was tender, loving, and passionate at the same time. In his arms, Katherine forgot about the world, about her mother. All she knew was Tom Marlow. All she wanted to know was Tom Marlow.

"Marry me," he whispered in her ear.

"Yes," she responded happily.

He reached into his pocket. "I've been carrying this around for weeks," he admitted a little bashfully as he opened the small box.

Katherine's eyes grew wide as he removed the diamond ring, and placed it on her finger. "I've already talked to your father. He gives his consent." He kissed her again. "It's just your mother…"

Katherine raised her hand in the moonlight. Even in the semi-darkness she could tell the stone was large.

"I thought about waiting to give you the ring until the night of the ball," Tom continued, "but I didn't want to take the chance of something interfering."

"I love it. I love you," Katherine cried fervently as she hugged him tightly.

Slowly, a sinking feeling invaded her. She wanted to spend eternity with him, right there in the melting snow, but her presence would be missed. It was time she got home.

Tom read her expression, and understood. Putting his arm around her, they started walking again, over ice and through slush. He drew to a stop at her fence. "Find a way to stay in Helena," he urged. "I'll look for suitable housing."

"Okay," she agreed.

He kissed her good night. It was brief, but heart felt. Then he turned, and headed home.

Katherine turned in her sleep as a knock persisted in her dreams. She woke as her father's footsteps descended the stairs. The hall clock began to chime. It was seven in the morning, and barely light.

"Katherine, it's for you," her father called.

Katherine reached for her house coat. Within moments she was stumbling down the stairs. At the bottom stood Lilly. Her father rubbed his eyes momentarily, and wandered out to the kitchen.

"I know it's early," Lilly apologized, "but we haven't much time. Can you come skating with us?"

Suddenly Katherine remembered Ed Holter. "Yes, I'll get dressed right away. Where shall I meet you?"

"I'll wait for you. We've already missed the streetcar, so Ed's bringing the sleigh around." Her voice dropped to a whisper. "He's over picking Tom up right now."

Katherine ran back up the stairs, ripping off her night clothes as she shut herself in her room. She could hear her mother calling her, but she ignored her as she hurried into her warm woolens, and grabbed her mittens. Mrs. Sligh appeared at the door.

"What's going on?" she asked.

"I'm going skating with Lilly," Katherine answered. "She waiting downstairs."

"It's barely light out, and you were up late last night," Mrs. Sligh protested.

"So was Lilly. I've got to go," Katherine replied quickly. "See you later."

Mrs. Sligh watched her daughter disappear back down the stairs, and then wandered back to her bedroom. She did not appreciate such commotion so early on a wintry Saturday morning.

"Let's go, Lilly," Katherine urged as she grabbed her coat. The two young women quickly escaped through the front door as they made their way down to Dearborn Avenue.

"Look," Katherine cried as she momentarily stopped, pulling off her left mitten.

Lilly's mouth dropped open. "He finally asked you to marry him," she exclaimed joyously.

"Yes, well, mother doesn't know yet. ...and well, Tom and I have had an understanding for a while, except now with the end of the assembly coming up, and my parents leaving Helena... Well, he went ahead and gave me the ring," Katherine informed her friend.

"You're not going back to Granite, are you?" Lilly cried.

"I don't want to," Katherine replied, "but I can't stand the thought of living with Bessie."

"Oh, I don't blame you," Lilly responded, "but you've got to stay. Maybe I can talk to mother."

"You're so lucky to live here, Lilly," Katherine replied wistfully

"We'll figure out something," Lilly responded. "Don't worry." Her attention shifted as sleigh bells caught her ear. "There's Ed and Tom."

The sleigh ride through the white landscape was a memory that would stick with them for as long as they lived. The sound of the horses, the jingle of the bells, the soft swish of the sleigh's runners in the icy packed snow only added to the winter thrill of the sun rising higher and higher into the sky, and gleaming off the white world as their breath bellowed from their faces with the joy and laughter of being together, snug beneath heavy lap rugs.

The Broadwater Hotel became visible in the distance, and drew increasingly near. The snow had melted off its shingled roof, and provided a sharp contrast to the surrounding white scenery. The two couples climbed from the sleigh and hurried to the lake's edge, laughing and giggling as they tried to throw frozen snow clomps at each other. Suddenly they grew quiet as they came to stand side by side.

"Well there's not going to be any skating today," Ed Holter noted as he surveyed the pools of water gathering over much of the ice.

"We should have known," Lilly lamented. "It's been too warm."

Katherine placed a foot on the ice, and added weight. The ice snapped beneath her, and she withdrew. "Nope, no skating this morning," she agreed.

"Then how about some breakfast," Tom suggested. "I'll buy."

The dampened spirits immediately lifted, and the four headed back to the hotel.

"Maybe we should have gone tobogganing," Katherine suggested as they entered the dining room, and were seated. "I understand the Lawrence Street hill was grand Thursday night."

"Seven blocks of pure sledding joy," Ed agreed, "but it might have melted too much last night as well."

"How do you know how many blocks were good? You weren't even here on Thursday," Katherine retorted.

"I know from experience," he replied with a brilliant smile. "I spent many a winter on that hill. Then of course there's the Broadway hill, but that's suicidal if you miss the turn into Edwards street." He laughed.

"My father took that run last winter," Lilly responded gaily. "He borrowed some kid's toboggan on a dare with Mr. Cruse, and they both raced down the hill. Mr. Cruse won though because he was on the outside of the turn and had a straighter shot."

"But the longest run is from the Quarry, down Davis into Helena Avenue," Ed Holter continued, "and right through town. On a good day you can almost make the Northern Pacific Depot. It must be nearly a two mile run."

"It's great," Lilly laughed, "even if you're not on the sled because everyone, just everyone gets out of the way. It doesn't matter if Governor Rickards is in some kid's path. He moves."

Everyone laughed.

"So ladies, what's this I hear about your latest charity event having a scene in the buff?" Tom Marlow asked slyly as they ate. "I understand there's to be a portrayal of 'Venus at the Bath' in your Living Pictures fund raiser."

Katherine nearly choked as a red flush stole up her neck.

"Oh that," Lilly laughed. "Grace says it's a pure disappointment. They're going to put Charlie Word in a tub with his toes and arms hanging out." She smirked. "Yes, we have real nudity here. All Charlie's going to do is roll up his sleeves and take off his shoes and socks."

"Then why is Katherine turning so red in the face," Ed Holter asked.

"Because," Lilly explained haltingly amid new burst of giggles, "she and Charlie are bringing the first picture to life, entitled 'Wooing'."

"I tried to get out of it," Katherine stated as she turned to Tom. "Miss Burke wouldn't let me."

"Actually I'd like to hear more," Tom replied with a relaxed smile. "What poise do you and Charlie take?"

"I lean against a well," Katherine answered simply.

"She does," Lilly agreed, "but Charlie plays the rustic, star-crossed lover, full of passion, and ready to confess the sin of his desire."

"Lilly!"

"Oh Katherine, relax. It's only foolishness," Lilly laughed.

"Well, you can be certain, Charlie won't think it's foolish," Ed replied as he sat back in his chair. "Anything to show off his muscles."

"Wait a minute," Tom interjected, "isn't Venus a goddess?"

"Men play all the good roles on stage," Lilly retorted with a smile.
"But still..."
"Interesting commentary, isn't it?" Ed laughed

By noon, Ed Holter was standing on the depot platform with luggage in
hand as his family and friends saw him off. The train departed within
minutes, and the Holters turned to go.

Lilly climbed into the sleigh with Tom and Katherine. "Look," she
exclaimed softly as she grabbed Katherine's arm on the way home. A package
rested in her hand.

"What's that?" Katherine asked.

"Ed said it was my birthday present," she replied with a smile.

"Your birthday! When is it?"

"A week from Tuesday," Lilly responded. "It looks like a book, doesn't
it?"

"Herodotus," Katherine replied with a smile. "He did say he was going to
get it for you, remember?"

"Yes."

Wednesday evening Katherine arrived at the Auditorium to play her part
in the Living Picture Charity. She appeared in the first scene dressed as a
peasant girl in a light skirt with a red bodice. At center stage was a massive
gilt frame upon which a hundred incandescent lights were trained. Heat rose
from Katherine's skin as she poised against the fake stone well. Charlie Word
adjusted his stance so that he leaned toward her, beads of sweat glistening on
his neck and forehead. Then as the curtain was drawn, Charlie fixed his eyes
on Katherine, and his expression took on that of a desperate lover. The
artistry was complete as the picture took on the reality of living, breathing
humanity.

The audience exploded into applause. Until now, none had seen such a
poise except in a painting or etching. The curtain finally closed, and
Katherine let out a sigh of relief. Charlie Word broke into a smile.

"Wow, you've got the curves of a real Venus," Charlie exclaimed. "I
never realized."

"What are you talking about?"

"Your bosom," Charlie cried, "and the way the sweat trickled down into
the lacing of your red camisole."

Katherine flushed with anger. "It's not a camisole. It's my dress," she
cried.

"Again," Mr. Child called from right stage. The curtain opened again
before Katherine could leave. She panicked and froze.

The minutes ticked by as the audience applauded loudly. Sweat now
beaded over all her skin as Katherine hated every second This time, however,
Charlie Word was not staring at her bosom at all, but his eyes were fixed

passionately on hers. He formed a kiss in mid air. The crowd went wild. Katherine's stare turned into rage. The curtain closed.

"How dare you," Katherine screamed, and left the stage.

"It was for the audience," Charlie declared as he hastened after her.

Katherine turned. "This is a charity for the hospital and for the Sisters of Good Shepherd. It is not some brothel act."

"Ah, that explains it," he retorted in good humor. "That's why I get to sit in a bath tub, and let everyone imagine I don't have any clothes on."

"As if you don't love the approbation," Katherine retorted. "Is that why you work out? So you can look like a Greek?"

"What if I do," he asked. "It's not a crime to be fit."

"The Greeks were not Christian," Katherine fumed. "They were licentious and corrupt."

"But they had a good time." He smiled.

"A good time in hell," she retorted as her eyes flashed sharply. Charlie backed off. Her anger was strong.

Katherine headed for the dressing room. She wanted her coat. She wanted to leave. As she headed around the outside of the Auditorium, Tom Marlow met her.

"Charlie's a jerk," she declared emphatically. "I want to go home."

"Okay," he responded. "What about your folks?"

"They can come whenever they're ready. I told Grace I was leaving."

"So are you all right?" Tom asked as he hailed a cab. The streets were almost melted with only patches of ice and snow.

"I'm fine, but I'll be darned if I ever consent to being in something like that again," Katherine fumed. "I won't be humiliated in public, not by some jerk like Charlie."

"He didn't mean to insult you," Tom commented quietly, "it's just the way he is. He's athletic, and loves the human body."

"I don't care," Katherine retorted, "and he can keep his darn eyes off me."

"Shall I take you home then," Tom asked softly.

"I don't care," Katherine repeated, "as long as it is away from here."

Tom Marlow helped Katherine into the cab, and climbed in beside her. "Was Lilly there? I don't remember seeing her."

"No, she wasn't," Katherine responded. "She thinks all this charity stuff is stupid."

"But she likes the theater," Tom countered.

"She likes serious theater," Katherine replied. "This would have made her sick."

"But wasn't she the one that was laughing about Charlie the other day," Tom ventured cautiously, "something about all the foolishness?"

Katherine glanced quickly at him. He was right. They had all laughed about the silliness of it all.

The following evening, Katherine was expected to attend a birthday party for Mr. Lindley. Her heart was not in it. It was Valentine's, and she wanted to spend it with Tom. Not only that, she did not know anyone attending the party. But her mother insisted, and she went. Katherine was given half a heart upon arrival, and this was matched during the evening to Mr. Farmer's. A cupid's quotation was written on the two halves, but she didn't care. Even the arrow shooting didn't interest her. She was bored and impatient. It was time to her mother learned of her engagement.

On Tuesday Katherine was invited to dinner at the Cullens along with Lilly's sister, Violet and her husband. In total nine people gathered, all family except Katherine. Lilly was celebrating her seventeenth birthday. There was cake and ice cream for dessert, and gifts from everyone.

"Where's your package from Ed," Katherine asked discreetly. "Have you opened it yet?"

"It's upstairs, and yes, I did open it first thing this morning," Lilly replied with a smile. "It is Herodotus."

"I knew it," Katherine responded.

Friday night was the Grand Ball at the Electric Hall, and Tom Marlow arrived with Katherine on his arm. "You haven't told your mother yet about our engagement," he asked anxiously as they entered the building.

"No, but I've been sorely tempted," Katherine replied. "She's been insufferable, and that Valentine's birthday party last week..." Her voice fell off.

"I know it's been hard," Tom acknowledged, "but if tonight goes well, and it should..." He smiled. "...we'll announce our plans."

"Without telling her first?" Katherine asked.

"Without telling her first," Tom confirmed with a smile. "How can she disapprove in front of the governor and all the assembly?"

A smile crept into Katherine's face as she gave up her cloak. The two wandered inside as Katherine looked around her. This was the first time Katherine had been to the Electric Hall, and she was duly impressed. Strings upon strings of electric lights draped across the ceiling, alternated by streamers of red, white, and blue. The paneled walls were covered in election buntings. The orchestra was to the right on a raised platform, dressed in their evening attire; tables lined the opposite wall; and in the middle was the largest dance floor Katherine had ever seen.

Tom Marlow greeted several friends. Tom was on the reception committee, and therefore they were early. Katherine said hello to Norman Holter, and then was introduced to Mr. Fiske, to Mayor Weed, and then to the governor. They wandered over to the refreshment table as the orchestra began to warm up, tuning their instruments and working the cold from their fingers.

"We should take our places in the reception line in about ten minutes," Norm Holter told his friends with a nervous smile.

"Right," Tom affirmed. "Is everything ready?"

"As far as I can tell," Norm confirmed.

"Good."

The orchestra began playing a portion of one waltz, and Governor Rickards pulled his wife out into the middle of the room, and began to dance as he flagged the others to join them. Several did, amid laughter and chatter. The director was unaware of this as he prepared his musicians for the evening, and abruptly terminated the piece. The dancing ceased, and in good humor, the governor applauded. The director turned in surprise, and everyone broke into laughter.

Ten minutes passed, and everyone migrated to the reception line. Tom and Katherine took their places next to Mr. and Mrs. Fiske and Mr. and Mrs. Setigman as they idly chatted. Another ten minutes went by, and then half an hour. Several new couples arrived, Senator and Mrs. Folsom from Meagher and the members of the invitation committee and their wives. Over the next half hour four more couples arrived.

Mr. Fiske looked at Tom Marlow. "Where is everyone?"

Tom looked a bit bewildered.

"The invitations were sent?" Mr. Setigman inquired as Mr. Kleinschmidt joined them.

"Of course they were," he replied. "I was on the committee."

Tom Marlow's attention focused on Katherine. "Your folks aren't here."

"They said they would be a little late," she replied quietly. "They said something about stopping by the Auditorium on the way."

Tom Marlow's expression fell as he remembered the Masquerade Ball. At the time he hadn't given it much thought, but now he realized it had been scheduled for that very night.

Katherine knew Tom was counting on the evening to be a success. He thought it would be a certainty. She glanced at the dance floor. Only a half dozen couples were enjoying the orchestra's waltz. The hall was virtually empty.

Chapter Eighteen

"We heard the ball was postponed," Judge Cullen stated as he and his wife greeted Marlow an hour later. "It wasn't until Lilly told us otherwise that we came on down."

"Postponed?" Tom exclaimed.

"Yes, I heard it at the legislative tea last week," Mrs. Cullen offered. "Everyone was rather disappointed."

"Well that explains a lot," Norm Holter decided as he overheard. He promptly left the reception line. "Mr. Keinschmidt, Mr. Parchen, we need everyone from the Invitation Committee here, now."

The men left their wives and congregated in the back corner of the room. They talked for several minutes, and returned momentarily to their spouses. Then they vanished from the hall.

Tom and Katherine now followed the judge over to a table, and ordered drinks as Mrs. Cullen turned to Katherine. "Lilly tells me you have some good news," she offered with a smile.

"Yes," Katherine agreed as she willingly displayed her engagement ring, "but I haven't told mother yet. We were going to do it tonight, but it's turning out to be a disaster."

"Oh my dear, the night is still young. Don't loose hope," Mrs. Cullen encouraged as she glanced around. "Your folks are coming, aren't they?"

"They said they would," Katherine acknowledged.

Mrs. Sligh had told her daughter they would be by later, but she hadn't told her about the rumor at the Legislative Tea. Would she really come, or was she just waiting for Katherine to come home defeated? She knew of Tom's involvement in arranging the ball.

Governor Rickards now joined the table as he and Judge Cullen found much to discuss. Within minutes several other men joined the conversation as well. Their wives had migrated into their own groups. The orchestra played softly in the background.

A few people left. A few more arrived. Then more came, including the return of those on the Invitation Committee. By eleven o'clock the hall was filled. The grand march was led by Governor Rickards and Mrs. Hersey, and then the dancing began.

"I still don't see your parents," Tom Marlow worried as he danced with Katherine.

"No, I don't either," Katherine replied as she silently fumed. Eleven o'clock was the time most of the parties ended. She would be expected home soon, but she wasn't going. With the ball just picking up momentum, she was going to stay until the very end.

Katherine tried to shove the thoughts of her parents out of her head, and concentrated on her dancing, her Tom, and the wonderful company they were in. Governor Rickards had spoken to her. Mrs. Weed had complimented her on her gown. Mr. Fiske had actually asked her opinion on some trivial matter. Her mother would be envious.

Katherine sighed in disgust. Why couldn't she keep her mother out of her thoughts.

"What's the matter?" Tom asked quietly.

"My mother," she replied.

"She just came in," Tom informed her. "Your father looks frustrated." Katherine's attention darted to the door. Her parents had arrived.

"Maybe we should go over and greet them," Tom suggested.

"No, they don't deserve it," Katherine responded. "Let's stay back here out of sight for a while."

The two waltzed for a full half hour as Katherine tried to enjoy the evening. The music was wonderful. Tom was wonderful. The company was wonderful, and now it was also complete. Her parents had finally arrived.

"Shall I make a public announcement of our engagement?" Tom asked quietly.

"No," Katherine responded. She could hear the uncertainty in Tom's voice. He had planned to, but that was before the evening had gotten off to such a grim start. "A public announcement is no longer necessary for my mother," Katherine continued. "We can just tell her at the end."

"Are you sure," he asked.

"Yes," Katherine answered. "My mother had no intention of coming tonight. I know that now. Her insult is undeserving of any consideration. We will just tell her."

"We can do it now, if you wish," Tom replied softly. "Here they come."

Katherine turned, her dancing stopped. Her mother and father were dancing in their direction. Katherine reached for Tom's hand, and led him to the refreshments.

"Your father does not deserve to be shunned," Tom commented as he handed Katherine a drink.

"True," she agreed. "I'll have to apologize to him…later."

"Or now," Tom offered. "They're not letting us get away."

"Katherine, there you are," her mother greeted. "We thought you'd gone home already."

Katherine forced a smile. "Daddy, how wonderful to see you," she greeted as she ignored her mother. She reached over, and gave him a hug.

"Katie, she told me the ball was canceled," her father whispered in her ear.

"I know," Katherine replied with a smile as she let go of her father. "Daddy, would you like to see my engagement ring? Tom finally proposed."

Her father's face brightened as Katherine held out her hand. His eyes immediately turned to Marlow as he embraced his future son-in-law.

"Proposed?" Mrs. Sligh gasped. "You didn't accept, Katherine… I mean…" Her voice fell off as devastation overcame her expression. "No…"

"Yes mother, isn't it wonderful," Katherine responded as she showed her diamond off. "Tom is so very thoughtful and generous. Don't you think so?"

"I..." Her mother's voice fell off as surrounding people noted Katherine's engagement ring, and warmly congratulated her. The news spread like wildfire as the orchestra took a break, and refreshments were in demand.

Suddenly Governor Rickards was congratulating them and Mayor Weed, and then Norm Holter was there smiling broadly. Katherine gave him a big hug. "Thanks for being my protector. I only wish you could have been at all the parties."

"I did my best," he responded, pleased. "You know, I don't think Power ever did figure out who spilled that drink on him."

Katherine laughed. It felt good.

She glanced at her father. He was smiling. She looked then at her mother. She had tears in her eyes. Katherine turned to Tom. "Maybe your aunt knows someone who needs a companion. That would allow me to stay in Helena."

He smiled. "I'll ask her."

The orchestra resumed their music, and the dancing recommenced, lasting long into the night. Katherine danced now with pleasure. The weight on her mind was gone. Her mother knew of their engagement; and with everyone else knowing, there was nothing she could do. Finally, Katherine was safe in Tom Marlow's arms, and she didn't care if they danced until morning.

By the time the orchestra called it a night, half the hall was empty. Katherine lingered beside Tom, scanning for her parents.

"They're not here," he informed her quietly. "Let's go home."

He led her out, wrapping her evening cloak around her as they emerged into the cool night air. Stars twinkled in the clear midnight blue sky. The smell of evergreens drifted down from the nearby hills. It was so quiet.

"Helena is asleep," Tom commented as he led her to their awaiting carriage.

Katherine didn't answer. She was tired from the strain of the evening, but she felt wonderful. The news of their engagement was out. Tom Marlow was hers.

"When do you want to get married?" she asked sleepily as he sat down in the carriage beside her.

"Tomorrow," he replied with a chuckle, "but isn't it customary to wait a year or two?"

"It's preferred," Katherine replied softly, "but I don't know by whom. Certainly not me." She smiled.

"By your mother then," Tom laughed. "I don't think we should rush it."

The horses took them home. As they pulled to a stop outside the Sligh's, all was dark except one room upstairs.

"Are they waiting up for you," Tom asked quietly.

Katherine looked up at the window. She could make out a silhouette as it paced across the room, and then turned and assumed a stand. It faced the bed.

"No, they're having an argument," Katherine replied. "I doubt they even know I'm home."

"I'm sorry," Tom responded.

"Don't be," Katherine replied. "Daddy and mother have never seen eye to eye on certain things."

"Like me," Tom stated.

"Like you," Katherine agreed as she snuggled up against him. "Mother has always wanted to be society, the best society. Father sees life a little more practically."

"I'm sorry your mother doesn't approve of me," Tom noted softly.

"I'm not," Katherine responded. "If she approved of you, then I wouldn't."

"Why not?"

"Because then I would have to be a different person, and I like who I am. I don't want to change, at least not just to impress people."

"But you like your parties and your fancy houses."

"Absolutely," Katherine laughed, "but they aren't what's really me. They're what I enjoy. There's a vast difference."

Tom smiled approvingly. "How about if I walk you to the door?"

Katherine slept late the following morning. When she went downstairs for breakfast, only her father was at the table. He sat drinking a cup of hot water as he read the morning paper.

"Where's mother?" Katherine asked as she found something to eat.

"I don't know, maybe Bessie's," he answered as he finished the column. Katherine sat down as her father re-folded the paper. He now sat idly staring at her.

"You and mother had another argument last night, didn't you?" Katherine stated.

"A very long one," her father acknowledged.

"I'm sorry," Katherine responded quietly.

"Don't be. It's not your fault," Dr. Sligh retorted as a wave of his former anger escaped. "Sometimes I just don't know why I even listen to that woman. All she ever thinks about is appearances, that and loosing you."

"Me?" Katherine exclaimed. "She's worried about loosing me?"

Suddenly Dr. Sligh's expression softened. "You're the last daughter to fly the nest," he answered quietly. "When you're gone, the only one left is Charles, and suddenly we aren't as young as we once were."

"You're not old, daddy," Katherine replied.

He smiled softly. "We're not young either. It bothers your mother. What will she do now that all her daughters are gone?"

"There must be something," Katherine exclaimed.

"Yes, there must be something," her father agreed. "I suggested she take up painting or some other hobby, but she doesn't think she has the talent. Maybe she should join a whist club."

"Is she terribly upset over my engagement?" Katherine asked.

"No Katie, not really. She just has some adjusting to do. You see, she really set her heart on marrying you to money. I told her you weren't going to tolerate being matched, but she didn't listen. So now she has to face me, her disappointment, and loosing her darling girl all at the same time. It's a blow, but things will come around. She just needs time, that's all."

"How much time," Katherine asked.

"Oh I don't know," he responded as he leaned back in his chair. "How long an engagement are you planning?"

"A year or two?" Katherine suggested.

"That should be plenty of time," her father replied with a smile. "She surely can't complain about that."

"But I don't want to go back to Granite County," Katherine stated. "I don't want to be that far from Tom."

"I'm sure he doesn't want it either," Dr. Sligh chuckled.

"So what am I to do?" Katherine asked.

"You can stay with Bessie," he answered simply.

"Bessie. Would you want to live with Bessie, the way she is now?" Katherine asked.

The smile disappeared from her father's face. "No, quite frankly I would not. But I would do it anyway, Katherine, I would move in with her on a dime, if I had the opportunity."

"Why?"

"Because maybe, just maybe, it would help her," he responded. "Maybe that's all she needs is a little support, a little confidence to stand up to those in-laws of hers."

"I never thought of it that way," Katherine replied.

"Well think about it, Katie. Bessie has become so preoccupied with the details of life, she's missing out on all the fun. Maybe you can loosen her up, and get her to relax a little, for her daughter's sake if not her own. Can you imagine having a mother strung so tight?"

"Yes," Katherine replied.

Her father's eyes focused sharply on her. "You can?"

"Do you think it was fun being a sister when Bessie was dating Don?"

Her father remained silent for several moments. "Third wheel, huh."

For two weeks Tom looked unsuccessfully for a place for his fiancée to live while Katherine pondered her father's words. She loved Bessie, and she felt sorry for her. Maybe she was being selfish. Fate seemed to agree. Tom Marlow found no suitable housing in all Helena during the days preceding the

Sligh departure for Granite County. Frustrated and disappointed he broke the news to Katherine.

"Don't worry," she replied with a soft smile. "I'm not leaving."

"But how..."

"I'm moving in with Bessie," she responded. "Daddy's arranged it."

"Your father? I thought you hated the idea."

"I do," Katherine replied, "but daddy thinks I might be good for Bessie. Maybe I can take some of the pressure off her."

"Are you sure, Katherine? My aunt did say you could visit her from time to time."

"I'm sure, Tom. I have to at least try for daddy's sake and Bessie's."

On March 8th Katherine moved into her sister's rooms at Mrs. Osterhout's boarding house as her little niece watched all with wariness. Within the hour Katherine said good bye to her parents, and turned to her sister. "You're having a dinner party tomorrow night for friends of the Davenport's?"

"Yes, they're from White Sulfur," Bessie responded. "They're staying at Mother Davenport's, and they had their big meal on Wednesday. It's our turn now. Mrs. Osterhout is letting me use the kitchen for a late supper."

"I've already made plans for tomorrow evening," Katherine responded. "It's Tom's birthday."

"Oh," Bessie responded in disappointment as she stowed her sister's things out of sight. "I was rather counting on you to help out. I've got so much to do." Then she smiled. "You don't know how glad I am that you're here."

"Maybe I can help until I have to go," Katherine offered.

A smile grew in Bessie's face. "I knew I could count on you," she exclaimed as she led the way to Mrs. Osterhout's kitchen, and got out the silver polish. "If you don't mind, Katie, the silver really needs a bit of a touch up."

Katherine took the polish and rag her sister held out for her.

"It's not like we can afford a place of our own yet," Bessie offered as she took a handful of knives and forks from the drawer. "That's why I won't tolerate even a speck of tarnish."

Katherine spent the next two and half hours rubbing piece after piece of Mrs. Osterhout's silverware. Then dousing handful after handful in soapy water, she washed the silverware, and put it all away. After that Katherine found herself washing woodwork. Little Margaret had left a few smudges on the door frames. But Bessie was not content to have only these few smears removed, she demanded all the woodwork glow with cleanliness.

Mrs. Osterhout just smiled and stepped aside. Katherine had never experienced such stringent standards in all her life. Even little Margaret was given the task of cleaning her toys. Everyone felt the pressure of the upcoming event. By the time Don got home from work, the whole boarding house smelled of cleaning solvent and furniture oil. The extra cooking would commence in the morning.

Katherine was only too glad to escape the pressures of her sister Friday evening. Tom's birthday was celebrated at the Broadwater Hotel amid family and friends. Norm Holter was present, along with Mr. Smith and several others. Mrs. Broadwater and Wilder made certain Katherine never felt left out when the men inevitably dove into business discussions from time to time. They diverted her attention to more feminine concerns, and on the whole, Katherine had a very nice time.

For a month, Katherine patiently endured her sister's routine at Mrs. Osterhout's, helping at every turn. But the more she helped, the more help seemed to be needed. Bessie was volunteering their combined efforts to her mother-in-law, who was finding endless self-less tasks to perform during the Lent season. Suddenly Katherine realized she was not making life easier for Bessie, but harder. More was expected.

"Bessie, no," she finally declared. "I've cleaned, I've polished, I've sewed, I've hauled box after box of this and that, I've helped you in every way I can think of, but enough!"

"Katie, you've been like an angel from heaven," Bessie told her, "but please, we must get this stuff boxed and delivered."

"No."

"No?" Bessie exclaimed.

"No," Katherine repeated. "I agreed to stay with you so I could help ease your load, but instead it's just gotten bigger. You have less time now than you had before." Katherine's eyes swung to her niece. "When was the last time you and your mother did something fun together?"

Margaret just stared at her aunt.

"See," Katherine exclaimed as her attention swung back to her sister.

"Katie, I've given my word. I must get this over to Mother Davenport's this afternoon."

"Then I'll do it alone. You take Margaret to town and buy her an ice cream, and just have some fun together."

"Katie, I can't do that," Bessie objected.

"You can. You can walk down together. I'll take the buggy, and make the delivery."

"Katie, I can't," Bessie repeated. "You'll never make it by three."

"Three? What if it's four when I get there? What is an hour?"

"An hour? You don't know Mother Davenport," Bessie exclaimed.

"But if I'm late, I'll take the blame, not you," Katherine replied with a smile. "Take your daughter for ice cream, Bessie."

"No, I can't," she repeated.

"Bessie, if you don't take your daughter, I will," Katherine decided as she noted the first look of hope she had seen in her niece's eyes since her arrival.

"If I go, then you'll have to face your mother-in-law. Wouldn't it be far easier if I just took the blame?"

"I'll have to face her later," Bessie stated quietly.

"Well, I won't be part of your misery any longer," Katherine decided. She turned to Margaret. "Get your coat. We're going for a nice long walk."

The child darted from the room. Within seconds she was back with coat in hand.

"Katie, if you leave now, if you leave me in this pinch," Bessie cried in growing desperation, "then you better have somewhere else to stay."

"Bessie, are you threatening me?" Katherine asked.

"Katie, you know I'm depending on you," Bessie told her.

"Yes, I know you're depending on me to become just like you. But I won't, Bessie, I won't." Katherine's attention shifted to her niece. "Got your hat?"

The child nodded eagerly.

"Then come on," Katherine urged. "Let's go."

"You two be back in time for supper," Bessie cried after them.

For a full hour Katherine and little Margaret walked and talked, and generally played on their way down to the Grand Central Hotel, one of the few places Katherine knew served ice cream. After they finished their treat, the two headed back outside, hand in hand.

"What do you want to do now?" Katherine asked.

"Go someplace."

"Where?" Katherine asked her niece.

"The toy store."

"Okay, but I haven't much money," Katherine warned.

"It doesn't matter. I just want to look," Margaret replied.

The two walked down to the Sands Brothers where Katherine proceeded to shop with her niece, carefully examining every toy on the shelves. The child was delighted as much with Katherine as with the toys. To have so much adult attention, without distraction, without time limits, Margaret was in heaven.

"How about if we buy this one," Katherine offered finally.

Chapter Nineteen

Katherine did not hurry home, but played with her niece and enjoyed the freedom of being out from under her sister. But as the dinner hour approached, she and Margaret headed reluctantly back. Bessie was not there when they arrived. But as they hung up their coats, Don came through the door.

"Where's Bessie?" he asked.

"At your mother's, I presume," Katherine answered as she closed the closet door. "We had an argument."

"An argument?" Don repeated.

"Yes, I'll make arrangements to leave this week."

Don stared at her. "You had quite a fight then."

"I realized that I don't belong here," Katherine stated quietly.

"But Bessie loves that you're here. She told me so," Don objected.

"So do I," Margaret chimed in as she hugged her daddy.

Katherine smiled. "Your daughter needs more of her mother," Katherine stated. "I thought I could help; but the more I do, the busier Bessie gets. She doesn't know what fun is any more."

"It takes a lot to run a household these days," Don replied.

"Especially when most of her time is taken up doing other people's bidding," Katherine responded as she held up her hand. "I know. I know. I'm saying more than I should. That's why I'm making arrangements to leave."

"Katherine..." Don fell silent. He didn't know what to say. He knew what she said was true. But if he took her side of things, he would have Bessie and his mother, both, down his neck. "I'm sorry you feel that way," he commented finally.

When Bessie got home, she joined the family at supper, idly chatting about various things of little consequence. But as the meal finished, and they again gained the privacy of their own rooms, she turned to Katherine. "Perhaps I have been expecting too much," she admitted. "You need more time for your fancy work. You have a wedding coming up, and you want to have the proper linens." She smiled sweetly. "Don't worry about what I said earlier. You are welcome here for as long as you wish."

"Thank you," Katherine responded. She did have handwork goals, but this was not foremost on her mind. Her sister had given ground, probably on the advice of her mother-in-law. Things had not changed, not substantially any way. The hopes of their father were not going to be realized. Bessie did not make a move without consulting her mother-in-law.

The following morning Tom Marlow picked Katherine up for church as he had for each of the Sundays that had passed since Dr. and Mrs. Sligh had returned home to Granite County. As Katherine climbed into the Broadwater coach, Wilder made room for her.

"Lilly's been sick, did you know?" Wilder asked.

"No," Katherine replied. "Is she bad?"

"They say it's appendicitis," Mrs. Broadwater offered quietly.

"Appendicitis," Katherine exclaimed. She knew most people died from it. Alarm took hold of Katherine. "When did Lilly start feeling poorly?" she asked.

"Friday wasn't it, Wilder?" Mrs. Broadwater asked.

"The doctor was out on Friday, but she started coming down with a fever on Wednesday," Wilder replied.

Katherine fell sullenly silent. She might as well have been home with her parents for all the news she'd heard of her friends. Lilly had been seriously ill for several days, and she was just now learning of it. Only on Sundays did she get to mingle with her own friends. Every other day of the week she was swallowed up with Bessie and the Davenports and their church.

The coach pulled up outside St. Peter's, and everyone got out. But Katherine could not follow the others inside. Lilly was ill, desperately ill. She could conceivably die at any moment, even before Katherine could get there.

"Are you coming in," Tom asked.

"No, I can't," Katherine objected. "I have to see Lilly."

"Let me tell my aunt, and then I'll drive you," Tom offered. He disappeared momentarily. Together they drove to the Cullens. Lilly's mother opened the door.

"Katherine, Mr. Marlow," she greeted, "hello."

"We heard Lilly is sick," Katherine blurted. "How is she?"

"Come in," Mrs. Cullen responded. She closed the front door behind them. "You've probably heard that it's appendicitis," she offered now. "The doctor has her on medication, and her fever is down a little, but she is still terribly ill."

"Can we see her?" Katherine asked anxiously.

Mrs. Cullen hesitated only momentarily. "Yes, of course," she decided, and led the way upstairs. Lilly's room was the last one on the right.

"Lilly, dear, Katherine and Mr. Marlow are here to see you," Mrs. Cullen offered as her youngest daughter rose from the chair. Puss had been keeping a watchful eye on her sister.

Lilly's eyes came slowly open. It took her a moment to rouse herself. "Katherine, hi," she greeted weakly. "Tom, thank you for coming."

"I didn't know you were sick until this morning," Katherine lamented as she took the chair Puss had vacated. "How are you?"

"A bit done in," Lilly responded with a faint smile. "I'm glad you're here, though. Can you stay, Katherine?"

"Of course," she replied as she took hold of her friend's hand.

"I need to talk to you," Lilly continued as she turned slightly in bed. Her face suddenly grimaced tightly as her head bowed. "Mother..."

"Puss, quick, the chamber pot," Mrs. Cullen instructed. She promptly turned to Tom Marlow. "You may want to wait downstairs."

He took the hint, and retreated to the hall as Katherine retrieved the pot, and held it for Lilly. As she finished wrenching, Lilly fell back against her pillow, totally spent. Puss then took over, covering the pot quickly with its lid as Katherine reached for the cloth lying on the edge of the wash bowl. She wet it, and cleaned up her friend's face, spreading the refreshing moisture over her skin.

"That feels good," Lilly muttered weakly as her eyes fell shut.

Katherine laid her hand across Lilly's brow, noting its warmth.

"Her fever is down to 100 point four," Puss offered quietly. "It was above 102 on Friday."

"How often does she..." Katherine asked.

"A few times a day. It's not as often now, but I wish it would stop," Mrs. Cullen worried.

"Can she keep anything down?" Katherine asked.

"Sometimes," Lilly's mother continued. "Dr. Dean has her own various tonics, and they have helped, just not enough."

Puss left the room with the chamber pot.

"I'm sorry," Mrs. Cullen now apologized to Katherine. "If I had thought Lilly would have another episode, I'd never have brought you up."

"I'm glad I was here," Katherine responded warmly. "I'd like to help, if I may. Lilly did ask me to stay."

"Are you sure?" Mrs. Cullen asked, skeptically.

"I'm quite sure," Katherine replied.

"Well, Puss could use a break. She's been confined to this room for days." She smiled. "Thank you, Katherine."

"Where is Grace?"

"At church with the men," Mrs. Cullen answered. "She's having a hard time with this. You see, she and Lilly had plans for this summer, but now..." Her voice trailed off. Then she smiled bravely, and headed out.

Mrs. Cullen found Tom Marlow leaning up against the hall wall, waiting and listening. He had not gone downstairs. Grave concern rested in his face. "You can go back in now, if you wish," she offered.

Tom's body slowly left the wall as Mrs. Cullen retreated down the hall. "Is she okay, Katherine?" Tom asked quietly as he hesitated at the door.

"For now, at least," Katherine answered.

"How long do you plan on staying?" Tom asked as he pondered his fiancée.

"As long as they'll let me," Katherine replied quietly.

"Then perhaps I'd better return to my aunt, and see that they get home okay," he noted tentatively.

"Yes, that's a good idea," Katherine agreed.

"Is there anything I can do?" Tom Marlow asked.

"No, I don't think so," she answered.

"Could your father help?"

"My father is in Philipsburg," Katherine replied.

"Yes, but could he help?" Tom asked.

"I don't know," Katherine answered as she rose to her feet, and pulled him back out into the hall. "I don't know if anyone can help, Tom," she worried. "I've never heard of anyone surviving appendicitis. Everyone I've known of was dead within the week."

"But Lilly's fever is down, and she is improving," Tom countered.

"Yes, that's true," Katherine admitted.

"Her doctor must be doing something right."

"I hope so," Katherine responded. Church bells began to ring in the distance. "You'd better go," she encouraged. "Your aunt will be getting out of church."

"Shall I drop back by later then, to take you home?" he asked.

"No, I can walk," she replied. "But Tom, could you let Bessie know?"

"I'll take care of it," he assured.

Katherine went back in to Lilly. She had awaken. "How are you feeling," Katherine asked softly.

"Better," Lilly responded.

"Do you like your doctor," Katherine asked now.

"Dr. Dean, yes I do. She's really nice," Lilly replied softly.

"She's a woman?" Katherine replied in surprise.

"Yes. She practices homeopathic medicine, like in the British Isles. She has an office near daddy's."

"She's a quack too?" Katherine retorted, shocked.

"No," Lilly cried, "she's good." Her eyes watered. "Katherine, I know your father is a doctor, but that doesn't mean he knows everything, and others nothing."

"No, no, I didn't mean it like that," Katherine replied in a softer tone. The hurt in her friend's weak eyes tore at her. "I'm sorry."

"So what does your father recommend for appendicitis," Lilly asked quietly.

"An operation," Katherine answered automatically. "If it's not done in time, the person..." Her voice fell off. She couldn't say the word to Lilly.

"Dies," Lilly finished for her. "And how many die who have the operation?"

Katherine stared at her. Most people she had heard of with appendicitis had usually died before the doctor ever got there. "I don't know."

"How many people die from operations in general?" Lilly asked.

"Most," Katherine answered reluctantly. The truth was awful.

"So what's wrong with a little homeopathic treatment?" Lilly responded. "The alternative hasn't anything to brag on."

Katherine fell silent, pouring fresh water into the wash basin. She dipped in a clean wash cloth, and wiped Lilly's face with the coolness.

"Thank you," she breathed softly, and again her eyes dropped heavily down.

Katherine continued to stare at her resting friend. Lilly had lost considerable weight over the last few days. Her features looked pinched, and her complexion was terribly pale. Yet underlying all the pallor of illness, Lilly's spirit was still in tact.

Appendicitis – Katherine racked her brain for all she knew of the illness. It wasn't much. She could name four individuals that had died of it during her life time. One fellow had it just two years before. He was a miner; and one week he was at work, and by the end of the next week he was dead. Her father had been called in on the case, but to no avail. She didn't know the particulars. She just remembered her father's frustration; and for months and months after the young man's death, she would find him reading on the subject.

Katherine stared at Lilly's sleeping form. Maybe her friend was right. Maybe one person couldn't know everything, maybe other doctors, even quack doctors knew something, something different, something that might help. Lilly had improved some. Maybe this was a step in the right direction.

Katherine's thoughts turned to Tom Marlow.

"Katherine, would you like some lunch?" Mrs. Cullen offered as she appeared with a bowl of broth. "I can help Lilly eat."

"Okay," Katherine responded as she rose to her feet. Downstairs she found the Cullen family at the table. Grace was waiting on everyone.

"Ah, Katherine is here for a little taste of our reality," Ernest grinned as he rose to help her with her chair. "I hope you have…a pen to cite us…with."

"Ernest!" Grace exclaimed. "Lilly's illness is no laughing matter."

"Oh relax, Grace, you're strung tighter than a violin."

She threw him a look of hatred.

"You'll have to excuse Grace, Katherine," Ernest retorted in good humor. "She had plans to go to Europe this summer with Lilly, but mom and dad won't let her go alone." He glared at his sister. "Poor Grace."

"That's enough, Ernest," their father admonished.

Grace's eyes were boiling with tears, and she instantly left the room. Katherine cautiously rose from her chair to follow. She met with no resistance.

"Grace," Katherine called softly, "are you all right?"

"I hate Ernest," she declared hotly. "Lilly is lying upstairs sick, and all he can do is make fun. I love my sister."

"I know," Katherine responded. "So is the trip off?"

"Everyone is going, everyone except me and Lilly. Even Wilder."

"Wilder is going to Europe? When did this happen?" Katherine asked.

"Oh, I don't know. Over the last couple of weeks, I guess, why?"

"It's just that I may as well have been in Granite County for all the news I've heard," Katherine mumbled.

"Bessie has been monopolizing most of your time," Grace agreed. "Even Violet has noticed."

"Well not any more," Katherine declared.

Grace smiled slightly. "Could you come to Europe?"

"Europe?" Katherine exclaimed. "Me? I hardly think my family can afford that. Besides, I'd die if I had to be away from Tom."

"Oh that's right, you're getting married," Grace responded. "Have you set a date?"

"Oh it won't be for a year or two," Katherine responded. "Couldn't you go to Europe with Wilder?"

"She can't go until June, but the Paynes are meeting us in New York the end of May. It's all been arranged."

"What about Violet? Couldn't she take Lilly's place," Katherine asked.

"She doesn't want to go without her husband," Grace replied, "and Puss is too young. Mother won't let her go."

"That leaves Ernest," Katherine noted. "Surely he's wouldn't mind seeing New York."

"No, not Ernest," Grace retorted, "to be cooped up with him on a train... I'd rather die."

"I'm sure Lilly would swap places with you," Ernest offered as he entered the kitchen. "Dad wants to know what's become of you. He wants his dessert."

"Here," Grace replied as she shoved the whole pie into his hands. "Take it."

"Okay," he smiled, and turned away.

"See," Grace stated.

Katherine said nothing as Puss entered the kitchen with two tiny kittens, one in each hand.

"Katherine, do you want to hold one?" she asked.

"When were these born?"

"About three weeks ago," Puss answered. "I thought I'd take them up to Lilly. Want to come?"

"Sure," Katherine responded.

"Mama kitty only had three this time," Puss informed her companion as they headed up the steps. "She's kind of small. That's probably why she's never had more than four kittens, ever."

"But she's had kittens every time I've been here," Katherine replied.

"Oh, she has kittens a lot, just not very many," Puss laughed. "Daddy says she never misses a chance to be a mother."

Mrs. Cullen met them at Lilly's door. "She's resting quietly at the moment," she informed them. She lifted one kitten's tiny chin, and smiled. "Lilly will like your little friends. Just don't get her excited, okay?"

"Okay," Puss responded, and went in.

"Will Grace have to miss out on Europe?" Katherine asked Mrs. Cullen.

"I don't know yet," she replied. "I hope not. She's waited an extra year already. You see Grace graduated from St. Vincent's last year, and this year Lilly is supposed to. Their trip was supposed to be their graduation present."

"Oh, to miss Europe," Katherine groaned in envy. "Is there anyone who could go with Grace, besides Ernest, at least as far as New York? She meeting someone there, isn't she?"

"Ernest," Mrs. Cullen repeated, "does he want to go?"

"Why wouldn't he?" Katherine replied. "New York, wow! Surely it holds as much appeal for a fellow as it does for us."

Mrs. Cullen smiled. "I suppose you're right. I hadn't thought of Ernest."

"Oh, I wasn't suggesting him," Katherine exclaimed quickly. "Grace doesn't want to go with him. He hasn't given her a moment's peace since I've been here."

"Ernest can get a little carried away," Mrs. Cullen responded warmly, "but his heart is good. I think he would be a fine traveling companion for Grace."

"Oh no," Katherine cried, "I didn't mean to... Grace will kill me if she, if he..."

Mrs. Cullen smiled. "Don't worry, Katherine," she admonished as she patted her young friend on the arm. "I won't tell them it was your idea...but it may be the only way for Grace to have her trip. I've been racking my brain for a way to let her go, and so far I've come up with nothing." She paused only momentarily. "When Lilly gets tired of the kittens, you send Puss downstairs with them. I kind of think Lilly would like some time alone with you."

"With me?" Katherine responded.

"She hasn't hardly seen you since your engagement. I imagine you have some boy talk to catch up on." Then she smiled knowingly. "You realize, don't you, that Lilly and Ed Holter have become regular pen pals." Without a further word, she disappeared downstairs.

Katherine walked into Lilly's room. Both kittens were on the bedcovers cautiously exploring their new terrain. Puss was making scratchy noises from under the blankets, but the kittens were too young to know they were supposed to attack.

"They are so small," Lilly noted as she stroked one's back. "Mama kitty doesn't mind that you brought them up, Puss?"

"She still has one," Puss replied. "It's a yellow one, a short hair with a molten spot across it's face. He looks like he stuck his head in a tar bucket, and then splattered the stuff all over. He's really ugly."

"You'll have to bring him up next time so I can see," Lilly replied with a soft smile. Then her face lifted. "What color cats do you like, Katherine?"

"White ones with blue eyes," Katherine replied.

"They're hard to find," Puss responded, "though Lilly Fuller's neighbor has one. It's a boy."

"I had one when I was little," Katherine recalled. "We called him Fluffy because he had the longest fur I've ever seen on a cat."

"He was a long hair?" Puss exclaimed. "They're even harder to find."

"Daddy brought him home to me," Katherine replied, "from one of his trips."

"Wow," Puss murmured, "I wish my dad would bring me home a special cat."

Katherine smiled as she turned to Lilly. Her friend was staring out the window, lost to their conversation. "Puss, why don't you take the kittens back down to their mother. I bet she's missing them."

"Okay," she replied. Within moments she was gone.

"Lilly, are you all right?" Katherine asked. "You're awfully quiet."

"I was just thinking," Lilly responded softly, "how much I would like to take a trip."

"I heard about your plans for Europe," Katherine noted quietly.

"Oh that," Lilly responded slowly with a smile, "that was Grace's idea. No, that's so very far away..." Her voice faded.

"Where would you like to go?" Katherine asked.

"Just away," Lilly responded. "It really doesn't matter where. Maybe somewhere I could find a long hair, white cat for Puss." She smiled, but there were tears in her eyes.

Chapter Twenty

That afternoon the Wilsons, the Hausers, and the Bachs called at the house, inquiring after Lilly and leaving small gifts. Grace and her mother presided over the social responsibility, but allowed no visitors upstairs. Lilly's earlier accident in front of Katherine was not to be repeated.

Then about four o'clock, Dr. Dean arrived and was escorted upstairs. Katherine was introduced. It would have been proper for Katherine to leave Lilly alone with her doctor, but this she did not do, watching over her friend with the scrutiny of a watch dog.

"Lilly tells me your father is a doctor, Katherine," Dr. Dean noted while she examined her patient.

"Yes, ma'am," Katherine responded.

"From Granite?"

"Yes," Katherine answered.

"He works for the silver company then?"

"He's a state legislator now," Katherine answered.

Dr. Dean paused. "Lilly, I need to examine your stomach. Your muscles are rigid and tight, and the inflammation has made you very tender. But its the only way I can check for any changes. All right?"

Lilly nodded.

The room fell silent as Dr. Dean examined Lilly. With deft fingers she placed deep pressure at various locations, causing Lilly to gasp in pain as involuntary tears ran from her eyes. "Lilly, can you feel this?" Dr. Dean asked. Her doctor guided Lilly's fingers down upon her bare abdomen.

"There's a soft welt," she responded in a strained tone.

"Yes, this is your inflamed appendix," Dr. Dean noted quietly. "I'm afraid, my dear, you aren't out of the woods yet. Yesterday I could hardly feel anything, not like the day before when it was huge. But today it's back, and though I rather expected it would be, the key is for it too stay small." She now pulled down Lilly's nightgown, and pulled up her covers. Then for the next twenty minutes, Dr. Dean talked with her patient, asking her questions, listening to Lilly's answers.

"I think we'll keep you on the same medicine," Dr. Dean noted, "but I want to add a tonic to discourage your inflammation while at the same time strengthening your immune system. Also you should be eating greens, and as much fresh produce as your mother can find." Then she smiled. "But when the cherries come on, don't eat so many you get a belly ache."

"That's still a month or two off," Lilly replied.

"True, but I can't imagine you would ever want to risk more abdominal pain," Dr. Dean replied with knowing smile. "Remember, eat a variety of fresh things, but each with moderation. Listen to your body." She turned to gather her things. When she finished, she took momentary hold of Lilly's hand. "Courage. We'll get through this." Then she smiled, and turned to Katherine. "It was nice meeting you."

"Yes," Katherine responded. She watched the doctor leave the room. Then her eyes shifted to her friend.

"What do you think," Lilly asked.

"I don't know," Katherine replied uneasily. "She did more talking, than looking."

"What was she supposed to do, look up my gluteus maximus?" Lilly asked with a sudden grin.

"Your what?" Katherine retorted.

"Oh, come on. You're a doctor's daughter, and you don't know what the gluteus maximus is?" A big relaxed smile rested on Lilly's face.

"No, what is it," Katherine asked.

"It's just the largest group of muscle tissue in your rump," Lilly replied.

"How do you know that?" Katherine choked.

Lilly pointed to her bedside stand. "I asked Dr. Dean for an anatomy book. She's letting me borrow it."

"You've been studying?" Katherine gasped.

"Only when I can't sleep," Lilly answered. "So, is that what your father would have done? Looked up my rump?"

A red flush rose up Katherine's neck. "I don't know."

"In any case, I bet he wouldn't have been as honest with me," Lilly noted quietly.

Katherine stared at her friend. Her father would never have spent so much time talking with Lilly. He would have simply asked her a few "yes or no" answers. ...and never, ever would he have told her where the risk of danger lay. He always said there were things the patient was better off not knowing.

"What is it, Katherine?" Lilly asked softly.

"Do you like knowing everything?"

"How can I understand my situation without it?" Lilly asked.

"But everything?" Katherine repeated. "Wouldn't it be better not knowing the worst? I mean, worry does its own damage."

"I would worry more if I didn't know all the facts," Lilly answered seriously. "If I thought Dr. Dean was holding back, it would worry me to death."

"So you like knowing that if your appendix grows again, you're really in for it?"

"Yes," Lilly replied. "I know where I stand. I know what my body is dealing with."

"But if it grows..."

"If it grows, then I really have something to be sick about." Lilly smiled slightly. "Katherine, it's all right. I'll just take it one day at a time, maybe one hour, or even one minute. It's not like hell. There is a time limit to the suffering, even intense suffering. If things get too bad, I'll simply pass out."

"Or die," Katherine thought to herself.

"Yes Katherine, or die," Lilly stated as she read her friend's expression, "but then that would he the pill in the jam, wouldn't it? Because then I wouldn't have to endure anything more, not even the suffering of recovery. I would be free of it all."

"You want to die?" Katherine choked. She stared at the smile on Lilly's face in disbelief.

"No dummy," Lilly responded as a twinkle almost re-emerged in her eye, "I want to live. There's a mountain of things I want to do, to experience. But at the same time, I'm not afraid to die, to loose my inferior body and become Christ-like, passing through walls at will, ascending and descending from heaven with the ease of a single thought. Katherine, think, how glorious!"

"Lilly, how can you know that," Katherine responded in shock.

Lilly stared at her friend momentarily in silence. "Church," she answered simply.

It was Katherine's turn to ponder Lilly. "Church?" she repeated.

"Reverend Love has often sermonized that we are children of God, that we will become like Christ after death."

"Yes," Katherine agreed, "but where did you get the 'passing through wall' stuff, and the 'in and out' of heaven? He never talked about that."

"Well, didn't Christ do it?" Lilly asked.

"Yes, but we will be confined to heaven."

"And where is heaven? What is heaven?" Lilly asked.

"In the sky," Katherine answered, "the good place."

"And does this good place have walls like a prison?" Lilly asked.

Katherine stared at her friend. "Lilly, don't be blasphemous."

"I'm not," Lilly responded with a grin, "because even if heaven had walls, we could go through them just like Christ. It is impossible for heaven to be a prison."

"I don't know," Katherine muttered in confusion.

"Some day you will," Lilly responded light-heartedly.

"You're in a good mood," Katherine noted.

"Why shouldn't I be," Lilly responded. "My exam is over, and maybe tomorrow I will be better, and it won't hurt so much."

"Aren't you tired out?" Katherine responded.

"Not yet," Lilly replied. "I think my pounding heart is still pumping too much blood."

"Katherine," Puss called as she entered the room, "mother says I'm to take over while you go downstairs for supper."

"Is it that time already," Katherine asked as she rose to her feet.

"I am a little hungry," Lilly noted.

Both turned to look at her.

"That's supposed to be a good sign," Katherine responded with a smile. "I'll tell your mother."

Katherine found Mrs. Cullen in the kitchen arranging Lilly's tray. She was glad to hear that Lilly's appetite was improving, and the two talked for several minutes.

"After you eat, Katherine, I'll have Ernest walk you home. You've been a great help today."

"Can I come back tomorrow," Katherine asked.

Mrs. Cullen paused before she picked up Lilly's tray. "That would be very nice, but can your sister spare you?"

"My sister and I are not seeing eye to eye lately," Katherine replied. "I was planning to go back to Granite County."

"Oh no, Katherine, really?" Mrs. Cullen cried. "You would be so far away. Lilly would miss you dreadfully."

"That's why I want to spend as much time with her as possible," Katherine responded.

"Did you and Lilly have a chance to catch up today?" Mrs. Cullen inquired.

"About my engagement?" Katherine asked. "No, the subject never came up."

"Funny," Mrs. Cullen remarked, "but of course Lilly is not Grace. I suppose I should have expected as much." She smiled. "Are you needed at home, Katherine, in Granite I mean? Or would you consider staying in Helena if other arrangements could be made?"

"I would love to stay in Helena," Katherine responded. "Have you heard of something new, someone who needs a companion maybe?"

"Possibly, let me look into it," Mrs. Cullen replied.

"I would really appreciate it," Katherine cried. "I hate to be so far from Lilly, and from Tom."

After dinner Ernest walked Katherine home along Dearborn Avenue. It was dark and quiet with only a soft breeze as Ernest turned to her. "This has been some Palm Sunday, hasn't it?"

"Yes," Katherine agreed softly.

"You were with Lilly most of the day. How do you think she's doing?"

"It's serious. There's no doubt about it," Katherine replied.

"Do you think she'll recover?"

"I don't know anyone that has survived appendicitis," Katherine answered quietly.

Ernest walked in silence for nearly half a block. "Lilly isn't an ordinary girl. Do you think it could help?"

"I don't know," Katherine responded. "She certainly has a funny outlook on things."

"She's told you her theories on the after life then," Ernest replied.

"You know about them?" Katherine asked.

"Sure, they're not new," he answered. "She's believed them for ages."

"They're really strange," Katherine commented.

"Maybe, but Lilly always bases her ideas on fact."

"It's certainly not how I pictured heaven."

"It's not how most people picture heaven," Ernest chuckled, "but it doesn't stop Lilly."

"What do you believe," Katherine asked.

Ernest smiled. "I don't know. I've never really given it much thought, didn't think I needed to, not yet anyway."

"Do you think Lilly knew she might need to? I mean subconsciously," Katherine asked.

"Na, I don't," he replied. "She's just always been one of those serious types. I kind of envied her from time to time. She never seemed to mind all the studying school requires. She would make a great attorney, better than me. She would make dad proud."

The following morning Katherine showed up on the Cullen doorstep by eight-thirty. "Oh, Katherine, you're here already," Mrs. Cullen greeted with a relieved smile. "I'm so glad."

"What's the matter?" Katherine demanded as concern engulfed her.

Mrs. Cullen pointed to the stairs. Sobbing was audible. "Grace is up there," she noted softly. "I was just on my way up."

The two hastened up to Lilly's room. No sooner did they reach the door than Grace burst through it, her face wet with tears. Both Katherine and Mrs. Cullen turned to Lilly. Her eyes were wet too, and she looked miserable.

"What's going on," Mrs. Cullen demanded quietly as she sat down beside her younger daughter, wiping her tears away with her own hanky

Katherine followed Grace to her room. Lilly's sister lay on her bed, sobbing hard. Katherine went in.

"I don't want Lilly to die," Grace cried as she suddenly turned. "I don't want her to."

"I know. I don't either," Katherine responded as she sat down. "Maybe she won't."

Grace's attention focused sharply on her friend. "Does she have any chance?"

"It's small, but yes, there is a chance," Katherine encouraged.

"How big?"

"Small," Katherine repeated.

"Then she probably will die," Grace decided as tears again welled in her eyes.

"I hope she doesn't give up so easily," Katherine responded quietly.

Grace stopped. "What do you mean?"

"I mean, we need to be strong for your sister. Her life is rough enough. She surely doesn't need our anguish on top of everything else."

"You're worried then, really worried," Grace replied.

"Yes," Katherine acknowledged, "but I won't tell Lilly that."

"You two seem to really get along," Grace noted with envy. "I wish we could."

"Personality differences, maybe," Katherine suggested.

"Probably," Grace agreed. "Still, she is my sister. I wish we were closer."

"Maybe you can be," Katherine offered.

"How?"

"By being strong for her now when she needs you most," Katherine answered.

"I don't know," Grace mumbled. "We're so different."

"That can be a good thing too," Katherine encouraged.

Forty-five minutes later, Katherine returned to Lilly's room. Mrs. Cullen met her at the door. "How is Grace?" she asked.

"Better," Katherine answered. "How about Lilly?"

"Lilly's fine. She always is," Mrs. Cullen answered with a soft smile. "She's just concerned about Grace."

"How about her fever? Has it gone up at all?" Katherine asked.

"No, actually I think she is looking a little better this morning," Lilly's mother replied, "aside from the tears, of course."

"Then she's improving," Katherine surmised.

"I hope so."

"Good. Would you like me to sit with her?" Katherine asked.

"I would appreciate it," Mrs. Cullen responded as her eyes wandered down the hall.

As Katherine quietly joined Lilly, Mrs. Cullen went to check on Grace. Within minutes two sets of footsteps descended the stairs together. Katherine's attention returned to Lilly.

"Grace is having a hard time with me," Lilly noted.

"It's not your fault," Katherine responded.

"Maybe, maybe not," Lilly replied.

"What do you mean?"

"I think maybe I brought on my own appendicitis," Lilly admitted.

"You? No," Katherine retorted. "No one knows what causes appendicitis."

"No one will see the obvious," Lilly replied in a still tone.

"What do you mean?" Katherine demanded.

"Dr. Dean brought by a couple of journals yesterday. The number of cases is on the rise."

"So?"

"So usually there is concern over the diet, but they can't find any common link. Appendicitis also often occurs after an illness, but they don't see the obvious there either."

"What is the obvious?" Katherine asked.

"Constipation," Lilly replied, "and how it's alleviated these days. I gave up sweets for Lent, and I did the job thoroughly. No fruit, no dates, no raisins, nothing that would prevent constipation...and I had problems, and I took the normal purge."

"Everyone does," Katherine responded.

"And that's why appendicitis is on the rise. It doesn't happen every time, not even most of the time. But it's the common link, I'm sure of it."

"But how?" Katherine demanded.

"I don't know how," Lilly replied, "but the coincidence is too convenient. I'm sure the enema is at the root of the problem."

"I can't believe it," Katherine responded.

"Well the whole process does defy nature," Lilly smiled, "and you know how mad mother nature gets when she's defied."

"Oh Lilly, be serious," Katherine chuckled.

"I am, Katherine," Lilly replied as her smile faded. "I'm afraid I've caused my own agony, and maybe Grace's too."

Conversation fell off between the two then as Lilly drifted into sleep, and Katherine became lost in thought. Could it be after all the hours and hours her father had spent pondering the illness, the answer was practically staring him in the face. Lilly had a talent for recognizing the obvious. Still, this was medicine. Surely with all the doctors that treated dying patients, they would never miss something so simple. No, Lilly had to be wrong. This time she had to be wrong.

"Katherine," Mrs. Cullen called softly so she wouldn't wake Lilly. She motioned for her young friend to join her in the hall. "Katherine, I talked to the judge, and we were wondering if you would consent to becoming Lilly's companion and nurse. We both feel it is something Lilly would like, and could ease things for the rest of us. You would still be free to attend any social functions you want."

"Lilly's companion?" Katherine gasped. "Yes, of course. I'd love the opportunity." A broad smile emerged on her face.

"Oh good," Mrs. Cullen responded with relief. "I thought Grace would be more help, but she just isn't up to it. ...and I can't handle everything alone, even with Puss."

"Don't worry," Katherine responded. "I'll help however you need me."

"Do you have many things at your sister's?" Mrs. Cullen continued. "Could Ernest move them over for you? We have a spare room."

"I don't have that much," Katherine responded easily, "and yes, Ernest would be a big help. Thank you."

That afternoon Lilly slept a great deal, her sleep growing more restless as time progressed. Katherine sat sentinel, noting the change as her worry grew. Finally she placed a light hand on Lilly's forehead. Her friend's eyes opened.

"You feel warm," Katherine noted.

"My stomach is queasy," Lilly stated uneasily. Her jaw quivered lightly.

"Should I get your mother?" Katherine asked.

"Get the pot," Lilly suddenly cried.

Katherine instantly obeyed, helping her friend through the ordeal. But as Katherine clapped on the lid and placed the chamber pot in the hall, Lilly did not fall back to sleep, but lay curled in misery.

"What's wrong?" Katherine cried.

"It hurts," Lilly responded.

"What hurts?"

"My side," she answered as tears boiled in her eyes.

Katherine immediately rang the bell Mrs. Cullen had provided. Within moments Lilly's mother was at her daughter's side.

"I don't know what to do," Katherine cried.

"It's a muscle spasm," Mrs. Cullen informed her. "Lilly had several episodes last week." She talked softly to her daughter, reminding her of the small things that might help.

"Should I get the doctor?" Katherine asked now.

"She's already due within the hour," Mrs. Cullen responded. "It's probably better that you're here. I might need you."

Chapter Twenty-One

"Lilly, your appendix isn't any larger," Dr. Dean noted as she released the pressure of her fingers. She smiled encouragingly. "Remember, I told you this could happen, that your symptoms could get worse."

"I remember," Lilly responded weakly. Her expression was taunt as she tried to smile.

Dr. Dean patted her shoulder. "You're doing fine. And as miserable and painful as the symptoms are, they're fighting for you. That's how the immune system works."

Dr. Dean turned her attention to Mrs. Cullen. "I know you're concerned about your daughter, and you should be, but her increased symptoms are really just her body's increased fight against the inflammation of her appendix. It's a positive step. It's good."

"How do we know if it should go the other way?" Lilly's mother asked.

"Her appendix will swell and get bigger, like last Friday. That's what we don't want," Dr. Dean replied. "That's what I'm hoping all Lilly's discomfort now is going to prevent."

"But she is in sheer agony," Katherine interrupted.

Dr. Dean turned to the young woman. "Katherine, isn't it?"

"Yes."

"Katherine, would you mind walking out with me?" She turned momentarily to Lilly's mother. "A ginger cookie might help her nausea." Then she gathered her things, and said good bye to Lilly.

Downstairs Dr. Dean led Katherine into the parlor, and took a chair.

Katherine sat opposite her. "How is a ginger cookie going to help Lilly's nausea? It's just something more to throw up."

Dr. Dean smiled. "You know, my worst critics are women."

"You didn't answer my question."

"First, answer one of mine," Dr. Dean responded. "Does your father ever prescribe chicken soup for a cold?"

"Yes, of course," Katherine replied.

"Does it help?" Dr. Dean asked.

"It seems to."

"What's the difference then between prescribing chicken soup for a cold, or a ginger cookie for nausea? Each seems to help."

"All right," Katherine conceded. "But Lilly has pain, and I don't see you prescribing laudanum...or anything else for that matter."

"First, do you know what laudanum is?" Dr. Dean asked.

"It's a pain killer," Katherine replied.

"It's a pain killer, a sleep inducement, and an intoxicant," Dr. Dean replied, "and it can be very addictive. Do you want Lilly to become dependent on a drug on top of all her other problems?"

"No, but she needs something for her pain," Katherine objected.

"I've been giving her anti-spasmodic medicine," Dr. Dean replied.

"You have?" Katherine responded.

"Yes, Katherine, I have. I don't like to see her suffer any more than you." Katherine remained silent.

"I am not the enemy here," Dr. Dean offered. "We're all trying our very best to help Lilly get well."

"Have you ever cured appendicitis?" Katherine asked quietly.

"Yes, once. It was a light case, and I was there from the very start," Dr. Dean answered.

"You cured appendicitis," Katherine repeated in disbelief.

"Yes, a light case."

"And you're sure it was appendicitis?" Katherine questioned.

"All the symptoms were there, except the fever," Dr. Dean replied.

"Then it could have been something else," Katherine concluded.

"Like what?"

"Like influenza along with a pulled muscle," Katherine fabricated.

Dr. Dean pondered Katherine for several moments. "Yes, I suppose you can believe whatever you wish. But a lack of fever is also a symptom of appendicitis, as it so happens. So was it just a sheer coincidence of symptoms? The patient didn't recall having done anything strenuous during the preceding days."

It was Katherine's turn to ponder in silence.

"Katherine, I've got to go. I have another patient to see," Dr. Dean stated as she rose to her feet. "I hope I've cleared up any misunderstandings. I know you're concerned about Lilly. We all are." She turned to leave, but suddenly stopped, reaching into her pocket. "I forgot to give this to Lilly. Would you mind?" she asked as she offered a home-made card. "It's from Lizzie Ralley. They go to St. Vincent's together, and I was over there this morning."

"I'll give it to her," Katherine assured as she accepted the card.

Dr. Dean let herself out the front door as Katherine slowly followed. As the door slammed shut, Katherine turned. Grace stood at the bottom of the stairs.

"I've made Lilly worse, haven't I?" she stated.

"No Grace, no," Katherine responded. "Lilly's not any worse. Her appendix is still the same size."

"But she's in such misery, just like on Friday. She's going to die, isn't she?"

"Her symptoms are worse, but Lilly isn't," Katherine repeated. "It's just her body's way of fighting the appendicitis, so she won't die."

"She's not going to die," Grace asked.

"We don't know yet for sure," Katherine responded. "But Dr. Dean has cured one case of appendicitis, that's more than anyone I know."

"Even your father?"

"Even my father," Katherine admitted.

"As long as she's not going to die," Grace responded with more confidence.

"I didn't say that," Katherine objected, "but maybe, just maybe she will get better."

"Thanks, Katherine," Grace responded with a smile. "I'm glad you're here."

Katherine glanced down at the card she still held.

"What's that?" Grace asked.

"A card from someone at school," she answered. "Dr. Dean asked me to give it to Lilly."

"You'd better take it up then," Grace coaxed. "It might encourage her to get well. Maybe I should take her a book."

"I don't think she can read today," Katherine responded. "Maybe later."

"Okay," she responded as Puss came through the door. "Where have you been?" Grace demanded of her youngest sister. "It's nearly supper time."

"Our whole class had to stay after," Puss pouted, "for talking."

"Were you doing it?" Grace demanded.

Katherine excused herself, and headed upstairs as Grace interrogated her sister on their way to the kitchen.

"Lilly's sleeping," Mrs. Cullen informed Katherine quietly. "Did you and Dr. Dean come to an understanding."

"Yes," Katherine answered softly as she set Lizzy's card on the bedside stand for Lilly to see. "Grace helped me."

"Grace?"

"It wasn't until I had to explain things to her that they suddenly made sense to me." Katherine smiled wanly. "Grace thought she made Lilly worse because of this morning."

"Oh dear," Mrs. Cullen responded. "Is she all right?"

"She's fine. She and Puss are bickering in the kitchen. I think they're starting supper," Katherine offered.

"Oh good, Puss is home," Mrs. Cullen breathed in relief. Then she lightly grabbed Katherine's arm. "Come here, I want to show you something." As Katherine followed her into the hall, Mrs. Cullen opened the door across from Lilly's room. "You can have this room," she offered.

Katherine walked in. The room was much like the one she had at the Eslers. The wallpaper was even the same color.

"The bed is already made up," Mrs. Cullen offered. "All you need are your things."

"That shouldn't take long," Katherine grinned. "I packed half of them the other night after Bessie and I had words. One trip should do it."

"Good, then Ernest can take you over tonight," Mrs. Cullen decided. "But you will try to smooth things out with your sister, won't you?"

"Don't worry," Katherine smiled. "We don't hate each other. I'm just not comfortable living with her."

Mrs. Cullen smiled knowingly. "My girls don't like staying with Violet for very long either. Puss says its like living with a stranger who has her sister's name."

After supper Ernest drove Katherine over to Bessie's, and carried her trunk and several boxes out to the carriage. Katherine, meanwhile, explained the severity of Lilly's situation, and begged for her sister's understanding. The two sisters parted in perfect sympathy.

It was nearly nine o'clock when Katherine sat down on her new bed and surveyed the pile of empty boxes stacked in the center of the floor. Suddenly a commotion rose across the hall. Lilly was again having a hard time. Katherine went to help.

For three days Lilly struggled with the reality of her inflamed appendix while Katherine devoted her entire existence to her friend's needs. Then on Good Friday, things eased.

"Lilly, what are you doing out of bed?" Katherine cried as she woke. She had fallen asleep in the chair.

"I didn't want to disturb you," Lilly replied as she placed the chamber pot out in the hall. She returned to the bed, taking Lizzy Ralley's card with her. She crawled in under the covers as she looked at it. A soft smile rose to her lips.

"You're feeling better," Katherine noted in amazement.

"Yes, I am," Lilly responded. "I should write to Lizzy."

"Where's your stationery?" Katherine asked as she rose to her feet.

"The bottom drawer of my dresser," Lilly replied.

Katherine retrieved the box of paper.

"It's all right, Katherine," Lilly responded gently. "You're not seeing a ghost."

"I know," Katherine replied quietly. "It's just so sudden. You look a lot better."

"I slept better too, at least this morning. I was terribly nauseous last night, but it seems to have eased." She smiled.

"It is so good to see you like this," Katherine noted with feeling. "You don't know how good."

"Yes, I think I do," Lilly stated softly.

"Are you hungry?" Katherine asked.

"Yes, a little," Lilly answered.

"What sounds good?"

"Maybe some oatmeal," Lilly replied.

"With apple and cinnamon?" Katherine asked. "Your father brought some apples home last night."

"That sounds wonderful," Lilly agreed.

As Katherine disappeared downstairs, Lilly took her stationery box and wrote a short note to Lizzy Ralley. This she tucked into an envelope and set on her bedside stand for someone to deliver. Now she pulled a letter from her box, and began reading it.

Katherine returned with a tray of food. "Who is that from?" she asked as she set breakfast down across Lilly's lap.

"Ed Holter," Lilly answered with a smile. "I should have written to him long ago."

"Well, it's not like you haven't had your reasons," Katherine replied as Lilly set her writing materials aside. Katherine reached and felt her forehead. "Your fever is gone."

"So is the nausea and pain," Lilly responded. "I just hope my appendix isn't swollen."

"Dr. Dean is supposed to be by this morning, isn't she?" Katherine asked.

"Yes," Lilly answered as she began to eat.

Puss emerged from the hall. "I heard voices," she stated.

"It's all right," Katherine smiled. "Lilly's feeling better."

"Really," Puss exclaimed as she bounded over. She was soon followed by each and every member of the family as they checked on Lilly before their day's duties claimed their attention.

Lilly's bowl sat empty, and her eyes drooped as she handed Puss the note she had written. "Would you give this to Lizzy when you see her at school?" Lilly requested.

"Sure," Puss exclaimed.

"You had better get ready, Puss," Mrs. Cullen reminded her. Then she turned to Lilly. "You're getting tired. You should rest, dear." She promptly shooed everyone from the room, including Katherine.

"You look like you could use a little time to yourself, Katherine," Mrs. Cullen noted. "I think Lilly will be all right on her own for a while. Dr. Dean will be by at ten. Why don't you get a little nap?"

"Lilly really does look better, don't you think?" Katherine asked.

"Yes, dear, but she looked better on Sunday too. Don't set your hopes too high," Mrs. Cullen warned.

Katherine made no reply as Lilly's mother bent to pick up the chamber pot, taking it downstairs. She wandered into her own room.

A smile grew on Dr. Dean's lips. "Your appendix has not grown," she announced as she released the pressure of her fingers. Lilly's taunt expression eased.

"I was hoping your exam wouldn't hurt as much today," Lilly responded.

Dr. Dean smiled. "In time, Lilly, in time. For now, let's just be grateful that you're feeling as well as you do."

"You mean I'm not over it?" Lilly cried in concern.

"Lilly, we've made progress, good progress. That's something to be very pleased about," Dr. Dean replied.

Katherine glanced at Mrs. Cullen. Her warning was evidently well founded.

"Then the swelling is not gone," Lilly concluded.

"No, Lilly. But, it has not grown either," Dr. Dean responded. "That was our goal, remember?"

"So now what?" Lilly asked quietly.

"Now you enjoy feeling better for a day or two, and get plenty of rest and nourishment while we watch things. Then we will proceed."

"Proceed, how?" she asked.

"We'll see if we can't get the inflammation to diminish some more," she answered cheerfully. "We're heading in the right direction, Lilly. The task before us is just not as quick or simple as we would like." Dr. Dean smiled warmly now. "We'll get through this, but we must be patient."

The doctor turned to Mrs. Cullen. "I'm very pleased with her progress," she stated as she now gathered her things.

"I'll walk out with you," Mrs. Cullen offered.

"Good, we need to discuss her medicine," Dr. Dean responded.

Katherine glanced at Grace. She stood by the door, silent as a tomb. The older women walked past her as she finally broke her pose. "Daddy will be pleased," she offered as she went over to her sister.

"Probably," Lilly replied.

Grace glanced at Katherine. She looked suddenly helpless and lost. "I'm sorry, Lilly. I'm sorry it's not all over," Grace blurted, and fled the room.

Tears welled in Lilly's eyes.

"It's all right," Katherine soothed as she sat down on Lilly's bed next to her. "You're making progress. Grace knows that."

"Everyone is so worried," Lilly cried. "It can't be good."

"No, Lilly, you're wrong. Your progress is good," Katherine stated.

Lilly's eyes became fixed on her friend.

"Stick to your logic. Consider the facts," Katherine reminded her. "Your inflammation has not grown. That was the goal. You've accomplished the first step. You can accomplish the next one."

"Yes," Lilly decided. "Yes."

Katherine placed Lilly's stationery in front of her. "Ed's waiting. Maybe you can get started on your letter before you get too tired." She smiled.

Lilly continued to feel better, and Easter Sunday dawned with new hope. Katherine stayed behind from church, giving Lilly her medicine and watching for any changes in her condition. Easter Sunday was the first day of their next battle. So while everyone celebrated Christ's resurrection, Lilly began again her fight against appendicitis. Dr. Dean did not think she could afford to loose another twenty-four hours in her recovery.

Again her previous symptoms reappeared, and intensified as the mood of the family again quieted, and tension mounted. For three days Lilly struggled. Dr. Dean visited her each day.

"Has it shrunk?" Lilly demanded as Dr. Dean finished her exam on Wednesday.

"A little," she replied.

"A little?" Lilly repeated.

"I was hoping for more," Dr. Dean replied, puzzled. "But at least it's progress, even if it's not as much as I hoped for."

"Let me feel," Lilly demanded.

"Are you sure?" the doctor asked.

"Yes."

Dr. Dean guided Lilly's fingers to the appropriate location.

"Yes, it's a little smaller," Lilly agreed in a strained, still tone, "but not much."

"It's just going to take longer than I thought," Dr. Dean commented. She glanced at Mrs. Cullen who had now become a permanent fixture in Lilly's room during examinations. They exchanged a look of forbearance. Then the doctor again gathered her things, and the two walked out together.

"You're still making progress," Katherine noted. "Don't loose sight of that."

Lilly's eyes rested on her friend. There was doubt in them.

Katherine smiled encouragingly, and pulled a letter from her pocket. "I have something for you."

"From Ed?" Lilly cried. "It came today?"

"Yes."

"Would you read it to me?" Lilly requested.

Katherine opened the envelope, and pulled out the pages

"Dear Lilly," it began. "I received your last letter with much trepidation. Are you all right now? Appendicitis is extremely dangerous, and I feel very far away." The letter went on to relay what was happening in Ed's life, and how he felt about it all. But in the end, he returned to his concern over her. "I am worried," Ed admitted openly. "Please tell me, should I come home?"

Katherine looked up from the letter. Lilly was staring blankly across the room. "Lilly?" she asked. "Are you all right?"

"Yes," she answered slowly. "Yes."

"What are you going to write back to him?" Katherine asked.

"I shall write that he should stay," she answered quietly.

"Will you tell him everything?"

"Yes," she answered.

"Do you love him?" Katherine asked.

"Yes."

"Katherine, you have to go tonight," Grace insisted. "Everyone will be there."

"I don't feel like going to the Hauser party," Katherine replied.

"But mother is staying home with Lilly," Grace insisted, "and so is Puss. Besides, Lilly had a quiet afternoon."

"It will do you good to get out," Ernest prodded. "Go on, get dressed. We'll wait."

"Please, go without me," Katherine cried. "I don't want to go."

"We won't take 'no' for an answer. Go get dressed," Grace insisted.

"I think you should go, dear," Mrs. Cullen added as she came down with Lilly's dinner tray. "A little cheering up would do you a world of good, and Lilly too."

"All right," Katherine conceded slowly.

She headed upstairs. It didn't take long to change into the blue crepe Grace had hung out for her. Katherine took a few moments in the mirror, and then left her room. Lilly was asleep as she peeked in. Puss smiled, and waved good bye.

"Finally," Grace noted with approval as Katherine again joined them. She immediately produced Katherine's cloak, and Ernest helped her on with it. Then the three left the house, walking the short distance to the Hausers in the warm night air.

Grace and Ernest chatted about anything and everything, trying to pull Katherine out of her mood, but Ed Holter's letter had touched her, and Katherine could not shake its hold. Lilly loved Ed, and she suspected Ed loved Lilly. But they were miles apart during the largest crisis of their lives.

The Hauser door opened, and the three were greeted with open arms. Ernest fielded the questions concerning his sister as Grace ushered Katherine inside and disposed of their outer wraps. Now slyly Grace guided Katherine down the eloquent hall not to the drawing room, but across to the music parlor where Tom Marlow stood talking with Norm Holter. Both turned at their entrance.

Katherine faltered in surprise, tears rising into her eyes.

Chapter Twenty-Two

Tom Marlow instantly took Katherine into his arms, and she broke down as Norm Holter and Grace quickly dropped the drapery over the two doorways, affording them as much privacy as possible.

"Katherine, what is it?" Tom asked as she sobbed against his chest. "I understood Lilly was making some progress."

"She is," Katherine choked.

"Then what is tearing you apart?" he pressed.

"She got a letter from Ed today."

Tom pulled Katherine back from him, and looked into her face. "What did it say?"

"He's hurting. She's hurting. And they're miles and miles apart."

"He can't come home?" Tom asked.

"She won't ask him."

Understanding entered Tom's face. "Of course she won't. She wouldn't." He paused momentarily. "But Lilly's not worse, is she?"

"No," Katherine replied.

Tom took her snugly back into his arms, and held her close. Slowly Katherine's tremors faded. It was only then that his lips sought hers. Little by little the weight of the world faded away, leaving only her love for Tom and his love for her.

"Excuse me," Ernest faltered as he came through one of the closed curtains. He took a deep breath. "Mrs. Kennett wants the piano."

Both Katherine and Tom looked up.

"I thought you two ought to be warned," Ernest offered quietly.

"Thank you," Tom replied as he took Katherine's arm. They left the music room, and joined the couples dancing in the drawing room.

Meanwhile, Charles Broadwater asked Grace to dance after inquiring about her sister, and Norm Holter watched all with his usual austere protective instinct, noting that his youngest brother, Albert, was finally starting to dance with more ease.

Every evening after that, Tom Marlow showed up at the Cullen house, inquiring after Lilly and spending time with Katherine. Slowly Katherine's melancholy faded as Lilly progressed, and her inflamed appendix shrunk to nearly half its original size.

Everyone was encouraged, none more than Lilly's father. He spent as many evenings with his daughter as his work would allow, talking with her when she was awake, reading and working while she slept. Katherine was impressed by the man's devotion. Even her father would be hard pressed to show such tenderness.

Then as the spring weather reveled in the world around them, Doctor Dean noted a growing uneasiness in her patient. "What's wrong, Lilly?"

"Nothing. Nothing's wrong," the young woman responded.

The doctor examined her closely. "Something is wrong," Doctor Dean insisted as she now barraged Lilly with a multitude of questions. Lilly reluctantly answered one after another until the doctor finally hit directly upon Lilly's concern.

"You haven't gone in how long?" Doctor Dean demanded.

"Three days," Lilly answered miserably.

"Why didn't you say something?"

"Because I thought it would take care of itself," she answered.

"You know better," Doctor Dean insisted.

"I know that the cure caused my appendicitis," Lilly replied quietly.

"Caused your appendicitis?" Doctor Dean stared at Lilly. "Appendicitis is caused by inflammation of the appendix membrane. It's caused by a seed or some other particle lodging itself into the tissue."

"I want to wait. I'm eating lots of fresh produce," Lilly insisted.

"You have been eating well," Dr. Dean agreed, "but stoving yourself up, will only slow your healing, maybe even reverse it. We must not tempt fate."

"Lilly, she's right. We can't take the chance," Mrs. Cullen reinforced.

Lilly glanced at Katherine. Her eyes pleaded for support.

"If the cause of appendicitis was as simple as you think, Lilly," Katherine responded, " some doctor would have discovered it by now."

"And if I still refuse," Lilly asked as she turned to her mother.

"I'm sure the doctor can give you something to calm your nerves, dear," she offered, "if that would help."

Lilly's jaw began to quiver. "May I at least wait until later?" she requested.

"Certainly," Doctor Dean responded, "but I would recommend it's done before you turn in for the night."

Lilly waited patiently for the doctor to finish, and watched intently as her mother again walked the woman out. Then she turned to Katherine. "You won't believe me," she accused.

"There's nothing to believe," Katherine responded. "You have no proof, only a suspicion. On the other hand, Doctor Dean has a point. You could be risking your recovery."

Tears formed in Lilly's eyes. She was tired. "Would you ask my father to come up as soon as he gets home," she asked quietly.

"That I will do," Katherine responded with a smile. "Why don't you rest? It will probably be an hour yet."

Lilly laid back and closed her eyes, but she did not rest as she went over and over a plausible line of defense. Her father was an attorney, and she would have to summon every ounce of logic and fact she possessed to convince him of the justice of her stand. An hour and a half slid by before he got home, and another fifteen minutes passed before he appeared in her room. As he sat down beside her, Katherine left.

"So how's my little girl?" Judge Cullen asked pleasantly.

The conversation followed Katherine as she crossed the hall to her own room. Both doors were open; and as she sat down on the bed, she could even see Judge Cullen's back

"Upset," Lilly replied.

"Upset, why?" her father asked.

"I believe differently than Dr. Dean," she replied as she fixed her eyes on her father.

"Ah yes, your mother told me all about it downstairs," he responded.

"So even you have joined their consensus?" Lilly asked. Her voice quivered.

"Not necessarily," he replied with an encouraging smile. "You know I always listen to both sides before I pass judgment."

"Then consider this," Lilly replied as she summoned her strength. "I may be of minor age, but God gave me the right of free choice. It is sacred. You know that. And I am at stake here, no one else. It is my life I am fighting for. It is me that will pay the consequences. I'm not an idiot, daddy. Don't treat me as if I was. Respect me enough to give me choice." Her voice faltered. "Please, Daddy?"

Judge Cullen stared at his daughter's tears as his heart broke. If anyone in his family understood the way law worked, it was Lilly. She knew she was at his mercy. She knew that in her present circumstance she didn't have a legal leg to stand on. That was why she had appealed to the higher law, God's law.

"How long do you think it's wise to wait?" he asked her quietly.

"At least another day or two," she replied. "Please."

"If we wait that long, and you have no success, will you submit then to the doctor's advice?"

"Yes," she replied.

"You have considered the risk involved?"

"Yes," Lilly answered.

"All right then, you have forty-eight hours," Judge Cullen stated.

Lilly's father shifted uncomfortably, as if he wanted to take her in his arms, to hold her, to give her everything, but something within stopped him. He had just rendered a decision. It might require consequences. He could not coddle her, not just now. He rose to his feet, smiled briefly at his daughter's relief, and left the room.

Lilly sunk back against her pillow as tears of relief streamed down her face. She had forty-eight hours. Surely, that would be enough.

Katherine sighed. Lilly had won. She hoped it would be for the best.

But the more Lilly tried to relieve herself, the more excruciating her pain became until even she was willing to waive her own constraint. But submitting to the enema did not bring anything but superficial relief. Her appendix had swollen again, larger than before, and things were looking bad.

"I'm afraid Lilly needs surgery," Dr. Dean told the judge late the following afternoon. "Your daughter's condition is getting critical. If her appendix bursts, she'll die."

"When should it be done?" Judge Cullen asked.

"The sooner the better...but in a case like this, I would prefer a second doctor be involved. Perhaps you'd like to call in Dr. Sligh."

"Dr. Sligh, yes, I like him," Judge Cullen responded, "and I believe he's back in town."

Surgery was scheduled for the following morning as Katherine maintained vigilance at Lilly's side. The young lady was now in constant pain, relieved only by the strong pain killer Dr. Dean gave her. Katherine suspected it was laudanum.

Groggy and a little disoriented, Lilly turned to Katherine, focusing all her concentration on the young woman. "Katherine, you have to do something for me," she pleaded.

"What?" she responded.

"In the bottom drawer of the dresser, under my stationery, there's another box. Get it, please."

Katherine retrieved the flat brown box, and gave it to Lilly.

"Inside," Lilly began now with effort, "are letters. I want you to keep them for me, and if anything happens tomorrow, if I don't come through the surgery...burn them."

"Letters," Katherine repeated. "Ed Holter's?"

"Yes," Lilly answered as her eyes fell shut.

"Should I write him?" Katherine demanded.

"Only if I die," Lilly muttered, and faded into sleep.

Katherine looked down at the box. In her hands was all that had passed between Lilly and Edwin Holter in their absence from each other. Here was the story of their love. Katherine retreated to her room, opening her trunk and placing the box safely in its deep recess. Her eyes wandered back to her friend's room. Katherine was worried, deeply worried. She knew surgery had its risks, but she also saw the agony and torment Lilly was suffering, and had suffered for weeks. The whole situation was a horrible nightmare that refused to give peace. Katherine had grown to love Lilly. She was so strong, so wise, so patient. She didn't want to loose her friend, but the agony of it all... Maybe Lilly was right, maybe if she died she would have the pill in the jam, and be free of it all. What had Lilly said? Think of the glory of it all, Katherine, to ascend or descend through the heavens curtsey of a mere thought. Tears rose in Katherine's eyes and streamed down her face as she shut her door. Her heart was breaking.

"Don't worry, Katie," Dr. Sligh told his daughter after Lilly had been transported to the hospital that evening. "Doctor Dean has the best recovery rate in the city. Lilly is in good hands." But Katherine could see the worry in his face. Appendicitis had plagued him before, and claimed his patients sooner or later, usually sooner.

"Katherine," her mother informed her, "I really think you should return to the boarding house. The Cullens won't need you now that Lillian is in hospital. You'll just be in the way."

Katherine had a sudden urge to stick out her tongue at the woman. Her mother infuriated her at times, but she controlled the impulse. Only her eyes narrowed slightly. "I'm not staying with Bessie," she announced quietly.

"Of course not, not until after we go home anyway," Mrs. Sligh replied.

"Not after you go home either," Katherine responded firmly.

"Why doesn't Katherine stay with me," Mrs. Osterhout suggested as she joined them. "At the moment, I have an extra room downstairs."

Katherine attention focused on the woman. Mrs. Osterhout had been visiting a friend at the hospital, and become quite concerned to learn that young Lillian Cullen had been admitted as well.

"Oh how wonderful of you," Mrs. Sligh responded immediately. She turned to her husband. "Katherine would be close to Bessie, but not underfoot, and she could hear all the news of Lilly through Violet. It would be perfect."

"Good," Mrs. Osterhout concluded. She smiled warmly at Katherine. "I'll expect you some time this weekend, shall I?"

"Yes, yes," Mrs. Sligh responded for her daughter.

Katherine sat down. She was too overcome with worry to reason herself out of the situation. Besides, she couldn't think of an alternative. Her mother was right about the Cullens. They didn't need her now, and when Lilly came home they would want an experienced nurse. Lilly had to come home.

It was close to two hours before Katherine's father finished his consultation on Lilly's case. Mrs. Sligh had already left; the Cullens were with Lilly; and only Katherine waited in the hall.

"Ready to go?" her father asked as he finally returned to his daughter.

"No daddy, I think I'll stay," Katherine responded.

He took a seat beside her. "You've become pretty close friends with Lilly over the past few months, haven't you?" he commented.

"Yes."

He fell silent for several moments. "You know, I keep thinking of that young man from the mine. He died, what was it? Two years ago?"

Katherine made no response.

"Well, anyway," he began again, "it really bothered me. Maybe it was because he reminded me of a good friend I had when I was young, I don't know. But after he died, I couldn't stop hunting for his cure, a clue, anything that would have saved his life."

"Did you find it?" Katherine asked as she turned.

"No honey, I didn't," her father admitted honestly, "but what I did find was a mass of information from other doctors, their experiences, their knowledge. I don't know if it will help. There seems to be no magic cure for appendicitis, but at least we're not as ignorant as we were."

"Thank you, daddy," Katherine responded as she suddenly embraced him. "Thank you for not forgetting Louis."

Dr. Sligh held his daughter close, the sweet scent of her soap mingling with the softness of her hair against his cheek. "Perhaps we should go," he suggested after a moment.

"You go," Katherine replied. "I have to stay."

Her father responded with an understanding smile. He rose to his feet, but his eyes did not leave his daughter. "I love my girl, you know," he stated softly.

"I know, daddy, and I love you too."

The Cullens prepared to leave forty-five minutes later as Grace turned to Katherine. "Did you get a chance to see Lilly?" she asked.

"Briefly, over your shoulders," Katherine answered quietly.

"Good, I'm glad you at least got that," she replied.

Katherine could see Grace's throat choke up. It was obvious she wanted to say more. It was obvious she felt a great deal more. But this was not the time. Grace simply mustered a small smile, and left.

"Thank you for coming, Katherine," Mrs. Cullen responded. The judge nodded his greeting, and Puss and Ernest followed them out without a word.

Suddenly Katherine was alone in the hall.

"Visiting hours are over," a nurse informed her. "I'm afraid it's too late to see anyone."

"I'm won't disturb a soul," Katherine promised. "I just want to stay a bit longer."

The nurse seemed to understand, and left her to herself. Katherine leaned back in the wood chair, and closed her eyes. Lilly was in the next room, probably asleep. Her pain medicine made her drowsy, and after the trip to the hospital, and all the people – she needed her rest.

Katherine wished she could sleep. She hadn't gotten much over the last day or two. She felt exhausted. She felt tormented. Thoughts of losing Lilly constantly plagued her. She didn't know why Lilly had grown to mean so much to her in such a few short months. She didn't know how someone so much younger could possibly have that much in common with her, especially someone so bookish. But the truth was, Lilly had become a good friend, a true friend. ...and those were few and far between.

"There you are," Tom Marlow cried as he suddenly appeared. "I've been looking for you, Katherine. You weren't at the Cullens."

"Tom," Katherine greeted with a smile. She was glad to see him.

"They almost wouldn't let me in," Tom responded. "Visiting hours were over long ago."

"I know," Katherine replied. "I just couldn't leave."

Tom sat down next to her. "Have you had anything to eat?"

"No," Katherine responded, "I'm not very hungry."

"How's Lilly doing?" he asked.

"Fine, I guess. She's probably sleeping. She's got a big day tomorrow."

"So why don't you go home?" Tom asked.

"The Cullens don't need me," Katherine answered.

"What about your family?"

"They're staying with Mrs. Osterhout. I don't want to be around Bessie, not now."

"So you're just going to sit here?" he asked.

"Yes," Katherine answered. She smiled softly as her hand stole into his. "Thank you for coming. It means a lot."

Conversation passed between them in spurts, erupting from a passing thought of one or the other. Katherine relaxed in Tom's presence. He appreciated their time together. Nothing needed to be rushed. The whole night stretched before them, and the minutes ticked by one after another until their eyes became so heavy that sleep finally overtook them.

When Katherine woke, Tom was no longer at her side. Doctors and nurses now traversed the hall with great frequency. Katherine glanced at the door to the beds. She wondered if Lilly was awake.

"Katherine, you're still here?" Dr. Dean greeted in surprise. She had just come on duty.

"Yes."

"Would you like to see Lilly," she asked.

"Is that possible?" Katherine responded.

Dr. Dean smiled. "She has a little time before we get started. It would probably do her good."

Katherine rose to her feet, and followed the doctor into the long room of beds. Lilly was the fourth one on the left. To Katherine's surprise she was awake and alert.

"Good morning, Lilly, you have an early visitor," Dr. Dean greeted. "How's the pain?"

"Not too bad," her patient answered. A small smile rose to her taunt lips as she saw Katherine.

"Hi," Katherine greeted.

Chapter Twenty-Three

"I'm glad you're here," Lilly stated quietly. "I wanted to talk to you yesterday, but there were so many people."

Dr. Dean left them.

"And by the time they left, you were exhausted," Katherine responded.

"And visiting hours were over," Lilly agreed. "Katherine, would you write Ed for me after all, and let him know about the surgery and how it goes. I probably won't be up to it for a while even if everything turns out well."

"It will go well, Lilly. It has to," Katherine responded.

Lilly smiled slightly. "You'll write to him, then? His address is on the letters I gave you."

"Of course."

"Good. That's good," Lilly responded. Her eyes shifted behind Katherine.

"Good morning, Lilly," Dr. Sligh greeted. "How are you feeling?"

"Nervous. Very nervous," she replied.

"Well, today is the big day." He smiled. "How about if we make you all well again. Does that sound good?"

"It sounds wonderful," she answered.

"Good, good," his voice fell off as he looked over her chart. Within moments, Dr. Dean joined him, and Katherine excused herself.

"There you are," Tom Marlow responded. He rose to his feet at Katherine's appearance.

"I thought you'd gone to work," Katherine replied.

"Not yet," he smiled. "I just went out to get us something to eat." He handed her the bakery sack. "I was hoping to get back before you woke."

"They let me see Lilly for a few minutes," she offered as she refused the food.

"Katherine, you've got to eat something," Tom protested. "You skipped supper last night."

"I will later," she replied.

"No, eat something now," he urged. "You don't want to faint again, do you?"

Katherine's eyes met his, and she obediently reached for a doughnut.

"I can't stay much longer," Tom stated. "Are you going to be all right here on your own?"

"Daddy's already here, and Lilly's family will be shortly," she replied as she ate. "I'll be fine."

Tom sat with her for another ten minutes, and then left for work. Katherine finished her second doughnut. She hadn't realized how hungry she was.

"Katherine, good, you're here already," Grace exclaimed as she and her family arrived. "Have you heard anything?"

"I saw Lilly briefly. She was alert," Katherine responded as she watched Judge and Mrs. Cullen stop at the nurse's station. Puss and Ernest wandered over.

"Katherine, we thought you were going home with your parents last night," Mrs. Cullen exclaimed, "but the hospital staff tells us you never left."

"I couldn't," she stated simply.

"You stayed all by yourself?" the judge asked.

"Tom Marlow was with me," Katherine answered.

"Mr. Marlow was here all night?" Puss gasped.

"Yes."

"Katherine, the hospital has a waiting room for the families of patients," Judge Cullen offered. "We would be pleased if you joined us."

Katherine could see the worry in the man as she answered in the affirmative. The judge held out his hand, personally escorting her along with them.

Katherine was instated with family status as they now waited out the surgery. Grace withdrew within herself, sitting with her knees drawn up under her chin on the huge chair that dominated one corner of the room. Ernest tried to read, but was having a difficult time of it. Puss fidgeted with one thing after another, frequently demanding her mother's attention. Lilly's father sat austere and alone by the door where he had a limited view of the hall. No one talked to him. No one dared interrupt his tense preoccupation. For close to two hours they waited and wondered and worried. Ernest became restless, and took to his feet, pacing nervously as his mother and sister erupted in complaint. The judge woke from his state as well, and retreated back into the room, sitting down next to Katherine.

"I appreciate what you and Tom did last night," he commented. "Thank you."

Katherine found the judge's eyes resting on her. They were moist, but clear. "I... I couldn't leave," Katherine faltered.

"I know," Lilly's father responded. He placed his hand over hers. "You've been very loyal to Lilly. She's lucky to have you for a friend."

At that moment Dr. Dean and Dr. Sligh appeared, and everyone rose to their feet as the judge walked directly to them. They talked for several minutes while the residents of the room strained to hear every word.

Lilly's surgery was successful. Relief flooded everyone as the strain of the last hours exploded into happiness. Lilly had withstood the operation well. She was resting comfortably, and if all went according to plan, she would be able to go home in a week or so.

Dr. Sligh gave his daughter a big satisfied hug. His face was radiant as he whispered in her ear, "I think this time we've finally done it. Lilly should be okay."

"Thank you, daddy," Katherine responded as she squeezed him tightly.

He pulled back, staring into her happy face, and then embraced her tightly again. Dr. Sligh felt wonderful. Finally, it seemed, they were making progress in their fight against appendicitis.

"How about some lunch?" Judge Cullen finally announced. A broad smile rested on his lips as he finished his discussion with Dr. Dean. "I'm starved."

A general consensus rose from the room as Dr. Dean excused herself. The judge was now shaking Dr. Sligh's hand, thanking him for all he'd done, and inviting him along for the meal. Katherine's father accepted.

"We're planning to move Katherine's things back to Mrs. Osterhout's," Dr. Sligh announced as the two gentlemen walked out together. "That way you can hire an experienced nurse to oversee Lilly's recovery. We don't want to take any chances."

Judge Cullen stopped in his tracks. "You're taking Katherine away from us?"

"She can still visit," Dr. Sligh responded with a big smile. "We just want the best possible care for Lilly."

"Yes, yes, I see," Judge Cullen responded as he turned to his wife. "Katherine's leaving us."

"Oh no," Mrs. Cullen replied, "not now."

"Dr. Sligh thinks Lilly should have an experienced, professional nurse," her husband explained. Then he turned to Katherine. "But you know, you're welcome any time."

"Thank you," Katherine responded. So it was fact. She was moving. Her mother had succeeded in removing her from the Cullen household.

It wasn't until evening that Katherine got to see Lilly as she accompanied her father on his rounds. She waited patiently as Dr. Sligh looked his patient over, and asked Lilly various questions. Then making a few notes on her chart, he finally turned to Katherine.

"I need to check a couple things in the dispensary. I won't be long."

Katherine watched him leave as she sat down in the chair next to her friend. "How are you feeling?"

"Not too bad, considering," Lilly responded with a faint smile.

"Lilly, I'm moving back to Mrs. Osterhout's tomorrow. I thought you should know. Do you want me to put your letters back in your dresser?"

"Why are you moving?" Lilly asked.

"Daddy thinks you need an experienced nurse, and I don't want to be in the way," Katherine answered softly.

"No, keep the letters," Lilly decided.

"But the surgery was a success," Katherine responded with a smile. "I don't need to keep them any longer."

"Have you written to Ed for me?" Lilly asked.

"I'm almost done. I'll post it first thing Monday morning," Katherine promised.

"Keep the letters," Lilly repeated. "I trust you. I don't trust some nurse."

"Well, all right," Katherine agreed. "But when she's gone, you're getting them back." She smiled broadly. "I'm so glad you're all right. It's just great."

Lilly smiled. She enjoyed Katherine's exuberance, but she was tired too. Katherine saw this, and said good bye, joining her father down the hall.

"Are you ready to go?" Dr. Sligh asked.

"Yes."

The following day Dr. Sligh and Don moved Katherine's things to Mrs. Osterhout's as Katherine's mother made plans to return to Philipsburg with Bessie on Monday to square away things at Mrs. Sligh's recently acquired boarding house. Little Margaret was to stay behind, watched by Katherine, Violet, or Mrs. Osterhout during the day, and by her father at night. This arrangement seemed to suit everyone, including Katherine. She would be able to visit Lilly regularly, and have her evenings free to spend with Tom.

However expectation only partially met with reality. In truth, Katherine baby-sat her niece nearly all day, every day while she helped Mrs. Osterhout with the cooking and cleaning. But while she was able to visit Lilly regularly, her plans to be with Tom were less successful. Tom Marlow often worked late, as did Margaret's father. The time Katherine got to spend with her fiancé was almost non-existent during that week.

"You didn't come to the Plunge Party," Tom Marlow complained when he saw Katherine the following Sunday.

"Plunge Party, what Plunge Party?" Katherine cried.

"Last night at the Broadwater. Everyone thought you were coming," Tom responded. "You always go to the parties."

"I go when I'm invited," Katherine responded.

"No one invited you?" he asked.

"No, I didn't even know about it. And I had Margaret until late, and Mrs. Osterhout had a million things for me to do," Katherine replied. "I didn't even get over to see Lilly."

"She's going home on Tuesday," Tom Marlow announced.

"Really," Katherine exclaimed excitedly. "I was starting to wonder."

"Grace told me last night."

"Oh good. Did they get a nurse?" Katherine asked.

"Yes, I think so," he replied. "Can you get away today? It's the season's opening of the Broadwater Natatorium. They're having various sports events including a bicycle race, and then fireworks later. It should be a nice day."

"I've got to go see Lilly," Katherine responded, "but afterwards I can." She smiled. It sounded like fun.

"Katherine, there you are," Grace called as she joined them. "Practice starts tomorrow for the Gibson Picture Charity at the Raleigh's. You're coming, aren't you?"

"I don't know," Katherine replied. "Is it like the Living Pictures?"

"Exactly," Grace answered. "It should be great."

"Is Charlie Word in it?" Katherine asked hesitantly.

"Sure," she laughed. "Why do you think all the women buy tickets?"

"Then no," Katherine responded quietly.

"No," Grace retorted. "Why not?"

"Charlie flirts with her," Tom explained with a smile.

"He flirts with everyone," Grace replied. "Don't take it personally, Katherine."

"I don't care to take part," Katherine repeated firmly. "Besides, I have other plans for that night."

"Well all right," Grace responded, "if you're sure."

"I'm sure."

"What do you have planned for Saturday night," Tom asked as Grace disappeared among her many friends.

"I thought I might spend the evening with you," Katherine answered with a grin. "We haven't had much time together lately."

A smile broke across Tom Marlow's face. "I'd like that. What do you have in mind?"

"Surprise me," Katherine laughed.

"All right," he agreed. "By the way, do I get to take you home now, or are you riding with the Wilsons?"

"Actually I'm walking over to the hospital," Katherine replied.

"Then why don't I take my aunt home, and I'll come by there?" Tom replied. "I'd like to see Lilly."

Katherine and Tom parted paths at the church door, Katherine heading north and Tom west.

The hospital buzzed with a quiet energy as Katherine arrived. Many patients already had visitors. Lilly was one of these. Several friends from school were already in attendance, but Lilly's face brightened when she saw Katherine.

"Do you know Katherine Sligh," Lilly asked her friends. "Her father is our state senator from Granite County, and one of my doctors. Katherine, this is Sarah Horner, Cora Eschle, and Nellie and Mamie McNamara."

"I'm pleased to meet you," Katherine responded.

"Lilly, you hurry up and get well," Mamie McNamara entreated. "St. V's just isn't the same without you." She turned to her friends. "We'd better go."

As the girls left, Katherine sat down. "I didn't mean to shoo them off," she apologized.

"It's all right," Lilly replied. "They've been here a while, and I'm starting to get tired."

"Maybe I should go," Katherine offered. "I just wanted to see how you're doing."

"Don't you dare leave," Lilly retorted. "I waited and waited for you yesterday."

"I'm sorry," Katherine responded. "It's just that Margaret's father didn't get home until late, and Mrs. Osterhout was up to her ears in work."

"Then I'm the one that should be sorry," Lilly responded more quietly. She pulled an envelope from her bed sheets, and handed it to Katherine. "Read it," she prodded.

Katherine noted the return address. "It's from Ed?" she asked as she pulled out the pages.

"Yes."

Katherine scanned the writing. "He hasn't gotten my letter yet," she noted. "He doesn't realize..." She looked up. "He's looking for a job?"

"He's doing some ground work for when he graduates," Lilly explained. "He's got some leads to some pretty substantial firms."

"But how..." Katherine stared at her friend. "How can he come home then?"

"He can't, not just yet," Lilly answered, "but think if he lands even one of them." She smiled broadly.

"What if he does?" Katherine asked. "Where does that leave you?"

"Me?" Lilly repeated. "This is about him, not me."

"But..."

"Katherine, we're friends, that's all. And friends want the best for each other," Lilly replied.

"But you love him. You told me so."

"Yes, I do," she responded more quietly, "but you're the only one I've told."

"Doesn't it bother you that all the two of you have are letters? Don't you want to see him?" Katherine asked.

"Of course I want to see him," Lilly replied, "but how am I to do that? Invite him to the hospital? Or maybe to my bedside? Katherine, no, I don't want him to think of me like this. It's bad enough having to be honest in my letters."

"But if he loves you..." Katherine objected.

"I don't know that for sure," Lilly replied quietly. "He signs all his letters with love, but it may just be etiquette."

"I hear you're going home Tuesday," Katherine stated as she changed the subject, and stuffed Ed's letter back into the envelope. She handed it back.

"Keep it with the others," Lilly responded. "Yes, I'll be glad to get out of here."

"I understand they found you a nurse."

"Oh yes," Lilly replied, "a real peach of a woman, complete with facial fuzz."

"Oh Lilly, no," Katherine responded with a grimace, "is she that bad?"

"No," Lilly sighed. "She's just older, and she's not you."

"It probably won't be for too long. You'll heal fast. You'll see."

Lilly smiled sweetly, too sweetly. Katherine shifted uneasily. Something wasn't being said.

"Tom," Lilly greeted quietly with a smile, "it's good to see you." He inquired after her health, but their visit was cut short as others from church joined them.

"She doesn't look good," Tom noted as he and Katherine left.
"You don't think so?" Katherine replied.
"No."
"But she goes home on Tuesday," Katherine objected. "They wouldn't let her go home unless everything was okay."
"Either that, or they can't do anything for her," Tom suggested.
"No, the operation was a success," Katherine responded. "Everyone said so. It's just taking time for her to heal."
"I hope so," Tom offered quietly. "I truly hope so."

The grand opening of the Broadwater Natatorium was an event Katherine thoroughly enjoyed. The Broadwater grounds were a mass of people, participating in or simply observing the numerous sports events offered. Everything from swimming to bicycle racing captured the attention. Wonderful smells of foods drifted in the warm spring air: barbecued ribs, pop corn balls, candies of every description, and drinks, every thing from tea to hard cider.

Katherine walked arm in arm with Tom Marlow. They were often joined by someone they knew. Tom introduced her to numerous business associates. She introduced him to those she knew from her many parties.

"Would you like to go swimming," Tom asked as they found themselves watching the various water events.

"I suppose it would make a perfect 'surprise' for Saturday evening," she responded quietly.

"Oh no," Tom Marlow laughed, "a surprise is a surprise. "You can't plan Saturday night."

Tuesday at ten o'clock, Lilly was released from the hospital and escorted home by her family and friends. Katherine met Lilly's new nurse, and had to admit the woman was experienced. However, she also agreed with Lilly that the woman was not the sort to confide personal things to, least of all Ed's letters. Katherine had received a reply from Mr. Holter. Now if she could only find an opportunity to share it with her best friend.

Thursday evening Katherine joined the Cullens for dinner after attending the Larson reception. The household was again buzzing with activity. Their concerns for Lilly had been laid to rest. Grace was full of talk about the Gibson Picture Charity while Puss was getting ready for a cotillion the following afternoon.

Katherine enjoyed the tumult. It was almost as if Lilly's health had never been a concern. Then after supper, she stole upstairs. Lilly's nurse was across the hall in her old room.

Katherine quietly shut Lilly's bedroom door as her friend watched with anticipation. Then she handed over the letter.

"I knew it," Lilly exclaimed softly. "When did it come?"

"Tuesday."

"It's addressed to you," Lilly noted.

Katherine smiled. "Yes, but it's all about you. He loves you!"

Lilly looked up. "He does?"

"It says so in black and white," Katherine exclaimed. "That's why he's trying to set up that job. He wants to marry you."

A soft squeal exploded from Lilly, and her eyes instantly began reading, furiously and desperately. "Here. Here, this must be it," she exclaimed softly. Suddenly Lilly stopped, the letter falling from her hands. "No, no, it won't work. Oh, what a fool I've been."

Chapter Twenty-Four

"You, Lillian Cullen, are incapable of being a fool," Katherine retorted. "So what won't work?"

"Marriage, Ed Holter," Lilly gasped. "It won't work."

"Why not?"

"Look at me," Lilly cried. "This is not the girl that went to Salvini, that he enticed away from Tom Hauser's party."

"Ed knows you've been sick, that you've had an operation," Katherine responded. "If anything, it's made him appreciate you more. And you will get well again."

"Katherine, you're my dearest and best friend, but sometimes…"

"Sometimes what?" she demanded.

"Open your eyes," Lilly responded quietly. "Do I look better than a week ago?"

"Healing takes time," Katherine replied. "A bruise takes two weeks to heal completely, and a mountain climber my father knew once drank some bad water and nearly died. His problems took six years to disappear."

"Another week isn't going to cure me," Lilly replied quietly, "and I won't be here in six years."

"You'll probably be back east with Ed," Katherine agreed.

"No Katherine, open your eyes. I'm not getting better. I'm getting worse."

Katherine stared at Lilly. "What do you mean?" she demanded in a stunned voice.

"After the operation I had a low grade fever," Lilly offered quietly. "That didn't surprise either your father or Dr. Dean, but they expected it to go away. It hasn't. It's gotten worse despite all the medicine Dr. Dean gives me."

"How bad is it?" Katherine cried.

"Oh, it's not really up there yet," Lilly replied. "It's still low grade. That's why they let me go home. But the direction is wrong, and they haven't been able to alter it."

"Does your family know," Katherine asked.

"They know I have a small fever, but they haven't done their arithmetic." She smiled wanly. "They're so relieved I made it through the surgery, they think the whole thing is over. Grace and Ernest are leaving for New York on Monday."

"Monday? Grace didn't tell me," Katherine gasped.

"New York on Monday, Europe on the 29th," Lilly offered. "Once Grace joins up with her friends, Ernest will visit relatives for about a month, and then come home."

Katherine stared at Lilly in disbelief. As usual, her friend had a total grasp of reality despite her illness.

"Don't look so shocked, Katherine," Lilly responded now. "You knew my chances of recovery. You always knew."

"But medicine is improving all the time," she cried. "I thought…"

"You wanted to believe your hopes," Lilly finished for her, "for both me and your father."

Katherine stared at her.

Lilly handed back Ed's letter. "It's to you. I think you should keep it."

"But you haven't read it yet, not all of it," Katherine protested.

"I don't need to," she answered quietly, too quietly. "He loves me. He loves me, and because he does, he's going to hurt."

"What about you?" Katherine demanded.

Tears glistened in Lilly's tired eyes. "I already hurt."

"Katherine, would you cheer up. This is supposed to be fun," Tom Marlow complained with a devilish grin as he helped her into the carriage Saturday afternoon. "It was your idea."

Katherine sat down. "Where are we going," she asked.

"Not far," he answered as he climbed in beside her.

"Then why the carriage. We can walk," she countered.

"You'll see," Tom answered. He slapped the reins, and the horses moved off.

Katherine became lost in thought. It was two days since she had dinner at the Cullens, and still she could not shake Lilly's conversation from her mind She had thought the surgery was a success. Her father said it was. Could Lilly be wrong?

The carriage proceeded down Benton Avenue in the warm afternoon sun until Tom turned up a street, and pulled up in front of Lilly's house.

"What are we doing here?" Katherine asked.

"You'll see," Tom replied as he jumped out. "I won't be long."

Within minutes Tom Marlow emerged from the Cullen house with Lilly in his arms. He carried her down to the carriage as her mother followed with blankets.

"Mother, it's nice out," Lilly complained as Tom placed her in the rear seat. "You're going to smother me with all those blankets."

"You can't afford a chill, darling," Mrs. Cullen replied. Within minutes she retreated back into the house.

Lilly and Katherine exchanged awkward greetings, and Tom got under way.

"Where are we going?" Katherine asked again.

"Just up here," he smiled as he directed the horses up Gilbert Avenue. "There's a nice grassy spot under an old crabapple tree. I thought we'd have a picnic." He turned the horses left on Harrison Avenue, and stopped. Reaching into the back alongside Lilly, he grabbed the blankets and gave them to Katherine. "If you take these up there," he pointed, "I'll bring Lilly."

Katherine did as she was instructed.

"I love being outside," Lilly commented as Tom lifted her out. "Thank you for this."

"Well I do owe you for several past kindness," Tom responded with a smile. "I'm just happy you could accept." He carried her up under the crabapple tree, and set her down on a blanket. Then he took a moment to survey their vantage point. "Nice view," he decided, and headed back down the incline to get the picnic basket.

Katherine turned to Lilly. "Are you warm enough?"

"I'm fine," Lilly responded as she looked around her. "I used to play here, you know. Ernest and I used to climb this tree and spy on Grace and Ella Hauser. They were always talking about boys, and we used to listen in until we couldn't hold back the laughter. Grace used to get so mad at us."

Tom returned with the food, and Katherine opened the basket, taking out the plates.

"You're awfully quiet, Katherine," Lilly noted softly. She caught Tom watching her friend as well. Concern rested in his expression.

"What do you want me to do?" Katherine retorted. "Pretend?"

"No." Lilly's eyes dropped. She fidgeted with the folds of her skirt.

"Katherine, I think…" Tom Marlow's voice fell off as her eyes swung violently to him.

Katherine rose to her feet, striding through the long grass, away from her friends.

Tom rose as well, hesitant, wondering if he should follow.

"Let me," Lilly offered as she struggled to stand up.

"Allow me." Tom offered his hand. "Are you sure you're up to it?"

"I have to be," Lilly replied. She now picked her way through the grass, slowly and laboriously. By the time she reached her friend, Katherine's cheeks were wet with tears.

"I wish this wasn't happening," Lilly offered gently. "I hate causing so much pain."

Katherine turned. "It's not your fault."

"Not my intentional fault," Lilly agreed, "but I did cause the problem. If I had only…" She stopped. "Ignorance is no excuse, you know. But it happens, and we pay, sometimes dearly."

"Lilly, how can you be so calm. I would scream bloody murder if I were in your shoes," Katherine protested. She wiped her nose.

"I've had my moments," Lilly confessed, tears rising also in her eyes. "Hope is forever plaguing me, but reality is relentless." She placed her hand on Katherine's arm. "The thing that really helps though, is knowing that our earthly existence is not what life is really all about, that our humanity was never meant to be anything more than temporary."

"But it's all we know," Katherine replied.

"Yes, and we cling to it," Lilly responded, "sometimes too much. I think that's why we often bring these things on ourselves. We get so caught up in what we're doing, we forget just how fragile our humanity is."

"I don't want to loose you," Katherine cried softly.

"I'll miss you too," Lilly responded as they embraced. "But you have your future, Katherine, and Tom is going to make a fine husband. He's a good man."

"So is Ed."

"Yes," Lilly agreed. Her hand disappeared into her pocket, and she handed Katherine a letter. "Would you mail this for me? I'm afraid with all the commotion of Grace and Ernest's trip, it might get lost."

"Sure," Katherine responded. "What did you tell him?"

"Nothing," Lilly answered quietly. "I want Ed to keep his eyes on his future." Her face turned. "Tom looks a bit lost. Perhaps we should go back."

The two linked arms and walked back through the tall grass together, pausing from time to time as Lilly rested, and Katherine picked wild bluebells. Tom Marlow let out a sigh of relief. Katherine had been out of sorts since he had picked her up, but now things were okay again. He was glad. He was glad that Lilly could now enjoy the afternoon, and Katherine could enjoy Lilly.

After a light meal, Lilly rested in the afternoon sun as Katherine and Tom nibbled at the left-overs, and talked about the load of apples Tom had hauled into Helena one time. The weather had turned cold, and he had to keep stopping to build fires under the wagon so the fruit wouldn't freeze. It was a very long trip, but the apples sold for a dollar a piece.

"My grandmother used to dry apples," Lilly offered as she listened. "I kind of miss them. They were always so sweet and chewy."

"Doesn't your mother dry fruit?" Katherine asked as she reached for her bouquet of wildflowers, and began weaving stem after stem into a garland of blossoms.

"Yes, but it comes out hard and brown. My mother always tries to hurry things along with the wood stove. She never had the patience for Grandma's way. So, where are you and Tom going to live after you're married?" Lilly asked as she changed the subject. Katherine handed her the ring of flowers, and began another.

"She's going to move in with me above the bank," Tom answered pleasantly, "until we can put away enough to build a house."

Grace and Ernest left for New York on Monday amid a crowd of family and friends. Lilly, of course, said her good byes before they left the house. Katherine kept her company as everyone followed the brother and sister to the train depot, wishing them a good journey and saying good bye there. Lilly tried to distract herself from the empty house, but Katherine could tell she was feeling left behind. Then as a train whistle broke the silence, Lilly's face turned eastward.

"Katherine, have you ever counted all the whistles?" she asked. "They blow more frequently than the church bells ring, especially at night."

"So true," Katherine agreed. She pulled a letter from her pocket and handed it to Lilly. "It came just minutes before I left Mrs. Osterhout's."

"You didn't open it," Lilly replied as she looked up. "It's addressed to you."

"I'm sure Ed just didn't want your nurse to get it," she responded with a smile. "Open it."

Lilly tore open the seal and removed the pages. Inside she found a letter to her, as well as a shorter one to Katherine. She handed Katherine hers, and began reading her own. "Ed's got a job," Lilly exclaimed, "with a prestigious accounting firm." A smile lit her face. "He doesn't know if it's just for the summer, or longer, but they seem to like him." She fell silent as she read further.

Katherine's attention dropped to her own letter. Ed Holter was asking her to write to him regularly. He had already figured out that Lilly was only telling him partial truths. Katherine refolded the page. She didn't know how she felt about the idea. She didn't want to play the spy, but at the same time she understood how Ed must feel.

A contented smile rested in Lilly's face as she finished her letter. "He's doing well," she noted. "What did he write you?"

Katherine slipped her letter into a pocket. "Just that you aren't telling him everything. He's concerned."

A shadow fell over Lilly's expression. "I tell him everything, just not right away," she replied. "It wouldn't have been fair to tell him about my operation when he was up to his ears in final exams."

"Nor fair to tell him that you're getting worse when he's landed a brand new job?" Katherine replied.

"Exactly," Lilly responded.

"What about choice, Lilly? Don't you think he should decide these things for himself?"

The young woman stared at Katherine silently for several moments. "I also have choice," Lilly replied quietly. "Ed wouldn't have to be facing such decisions if it wasn't for me. When I'm gone, he will still have to make his way in this world, and I can't stand the thought that he might pass up any opportunity because of me. Life is too short."

"But will he have regrets, Lilly? He loves you. Wouldn't you want to be there for him, if the situation was reversed?"

"He will only have regrets if he has choice," Lilly responded. "If I don't give him that, he has nothing to rebuke himself for."

"But wouldn't you want to be there for him, above all else?"

"Yes," Lilly admitted as her eyes watered, "and that's precisely why I won't give him the choice. I don't want him to watch me die. It's hard enough the way it is. Besides, it's not like you and Tom. Ed and I have learned to love each other through letters, not by being together."

"You would die alone?" Katherine gasped.

"Everyone dies alone," Lilly replied. "It's the last moments of living that are the hard part. How am I supposed to keep my eyes on God when I'm being torn with guilt for leaving Ed, and causing him so much pain? And it would only be worse if he made sacrifices for me."

"But wouldn't it be some comfort having him here?" Katherine asked quietly. "After all, you're the one who's sick, not him."

"So that makes it all right to think of nothing but my selfish needs?" Lilly cried. "That would indeed make me pathetic soul."

"I don't understand you," Katherine replied quietly. "I don't think I'll ever understand you."

"Don't judge me too harshly," Lilly responded now in a softer tone. "One day you'll eventually have to stand in my shoes, and then maybe it will all make sense, even if you do choose differently."

"I just hope that one night when I eighty five, I just die in my sleep," Katherine retorted. "It would make the whole thing a whole lot easier."

"Dying is not all bad," Lilly responded quietly. "It's a lot like winter. It is bleak and cold, but there's a strange and wonderful beauty to it too. I can't explain it exactly. I think it's fear that ruins everything, fear and panic."

"Lilly, I honestly don't know where you come up with this stuff. I swear that when I leave this earth, I will go out screaming and kicking."

"No Katherine, you have too good a heart for that," Lilly responded.

During the week Katherine's mother and sister returned to Helena as the elder looked around for a more permanent residence. Mr. Phelps's construction was nearing completion on his Lawrence Street house, and it was hoped that they might secure it. Then on Thursday, Mrs. Sligh again returned to her boarding house in Philipsburg, taking Bessie and little Margaret with her. Katherine breathed a sigh of relief. This time at least, she would not be constantly baby-sitting.

"Come on, Katherine," Wilder called. "If we don't hurry, we'll miss the streetcar."

"I'm coming," Katherine called as she broke into a run, following her friend as they both hurried toward the depot. The conductor shook his head in amusement as Wilder and Katherine leaped on. Tom Marlow waited inside, a smile resting on his face.

"I was afraid you weren't going to make it," he commented as they sat down beside him.

"We were afraid we weren't either," Katherine replied breathlessly.

The trip to the Broadwater went too fast. Katherine loved being with Tom, but inside she dreaded going to the Natatorium. Within minutes the crowd was pouring off the streetcar, and into the bath house. Reluctantly she followed everyone to the dressing rooms, and changed in the light of the round, stained glass window. Katherine was the last to emerge out to the edge of the bath. It's enormous size made her feel small and insignificant. The noise reminded her of the train depot.

Katherine focused on the crowd. Wilder was already in the water, swimming, splashing, and having a good time. She sat down on the edge, her feet dangling in the water as she searched for Tom. She scanned the fellows near her, stopping to watch one glide though the water with incredible ease, twisting and turning in the water with hardly a splash. He swam in her direction. Suddenly Tom emerged as streams of water dropped from him. His dark eyes twinkled as he wiped the water from his face, his hair plastered tightly to his head.

"There you are," he greeted. "I thought you'd gotten lost."

"You're a good swimmer," Katherine responded. She had never seen him wet before.

"My aunt and uncle always let me in free," Tom responded with a smile. "It helps to practice. Are you coming in?"

Katherine slipped from the side of the bath, appreciating the warmth of the water.

"Come on, I'll race you to the other side," he grinned.

Katherine shook her head. "I don't think so," she replied.

Chapter Twenty-Five

"Why not?" Tom demanded as he suddenly noticed how ill at ease she was in the water.

"I can't swim," Katherine replied.

"You can't... You can float, can't you?" he asked.

"Not very good," she replied, suddenly bashful.

"What's going on?" Wilder demanded as she suddenly emerged from the water on their left. "Do you want to dive off the platform with me, Katherine?" she asked.

"Katherine is going to practice her backstroke," Tom responded automatically. "She wants me to help her with her technique."

"Practice, ugh," Wilder responded. "Oh there's May. See you." She swam off.

"Thank you," Katherine breathed. "I haven't told her I can't swim."

"Well, that's the last we'll see of her for a while," Tom replied. "Wilder hates practicing anything. It's a good thing swimming comes naturally to her." He smiled as his attention shifted back to Katherine. "Now lie down on my arms, and pretend the water is a bed. I won't let your face get wet."

Katherine reluctantly obeyed. She didn't want to, but Tom just assumed she would. The young woman leaned back and felt his strong arms supporting her in the water. She relaxed slightly.

"Now take a deep breath, and put a big bubble of air in your chest," Tom instructed. "Lay your head back in the water until you feel it just touching your forehead. Now straighten your legs, point your toes, and flutter them in the water."

Step by step Katherine obeyed until Tom was walking to keep up with her.

"How does it feel?" he asked.

"Okay," she answered as her concentration remained on his instructions. Suddenly, she spotted his arms. They were now longer under her, but folded across his chest as she began to leave him behind. A broad smile rested on his face. She instantly sunk. Katherine's feet found the bottom of the pool, and she stood up, choking and sputtering, water running down her face.

"Why did you stop?" Tom cried as he closed the distance between them.

"You let go," she cried angrily.

"That's because you were doing fine on your own. You didn't need me." His eyes twinkled with merriment.

"You told me I wouldn't get my face wet," she accused.

"You didn't, not until you stopped," Tom laughed.

"But you let go," she cried.

"You didn't need me."

Katherine glared at him. He smiled at her.

"Katherine, look where you're standing," Tom noted. "That's how far you went without me."

Suddenly Katherine looked at the distance between where she was and where he had been. The ripples in the water still testified the distance. She was a good six feet away, and her accomplishment finally dawned on her. "I did that?" she asked.

"Yes. Let's try it again. This time I'll tell you when I let go, and I'll walk with you," he promised.

"You'd better," Katherine retorted. She laid back in the water, eager to learn, yet skeptical. Her eyes were on Tom, watching him closely as she repeated his directions. Again she began to float.

"All right now," Tom noted quietly, "you're floating, and I'm going to take away one hand and then the other," he told her as he walked beside her.

Katherine watched as each of his arms returned to the side of his body. "Now what?" she asked.

"Just keep going," he smiled. "I'm not going any place."

Katherine kept fluttering her feet as her eyes rested on Tom. He was doing the breast stroke now to keep up with her. From time to time he would remind her to keep her chest up or her head back.

"All right," Tom now instructed, "take a deep breath, hold it, and turn over, letting your feet drop to the bottom."

Katherine obeyed. Suddenly she was standing on the opposite side of the pool. Her eyes widened.

"See, it's not so hard," Tom smiled.

"Marlow. Hey Marlow," a voice called from the side. Norm Holter was walking briskly toward them, water running off his body. "We've got a bet going. Come on, we need you."

"Not today, Norm," Tom smiled. "I'm busy here."

"Hello Katherine," he greeted. His attention returned to Tom. "I'm sorry to interrupt old man, but I'm afraid you can't pass this one up. It's Charlie Word. If you can beat the length of his dive, he'll donate a whole month's budget to the boy's school, and you know they're running short on cash."

"And if I loose?" Tom asked.

"If you loose," Norm repeated. "Well if you loose, he wants an hour's time with Katherine."

"He wants what?" Tom cried.

"An hour's time," Norm repeated, "right here today in front of everyone. It's not like he can do much, now is there?"

"Why that son of a..." Tom retorted as his eyes flashed anger. "Excuse me, Katherine," he stated as he dove under the water, and disappeared down the length of the bath, re-emerging beside Charlie Word. The two men exchanged words. Then Charlie Word climbed out of the water, smiling, as Tom Marlow pulled himself onto the edge of the pool and grabbed a towel. Charlie Word walked up the platform steps, gauged the distance to where

Katherine stood talking with Norm, and dove in. The towel dropped from Tom's hands as he sprung to his feet, and dove in as well.

Tom Marlow's face broke the water in front of Katherine as he gained his feet. He was breathing hard as he turned, searching for Charlie. There was a turbulence in the water, and Charlie appeared.

"You son of a gun," Tom accused. "You were laying siege on Katherine the whole time. The bet is off. I'm not diving against you ever."

"You just did," Charlie smiled triumphantly, "otherwise you couldn't have gotten here so fast."

"The hell, you say," Tom seethed. "The bet is off."

"Quite the contrary," Charlie rebutted. He turned to Mr. Sparr, who was standing beside the pool. "How far did I dive?" he shouted.

"Here," he answered as he raised his arm to mark the spot.

"Charlie, you can't count the dive," Norm Holter objected. "Marlow didn't even use the platform."

"That's his loss," Charlie Word retorted. "Knight, how far did Marlow make?" he shouted.

The young man swam to the side, and raised an arm. He stood in front of Sparr.

"That can't be," Charlie objected. "Sparr, you're off," he shouted as he pulled himself out of the water, and retreated down the bath's edge. Norm swam off, investigating the circumstances.

"I don't like your bets," Katherine told her fiancé. "You know I don't like Charlie Word."

"It wasn't much of a contest, and the orphans need the money," Tom responded with concern. "If Word would just play straight..."

"If he played straight, he wouldn't flirt with every girl in the city," Katherine retorted. Her attention shifted. Wilder was diving off the platform at the other end of the pool.

Norm swam back to them. As he rose out of the water, a cheer erupted from several of the crowd. "Tom, you beat the pants off Charlie Word," Norm announced with a big grin. "You beat him by a good two feet."

"Two feet?" Tom retorted. "That's impossible."

"But it's true," Norm laughed. "The boys over at St. Aloysius won't go hungry this month."

Over the next three weeks, Lilly's health continued to deteriorate as her fever rose, her appetite dwindled, and her complexion sallowed. Concern rose in everyone. Dr. Sligh was called back from Granite County to consult with Dr. Dean, but neither could offer more than suggestions. Their best one was a referral to a hospital in Victoria, B.C. that had experience and limited success in abdominal surgery.

The Cullens' friendship with the Hausers, however, provided a more promising option. Governor Hauser knew influential people nation wide, and he was sure that with a little inquiry he could set Lilly up with a renowned surgeon.

To this end, everyone directed their efforts. Puss was out of school now for the summer as Lilly's parents looked into travel arrangements, keeping their plans out of the limelight as much as possible. Everyone was told they were simply taking Lilly to a lower altitude in hopes that it would help her recover from her sick bed. The Hausers also made plans to travel to the coast on the same train. Afterwards, all the Hausers except the governor would sail north to Alaska.

"You're going to have surgery?" Katherine asked Lilly as Mrs. Cullen left the room with the nurse.

"Yes, I think so," she answered. Lilly mustered a smile. "Your father is pretty impressed with the physician I'm supposed to see."

"And what does Dr. Dean think?"

"She thinks there is considerable risk in the whole idea," Lilly answered softly, "but she's about at her wits end with me. She can't seem to alter the course of things, and it frustrates her terribly."

"And what do you think?" Katherine asked now.

"What I've always thought," Lilly responded quietly.

"If you don't think it will do any good, why go?" Katherine demanded.

"Because Katherine, everyone is consumed with worry over me, including you. No one, absolutely no one, accepts my fate for what it is." Lilly's face was flushed, her eyes glassy bright.

"Your father isn't making you go, is he?" Katherine inquired softly.

"No," Lilly responded as she grew quiet, fighting her increased pulse.

"I'm sorry. I shouldn't have upset you," Katherine responded as she rose to her feet.

Lilly's eyes darted to her. "Don't you dare leave."

Katherine sat down again, startled.

After several moments, Lilly was strong enough to continue. "I leave Helena tomorrow. We have to talk. This may be our last chance."

Katherine remained silent. There was an unexpected edge to Lilly's voice.

"I'm sorry if I seem harsh," Lilly stated now, "but it's hard to think of everything I need to deal with in such a few short hours." She bit her lip as worry descended over her demeanor. "I should have talked to Grace more before she left. I... Well, it's too late now," she concluded.

"I can write a letter for you," Katherine offered.

"I've already done that," Lilly responded. "I hope it's enough." Her eyes settled on Katherine. "Ernest will be okay, and Puss will be with." She stopped as her eyes now wandered aimlessly.

"What about Ed?" Katherine asked quietly.

"I wrote him yesterday. Mother promised to mail it this morning."

"And did you tell him?" Katherine pressed.

"No."

"Lilly, what is he supposed to think?" Katherine cried. "He won't get a letter from you next week."

"Nor the week after," Lilly agreed. Her jaw quivered slightly. "I know you two have been writing. I hope you haven't said anything to Ed that might..." Lilly's voice fell off. Tears boiled in her eyes. "His job is important. I don't want to ruin it for him."

"I haven't said anything," Katherine replied, "though I've been tempted a thousand times."

"After you receive word," Lilly began now as she mustered some composure, "you can tell him whatever you want. Just tell him his dreams are all I have left in this world, and not to let anything happen to them. Okay?"

"I can do that," Katherine agreed.

"And then there's you," Lilly stated quietly. "You have been the dearest friend I could possibly have, and I cannot think of a way of returning even a portion of your kindness."

"You don't need to," Katherine responded as her voice choked. "Are you really going to do this? Are you really going to leave Helena?"

"It's my last chance to travel," Lilly responded with a wane smile.

"Tell me at least where you're going," Katherine cried.

"No... I can't. Ed mustn't know," Lilly responded, "not until after it's too late." She paused only momentarily. "I have to do this, Katherine. I have to end it. It's the only way for everyone to regain their lives again. It's been over three months. Besides, they think I'm being brave. Can you imagine? If I were truly brave, I'd wait this thing out."

"Does your father understand what you're doing?" Katherine asked. "Does anyone?"

"Dr. Dean does, I think," Lilly answered, "but she's the only one. We had a nice talk yesterday."

"So is there anything I can do," Katherine asked quietly.

"You've already done it," Lilly responded as she took her friend's hand. "Thank you. I only wish there was something I could do for you." Then she paused. "Tell Tom good bye for me."

Katherine embraced Lilly, and left her friend to rest. The conversation had taken its toll, and Lilly needed her strength for the trip the following day. Katherine stepped out into the hall as Mrs. Cullen appeared.

"Lilly's resting?" she asked.

"Yes."

"Katherine, your mother is staying at Mrs. Osterhout's again, isn't she? I heard construction on the Phelps house is running behind schedule."

"Yes she is, and Carrie arrives tonight," Katherine replied.

"Does the boarding house have enough room?"

"We'll probably be a bit crowded for a week or two."

"Then why don't you stay here. We need someone to take in the mail, and look after things while we're gone."

"That's very kind of you," Katherine replied.

"Nonsense," Mrs. Cullen retorted, "you'd be doing us a favor...again."
She smiled. "The judge can only be gone two weeks, but we might stay
longer, depending on Lilly's recovery time."

"I understand," Katherine responded.

"Good," Mrs. Cullen sighed in relief. "Violet has her hands full right
now with her in-laws. They have health problems of their own, and this will
definitely ease her mind."

"And let it ease yours," Katherine responded. "I'll bring my things over
tomorrow after you leave."

"Thank you, dear. Thank you," Mrs. Cullen replied gratefully. "Oh by
the way, we have two new kittens on the back porch. Puss will want to talk to
you about them before we leave," she continued as they walked down the stairs
together.

The train personnel was very accommodating when Lilly was transported
on her sick bed to the depot the following morning, promptly taken to a state
room, and tucked in a berth. All of this was done ahead of time, and gave
Lilly a chance to briefly rest before her many friends came to wish her well
and a safe trip. Katherine, too, was on hand, lingering with the family until
the last minute. Then as Violet and her husband said good bye, she was also
forced to leave. Lilly reached for her book, and clung to it tightly as her final
visitors left. Katherine was nearly off the train before she realized the book
was Lilly's copy of Herodotus.

"Katherine, we'll be seeing you then, all right?" Violet called as the train
began to move. She paused to wave at her sister's passing window.

"Yes, I'm sure," Katherine responded without thought. She lingered
where she was, watching the train grow more and more distant. When she
turned, she was alone. Her eyes returned to the disappearing train. The
moment had finally arrived. Lilly was gone. The thought was frightfully real
as a cold emptiness invaded her.

Katherine now looked around her in a daze. Her best friend was gone.
She would never see her again. She felt confusion and loss as she left the
platform, returning through the depot without conscious thought of her
surroundings. When she reached the street, she walked. Her direction was
not back to the Cullen house, nor to Mrs. Osterhout's. She just walked. Block
after block passed under her feet until she found herself outside Montana
National Bank. She went in.

"Miss Sligh, I'm afraid Mr. Marlow isn't in," Mr. Smith announced as
Katherine approached the rear offices. "Is there anything I can do for you?"

"No, I'll just wait," Katherine responded blandly. She sat down in the
same chair she had once sat with Wilder.

"But he's at lunch, it could be a while," Albert Smith objected.

Katherine made no response. She just sat quietly waiting, her eyes fixed
blankly in front of her as her mind retrogressed to her first memories of
meeting Lilly.

Forty-five minutes passed when Katherine suddenly got to her feet, and left the bank. Mr. Smith stared after her in surprise. The young woman had hardly spoken.

"Smith, any messages?"

"Marlow, where did you come from?" Albert Smith gasped in surprise. "You just missed Katherine."

"Katherine was here?" Tom inquired.

"For almost an hour," he answered, "and then she just got up and left without a word. She seemed distracted. Is everything all right?"

"I don't know," Tom responded. "Which way did she go?"

"She turned left at the door," Albert Smith replied.

Tom Marlow hastened back through the bank, heading north at the street. He spotted Katherine a block ahead of him, and broke into a run. He caught her at the following intersection.

"Katherine," he called as he now reached for her arm.

The young woman turned, her face brightening as she did. "Tom," she exclaimed softly.

"I heard you were at the bank," Tom responded breathlessly. "I'm sorry I missed you."

"Lilly's gone," Katherine announced. "She wanted me to tell you good bye."

"When will she be back? I heard she was going to a lower altitude for a while," he responded pleasantly.

"She won't be coming home," Katherine replied in a still voice.

"But I thought..." Tom's voice fell off.

"She's gone," Katherine repeated. "I won't ever see her again."

The gravity of Katherine's tone was undeniable. "How do you know this?" Tom demanded softly.

"Lilly told me," Katherine answered. "You were right. The surgery wasn't successful, and now Lilly's going to a specialist, but that won't be successful either. Lilly allowed it only to end things sooner."

Tom stared at her in disbelief. "She's really gone?"

Chapter Twenty-six

"I told Mrs. Cullen I would stay and look after the house while the family is away," Katherine offered now.

"Do you need some help moving your things over?" Tom asked quietly.

"Please," Katherine responded, "I would really appreciate the moral support. Mother thinks I spend too much time at the Cullens as it is."

"I'll come over tonight then."

Katherine's mother was not happy about her daughter moving back to the Cullen residence, but she could not deny the extra room would be welcome at Mrs. Osterhout's.

Over the next week, Katherine slowly came to terms with circumstances. Various girls from St. Vincents dropped by the house, all hoping for news of Lilly. But they also seemed to enjoy Katherine's presence, Lilly had left a void in many people's lives.

Tom often came and took Katherine somewhere. Friday night it was the circus. Sunday night it was church. The other nights they went to one friend's or another's. During this time, their relationship tightened and strengthened, and they talked about getting married more and more. Suddenly Katherine dared to think about eloping, but Tom discouraged it, thinking of his future in-laws. Mrs. Sligh wasn't that fond of him in the first place.

"I don't care what mother thinks," Katherine declared.

"I know, but I do," Tom replied. "She's family." He smiled. "What if we just move the wedding date up...say spring?"

"Why not Thanksgiving?" she responded.

Tom smiled. "I'd love to marry you tomorrow, but I want to do this right."

"You like my social standing," she suddenly realized.

"Katherine, maybe you don't care what your mother's friends think, but it could have a direct effect on our future. I know, I've been fighting prejudice all my life."

Katherine knew what Tom said was true. He had struggled long and hard to get where he was, and only since their engagement had he started receiving more invitations to parties. "All right, we'll do it your way," she agreed softly.

He kissed her. "Thank you."

Late Thursday afternoon Katherine returned to the Cullen house. She had just come from St. Vincents where she had stood in for Tom's aunt, spending much of the day helping the sisters do an unexpected inventory of their linens. Mother Superior had received an ultimatum from her higher authority to furnish a complete listing of every piece of cloth in the academy, post haste.

Katherine let Puss's mama cat outside for a brief repose as she headed to take in the mail. She opened the front door. Ed Holter stood outside, his hand raised to knock. "Ed," she exclaimed in surprise, "what are you doing here?"

"Where's Lilly," Ed Holter demanded softly as his arm returned to his side. Concern engulfed his face.

"She's not here," Katherine replied.

"Where is she?"

"I don't know. Her family took her to a lower altitude for an operation."

"An operation? Where?"

"I don't know."

"Katherine, you must know," he exclaimed.

"Come in," she responded. She shut the door behind him, and led him into the parlor where they sat down.

"Ed, I didn't expect you. I don't know what to say," Katherine admitted.

"You can tell me the truth," he replied.

"We've always told you the truth," Katherine responded, "just not in the most timely fashion."

"So I gathered," he stated. "I asked for your help. I expected you to keep me informed."

"And I tried," Katherine responded. "But Lilly..."

"She found out?" he demanded. "Who told her?"

"I did."

"You told her," he exclaimed as his eyes widened with anger. "Then you owe me the truth. Where is she?"

"I told you. I don't know. All she said was that they were going to coast, but she wouldn't tell me exactly where."

"She didn't tell her best friend where the operation was to take place?" Ed asked in disbelief.

"No," Katherine replied, "she was afraid I'd tell you."

Pain entered Ed's expression. "Why wouldn't she want me to know? I don't understand," he cried softly.

"Lilly didn't want you to watch her die."

"Die?" Ed Holter fell silent. A look of utter shock filled his face. "Is she that bad?"

"She hasn't done well," Katherine informed him quietly. "That's why they took her to a specialist."

"She said she was carrying a little fever, but she made it sound routine," he responded. "Can't the specialist help her?"

"He can try," Katherine replied.

Ed stared at her in horror.

"How's your new job?" Katherine asked quietly.

"I quit," Ed retorted as he rose to his feet. "Are you sure you don't know where she is?"

"Yes," Katherine answered.

"So who would know?" he pressed as a certain amount of desperation rose in his face.

"Everyone here was told they were going to the coast for the sea air and the lower altitude," Katherine replied, "everyone except her doctors."

"Then we can ask them," Ed responded automatically.

"I've tried, but Lilly anticipated that. I couldn't get anything from them, and one is my own father."

"Your father?" Ed repeated. "Even he won't tell you?"

"No. I'm afraid there's no one that can help," Katherine admitted softly. "I'm sorry."

"When was the operation to take place," Ed asked.

"I don't even know that," Katherine replied without pleasure.

Ed fell silent.

"I tried to get Lilly to change her mind," Katherine cried. "I tried to get her to tell you everything, but she only became more determined. ...and I'm afraid that's what finally convinced her to have the operation. She wanted all of it to end."

The color drained from Ed's face. "She didn't want the operation?"

"Operations have risks," Katherine replied quietly, "high risks, and they don't diminish with repetition. Lilly knew that."

"Then why? No one forced her, did they?"

"No," Katherine answered, "her father would never allow that."

"Then maybe she thought the risk was worth taking, that recovery was possible," he offered.

"No Ed, she knew the truth. She knew that despite all the hopeful words, it would only make things worse. It was everyone else that pinned all their hopes on the operation. But Lilly knew, Lilly knew that it would hasten the inevitable. She knew she wasn't coming home alive."

"Not coming home alive?" Ed repeated hoarsely. He turned, faltering in the move. In a dazed state he now retreated to the door. But as his hand reached for the knob, he realized he had nowhere to go, nothing to do that could possibly ease his misery. Total agony crashed over him as his breath became choked and labored. Katherine was the only one that knew of his love for Lilly. He couldn't go home. His family didn't even know he corresponded with his childhood friend. Slowly his legs buckled beneath him, and he slid helplessly to the floor as his head bowed over his outstretched arm, his hand still grasping the door knob.

Katherine knelt quietly beside him, taking him into her arms. His shoulders quivered with grief as heart wrenching, horrible, pathetic tones escaped his throat. They tore at Katherine as Lilly words came to mind, echoing in her ears. This was what Lilly had been trying so hard to insulate Ed from, and insulate herself from as well. Even in her frail state, Lilly had tried to spare each of them the memory of a last pathetic moment.

Katherine's thoughts were on her friend. Had Lilly already had her operation? No word had come yet, no bad news. Then she wondered where news would be sent. Lilly's family was gone, Grace to Europe, Ernest to New York, and everyone else was with Lilly -- all except her married sister, Violet.

"Violet might know," Katherine suddenly cried.

"What?" Ed responded.

"Lilly's sister, Violet. She might at least know if Lilly has had the operation yet. They would tell family. They would send a telegraph."

"She might even know where Lilly is," Ed responded with sudden hope. He was instantly on his feet, pulling Katherine with him through the door. Within ten minutes they were at Mrs. Osterhout's, standing outside the Wilson door. Violet's husband answered.

"We need to see Violet," Katherine cried. "Is she here?"

"Well yes," he answered. "Violet," he called over his shoulder. Within moments his wife appeared.

"Hi Katherine, Ed," she greeted.

"Violet, has Lilly had the operation yet?" Katherine demanded.

"Well yes, two days ago," Violet answered. "She's doing fine. It was a little touch and go at first, but she's over that." Violet smiled. "You didn't know, Katherine?"

"No," she responded in shock.

"But she's fine?" Ed repeated.

"Yes, she seems to be," Violet relayed.

"Where is she?" he asked.

"I don't remember the name of the hospital," Violet responded, "but it wasn't in Tacoma like they planned."

"What do you mean?" Katherine demanded.

"Governor Hauser's doctor wouldn't see them." Violet frowned. "Maybe I've said too much. Lilly made us all promise not to tell anyone where she is. But she is doing okay."

Ed turned away without a word, walking through the boarding house and back outside. Katherine hastened after him.

"You said she wasn't coming home," he accused as he spun to face her in the street.

"She hasn't," Katherine responded.

"Whose side are you on?" Ed demanded.

"Lilly's."

"Then what the blazes is going on? First you tell me she's as good as dead, and now I find out she is doing fine in some mystery hospital."

"I didn't know," Katherine anguished.

His eyes bore into her. His face was tense. Every muscle of his body was rigid and taunt. Suddenly he turned away, striding swiftly off into the night.

Katherine turned toward home, confusion and guilt rising within her. Lilly had told her good bye. It was a final good bye. Yet she hadn't died in the operation. She was alive, and according to Violet, doing fine. Hope sprung within Katherine. Maybe everything was going to turn out. Maybe her father had been right after all. Her pace picked up, her spirits rose. Her encounter with Ed still bothered her. But if Lilly made it through the operation and came home, he would still love her, wouldn't he? He may hate Katherine from now on, but that was a small price to pay considering Lilly's life. A smile rose to her lips.

The following week Judge Cullen returned to Helena, and Katherine's mother secured a house at Oro Fino Terrace. Katherine moved into the bedroom with Carrie, and attended the Greene Afternoon on Tuesday and the Seligman Evening Thursday night. Ed Holter attended both.

"Lilly's at Jubilee Hospital in Victoria, B. C.," Katherine told Ed quietly as she joined him to watch the Seligman fireworks.

He turned. "How do you know?"

"The judge returned home," Katherine answered.

"And how is Lilly?"

"I'm told she is slowly recovering."

"I hope so," he stated bluntly, and turned away.

When Katherine got home, Carrie was waiting up for her.

"So... How was it?" she asked.

"Terrible," Katherine groaned, "I hate parties anymore."

"Well maybe it's because we aren't the ones giving them," Carrie grinned. "We could hold a party out on the lawn in front of the building. I've already talked to the neighbors. They don't mind."

"At least you'd be there," Katherine replied.

"We'll work on the invitations tomorrow," Carrie decided.

Mrs. Sligh loved the idea, and the party was set for the evening of July 16th. It was an informal affair held in the open air with dancing and refreshments. Fourteen of their friends shared the entertainment. Katherine tried to ignore the fact that Albert Holter was the only member of his family to show up. Norm, she knew, was with Tom at a trade conference. But Ed had given no excuse, and had not come. At least Katherine had the Murphy girls to talk to. The topic was Thursday night's dance at Electric Hall. Weber's Orchestra would be playing, and the weather promised to be cool enough to make the evening enjoyable. Katherine planned to go, though Tom Marlow would be late in arriving. He had been cornered into attending several dinner parties during the week, and Thursday night was one of them.

Katherine wore a blue and white organdy dress with blue ribbons as she made her appearance at Electric Hall. She saw at a glance that Norm, Ed, and Albert Holter were all present, so was Ernest Cullen. Her heart skipped a beat. Ernest was home. Katherine made her way to him.

"Katherine, hi," he greeted with a big smile. "I didn't see you come in."

"I just got here," she replied. "It's good to have you back."

"Well, thank you," he responded with a smile.

"Have you heard how Lilly is doing?" Katherine asked.

"About the same as I understand it," Ernest replied.

"And where is Grace by now?" Katherine inquired.

"Oh, who knows," he responded with disgust. "Those friends of hers are in one place and then another with hardly a moment's notice. She contacts us, not visa versa."

"She knows about Lilly, doesn't she?" Katherine asked.

"The operation, yes," he replied, "but we don't hear much from her. Maybe mother does." He paused momentarily. "Katherine, are you here alone," Ernest asked. "Would you like to dance?"

"I'd love to," she responded. "Tom won't be here until later."

Ernest led her onto the dance floor. "Gees, what's going on here," he asked as they passed the Holter boys, "Norm and Ed look like they both ate something sour."

Katherine ignored the question. "Does anyone know when Lilly may be coming home?"

Ernest's attention shifted back to her. "No, not yet. Maybe next week."

"You will let me know if you hear anything, won't you," Katherine now pleaded. "I've moved, you know. Mother has taken a home for us in the Oro Fino Terrace. You'll remember, won't you?"

"Sure," he responded with a smile. "We can't let Lilly's best friend go without news."

Katherine fell silent as they danced. It felt good to have Ernest back. It would feel even better when the rest of the family returned. Her daydream was cut short. Norm Holter cut in, and suddenly Katherine was dancing with him.

"Evening, Katherine," he greeted with a reserved smile.

"Good evening, Norm," she replied pleasantly.

"Tom is coming later?" he asked.

"Yes."

"Katherine, I was wondering if we could talk," Norm stated.

"Certainly," Katherine replied with a smile. "What's on your mind?"

"I think you know."

Katherine's attention focused on her dancing partner. "Does this have something to do with Ed?"

"You know it does."

Katherine's head turned, her eyes searching for Norm's younger brother. She spotted him getting a cup of punch. His back was toward them. "What do you want to know?"

"Ed's been out of sorts ever since he got home," Norm stated. "I thought maybe he'd fallen for some girl back east, and gotten jilted, that is until I started noticing him at a few parties. Every time he lays eyes on you, Katherine, he bristles like a porcupine. Why?"

"We had a misunderstanding," Katherine replied quietly.

"I didn't even realize he knew you," Norm retorted.

"We went on a double date last year," Katherine offered.

"A double date? Oh, you mean that time with Tom," he acknowledged.
"Yes."
"So what was your misunderstanding about?" he asked.
"You haven't asked him?" Katherine replied.
"Sure I've asked him," Norm responded, "for all the good it's done. Why do you think I'm asking you?"
Katherine looked away.
"Katherine?"
Katherine now met Norm's eyes. "I can't tell you. Ed would kill me."
"It's not like you're his favorite person now," Norm retorted.

Chapter Twenty-Seven

"I still can't tell you," Katherine responded. "You'll have to talk to Ed." Norm's dancing ceased. "Katherine, I need to know what's going on."

"Norm, I would tell you if I could. But Ed would hate me for all time, maybe even you. I can't make things worse."

"What things?" he demanded.

"Norm, wait, just wait," she pleaded as she coaxed him to dance again. "Give it some time, please." Her face turned as Ed walked past. Why was he still here? Why hadn't he gone to Victoria? It had been two weeks since she told him which hospital Lilly was in. Katherine's attention shifted back to Norm. "Has Ed made any trips lately?"

"Trips? No, why?" he asked in surprise.

"I don't know," Katherine responded. "I just thought..." Her voice fell off. "I don't know, Norm. I wish I did."

"Maybe we could figure it out together, Katherine," Norm offered

"I can't, Norm. I'm sorry," Katherine responded as she suddenly broke free of him. Leaving him standing on the dance floor, she hurried toward the door. Ed was leaving. "Ed," she called as she hurried after him, "Ed Holter."

Ed stopped, and turned. "What do you want?"

"Why haven't you gone to Victoria?" Katherine cried. "It's been two weeks. I told you what you wanted to know."

He made no immediate reply.

"Ed?"

"She doesn't want me there," he stated finally.

"She loves you," Katherine responded

"She has a funny way of showing it."

"Maybe that's why she clung to her copy of Herodotus even when she was too sick to read it," Katherine responded.

Ed's eyes dropped away from her.

"She didn't want you to leave your job," Katherine cried. "She said your future is all she has left in this world, and she wants the very best for you."

Ed's eyes rose again, this time focusing on something behind and above Katherine. He abruptly walked away.

Katherine turned. Norm Holter stood in the doorway of Electric Hall. "How much did you hear?" she asked quietly.

"Most of it," he answered. "So he is in love. Who's the girl?"

"I can't tell you," Katherine replied.

"Katherine, I've never known you to be so exasperating and so stubborn..." Norm's attention shifted. "Tom," he greeted automatically.

Tom Marlow joined them. "Have I missed the entire dance?" he asked with a smile, "or is this some clandestine meeting?"

"Tom, you're here," Katherine greeted as they briefly embraced, "I'm so glad."

He looked at her a moment, and then turned to Norm. "What's up?"

"Oh, just my fool brother," Norm answered. "I guess he's in love."

"You didn't know," Tom chuckled.

"You did?" Norm demanded.

"I do have eyes and ears, Norm," Tom retorted.

"So who is she?" Norm asked with renewed interest.

"Ed hasn't told you?" Tom asked. "He's been home, what, two weeks?"

"No, he hasn't told me," Norm answered. "He hasn't told anyone."

"Well give him time," Tom responded. "He'll work it out eventually."

"It would help if I knew what was going on," Norm replied.

"I'm afraid, old man, you're going to have to wait until Ed's ready to talk. It's not my place to say anything."

A scowl rose on Norm Holter's brow, and he strode back into the dance hall. Tom smiled at Katherine, "A rough night?"

"Yes," she answered, "but Ernest is home."

"Good," he responded. "Two of the family are back. Four to go." He smiled encouragingly.

Knocking sounded from the dark front room late Monday night as Carrie sat up in bed, rubbing her eyes. "What's going on?" she cried as she nudged her sister. The thuds were again audible.

"What time is it?" Katherine asked as she woke.

"I don't know," Carrie answered. "Maybe one or two."

"I think someone's at the door," Katherine decided as the noise came yet again.

"Should we answer it?" Carrie asked.

"I think mother's got it."

The sisters heard the muffled sounds of talking, and then Katherine's name was called.

"What's going on?" Carrie repeated as both sisters got out of bed. Katherine grabbed her robe, and hastened to her mother.

Ernest Cullen stood at the front door. His appearance was disheveled. His expression urgent. "Katherine, you've got to come," he begged in exasperation. "Something's wrong, really wrong. I've never seen dad like this. You've got to come. Please."

"I'll come," Katherine responded immediately. She retreated quickly to her room, and threw on some outwear.

"Katherine, it's not your place," her mother objected from the doorway. "You're not a doctor. I wish your father was here."

"I wish he was too," Katherine replied as she brushed past the woman. "I've got to go." She joined Ernest, and the two headed out the door.

"I really appreciate this," Ernest exclaimed as he climbed on his horse. He reached down to Katherine, and pulled her up behind him. Within moments they were galloping up to Dearborn Street, and then made a straight shot down to the Cullen house. They reached it, slid from the horse, and went in.

"I've never seen dad like this, not even after the fire," Ernest stated now

"What fire?" Katherine asked.

"Four or five years ago," Ernest answered as he shut the front door, "we almost lost the house. We would have, if it hadn't been brick." A light burned from the library, thick cigar smoke drifted into the hall. "Gees," Ernest responded as they hurried to the library. Suddenly Ernest hesitated, reluctant to open the door.

Katherine grabbed the brass knob as the tall wood door swung silently open on its hinges. Judge Cullen sat at his desk, cigar in hand, staring at a telegram. A saucer held the butts of four former cigars. Katherine walked boldly into the smoke-filled room, and opened the window. Then she crossed to the desk, took the cigar from the judge's hand, and put it out in the already crowded saucer.

"Katherine, what are you doing here," Ernest's father responded in surprise.

"Putting out a fire before it starts," she answered quietly as she took the brimming saucer to the fireplace, and dumped it safely into the ashes.

The judge watched her, and noticed his son standing in the doorway. "I'm glad you're both here," he commented finally.

They waited for him to continue, but he did not. Instead his attention returned to the telegram. Katherine crossed to the judge. "You got some bad news, didn't you?"

The judge looked up. "It came at midnight. The hall clock was striking."

"From Victoria?"

"Yes." The judge looked away. It was a slow laborious movement.

"Well, what did it say?" Ernest demanded as he finally entered the room. Concern rested in his expression, anxiety in his words.

His father stared in front of him, unable to say the words.

"Lilly is at peace," Katherine explained softly.

"Yes," the judge agreed.

"Dead?" Ernest cried. "No." Desperation and panic filled his face. He grabbed Katherine by both arms, turning her until he looked straight into her face as he searched for something that could throw doubt on the fact. "No, Katherine, it can't be. Not Lilly. I know she hasn't been well, but they said...they said the operation went well. This can't be. This just can't be. Lilly has to come home."

"She is home," Katherine responded quietly, "just not this home. ...and her suffering has finally ended."

"No," Ernest shouted, and he left the room.

"I didn't know how to tell him," Judge Cullen confessed now. "I just didn't know how to tell him. They were so close."

"How are you doing?" Katherine asked as she leaned over the judge.

He looked up. "Not real well," he admitted. "I know Lilly is finally at peace, but I can't help feeling that I should have protected her better, kept her safer in this world, so she wouldn't have to leave it so very early in life."

"You did what you could," Katherine responded.

"No, no, I don't think so," Judge Cullen replied quietly as his eyes dropped. "Your father and Dr. Dean were right. The operations were risky, too much so. But I wouldn't listen."

"There must have been a reason," Katherine suggested.

"I wanted to believe that Lilly could be helped, and her suffering stopped. I wanted to believe that all of it could be miraculously done by an operation. But I was wrong."

"What happened?" Katherine asked softly.

Judge Cullen's eyes returned to Katherine, and he stared silently at her for several moments. "I thought Sam Hauser's connections were the answer. I thought his doctor could make Lilly well again. I wanted it so much. But Hauser's doctor wouldn't even see us. I'm still not sure why. Sam had words with the man. I had words with Sam. But none of it changed anything. The doctor simply refused to see Lilly."

"Why?" Katherine gasped.

"It hardly matters now," the judge noted quietly. After a moment he rose from his chair. "I'd better find Ernest," he commented. "It's time we talked."

He turned back momentarily as he reached the door. "It's the middle of the night, Katherine, and not a good time to walk home. Maybe you can find a place upstairs to get some rest."

"Sir, your wife will be coming home, and Puss...and there's the funeral arrangements, and all the people. Would you like me to stay?"

A look of appreciation rose in the judge's eyes. "Thank you." He disappeared then out into the hall, and headed upstairs to Ernest's room.

Katherine followed, turning instead for the kitchen. It had been two weeks since she had been a resident. Dishes were piled in the sink, and the larder was nearly empty. Mrs. Cullen should not have to face disorder on top of everything else. Katherine rolled up her sleeves, and went to work. When she finally finished, she headed upstairs to get some sleep.

Everything was quiet, though both rooms on the north side of the house still had lights shining from beneath their doors. Katherine headed down the hall to her old room, hesitating outside Lilly's open door. The bedroom was dark as memories flooded Katherine's mind. She stepped inside and the familiar smells and shapes wrapped themselves around her. The room felt like home, warm and secure. It was everything that reminded Katherine of Lilly. Hot tears rose in Katherine's eyes, and she grieved for her lost friend. She walked over to Lilly's bed, laid down, and wept.

When Katherine woke, the sun shone through the window as it often had during Lilly's extended illness. Katherine sat up and found an envelope lying beside her. It contained a brief note from the judge, and some money to carry out her volunteered tasks. Lilly's father was leaving to meet the train from Victoria. Katherine slipped the envelope into her pocket, and went downstairs. The house was empty

Katherine returned to Oro Fino Terrace just long enough to explain things to her family, and gather a few things. Then she returned to the Cullens, and set to work. The house needed to be cleaned and arranged for the crowd of people that would attend Lilly's funeral. Katherine rented the chairs, prepared the food, and overlooked nothing. It was her final tribute to her best friend, and she could not do less. By Thursday afternoon the house was ready for the family's return. The large parlor was only waiting for Lilly's casket. Many flowers had already arrived, pouring in with the city's sympathy.

Katherine closed the front door after accepting yet another bouquet of flowers. She was starting to feel the strain. Without conscious thought, she retreated through the house and out into the back yard. She needed air. She needed to collect herself.

"So you were right after all," a masculine voice commented quietly.

Katherine turned. Ed Holter sat on a bench a mere six feet from her. It appeared he had been there for some time.

"I would give anything to have been wrong," Katherine responded.

"Yes," he replied, "I would too."

"You read about it in the paper?" she asked.

"Yes."

"I wanted to tell you, but I thought it might make things worse," Katherine offered quietly.

"It may have," Ed admitted. "But you were right, I should have gone to Victoria. I should have been there."

"No," Katherine responded, "Lilly didn't want that. She didn't want you to have those horrible memories. She didn't want you to have regrets."

"Too late," he responded.

Katherine walked over and sat down beside him. "Lilly didn't want you to watch her die, but it wasn't just on your account, Ed. She was afraid for herself, afraid it would be too much for her."

"What do you mean?" he demanded in a still voice.

"Lilly knew you loved her; she also knew the futility of it; and she knew that you were going to hurt...because of her. It tore her up inside. I think she feared your pain above all else."

"Above death?"

"Yes, I think so," Katherine affirmed. "Death didn't seem to bother her as much."

Ed stared at her. "Everyone fears death."

"I don't think Lilly did," Katherine responded. "She saw it more as an escape from her suffering. She talked about the glory of it all."

"Glory? What glory? Appendicitis killed her," Ed retorted.

"But in death there is no more suffering," Katherine responded as she found herself repeating something she'd heard in church. The thought startled her. Lilly had said that church was where she got her ideas.

"What's wrong," Ed asked as he watched her expression change.

"Nothing," Katherine responded. "It's just I remembered Lilly talking about the after life, about having a body like Christ's. She thought she would be able to move through space by means of a mere thought. She had some pretty strange ideas."

"Yes, I remember," Ed noted.

"She told you about them?" Katherine exclaimed.

"In detail," he responded. "They were pretty irrefutable too."

"Then you believe them?" Katherine cried.

"I don't know. Maybe," he replied.

"Maybe we should be happy for her," Katherine suggested.

"Happy! Happy that I lost the woman I love? I only got to spend two lousy evenings with her. That's all. We didn't even get to go skating that next morning," he exclaimed.

"But you knew each other as children," Katherine replied.

"Children," Ed scoffed, "we fought as children. She would ignore me, and I would torment her until she couldn't take it any more, and then she would let fly a string of words that would always get me into trouble with the grown ups. We were always at each other."

"But you have her letters," Katherine reminded him. "That's how you two fell in love with each other, isn't it?"

"Lilly loved me?" Ed asked.

"You didn't know?" Katherine cried.

"I knew I loved her," he responded, "but no, I didn't know, not for sure. I hoped."

"Well she did. She told me so. I just can't believe she didn't tell you," Katherine replied in exasperation. "But I guess," she continued more slowly, "she wasn't sure of your feelings until she realized she had no future to give you."

The two fell silent.

"I'd better go," Ed decided.

"Wait," Katherine objected, "how did you know to come home?"

"Mrs. Cullen wrote me," Ed answered. "She knew about our letters, and thought I should know that her daughter was undergoing a serious operation. I panicked, and came straight home. Only Lilly wasn't here."

"She didn't want you to quit your job. Lilly was really excited about it."

"It suddenly didn't seem very important," he replied.

"Not important," Katherine cried, "it's all Lilly could talk about. Her hopes and dreams were dissolving before her eyes, but yours, yours were happening. You got hired by that big east coast firm. She was so pleased. You were her hope."

"No," he responded, "no. None of it is worth having without her. She's why I got the job in the first place. Now it doesn't matter. She's gone."

"You still have her letters," Katherine reminded him.

Ed Holter rose to his feet. "Just one or two," he responded. "I didn't know she was going to die."

"I have yours," Katherine offered carefully. "I haven't read them. Lilly gave them to me to destroy if anything happened, if she didn't come home. Do you want them?"

"She kept my letters?" he asked.

"Yes, every one of them," Katherine answered. "Do you want them?"

Ed Holter stared at her thoughtfully for several moments. "No," he finally decided, "burn them." He walked away then, out of the yard, and down to Benton Avenue.

Katherine returned to the house, and went upstairs. Retrieving Ed's letters from her things, she took them to the nearest fireplace, and struck a match. If both Ed and Lilly wanted them burned, she had no alternative. Flames licked the edges of the envelopes, turning them to ash. Katherine rose to her feet, and left the room.

It was growing late. The judge had expected to return that evening with his family, but nine o'clock arrived without him. Even Ernest came home and left again to wait at the train station. Katherine gathered her things to return to Oro Fino Terrace. Everything was done and waiting for the Cullens arrival. She was needed no longer.

Lilly's funeral was held Friday afternoon at four. The train was delayed, and the Cullens had not gotten in until the wee hours of the morning. But all the family was now home, except for Grace, though looking worn and exhausted.

Reverend Love tried to be strong for them, but Lilly had been such a favorite parishioner that he found difficulty in performing his duties. People came in throngs to show their respect, none more so than the pupils of St. Vincent's Academy. They brought generous offerings of flowers and placed them on Lilly's casket until it was totally covered. White flowers proliferated everywhere casting their heavy sweet scent throughout the house as everyone walked around in a state of disbelief.

The funeral service was not long. Reverend Love could not keep his voice steady as wrenched sobs broke from Lilly's parents. It was followed by a procession to Forestvale Cemetery, where Lilly's body was laid to eternal rest beside her grandmother's grave.

"Just bury me under some tree," Puss repeated at the end of the grave side service, "that's what grandma always used to say."

Katherine looked at the old woman's grave. It possessed only a small simple marker, no tree, not even a flower grew there.

"I don't suppose Lilly will get a tree either," Puss concluded too loudly. She earned a swift scowl from her mother's tear drenched face.

Her father bent down to his youngest. "There will be a fine family stone," he told Puss as he pointed across the lawn to an example, "and each grave will have an inscription on it. Okay?"

"What about grandma's tree?" Puss demanded.

"The cemetery doesn't allow plantings over the graves," her father stated.

The crowd was already dispersing as friends took the opportunity to briefly express their sympathy to Lilly's parents. Both were struggling under the strain as Violet and her husband tried to intercede where they could. Ernest, on the other hand, made a quick departure. Grace, of course, was still in Europe.

Katherine's eyes were on Ed Holter. He stood with his family, solemn and very silent. Norm was never far from his side, and it was obvious that he now understood things. Katherine wondered if the two brothers had talked, or if Norm had just finally been able to figure things out.

"I'm going to miss her," Tom commented quietly.

Katherine turned. "Me too. I'm still having a hard time realizing that I will never see her again."

"A lot of people seem to feel that way," Tom replied sadly.

Katherine glanced at her family. Her father was in one of his moods. It was the same mood that always occurred when he lost a patient, though this time perhaps a bit more intense. Mrs. Sligh was fussing over him as they walked away. Bessie, Don, and little Margaret followed.

Judge Cullen came up to Katherine. "You're coming back by the house, aren't you?"

"Yes."

"Good," he responded. "We'll see you there then." He turned and walked back to his family.

Chapter Twenty-Eight

Tom Marlow and Katherine joined the Broadwaters as they returned to their carriage, and drove back into town. Numerous families, including the Slighs, were already at the Cullens, quietly sharing a light supper. Conversation ebbed and flowed. Mrs. Cullen looked a little better, though the last few days had definitely taken their toll.

"Katherine, the house looks wonderful," Mrs. Cullen noted as she took the young woman aside. "How can we ever thank you? I honestly don't know how we would have managed without you."

A soft smile rose to Katherine's lips. "I wanted to do it...for Lilly, for all of you. You've been so good to me."

"Oh Katherine," Mrs. Cullen responded, "thank you. Is there something of Lilly's you would like? Something to remember her by?"

"I... I haven't a picture of her," Katherine suddenly choked.

"Of course, you'd want one," Mrs. Cullen responded kindly. "I'll see what I can find. But that isn't very much, is there something else? Maybe a necklace or something."

"She had a book," Katherine began now. "Herodotus."

"Herodotus, yes, she had it in Victoria with her," Mrs. Cullen responded.

"Yes, I believe so," Katherine replied.

"I'll see if I can locate it," Mrs. Cullen offered as she now turned away.

"Wouldn't you love to grow up in a house like this," Carrie noted as she joined her sister. "We could have each had a room of our own."

"Yes, it would have been wonderful," Katherine agreed quietly as she set aside her dinner plate. Mrs. Sligh was approaching.

"It's time to go," their mother informed them. "You girls have to change yet before you go to the Atchisons."

"Mother, I can't go to a party," Katherine retorted. "We've just come from a funeral." She noticed Ernest standing a little way off. He was listening.

"I want to go to the party," Carrie responded. "It's supposed to be a good one."

"Katherine," Mrs. Sligh stated in an even, but firm tone, "it's expected. You haven't given them any excuse."

Ernest abruptly walked away.

"I didn't know about it until now," Katherine replied softly.

"If you'd been home, you would have," her mother responded. "Come on, we're leaving."

"What about Tom?" Katherine protested.

"He can stay if he wishes," Mrs. Sligh responded. "I've already informed him that you have other commitments."

"Mother," Katherine exclaimed.

"Not here, Katherine. This is not the time or place to make a fuss," her mother reprimanded quietly. "The Cullens have been through enough."

Katherine's mouth fell shut as she followed her mother to the door. She was given just a few minutes to say her good-byes, and then they were gone.

The Atchison evening was considered by all to be a very pleasant fete champetre. The weather was not too warm, and dancing took place both in and outside the house. Japanese lanterns enhanced the grounds, and numerous easy chairs were placed outside to take advantage of the gardens.

Katherine preferred the out of doors as the mood of the funeral hung over her. She was not the only one to attend both events; the Murphys, Rosenbaums, Greens, Corys, Carpenters, and Holters had also shared her company. Katherine watched as Norm stuck to his younger brother like glue. Ed seemed quiet, but not unduly so, and his older brother was making sure that he danced and ate and talked.

Katherine sat down in one of the easy chairs that overlooked the outside dancing. The cool evening air was refreshing. Carrie and was inside enjoying herself, and Katherine was finally left to her own amusement. The pleasantries did much to lift her spirit. Life, after all, did go on.

Norm sat down beside her.

"Where's Ed?" she asked.

Norm pointed to where Virginia Atchison had the young man cornered in conversation.

"So the two of you finally talked things out?" Katherine asked.

"Yes," Norm responded, "though I hardly expected what I learned. But you already knew all about it."

"Pretty much," Katherine responded.

"Well I would never have guessed that two dates would precipitate so much," he sighed, "not after the way those two plagued each other growing up. Lilly used to come up with the most sophisticated insults I have ever heard, and so easily. Ed would have to look up the words half the time, and then he used to just burn with anger. I would never have thought those two could fall in love."

"Does anyone else know?" Katherine asked.

"No. Ed asked me to keep it that way."

"So now what?" Katherine responded.

"Now we take it one day at a time," Norm replied quietly. "I thought maybe I'd try and get him out a little, something physical, maybe some biking."

"Is he going back east again?"

"Maybe," Norm responded. "School would probably be good for him at this point, you know something structured, something familiar."

"I thought he graduated from Yale," Katherine responded.

"There's always law school," Norm smiled. "It never hurts to have an attorney in the family."

A small group of young ladies strolled past. "She was such a dull little thing. She hardly ever came to any of the events. I doubt anyone but her own family is going to miss her. I'm glad it wasn't Grace."

Katherine looked up sharply, but she could not distinguish which one had spoken the words. Norm's restraining hand came to rest on her arm. Her face turned.

"Let it go," he urged softly. They both knew the young women were talking about Lilly. "You know," he continued with a gentle smile, "people have said worse things about me, and I'm still alive."

"And you let it go?" Katherine asked.

Norm now broke into an easy smile. "Of course, what else could I do?" The question was rhetorical.

Church on Sunday was attended by a small summer crowd. Many of the members were out of town, either on trips or off in the countryside camping. The Slighs took their customary pew behind the Broadwaters. It too was empty aside from Wilder's brother and Tom Marlow. Wilder and her aunt were still in Europe. Katherine's eyes shifted to the Cullens. Only the men of their family were present. Reverend Love finished his sermon, and the congregation rose for the final hymn.

As people filed out of the pews, Ernest came up to Katherine. "Mother wanted me to give you this," he stated as he handed her a book. "She wanted you to know that she looked high and low for Herodotus, but she couldn't find it. She must have gone through the luggage a hundred times."

"Thank you," Katherine murmured. She stared at Lilly's name inscribed on the front of the leather binding.

"The photograph is inside," Ernest continued. "Dad thought Lilly's Bible was about as good a substitute for the missing book as we had. We hope you don't mind."

"No, the Bible's fine," Katherine replied as she opened it to where the photo stuck out.

"The picture was taken last summer," Ernest offered.

Katherine suddenly looked up. "Thank you Ernest."

He smiled softly. "I hope... I don't suppose you'll have much reason to come over any more?"

"When is Grace getting back?" Katherine asked.

"She probably won't leave for a couple of weeks yet. She has to return to Liverpool."

"That long," Katherine replied. "I really miss her."

"We do too," he responded quietly.

"You let me know when she plans to sail, will you?" Katherine requested as she presented a cheerful countenance.

"Sure," he responded.

"What have you got there?" Mrs. Sligh interrupted.

"A photograph of Lilly," Katherine answered as she watched Ernest disappear down the aisle.

"Well don't go leaving a picture of that dead girl laying around," she admonished strictly. "Your father feels bad enough about things as it is."

Katherine glanced incredulously at her mother. The woman was already busy greeting a friend.

The following week Katherine attended three different functions. Tom took her to the Plunge Party Tuesday evening, and together they worked on her swimming. Charlie Word was not there, and Katherine enjoyed the water without incident. Wednesday night, Tom took Katherine, Carrie, and their mother to the Electric Hall Party. Bessie was there, as was Pearl Davenport. Norm and Ed Holter were also present.

"Looks like Norm is looking after his brother," Tom noted as he and Katherine danced.

"Ed looks bored and restless," Katherine noted with concern. "They were both at the Atchison party, but Ed didn't look this bad."

"He's had time to realize the reality of Lilly's death," Tom replied quietly. "I understand Norm is planning a bike tour of the national park."

"I hope it's soon," Katherine responded.

May Word's Debut took place Friday evening at their residence on Madison Avenue. Katherine couldn't help be a little excited, despite the probability of seeing Charlie. The house had always fascinated her with its fairy tale appearance, and she wasn't disappointed when she was escorted inside. A profusion of flowers greeted the guests. Red poppies, carnations, and roses graced the mantel, tables, and every vacant corner of the hall. Similax heavily festooned the chandeliers. The guests were received in the front drawing room where a great profusion of roses, carnations, sweet peas, and marguerites exploded, all in white. It was a virtual bower of fragrance and beauty.

Katherine gasped at the heavy scent as her mind returned to Lilly's funeral. The air at the Cullens had been thick with the same oppressive sweetness. The flowers were the same color.

"What's wrong?" Carrie demanded.

"Nothing," Katherine responded gloomily.

"You don't look so good," Carrie noted. "Are you sick?"

"No," Katherine replied quietly, "I'm okay."

The sisters made their way through the receiving line to find themselves in the rear drawing room. Both it and the dining room were decorated in pink and green, but Katherine hardly noticed as they finally met up with Tom Marlow and numerous other friends. They proceeded upstairs to the ball room. The flowers were less profuse here, and Katherine breathed a little easier as she noted its tasteful decor. The windows were festooned only in vines, their seats cushioned. Persian rugs, easy chairs, and divans were scattered about for convenient tête-à-têtes, and Weber's orchestra was in its best form.

Charlie Word came up to them. "Katherine, it's good to see you. Would you care to dance?" His eyes rested tauntingly on Tom Marlow.

Katherine accepted his hand. It would be far from proper to refuse him in his own house.

"Why Katherine, you don't look happy to be dancing with me," Charlie Word commented. "Here you are in Helena's finest private ballroom, dancing with me, and I don't even see a smile."

"I'm sorry," Katherine mumbled, "but I'm not feeling very well."

"Katherine's ill?" Charlie Word responded. "Oh poor Marlow, now he won't want to find some private corner to be alone with you." Charlie purposefully lead her to the far side of the room.

Charlie Word received a tap on the shoulder. It startled him. "Oh Power, it's you," he exclaimed in disgust. "Can't you leave well enough alone?"

"Sorry old man," the Power heir responded. "Katherine looks like she could use a change."

As Word reluctantly ceded over his dancing partner, Katherine breathed a sigh of relief.

"You don't like Charlie Word, do you?" Power decided.

"He is not my favorite person," Katherine replied diplomatically.

"Oh, I think it's more than that," Power pressed. "I think you're repulsed by him." Katherine made no reply as a gradual smile worked its way into Power's face. "Well, so be it," he decided.

"Ah, there's your fiancé way over there," Power continued as he made no attempt to guide their dancing in that direction. Instead he watched Katherine. "My dear," he began now thoughtfully, "I am interested in how you truly feel about this Tom Marlow of yours. Do you love him?"

"Yes," Katherine responded automatically as her eyes rose to meet Power's. "Why?"

"Oh I just wondered. I've heard some talk, and I..."

"What talk?"

"Oh, sensitive," Power responded.

"What talk," Katherine repeated, quieter.

Power smiled. "Katherine, you're very lovely, and I only wondered why you set your cap for Marlow."

"Why shouldn't I?"

"No reason," Power responded as he tried to keep her temper from flaring. "Katherine, you look a little flushed."

"I'm not feeling very well," Katherine admitted. "I shouldn't have come today."

"Then perhaps you'd like to sit down," Mr. Power replied, remembering her kindness to him.

"I'd like to return to Tom Marlow," Katherine stated softly.

"By all means," Mr. Power agreed as he escorted her off the dance floor. This time he took her directly to her fiancée, and promptly excused himself.

"What was that all about?" Tom asked with a cocked head. "Power acted like he was making a delivery."

"He was," Katherine replied quietly.

"Well, I'll have to thank him," Tom responded with a smile. Then he paused. "Katherine, you look a little flushed. Are you all right?"

"I could use some fresh air," she responded.

Tom Marlow escorted her downstairs. At the bottom, the pungent scent of all the flowers again began to suffocate Katherine.

"Now you look pale," Tom noted with concern.

"I need some air," she repeated.

He quickly escorted her outside. As they strolled along the base of the house, Katherine's color began to return. "Finally you're looking better," he noted after several minutes.

"It was the flowers. Their scent is so strong," Katherine explained.

"Do they always bother you?"

"No, I love flowers," Katherine responded. "It's just that..." Her voice fell off.

"Lilly's funeral had a lot of flowers."

Tom and Katherine both turned. Ed Holter sat on the side steps.

"I didn't see you there, Ed," Tom responded.

"I needed some air too," Ed replied without expression.

"Where's Norm?" Katherine asked softly.

"Dancing with Ella Hauser," Ed replied.

"Does he like her?" Katherine asked now. "Ella seems to really like him."

"Norm? Na, he's just being nice. You know old Norm," Ed replied.

"So when are you and Norm off for the park?" Tom asked.

"Tonight's train," Ed responded with a little more life, and then a sly look invaded his expression. "We're taking Louie Sanders and Charlie Word with, so in about an hour you can relax, Katherine, and enjoy the evening again. It's not like you don't deserve it." He smiled.

"Charlie's leaving his own sister's party?" Katherine exclaimed as a certain amount of relief swept her.

Ed smiled. "You and Tom can dance the evening away. It's a nice party."

True to Ed Holter's word four of the men from May Word's debut made an early exit, leaving on the Northern Pacific. Several of the girls were disappointed by the fact, none more than Ella Hauser. This was the first social event she had attended since her family's return from Alaska.

Katherine now danced undisturbed in Tom Marlow's arms as she noticed the young woman. "Ella Hauser is looking a little lost without Norm," Katherine commented.

"I imagine she's looking a little lost because of more than just Norm," Tom Marlow countered.

"What do you mean?"

"The Hausers and the Cullens were close friends, but I didn't see any friendship at Lilly's funeral."

Katherine stared at Tom. "I didn't either."

"They were in Victoria at the same time, weren't they?" Tom asked.

"Yes."

"And Lilly died," Tom responded. "Something snapped between them."

Katherine fell silent as they continued dancing. Ella and Grace had been best friends. What would happen when Grace finally got home?

"Hurry up, Katherine. We're going to be late for church," her mother scolded Sunday morning as Katherine darted back into the bedroom and grabbed her Bible and shawl. She ran for the door.

Services had already started when the Slighs entered the sanctuary. Dr. Sligh scanned for an empty pew as he guided his son forward. All the seats were taken in the back, and they had no choice but to reclaim their customary seats during the opening hymn.

Katherine followed her family as she scanned the congregation. This week Ernest and his father were at services, and the Broadwater pew was completely empty. Tom Marlow had left the evening before so that he could be at an out of town meeting first thing Monday morning. She didn't know where Charles Broadwater was.

The Slighs took their seats as Reverend Love began the liturgy. Katherine's thoughts wandered to Tom as the congregation reached for their Bibles. Reverend Love prepared to read the epistle for the day.

Katherine opened her Bible as notes upon notes emerged between the pages. She shut it again, turning it over. Lilly's name was on the front.

Reverend Love again announced the passage, and Katherine quickly turned to the appropriate verse. But as the passage was read, Katherine's attention focused on the notes Lilly had secured on additional, smaller sheets of paper glued into the binding. Here in Lilly's Bible was an organized outline, delineating the priority system of divine doctrines. It didn't take a theology scholar to recognize the simple logic of it all. Katherine found additional charts in back of the Bible where Lilly's picture had been. Her heart pounded. Her friend's approach to scripture laid open the very genius of the Bible. Lilly had always seen the obvious.

"Katherine," Carried hissed.

Katherine rose automatically to her feet as the congregation sung the final hymn, and then began to disperse. She looked around her in a daze. Where had all the time gone?

"Are you coming?" Carrie demanded. The pew had emptied of people.

"In a minute or two," Katherine replied as she sat down. She wanted to make sure all Lilly's notes were in order.

"My daughter was always the last one out of the pews on Sunday mornings too," Judge Cullen commented as he sat sideways on the bench in front of Katherine. He smiled. "Lilly's Bible?"

Chapter Twenty-Nine

"Yes sir," Katherine responded.   "I grabbed hers by mistake this morning."

"She always did have it so full of stuff that the cover refused to lay flat. I suggested she use a notebook, but she never liked the idea."

"Do you know what's in here," Katherine asked now.

"You mean all her notes," he replied.

"No sir, I mean her system of organization.   It's so simple; it's pure genius. I have never seen anything like it. Does Reverend Love know about it?"

"Lilly used to heckle him about her theories quite often," Judge Cullen responded with a hint of pride, "so I suppose he does."

"And he did nothing about it?" she asked.

"What should he have done?"

"Shown it to Bishop Brewer, and then to the archbishop," Katherine responded. "Lilly would make most theologians look confused."

A large benevolent smile emerged on Judge Cullen's face. "Katherine, I appreciate your interest, but Lilly's notes were for Lilly's understanding. You can't expect a young girl to make any real impact on the Church. Women are to keep still, remember?"

"She did," Katherine responded, "but now..."

"Now she's gone," Judge Cullen replied, "and her Bible belongs to you. Learn from it what you can, pass on what you think is right and good, but remember keep silent in church. God provides opportunity, but not always in the most expected places."

"How is your wife?" Katherine asked as she now closed Lilly's Bible. "I thought she would be in church today. I wanted to thank her for Lilly's photo and this." She indicated the Bible.

"Not as good as I hoped," Judge Cullen replied quietly. "She's taken our loss quite hard."

"What about Puss?"

"She's fine, though awfully worn out. She's trying to be three daughters to her mother, and maintain the house at the same time. That's what I wanted to talk to you about. Is there any possibility you can come back to us, and take some of the load off Puss? It would just be until Grace gets home, and it wouldn't be as demanding as before. You'd be much more free to come and go."

Katherine glanced to the back of the church where her mother was deep in conversation with several women. Her father stood idly by the door waiting with her brother, who was teasing Carrie.

"Yes sir, I will come," Katherine decided. Her attention returned to Judge Cullen. He was pondering her family as well.

"Will your mother allow it?" he asked softly. "I understand she wasn't too happy about things before the funeral."

"If she won't, my father will," Katherine replied quietly. She smiled then. "Why don't you speak to him?"

Judge Cullen rose to his feet, and headed down the aisle to her father. Within minutes the matter was settled. Katherine would go home with the Cullens, and Dr. Sligh and Katherine's brother would bring her things over that afternoon. Mrs. Sligh was not pleased, but did not interfere.

"Puss, guess who's here," Ernest called as they entered the house.

The youngest of the Cullens emerged from the kitchen. "Katherine," she exclaimed in delight, and ran to her.

"How are the kittens?" she asked.

"Old enough to find homes," Puss laughed. "They're getting into everything."

"Puss, Katherine's going to stay with us until Grace gets home," her father offered. "I thought you could use a little help."

A large smile broke across Puss's face, and she instantly embraced her father. "Thank you, daddy," she murmured softly.

"Have you got lunch ready yet?" Ernest demanded.

"I would if you would only help," Puss retorted.

Katherine grabbed both siblings by the shoulders. "Come on you two, lunch won't make itself."

Judge Cullen took the opportunity to go upstairs to his wife.

The Cullens had always eaten fairly light on Sundays, and fixing a lunch was not difficult as Katherine began to wonder about the following day. The staples were in very short supply, and they would be lucky if the milk and butter lasted out the day. Still as the three set the table, Katherine was glad to be there. She always felt comfortable among the Cullens.

The three looked up as the judge ushered his wife into the dining room. Mrs. Cullen looked exhausted and pale, but a smile emerged on her lips as she spotted Katherine. She promptly embraced her.

"It's good to see you," she noted softly.

"It's good to be here," Katherine responded gently.

"Your mother is joining us for lunch," Judge Cullen announced. He glanced at Katherine with a big smile.

"So did you go to May Word's debut," Puss asked Katherine eagerly. "It was Friday, wasn't it?"

Katherine glanced at Mrs. Cullen. Interest rested in the woman's face. "Yes, it was Friday," Katherine agreed. "They held the dancing up in the ballroom."

Dr. Sligh and his son, Charles, brought Katherine's things by at four-thirty that afternoon. Carrie tagged along bringing Katherine's invitations for the various social events of the week, and to ask if her sister was planning to make the Mount Ascension Climb the following day with their friends. Katherine declined the next day's hike, but promised to attend the three afternoon functions she had been invited to with her sister. Puss listened in with great interest. The preceding week had been a glum one for her.

Katherine ran errands for the Cullens the following day. The wash had to be sent out, groceries purchased, and miscellaneous other things. Just before the noon hour, though, Katherine stopped in at Montana National. Tom Marlow immediately invited her into his office.

"I was going to come by this evening," he announced.

"I've moved," Katherine smiled.

"Again?" he retorted pleasantly. "Where to this time?"

"Back to the Cullens," Katherine replied. "The judge asked if I would. It seems his wife is taking Lilly's death pretty hard. I'm staying until Grace gets home."

"So how are you doing?" Tom asked his fiancée.

"Pretty good," Katherine responded.

"I wondered if you would like to go out to the cemetery?" Tom suggested. "It's been over a week since the funeral."

"Yes, I'd like that," Katherine responded, "but what about flowers?"

"Don't worry, I'll pick something up," Tom promised. "What time shall I come for you?"

"How about seven," Katherine suggested.

That evening Katherine and Tom invited Puss to go out to the cemetery with them while the others spent a quiet evening at home. Puss was only too happy to get out, anything to get away on the warm summer evening. At the cemetery, Tom handed a large bouquet to Katherine. She would have laid all the flowers on Lilly's grave, but Puss pulled out several large blossoms and placed them at her grandmother's marker.

"I still don't understand why they won't let us plant a tree over grandma," Puss complained with a frown.

"Because trees get pretty big over time, and your grandmother would not have a grave left," Katherine explained to her young friend.

"But it's what she wanted," Puss replied.

"Perhaps," Katherine agreed, "but I'm afraid she's going to have to settle for your flowers." Katherine's attention shifted. There was a granite base block at the head of Lilly's plot with the family name inscribed into it. She frowned. The marker was hardly what she imagined for her friend. "Did Lilly ever tell you what she wanted?" she asked as Puss joined her.

"White marble," Puss replied.

"In what shape?" Katherine asked.

"Oh, she didn't care," Puss responded. "She just wanted something in white marble. She used to think grandma's tree idea was a bit barbaric."

"White marble would be nice," Katherine agreed, "maybe something classic or Greek." She smiled as Tom joined them.

"Like a Parthenon pillar or statue?" he asked.

"A statue of Lilly, of course," Katherine exclaimed. "She always did have a way of just being present."

"Daddy says we're getting one of those," Puss stated as she pointed to a tall gray obelisk.

Katherine glanced over at the austere stone. It had a frightful coldness about it. "I miss Lilly," she stated softly.

"Me too," Puss lamented. "I can't believe I'll never see her again."

Katherine and Tom both turned. It was their sentiment exactly.

Katherine attended each social event that week, and brought home a glowing report of everything that went on, tactfully forgetting to mention Mrs. Hauser's presence at Power's afternoon reception. Puss ate up every detail as her mother's interest in life seemed to be slowly budding. The following week Katherine received no invitations, and she contented herself with her duties and some fancy work on the linens she was preparing for married life. Tom Marlow visited her regularly in the evenings, and it was from him that she learned that the Holter brothers returned home on Tuesday even as Ernest left on a two week hunting and fishing trip. Life went on.

Wednesday afternoon, a knock came at the front door. Katherine hurriedly wiped the flour from her hands and hastened from the kitchen. Puss was over at a friend's, and Mrs. Cullen, as usual, was reclused in her room. Katherine opened the door. The matronly figure of Mrs. Hauser stood before her.

"Miss Sligh, I didn't realize..." Mrs. Hauser exclaimed in surprise as she offered her calling card. It was only momentary. "I would like to see Mrs. Cullen, please," she requested.

"Come in," Katherine greeted as she opened the door wider. She led the stout woman into the small sitting parlor. "Mrs. Cullen is upstairs. I'll go tell her you're here."

"Thank you," Mrs. Hauser responded.

Katherine hastened up the stairs as trepidation rose within her. Nothing had been openly said about the rift between the Cullens and the Hausers, but much could be speculated on. Judge Cullen's comments the evening he received Lilly's tragic news came to mind.

Katherine knocked softly on Mrs. Cullen's door.

"Come in."

Katherine opened the door, and came to a stop beside Lilly's mother as she sat in a chair by the window. Katherine didn't know what to say. She stared at the calling card in her hand.

"What is it?" Mrs. Cullen asked as her attention focused on the young woman.

"Mrs. Hauser is downstairs," Katherine announced quietly as she offered the woman's card. "She would like to see you."

"Tell her I'm not feeling well," Mrs. Cullen instantly replied as she looked away. She never accepted the offered card.

Katherine didn't move.

After several long moments, Mrs. Cullen turned back. "What are you waiting for?"

"You were close friends, weren't you?" Katherine asked now.

"Once."

"Then why? Didn't the Hausers do their best..."

"Their best?" Mrs. Cullen hissed. "Sam Hauser has the ears of the nation's top men. He promised to get the most prestigious doctor on the entire west coast. He failed."

"But surely not for a lack of trying?" Katherine cried. "Didn't they go with you to the coast? The paper said Mrs. Hauser was even in Victoria."

"Yes they were there, always believing, always assuring, always assuming the best – never even considering there was any other possibility, never allowing us to consider any other possibility." Tears boiled in Mrs. Cullen's eyes. "It didn't happen that way. I should have known better."

"Maybe they were afraid of any other possibility." Katherine's voice fell off.

"It wasn't their daughter."

"Can you hate them for wanting the best for Lilly," Katherine asked softly.

"Lillian is dead. An operation could have saved her life, the operation Sam Hauser promised us, the operation that didn't take place. We had to go clear to Canada to find another surgeon, and by then Lillian was so weak." Her voice fell off momentarily. "It killed her," Mrs. Cullen anguished.

Katherine stared at the card as she turned it over and over in her fingers. She no longer could read the name printed on it. Her eyes were too full of tears. "Lilly knew the risk of the surgery," she stated quietly. "She never planned to come home."

"What?" Mrs. Cullen cried as she turned.

Katherine made no reply.

"No," Mrs. Cullen responded as she rose out of her chair, shaking her head in disbelief. "The operation was her one chance. If only Sam Hauser..."

"Lilly didn't think so."

Mrs. Cullen turned sharply, staring incredulously at Katherine. "How dare you!"

"Lilly told me herself," Katherine responded quietly.

"Lilly told you..." Mrs. Cullen stared at Katherine. Her face went pale, her expression taunt. "No, Lilly never objected to going. She believed in the surgery."

"Lilly believed it would end her suffering, and your suffering. She wanted it all to end. She did not fear death."

Mrs. Cullen's mouth dropped slightly open. She stared at Katherine in shock. "She told you that?" she whispered.

"Yes."

"Dr. Dean was skeptical," Mrs. Cullen recalled slowly, "but Lilly was suffering so. And Sam Hauser swore his doctor could solve everything."

"Perhaps he wanted to believe it," Katherine offered quietly.

"Yes, perhaps we all did," Mrs. Cullen now agreed.

"Will you see Mrs. Hauser?" Katherine asked after several still moments.

New pain filled Mrs. Cullen's expression. She did not answer, but returned to her chair, staring out afresh through the window.

"Mrs. Cullen..."

"I don't hate Ellen, you know," Mrs. Cullen began now in a still tone. "I just can't face her."

Katherine went back downstairs. "Mrs. Hauser, I'm awfully sorry to leave you waiting so long."

"Mrs. Cullen won't see me, will she?" Mrs. Hauser responded.

"She asked me to tell you she wasn't feeling well," Katherine replied quietly. "Is there anything I can do?"

Mrs. Hauser patted the chair beside her. "I'm afraid you already have by the looks of those red eyes, dear," Mrs. Hauser responded kindly, "but I'm afraid when one loses a child..." She smiled wanly. "And Cullie might be right. Lillian's death might have been avoided if she had gotten the operation in Tacoma, and yet... You know it seems strange that the doctor wouldn't make time for her. I can't help wondering why."

"He didn't say?" Katherine asked.

"Not really. You would think that after traveling all that distance, he would have at least looked at the girl."

"I thought all the arrangements had been made before Lilly left," Katherine commented.

"We did too, dear. We did too." Mrs. Hauser rose to her feet then. "I've left an invitation for a dance we're having next week on the table for you, Katherine. I realize the Cullens are still officially in mourning."

"I appreciate it, Mrs. Hauser, but under the circumstances I don't think I will be attending."

"I understand, dear," she replied as Katherine showed her out.

Katherine returned to the kitchen, and to the bread she was making. The sour dough starter had already caused her dough to rise. She punched it down, and kneaded the mixture until the flour was nicely blended.

"Did Lilly want to leave Helena?"

Katherine turned. Mrs. Cullen stood in the doorway.

"I don't think she minded," Katherine replied. "She said it was her last chance to travel."

Mrs. Cullen wandered in, and sat down at the table.

"I don't think Lilly was really afraid," Katherine repeated. "She always seemed so strong."

"Yes, she was that," Mrs. Cullen replied. "She was like her father, always there, always steady as a rock."

Katherine smiled. This was the first time Mrs. Cullen had emerged on her own from the cocoon of silence she had imposed upon herself since the funeral. Maybe things were finally starting to return to some sense of normality.

"I thought I would make a few extra rolls," Katherine offered as she tried to keep the conversation from dying.

Mrs. Cullen pulled a telegram from her pocket. "Grace is sailing home from Liverpool on Saturday."

"Saturday," Katherine exclaimed, "oh good. She's finally going to be on her way."

"Estelle Swann is traveling with her from New York. She used to live in Helena," Mrs. Cullen noted. "I understand she's engaged to be married, like you." She smiled softly.

"Sometimes I wonder if my wedding is ever going to take place," Katherine replied quietly.

"What makes you say that?" Mrs. Cullen responded with concern.

"Tom and I moved the date up to April, but mother has done nothing about the arrangements. ...and mother's dressmaker is notorious for missing deadlines. Plus, I've re-worked my white silk dress so many times, I don't think it's fit for a wedding, even with additional lace."

"You have several months yet," Mrs. Cullen noted

"Not if mother doesn't schedule a fitting," Katherine responded.

Chapter Thirty

"You do exquisite handwork, Katherine," Mrs. Cullen noted. "Could you sew your own wedding dress?"

"My own dress?" Katherine echoed.

"Perhaps it's not done in your family," Mrs. Cullen replied.

"No, it isn't," Katherine responded. "None of my family are decent seamstresses, and it would take forever without a sewing machine."

"You could use ours," Mrs. Cullen offered.

"You have a sewing machine?" Katherine asked.

"We have a whole sewing room in the attic," she replied. "You don't raise four daughters without one." She smiled. "We could hire a seamstress, if you don't think you want to undertake the job yourself."

"But that would take money," Katherine worried. "I don't think mother would approve."

"Do you know what kind of dress you want?" Mrs. Cullen asked.

"Oh yes," Katherine replied with a smile.

The two fell into a lengthy discussion as Katherine finished up her baking, and the two began the clean-up together. By supper Katherine had even sketched out what she wanted in her wedding dress, and all that remained was the question of money.

Judge Cullen shoved his empty dinner plate aside, pulled the billfold from his coat pocket, and placed several large bills on the table. These he passed to Katherine.

"What's this?" she gasped.

"You never asked for a penny all the time you spent in this house, watching over Lilly, watching over us. If this will help with your wedding gown, then here it is," he responded softly. "You earned every penny."

"But..."

A gentle smile rose to the judge's lips. "Take it Katherine. We want you to have your wedding dress. Has Tom decided where he's taking you on your honeymoon?"

"New York," Katherine responded as she mentally tabulated the amount of money. It was more than enough for her dress; and if she made the gown, the money would go even further.

Over the next three weeks, Katherine not only purchased the fabric for her wedding gown, but worked on it during every spare moment as Mrs. Cullen increasingly reclaimed her position in the household. The elder still tired easily, but found refreshment in the attic as she encouraged Katherine in the huge task before her.

"Where did you learn to sew," Mrs. Cullen asked one day.

"School," Katherine replied. "I had a teacher who took special interest in me."

"Was that in Granite?"

"No, Helena. I spent a couple years here before completing my education in Illinois," she answered.

"But surely we would have met," Mrs. Cullen objected.

"I do think I remember you from church," Katherine replied with a smile, "but I didn't get out much back then. My health wasn't terribly strong."

Tom took Katherine to the dance at Electric Hall on Labor Day Weekend. Charlie Word was there, and Tom made a point of always dancing in the opposite direction. The Holter boys were also all present. Ella was dancing with Norm as Katherine scanned for Ed. He sat against the wall by himself. Albert was talking to the Ashby girl.

Suddenly the lights flashed, and then an entire section went out as cries of alarm escaped the crowd. Norm Holter instantly began to reassure the dancers as Tom excused himself, and headed downstairs. Katherine wandered over to Ed.

"Are you going back east this fall?" she asked as she sat down beside him.

"Yes," Ed answered simply.

"Do you think they'll give you back your job?" Katherine asked.

"I'm not going to ask them," Ed replied. "Norm's convinced me to go to law school."

"Law school, that's great," Katherine responded.

"Yeah, Lilly would probably approve," Ed replied.

"I'm sure of it," Katherine responded. "So when do you leave?"

"Next week," he answered as the entire hall went suddenly black. It was momentary, and then most of the lights came back on.

"Tom," Katherine gasped. She rushed away, heading down into the basement. A single light guided her back into the semi darkness. She spotted an empty ladder, and then her eyes dropped to the figure sitting in the dirt.

"Tom?" she cried softly as she knelt beside him, "are you all right?"

"I think so," Tom Marlow replied, somewhat shaken.

"What happened?"

"I must have touched the wrong thing," he replied slowly as he struggled to his feet.

"Marlow, I've got the spare light bu..." Norm's voice fell off. "What happened to you?" He stared at Tom's dust covered evening clothes.

"Got knocked off the ladder," Marlow explained. "I don't think the light bulbs are the problem, Holter. We've got a short, a bad one."

"Well let me pull the fuse, and we'll take a look," Norm decided. Within moments he was up the ladder looking for the break in the wire.

"It's on the far side, to your left," Tom Marlow guided. "Do you see it?"

"Got it," Norm replied. He pulled a roll of wire wrap from his pocket and fixed it. Then he descended the ladder again, and headed to replace the fuse.

"Are you really all right," Katherine asked now. "You seem a little unsteady."

"Electricity does that to a fellow," Tom responded with a faint smile. "I think I'll sit the next dance out."

"You can't go back upstairs like that, old man," Norm objected. "Your clothes are a mess."

"Maybe if I brush them off a bit," Tom offered.

"All the brushing in the world isn't going to do the trick," Norm responded. "You need to change."

"You're probably right," Tom decided as they started back for the stairs. "Would you look after Katherine for me? Charlie Word's upstairs, and you know how she hates dancing with him."

"Don't worry about Katherine," Norm admonished. "My brothers are upstairs. We'll look after her."

"All right then, I'll head home and change," Tom replied as he reached the door.

For nearly the entire evening Katherine danced with one fellow after another; and every time Charlie Word made an attempt to cut in, one of the Holter boys interceded. Charlie Word's repeated efforts caused him increasing frustration as the Holters found sport in the situation. Even Ed got caught up in the game, forgetting his melancholy for a time.

However by the time the dance ended, Tom Marlow had not returned. Norm and his brothers saw Katherine home to the Cullens, and found Tom waiting on the front steps.

"Marlow, where have you been?" Norm demanded. "We've been waiting for you?"

"I didn't have a shirt to change into," Tom Marlow replied. "I forgot that I'd sent my spare out to be cleaned."

"Tough luck," Albert responded. "You missed all the fun. We really had old Charlie Word going. Every time he tried to dance with Katherine, one of us would beat him to the punch. Wow, was he mad."

"Thanks," Marlow responded with a tired smile.

"Well, we're off," Norm announced. Ed was suddenly looking very ill at ease.

Tom turned to Katherine. "I'm sorry I didn't come back, but I figured they would probably see you home. That's why I came here. I didn't want you to think I'd totally deserted you."

"Would you like to come in?" Katherine asked.

"No, I don't think so," Marlow replied as he struggled to his feet. His hand reached unsteadily for the rail, and then he sat back down on the step.

"Stay there," Katherine ordered as she left his side. She entered the house, heading for the light shining from the library door. Judge Cullen sat at his desk.

"Katherine, you're home," the judge responded as he turned. "Did you have a nice time?"

"Sir, Tom Marlow is outside. He took a jolt of electricity at the dance. Could you come?" Katherine asked.

Judge Cullen immediately rose, and followed her outside. Tom Marlow had not moved, though he now leaned against the side of the stair casing. He made another attempt to rise as Judge Cullen placed a restraining hand on his shoulder.

"I hear you took a swig of electricity," the judge offered as he sat down beside him.

"Knocked me off my ladder," Tom acknowledged.

"That bad," Judge Cullen mused. "Powerful stuff, that electricity, powerful stuff. Why don't you come in for a bit? It's getting cold out here." Judge Cullen helped Tom to his feet, ushering him into the parlor. Then he squatted down in front of Marlow, examining his face. "You're feeling a little unsteady?"

"Shaky, yes," Tom acknowledged.

"Do you need a doctor?" the judge asked. His face turned upward. "Is your father in town, Katherine?"

"No," she answered softly.

"I don't need a doctor," Tom responded. "Just a night's rest."

"I don't think you're in any condition to walk home," Judge Cullen noted. "Why don't you use the couch here? You'll probably feel better in the morning. What do you think, Katherine?"

"I agree," she answered.

"Then I'll just run upstairs and see if I can't find a pillow and a couple of extra blankets," he decided. "Do you need anything else, Tom?"

"No, thank you," Marlow responded. His eyes shifted to Katherine. "Some evening this has turned out to be."

The house turned in for the night as Tom Marlow made himself comfortable on the couch. Katherine slipped into Puss's room. The young girl had insisted that Katherine share her room when she moved back. Puss was feeling her sisters' absence.

"How was the dance?" Puss asked sleepily as Katherine climbed into bed.

"Fine. I'll tell you all about it tomorrow," Katherine replied.

Puss drifted back to sleep as the day's fatigue slowly caught up with Katherine.

Panicked screams woke Katherine, and suddenly she realized they were coming from downstairs. She jumped from bed and ran for the stairs as her thoughts turned to Tom. Judge Cullen and his wife were already racing down the steps.

They found Puss in the parlor, screaming hoarsely as Tom Marlow stood in front of the couch, his hands extended, his voice pleading softly with her.

But Puss was not listening. She turned at her father's entrance, falling into his arms as she babbled incoherently.

"Puss, it's all right," Judge Cullen consoled.

"No, no," she screamed, "he's going to set the house on fire."

"There's no fire," Mrs. Cullen reassured. "It's just Katherine's Tom. He wasn't feeling well, so he stayed over."

"Katherine's Tom?" Puss repeated as she finally began to quiet. She turned to stare at Marlow as he held his fiancée in his arms.

"You've just had another nightmare," Mrs. Cullen consoled. "No one's going to set the house on fire."

"Tom, I'm sorry," Judge Cullen offered. "Puss has had these nightmares for four or five years now, ever since we nearly lost the house. The dreams don't come as often, nor usually this dramatic." He smiled wanly. "I'm really sorry. You didn't need this on top of everything else."

"It's okay," Tom muttered.

"I think I'll get a midnight snack," Ernest decided from a nearby chair. "Does anyone want to join me?"

Grace returned home on the 21st of September, and Katherine returned to Oro Fino Terrace. For two and a half weeks Grace's companion, Estelle Swann visited friends and relatives. Then on the 9th of October, Grace and her mother accompanied her as far as Chicago. There, Miss Swann was to meet up with friends who would escort her the rest of her way home to Berryville, Virginia.

Meanwhile Mrs. Sligh played whist, and encouraged her daughter to do the same. Katherine attended four whist parties during the Cullen absence, two in the company of Tom Marlow. Grace and her mother returned home on the 26th, but Katherine saw none of the Cullens before Amy Rosenbaum's Halloween Party. This year Katherine was not without an invitation.

Katherine finished dressing, and looked at the clock. She was looking forward to All Saint's Eve. Many of her friends would be at Amy Rosenbaum's, even if Tom wouldn't. She sighed. Maybe after they were married, he would be automatically included in the invitations.

Katherine delayed just long enough to be fashionably late. However when she arrived at the Halloween party, it had already started, and she was shown into the drawing room where a large gathering of guests was already seated beneath the dim sepulchral light hanging from the center of the ceiling. Candles flickered at her appearance as heads momentarily turned beneath the ghoulish light of the pumpkin's distorted face. The crowd's attention returned to Ernest Cullen as he continued weaving his dark tale of the after world, sending shivers up spines, and goosebumps down arms.

Shadows danced across Katherine's head as she noticed the many suspended objects hanging from the ceiling. They were smaller and darker than the central pumpkin, causing the imagination to wonder if vampire bats might suddenly fly out of some niche. Ernest's voice became soft and wary.

Suddenly he jumped to his feet, and grabbed one of the objects in his teeth as screams escaped several girls. Ernest broke into a sinister smile.

"The apples tell your future," he declared in a low tone, "but only if you men can give them the vampire bite." He laughed hauntingly now, and withdrew from the light of the ghoulish pumpkin.

Katherine watched Ernest retreat to the rear of the crowd as the fellows all rushed to bite into the suspended apples. The fruit swung violently away from faulty attempts, banging back into distracted faces as the girls broke into laughter.

Ernest broke his apple open, and pulled a small piece of paper from its core. Unfolding it, his eyes traveled over Amy Rosenbaum's guests until they settled on Katherine. He refolded the paper, and placed it in his pocket.

Stephen Carpenter backed into May Franklin as he pulled his apple free of the ceiling, falling into her as both collided with Katherine. Laughter exploded from their lips. When Katherine looked up, Ernest was gone.

"I've got Katherine's name," Charlie Word declared.

"Let me see," Katherine demanded.

"Ah, I can't do that," Charlie Word objected. "It's between me and the spirits of good fortune."

"Then it can't be my good fortune," Katherine retorted as she called his bluff. "You must show proof."

Laughter broke from the Murphy girls as they demanded to see Charlie's paper. He held it high over his head as he tried to evade all attempts at capture, laughing and grinning with all the attention. Katherine rose to her feet, and left the room. She wanted to escape, to get away from Charlie Word. She thought Ernest had her name, but she must have been wrong. Thoughts of the previous year settled over her as she retreated into the kitchen.

Chapter Thirty-One

"You're going to miss all the fun."

Katherine turned to find Ernest sitting squarely on the surface of the kitchen queen. "I don't like the thought of being Charlie Word's fate."

"Charlie Word's? You're not," Ernest retorted.

"He says I am," Katherine replied.

"He's wrong. I have your name," Ernest stated.

"You?" Katherine responded.

A grin rose to Ernest's lips. "Yeah, who would have guessed. Maybe, we're doomed to spend our Halloweens together."

"I enjoyed last year," Katherine commented.

"I did too, more than now."

"A lot has happened," Katherine noted softly.

"Yeah."

"How come Grace isn't here?" Katherine asked.

"She's still getting used to a house without Lilly," he answered quietly. "She's got mom crying again."

"How's Puss doing?"

"She's over at a friend's. We both decided we had to get out tonight."

"And your dad?"

"He's down at the office," Ernest replied softly. "The bills have mounted to a pretty substantial sum, but I think it's more than that. I think the house has too many memories. He's doing more and more traveling too." He paused. "You know how Lilly was always there, ready and willing to talk about anything. Sure she always had a book handy, but..." Ernest looked away. The hurt in his expression said it all.

"You're the one she thought would be okay," Katherine commented after a few moments.

Ernest looked up. "What?"

"Lilly was really concerned about Grace, but she thought you would be okay."

"You mean with the operation," Ernest replied.

"With her death," Katherine responded quietly.

"You mean, she knew?" he demanded.

"Yes."

Ernest stared at Katherine in disbelief. "Why would she think I would be okay? Why would anyone be okay? Why did it have to be Lilly at all? Why couldn't it have been me instead?"

"Lilly blamed it on her diet," Katherine responded. "She gave up fruit for Lent."

"So did half the world," Ernest retorted. "That's no reason."

"The reason came after," Katherine replied quietly.

"What reason? So she stoved up her plumbing a little. Everyone does from time to time. It's not fatal. It's not the end of the world. You simply take care of it."

"And it doesn't happen every time, not even most of the time, but it's the one thing that each appendicitis seems to have in common with the rest," Katherine quoted. "That's what Lilly said once."

"You're pulling my leg."

"That's what Lilly told me," Katherine repeated. "I didn't know what to think of it at the time."

"What do you think of it now?" Ernest demanded.

"There may be some merit to it," she replied, "but sometimes there's hardly any other choice, is there?"

"No," he replied quietly.

Katherine mustered a smile. "She believed in you, Ernest. She knew you would be okay." She paused momentarily. "How about if we try and enjoy the party a little? The Rosenbaums went to a lot of trouble."

Each day after that, Katherine had practice at the Auditorium. The ladies from St. Peter's Episcopal Church were arranging the newest and most anticipated charity event yet, two Evenings With Tennyson. As many well known characters stepped out of the poet's pages and on to the Auditorium stage, Helena presented men and women who aptly posed, or appeared in pantomime, while Madame Medini read the corresponding passage of text. Handsome knights in all the bravery of silken doublet and hose, swinging cape and nodding plumes, and shining helmet and shield complimented the ladies in flowing robes, jewels, and floating hair. The two nights differed, however. Katherine was cast for Monday night's scene entitled Merlin and Vivian. Norm Holter was chosen for Tuesday's Gareth and Lynette. Ella Hauser was an attendant to Jeptha's Daughter for both evenings.

Katherine poised for her part as Vivian under the stage lighting as Louis Sanders portrayed old Merlin. Louis's make-up was so thick, and his wig so gray that Katherine had to stifle a laugh. This was not a repeat of her situation with Charles Word by any stretch of the imagination. Katherine could enjoy her part as the words of Tennyson brought the pantomime to life.

"Good job," Louis Sanders congratulated as they left the stage.

"You too," Katherine responded with a warm smile.

Norm Holter stood back stage talking with the attendants of Jeptha's Daughter who were finished for the night. Ella Hauser was among them, but Norm Holter wasn't talking to her, but to Miss Jefferies. Katherine drew to a stop. Ella looked upset, and Katherine's eyes focused more intently on Norm. His eyes glowed; his smile was warm; and his attention was securely on Miss Jefferies. Katherine smiled to herself. Norm Holter had found someone he liked.

Katherine bolstered her courage, and went over to Ella, drawing her away, distracting her with a costume problem. Ella Hauser was reluctant to leave, but Katherine's close association with the Cullens helped.

"Have you seen Grace lately," Ella inquired anxiously.

"Not since she got back from Chicago," Katherine replied.

"I need to talk to her, but after everything that's happened..." Ella's voice fell off. "You were there when mother called on Mrs. Cullen. She wouldn't even see her."

"I know," Katherine responded. "The Cullens are having a hard time with their loss."

"Their loss! I'm losing my best friend, and she didn't even die," Ella retorted. "And it's not like we didn't do everything in our power to help Lilly. She just shouldn't have died. It's not fair."

"I understand the Cullens have been invited to the King Reception. Maybe Grace will go to that," Katherine offered gently.

"Have they? Then maybe I will get a chance to talk to her," Ella decided. "Thanks, Katherine." She broke away, returning to the stage.

Katherine turned. Tom stood a half dozen paces from her. She glanced back at the empty stage. The curtain was down.

"Hi," he greeted.

"Hi," she responded. "I didn't realize the applause was the final one."

"How is Ella doing?"

"She's kind of at loose ends. She wants to see Grace, but I think she's afraid to go over to the Cullens."

"She's probably right," Tom noted. "They haven't been exactly sociable lately, and considering the Hausers involvement... Frankly, I doubt they will ever mend their fences completely. There's been too much water under the bridge."

The two walked out together. Katherine's family met them in the lobby, congratulating Katherine on her performance, greeting Tom cordially. Even Bessie and her husband were there.

After the second evening of Tennyson, Katherine turned her attention back to her wedding dress and trousseau as her mother played more and more whist, and brought home more and more prizes. Katherine pondered this new side of her mother. Mrs. Sligh was displaying more than just an aptitude for the game now. She was becoming more and more preoccupied with winning, claiming prizes even when she hosted the game. It was as if she had something to prove to these city ladies. Katherine could only sigh. Raising five children in a small company house had not been without an effect on her mother.

Two weeks later the King reception drew a constant throng of Helena's most prominent people. The women's gowns were extravagant both in design and fabric, and sported pearls and diamonds as they arrived at the Spruce Street residence. The house was richly decorated with chrysanthemums and similax, festooned with yellow satin ribbons. The guests were provided with sandwiches, beaten biscuits, chicken salad, olives, coffee or chocolate, ice cream, and cakes – all favorite foods – while Madame Ericke's orchestra played.

Near the door Katherine talked to Katherine Carpenter as Mrs. Cullen arrived in the company of her daughter, Violet Wilson. Mrs. Cullen wore black silk of a basic design with no jewelry. Grace followed behind. Her attire was also dark and plain. Katherine's attention shifted to Ella Hauser. She was standing with her mother, her eyes wandering over the crowd.

Katherine excused herself from Miss Carpenter, and greeted the Cullens, commenting on the size of the crowd as she tried to make them feel comfortable. This was the first time Mrs. Cullen had appeared socially since Lilly's funeral, and the woman looked ill at ease, more so when she spotted Mrs. Hauser. Mrs. Knight joined them, engaging Mrs. Cullen in conversation as they moved inward to pay their respects to the Kings. Grace was now free.

"Ella really wants to talk to you," Katherine told her.

"Where is she?"

"Near the orchestra," Katherine replied.

Grace spotted the Hauser girl. Then she hesitated. "What do I say to her?"

"Anything that comes to mind," Katherine encouraged. "You've been friends since you were children, haven't you?"

"Yes," Grace acknowledged as she watched Ella approach. Suddenly she turned, searching for somewhere private.

"Grace, you're here," Ella declared "We have to talk."

Grace grabbed Ella's hand, leading her out to the hall and up the stairs. Katherine let out a sigh of relief as she noticed her mother. Mrs. Sligh was busy talking with Mrs. Word as she reached out for Mrs. Power's arm. Mrs. Power ignored her, and passed on as she and Mrs. Hunt joined forces and returned to the Kings. Katherine grimaced. Her mother had just been slighted, and probably deservedly so. She had assumed she could claim Mrs. Power's attention at will, a presumption Mrs. Power had not honored. Katherine bit her lip. Had her mother even realized the breach of etiquette she had just committed? Probably not.

Katherine now joined Miss Murphy and Miss Atchison as they each obtained a cup of chocolate. It was cold outside, and the warm drinks steamed as the liquid was poured from the yellow and white china service. Conversation flowed freely among the young women. Katherine marveled at how easy it had all become when she spotted Bessie's mother-in-law. Mrs. William Davenport was again the essence of everything prim and proper. Katherine tensed.

"What's wrong, Katherine?" Addie Murphy asked.

"I don't mean to be unkind, but Mrs. Davenport makes me nervous," she replied quietly.

Addie turned and noted the woman. "She looks positively sinister. How does your sister ever stand it?"

"I don't know," Katherine answered.

"So have you met your future in-laws, Katherine?" Virginia Atchison asked.

Katherine's attention turned to the young woman. "No, I haven't," she replied as her thoughts turned to Tom.

"Katherine," Violet called as she pulled the young woman away from her two friends, "where's Grace? Mother no sooner paid her respects to the Kings than she bumped into Mrs. Hauser. She's ready to leave, and I mean now."

"I'll see if I can find her," Katherine responded.

Katherine slipped through the crowd, and up the stairs. Normally the upper portions of the house were considered off limits unless one was invited there by a family member, but Grace and Ella had to talk, and there was no privacy to be found downstairs. Katherine found the two in the sitting area of the upper hall, deep in conversation.

"Grace, your mother is looking for you," Katherine cried urgently. "She's ready to go."

"Already," Ella groaned, "we've hardly had a chance to catch up."

"Thank you, Katherine," Grace noted as she rose. "I'm sorry, Ella, but it's just the way things are." She mustered a small smile. "I've got to go."

Katherine's attention shifted to Ella as Grace quickly disappeared downstairs. "Did it help at least a little?"

"Precious little," Ella responded. "I think I've lost my best friend."

Saturday night Norm Holter gave an elaborate dinner for what he termed "the members of the mess", seven gentlemen in all. Tom Marlow was one of them. Sunday morning services at St. Peter's were canceled due to the renovation work being done on the church building, and Katherine finally walked into the bank on Monday morning in order to see her fiancé.

"Katherine," Tom greeted as he rose from his desk, "I was just thinking about you."

"Mother wants you to come to dinner on Thanksgiving," Katherine announced.

"Really," Tom replied, "well, I guess that's a step in the right direction." He smiled. Then it faded. "You're not pleased."

"I've been wanting to talk to you since last week," she responded. "This is the first chance I've had."

"Then talk," Tom encouraged as he now closed his office door. "What's on your mind?"

"Your family. I haven't met them," she replied.

"I know," he acknowledged. "You'll meet them on our honeymoon."

"But what if they're like Bessie's in-laws? I don't think I can marry into something like that."

"Katherine, they don't live here. You're marrying me, not my family."

"Bessie married both."

"Bessie is not you. I am not Don. I came west to be on my own. So even if you don't like any of my relatives, it doesn't matter. I love you. We'll simply live some place they don't."

"Really?" Katherine asked.

"Really," Tom assured as he took her in his arms. "You and I are what matter." He kissed her gently. "So now about Thanksgiving…"

The Slighs, with the exception of Katherine's mother, attended the eleven o'clock service at St. Peter's on Thursday. Mrs. Sligh excused herself in order to look after the turkey she had roasting in the oven. The rest of the family, including Tom, worshipped in the newly finished sanctuary. Both the Broadwaters and the Cullens were missing

Katherine opened Lilly's Bible for the reading of the epistle. Reverend Love's words ceased to penetrate Katherine's ears as her eyes shifted to Lilly's notes. It was almost like Lilly was present, her thoughts becoming accessible to Katherine as the young woman understood more of what Lilly had tried to convey months earlier. Katherine became oblivious to everything around her until suddenly Reverend Love's voice penetrated her concentration.

"The congregation is now requested to remember that this morning's Thanksgiving offering goes to St. Peter's Hospital," he announced as the elders distributed the offering baskets.

Katherine's eyes darted to the empty Cullen pew. They must have known the special offering was to be taken. The Cullens had such hopes for Lilly when she was at St. Peter's Hospital. She had such hopes. The offering plate was passed to Tom as he placed some money in it, and then he handed the plate to her, and she to her brother, and he to their father. Katherine leaned forward. Dr. Sligh also placed money in the plate as his face suddenly turned toward her. His eyes were sad; and suddenly Katherine remembered the raw hurt of Ernest's eyes on Halloween night. How much more would Lilly's own father feel when asked for such a simple thing as an offering to St. Peter's Hospital!

The congregation continued singing.

Katherine's mother had Thanksgiving dinner on the table and waiting by the time the family got home from church. It wasn't a big gathering. Bessie and her family were spending the holiday at the Davenports, and Carrie had decided to stay in Deer Lodge over the extended weekend. Nothing was said, but Katherine wondered if there was a man involved.

Dinner was conducted with all the civility appropriate to the occasion as Mrs. Sligh actually entered into conversation with Tom Marlow. He responded warmly and openly as he tried to gain her confidence. The mood improved as Katherine's brother added his youthful humor. Katherine glanced at her father. He smiled. Acceptance of Tom Marlow was finally coming about.

Mrs. Sligh finished her mince meat pie, and immediately rose from her chair, stacking empty plates on her own as she made her way out to their small kitchen.

"What's the hurry?" Dr. Sligh asked.

"Have you forgotten my whist club is meeting here tonight?" Mrs. Sligh replied. "I have a ton of things to do yet."

Dr. Sligh sighed heavily as he leaned back in his chair. His wife instantly removed his empty plate. "Katherine, do you and Tom have any plans for this afternoon?" Dr. Sligh asked.

"No."

Dr. Sligh turned to his son. "How about you?"

"I'd like to play whisk," Charles decided. "Mom, can I?" he called.

"Well maybe if someone doesn't show up," Mrs. Sligh answered from the kitchen.

"Finally," Charles exclaimed as he rose triumphantly from his chair. He ran for his room as his mother returned to remove the remains of the table.

"Katherine, something is on your mind," her father decided.

Katherine glanced at her mother. The woman left the room, and began scraping dishes. Her eyes returned to her father. "I know this isn't much like Thanksgiving, but I'd like to go out to the cemetery before the weather gets any colder."

"I don't see why not," he replied. He looked at Tom. "Any objections?"

"I can't think of any," he responded.

"Well it would get us out of the way," Dr. Sligh smiled. "Playing whisk on Thanksgiving -- I'm surprised anyone is actually coming."

"I haven't any flowers," Katherine realized.

"Not to worry," her father assured as he rose from his chair. He reached for the chrysanthemums in the center of the table. "I think these will do just fine. They always clear the table for whisk anyway. Get your coats."

Chapter Thirty-Two

The drive out to the cemetery was a brisk one despite the foot warmer in the bottom of the buggy, and the warm lap rugs. Snow dusted the landscape, and clouds threatened to bring more as the horses entered the cemetery gates. The gravel lane led them straight down to the Cullen plot. Katherine climbed out of the buggy as her father handed her the flowers. She came to a stop before Lilly's grave. Tom and her father joined her.

"They haven't changed the stone," Katherine stated.

"I imagine they've had some pretty steep expenses," Dr. Sligh replied.

"Maybe Puss was right," Katherine continued as she knelt to place her flowers at the bottom of the granite base.

"About what?" her father asked.

"About Lilly not getting her white marble tombstone. This granite base block is probably all she'll ever have."

Tom put his arm around Katherine, pulling her close as a soft smile emerged on his lips. "Don't loose hope. Some things just take time."

"But it's been months," Katherine lamented.

"Finding a good stonecutter can't be easy," Tom responded. "Look it's snowing."

For three days it snowed while all of Helena removed their carriage wheels and replaced them with runners. Jingle bells now dominated the city streets, warning pedestrians of on-coming traffic that might not otherwise be heard as the snow muffled the sound of the horses' hoofs and provided excellent slippage for the silent runners of the sleighs. Lawrence Street was closed, and sledding abounded as shops all around the city decorated their windows and interiors with evergreens and ribbons. Excitement grew in Katherine as she anticipated shopping. This year she would find something for Tom before Christmas, before the stores were picked over.

"Katherine, I'm off," her mother called from the doorway. "The Westside Whist club will be at Mrs. Sizer's. Your brother is going over to a friend's after school, but he should be home in time for supper. Your father won't be home until late."

"All right, mother," Katherine replied. She waited patiently for Mrs. Sligh to leave, and then hastened to her room, pulling her Christmas money from its hiding place. She had more than last year, a lot more, but she was saving the money Judge Cullen had given her for Tom. She had his Christmas, birthday, and a wedding gift to buy. Each should be special. Each should be perfect. But she also had a little money she had earned from Mrs. Osterhout, it would be enough to buy her family presents if she was frugal. She glanced out at their sitting room. Christmas would be cramped as usual, not like last year.

Katherine tucked her money in her handbag, picked up the Christmas greetings her mother wanted mailed, and grabbed her coat. She had three hours to herself, and she planned to make the most of them. Outside the sidewalks were clear of snow, and she headed down to Main, and then to Holter Hardware.

The display window on either side of the door held a Christmas tree with tools spilling from under the tree's branches on one side, and the latest in household items on the other. The store was bustling with people. Albert Holter raised his hand in greeting as Katherine entered. He was waiting on a customer as she brushed past several more. Katherine drew to a stop in front of the display case near the cash register. She was hoping to find a compass for her brother.

"May I help you, Miss," Mr. A.M. Holter asked.

Katherine smiled. She could see bits and pieces of all three of his sons in his face. "I would like to look at your compasses, please," she replied.

Mr. Holter opened the back of the display cabinet, and pulled out compasses from three different manufacturers. As he began to explain their differences, Norm appeared. He had a small crate in his hands.

"Dad, here's that order you were looking for." His eyes shifted to Katherine, and he smiled.

"Oh good," A.M. Holter exclaimed anxiously as he momentarily forgot Katherine. Then he turned back. "She was looking at compasses. Would you mind helping her, Norm?"

"My pleasure," he responded as his father headed to the back of the store. Norm quickly surveyed the items laying before Katherine. "That one," he pointed. "It's not as pretty as the others, but it's the most accurate."

"I didn't expect to see you here," Katherine commented as she examined Norm's choice. "I thought you would be tucked away in some office taking care of the journals."

"Not during Christmas rush."

"So how is Miss Jeffries?" Katherine asked as she slyly kept her eye on his expression. "You've been seeing her, haven't you?"

"Miss Jefferies?" Norm retorted. "No. I mean..."

"Florence seems very nice," Katherine continued as august Norm noticeably faltered, "and she obviously likes you."

"She likes me?" Norm repeated. "How do you know that?"

Katherine handed Norm the compass. "I'll take it," she stated.

"Oh yes, of course," he responded, a bit flustered. He took her money, and wrapped her purchase in a bit of brown paper. This he handed to her along with her change. "How do you know," he asked again, "about Miss Jefferies?"

"Katherine, I didn't know you were here," Addie Murphy called as she joined her friend. "What are you getting?"

"A compass for my brother," Katherine replied as she reluctantly turned from Norm. "You're out Christmas shopping too?"

"Oh no, I'm just picking up a new spool of twine. The clasp of one of our bags broke so mother is going to tie it shut. She swears she's going to buy a whole new set of luggage when we get to St. Louis."

"St. Louis, that's right, how soon are you leaving?" Katherine asked as she watched Norm turn to help another customer.

"We're taking the Monday night train," Addie answered.

"How long will you be gone?" Katherine asked

"Until spring. We're going on down to Jacksonville after the holidays."

"That long," Katherine groaned.

"It should be great," Addie replied. "Mother's promised us the best time."

"I'm sure," Katherine agreed.

"Oh don't worry, I'll be the one left at home this spring while you're off on your wedding trip," Addie giggled. "I would love to be in your shoes."

Katherine smiled. "I'd better get going. I've got more shopping to do. You and your sister have a good trip, okay?"

"Okay," Addie responded.

Katherine glanced quickly around for Norm as Addie headed for the household supplies. She spotted him helping a customer pick out the right size bolts. He pulled out one box after another, searching. Katherine went over, and as he bent over to pull yet another box from its shelf, she did the same. "It's her nervous smile," she whispered in his ear. "That's how I know."

He straightened as his eyes focused on her.

Katherine smiled. "I've got to go."

"She's a pretty one," Norm's customer commented. "You're one lucky fellow."

Norm turned back. "She's already engaged to my friend," he commented thoughtfully as he handed over a sample from the box. "Is that about the right size?"

By the time Katherine got home to start supper, she had only been able to obtain three of her gifts, the one for her brother, a smart pair of gloves for her sister, Bessie, and a great little book for her niece, Margaret. Katherine hurriedly stowed away her surprises, and headed for the kitchen as her mind lingered on all she'd seen.

Katherine had thought she would get Tom a set of gold cuff links or maybe even a watch chain, but she hadn't counted on finding a typewriter for sale. The P.O. News Stand had several in stock, and they fascinated her -- such modern expediency. The bank might have such machines at their disposal, but she would warrant Tom did not have one at home. The more she thought about the idea, the more she liked it; and it didn't hurt that the Williams typewriter had taken first prize at three different expositions. Modern technology was exciting, and she knew Tom Marlow loved it.

It was two full days before Katherine was able to return to her shopping. Household duties had increased tremendously with the approaching holidays. Katherine and her mother baked and decorated, and made the expected calls to their growing number of friends. When Katherine did return to her holiday shopping, the Williams typewriter was her first purchase -- however, getting it home was another matter. Too heavy to carry with her, the news stand promised to deliver it, but this poised another problem. Katherine didn't know if the Slighs were going to celebrate Christmas at home or at Bessie's. There was even talk of going over to the Davenport's. Katherine shuddered. She didn't want to give Tom his Christmas gift there, and she couldn't very well have it delivered to the bank. He'd think it was an office machine.

"Can you box and gift wrap it," Katherine asked at the News Stand, " and then hold it for me. I'm just not sure which address to have it delivered to, but I'll let you know by next week, okay?"

"That will be fine, Miss," the clerk responded.

The following Monday afternoon, Katherine's mother attended her whist club at Mrs. Hauser's while Katherine spent the afternoon putting whole walnuts on a loop of thread so she could paint them gold. The effort was time consuming and tedious as Katherine finally hung the last nut on her makeshift rack. Now at last she could gild them as ornaments for their Christmas tree. Katherine glanced out the window. The sun was low in the sky. She would have to hurry if she was to get done before her mother got home.

The clock chimed the three-quarter hour as Katherine glanced up. It was nearly six o'clock, and she still had four walnuts to paint, plus clean-up. She picked up another walnut as knocking came from the door. In frustration she laid aside her paint brush and went to answer it.

Tom stood outside. "I wanted to be sure you got this," he stated as he offered an invitation.

"What is it?" Katherine responded as she accepted the envelope. She promptly opened it.

"We assumed your family celebrated on Christmas morning."

"Yes," Katherine agreed. She looked up, puzzled. "The invitation is to the Ashbys for Christmas Eve."

"Yes, my aunt and cousins live with them. Didn't you know?" Tom replied.

"What about the Broadwater house down on Benton Avenue?" Katherine asked. "I thought they lived there."

"They did until my uncle died. Then Aunt Julia made some changes," Tom responded. "Accepting Mr. Ashby's offer to stay with them was one of them."

"Wilder lives in the Ashby mansion," Katherine exclaimed, "no wonder I saw her walking across from the Cullens so often. I just thought she was good friends with Phoebe."

"Can you come?" Tom pressed.

"Yes, yes of course," Katherine responded with a smile. "I'd love to."

"Good," he replied. "I can't stay. I just wanted to be sure this was settled. I'll pick you up on Christmas Eve right after the bank closes at four, all right?"

"Yes."

He smiled warmly, and left.

Katherine shut the door as her mind wandered to the Ashby house. It was a beautiful mansion, lacking in nothing. It would be a wonderful place to spend Christmas Eve, and she liked Mrs. Ashby. The woman had a certain practicality to her, a certain warmth. Other ladies in Helena were probably more refined in their airs, but she would never feel as comfortable with them.

The door flew open again as Mrs. Sligh rushed in. "Is Charles home?"

"Not yet," Katherine answered. She had just picked up her paint brush.

Mrs. Sligh came over and sat down at the table opposite her. "You won't believe what I just heard from Mrs. Allen."

"What?" Katherine replied.

"It seems that Mrs. Allen and Mrs. Kennett called on Mrs. Cullen," Mrs. Sligh reported.

Katherine's eyes lifted.

"Mrs. Cullen has quit the whist club. I know she hasn't attended since her daughter got sick last spring, but we all thought she would come back to us now that things are back to normal."

"I doubt she feels things will ever be normal again," Katherine responded.

"She's not the only one to loose a child," Mrs. Sligh retorted, "plenty of others have. She's just fortunate to have had her daughter so long. Many loose their children as babes in their arms. Anyway it's Christmas, and we thought with the holidays and all, she would want to get back into step with things. But she absolutely refused. Can you imagine! She wouldn't even talk about it."

"I can imagine," Katherine responded softly.

"Oh yes, I suppose you can," her mother continued. "You did stay with them an awfully lot. I don't see how you stood it so long. I'm so glad you're away from all that now."

Katherine said nothing as she carefully applied the gold paint to her walnut. Her heart was pounding, her muscles tense. Her mother was so flippant about Lilly's death. Katherine had never known anyone like Lilly, and honestly never expected to know anyone like her ever again. ...and the fact left a large emptiness within her.

"I've been invited to the Ashbys for Christmas Eve," Katherine announced as she desperately needed to change the subject.

"The Ashby's?" Mrs. Sligh's face turned in surprise. "Oh, you mean you're going to spend Christmas Eve with the Broadwaters. I thought for a moment you had secured an invitation to a party, and the Ashby's haven't thrown a proper one all year, not that they couldn't afford to. They're not hurting for money. Too bad their son is so much younger than you. Maybe you would have liked him. But the family is a difficult one, you would have your hands full with them."

Large flakes of snow were falling as Katherine headed to the street outside Oro Fino Terrace. A strong gust of wind slammed against her, and she faltered. Today was her last chance to shop, and she still had several people to buy for. She had taken care of the delivery of Tom's gift the preceding Friday, along with purchasing her gifts for the family. But there was now the question of taking gifts with her to the Broadwaters and the Ashbys, and she wanted to buy the Cullens something, at least Grace. The money for all this had bothered her all weekend, distracting her from everything, until her father had finally taken her aside and asked what the matter was. When she told him, he promptly reached for his bill fold.

"How much do you think you'll need?" Dr. Sligh asked.

"Daddy, I'm not asking for money," she responded.

"I know," he replied, "but you didn't ask for money when you bought your wedding gown either. I realize your mother has been slow in that regard, and I'm very proud of you for finding a way to go ahead with things." He pulled out several bills. "Here, buy what you need. We mustn't insult your future in-laws or their friends, and frankly, I still feel bad about Lilly. Do what you feel is right."

"Oh daddy," Katherine exclaimed as she instantly embraced him, "thank you."

The conversation had taken place shortly after church the day before, and now nothing would keep her from carrying out her objective. Katherine caught the street car and rode it down to the Sands Brothers where she would start her morning's shopping. She bumped into one acquaintance after another as she browsed through the merchandise, waited in line to pay for her purchases, and passed in the street. The atmosphere of the city was one of bustle and good cheer. Voices drifted into Katherine's hearing. Carolers were singing outside First National Bank as she hastened into Auerbach's men's shop. She wanted to get Charles Broadwater a wool neck scarf to wear to all the football games he liked to go to.

"May I help you Miss," the clerk inquired.

Katherine explained what she wanted, and the clerk helped her pick out a suitable item. The Ashby and the Broadwater gifts were now finished. But as Katherine re-emerged out into the icy weather, her eyes glanced up and down the street, searching for inspiration for her gift to the Cullens. Distant church bells announced the hour as she decided she would return to the Sands Brothers, and pick up a box of fancy wrapped pears she had seen there. This she would give to the family. Then all she needed was something for Grace.

By the time Katherine returned to the Sands Brothers, there were only two boxes of pears left. She picked out one, and immediately a lady snatched up the other. She had barely gotten there in time.

"Can you deliver this," Katherine asked as she paid for her purchase.

"Normally yes," the sales person responded, "but our deliveries are backed up so far that I can't promise it will get there in time."

"Then could you at least tie it securely with string," Katherine requested. The thought of carrying the heavy box along with her other packages didn't thrill her, but the string would make the awkward box a little easier to manage.

"Of course," the clerk responded.

Five minutes later, Katherine left the counter as she wandered past the jewelry counter. A beautiful moss agate ring caught her eye. She stopped, setting her box of pears on the counter as she slipped the ring onto her finger. It was snug as she realized that Grace's sapphire ring had fit the same way the one time she had tried it on. Katherine checked the price, and flagged a clerk. Her shopping was finally finished.

It was nearly six when Tom Marlow picked Katherine up Christmas Eve to take her to the Ashbys. Mrs. Sligh was in the kitchen preparing popcorn for decorating the tree as Katherine's sister poured cranberries into a bowl. Carrie had arrived that afternoon, and brought chocolates. Young Charles was already raiding them. Dr. Sligh helped Katherine on with her cloak, and gave his daughter a quick kiss.

"Enjoy yourself tonight," he urged with a smile.

"I will," Katherine promised, and turned to Tom. The two left the apartment.

Chapter Thirty-Three

The windows of the Ashby house glowed with warmth and activity as the cab drove up to the side door. Katherine and Tom were promptly ushered inside, and given warming drinks as they shed their wraps. The house was fresh with evergreen scent. Christmas greens and ribbons abounded everywhere, while candles chased away the winter gloom with their glowing effervescence. Katherine and Tom were led into the drawing room where an enormous fir tree dominated the room, decorated with candles and ornaments and garlands of snowberries.

"Tom, wait until you see the package that's under the tree for you," Wilder cried in excitement. "Phoebe says a delivery man brought it by on Saturday, and she had them leave it by the door. But when she went to take it in to the tree, it weighed a ton. She had to wait until Charles got home, so he could move it for her."

"A package for me," Tom Marlow questioned. "Who would send me a package here?"

"I don't know," Wilder continued, "but it's gift wrapped and everything." Her eyes danced with glee.

Tom now helped Katherine add her gifts to those already under the Christmas tree.

"Everything is so beautiful," Katherine commented as she surveyed the tree.

"Well it is one of the important times of year," Mrs. Ashby responded, "and we do try to make things festive."

Katherine reached to touch an ornament. "I've never seen one like this."

"Oh that," Mrs. Broadwater replied. "We got that little trinket this summer while we were in Europe. We have a miniature of the Eiffel Tower too. See?" She took the metallic ornament from the tree, and handed it to Katherine. "It's still all the rage you know, to see the Eiffel Tower, but personally I like London's Crystal Palace better. I always have. The Eiffel is too geometric, too rigid." She re-hung the ornament.

"It's that one," Wilder declared as she pointed out the heavy package to her cousin. "That's the one that weighs a ton, Tom. Try and lift it."

Tom Marlow reached for the package, humoring Wilder. "You're right, it does weigh a lot."

Christmas Eve dinner was served in the Ashby dining room, and frankly Katherine had never been invited to sit down to a meal of such eloquence. Five pieces of silverware rested on each side of the china, two more lay horizontally across the top. Three pieces of stemware waited in readiness to relieve her thirst. Everything sparkled in the candle light. Everything smelled wonderfully delicious.

Flat soup bowls waited atop each person's plate as a member of the house staff brought around the tureen, and served the soup amid lively conversation. Tom was talking with Charles and S C. Jr. about the recent football game in Butte, while Phoebe Ashby claimed Katherine's attention with talk of the latest fashion. Katherine watched which spoon Phoebe used for the soup, and followed suit.

Mrs. Ashby was now talking with Mrs. Broadwater and Mrs. Chumasero as they chatted about Europe. Everything they described was old and magnificent, and Katherine found herself fascinated by the conversation. Katherine's schoolbook knowledge was sparked into life, and she began to understand in some degree Lilly's enthusiasm for the ancients. Mrs. Ashby turned to momentarily help her young daughter, Gertrude, as her face disappeared behind one of the two elaborate candelabras festooned with greenery.

A six course meal followed. Katherine had never experienced anything quite so richly served. The wonder of the food, the warmth of conversation, the sheer eloquence of everything was unexpected to her, particularly when offered together. She had always secretly thought the rich tended to be greedy snobs, and true friendship belonged to the poor, but this proved otherwise. Mr. Ashby and his family believed in honesty, truth, and perseverance; and these ideals were credited to be the reasons behind all they had. The family had even taken in his mother and uncle in their old age, and tenderly looked after them until their death.

Katherine knew Mrs. Broadwater to be a kind person, and not just a little practical. Wilder was Wilder. Katherine loved her spirit. Her brother Charles had a bit of his mother's practicality in him. He was already gainfully employed in an assay office. Within an evening's time, Katherine got to know everyone better, including Tom Marlow. He was a gracious and accomplished guest. Katherine had never seen him in the presence of wealth.

As the family and guests of the Ashbys migrated into the drawing room, excitement boiled in the girls. Phoebe, Wilder, and especially Gertrude got caught up in the spirit of Christmas, distributing packages, laughing, teasing, and generally having a good time. Charles Broadwater tried to get his sister's attention, but Wilder's concentration was focused squarely on the box designated for her cousin.

"Tom, you've got to open the heavy one," she exclaimed.

"Oh do," Phoebe joined in. She turned to her brother. "Carry it over to him, will you? We have to see what it is." The portly gift landed at Tom Marlow's feet with a peculiar thud.

"Who is it from?" Wilder demanded.

"Probably someone at work," Tom replied as he detached the card. "They probably sent me a practical joke." He fell silent as he read the enclosure. His face turned to Katherine. "It's from you," he exclaimed quietly. His face was puzzled now, almost concerned.

"From Katherine," Wilder exclaimed. "I've got to see this." She came closer.

Tom removed the tie with his pen knife, and slit the wrapping paper. A wood box met his efforts. "Williams," Tom read, mystified. He pulled the lid off, and removed some packing.

"Bully," he exclaimed in utter surprise, "it's a typewriter."

"A typewriter, let me see," Charles exclaimed as he came over. "Wow, it is."

Tom lifted the machine from the crate and set it on the floor. His eyes were large, his touch appreciative. His attention turned to Katherine. "A typewriter...and a Williams. I saw this written up in the business journal we take down at the bank. It's won prizes at several expositions."

"I thought you might like it," Katherine responded. "I imagine you have a typewriter or two down at the bank, but this is for your personal use."

"The typewriters at the bank are utterly primitive compared with this," he stated as he suddenly kissed her in front of everyone.

Wilder instantly squealed as Tom looked up in surprise, and then realized what he'd done. A sheepish expression stole over his face.

Mrs. Broadwater now pointed under the tree, and Gertrude retrieved a package for her. This she handed to Katherine. "It's your turn," she stated softly.

"All right."

Charles threw a package at his sister. "Open it," he commanded.

"I want to see what Katherine gets first," Wilder exclaimed. Her face was all smiles and laughter as she now set to teasing her brother about the gift he was getting from her.

Katherine opened her gift from the Broadwaters. It was a beautiful batiste blouse with exquisite lace work. Katherine inhaled sharply in appreciation.

"Do you like it, dear?" Mrs. Broadwater asked.

"It's gorgeous," Katherine exclaimed.

"Oh good," Mrs. Broadwater responded. "I do hope it fits. But if it doesn't, I've already talked to my dressmaker, and she's agreed to make any adjustments necessary."

"Thank you," Katherine responded.

"We got it in Paris," Wilder offered as she tore open her package from Charles. "Ooh, Charles, your heavy old wool socks, how can I ever thank you," she responded facetiously.

He grinned. "They're just the packing. Look inside the top one."

"Ooh..." Wilder's tone changed instantly. Inside was a bottle of perfume. "Oh, Charles, thank you," Wilder exclaimed in delight. "I didn't think you even knew what I wanted."

"The whole world knew what you wanted," her brother retorted with a grin.

Wilder wrinkled her nose at him, but the delight in her eyes was obvious.

Similar excitement was exploding from the others. Phoebe had gotten her sister a necklace, and her parents were exchanging their gifts to one another.

Tom handed Katherine his gift as he smiled warmly. Then a slight nervousness entered his expression. "I hope you like it," he commented hopefully.

Katherine opened one end of the wrapping, pulling the long narrow box from the paper. She removed the lid. A strand of perfect pearls met her eyes, each one separated from it neighbor by a delicate knot, each one glowing in its natural luster.

"Oh Tom, how beautiful," she exclaimed, "my own pearls."

The anxiety left his face, and a smile returned. His dark eyes twinkled.

"Oh Katherine, thank you," Wilder exclaimed as she held up a dainty pair of ear rings. "I love them."

"Katherine thank you for the lovely broach," Mrs. Broadwater responded now. "It's such a nice practical gift."

Katherine turned. The words were a compliment.

Church bells began ringing in the distance as everyone gave pause. The sound was soft and vibrant as the bells resonated beautifully across the frozen outdoors, bringing together the thoughts of the whole city. It was Christmas.

The same bells rang the following morning as the Slighs left for church. They attended the early service so they could join the Davenport's afterwards for their Christmas morning celebration. Katherine tried every excuse possible to get out of the commitment, but to no avail. Even her father thought she should attend.

Bessie met them at the Davenport's front door, ushering them in, and guiding them into the parlor. Katherine looked around her. Nothing had changed since she had been at the house several years before for a baby shower on her sister. The same boring correctness prevailed, the same dull arrangement of the smallest items. Even the holiday decorations were in minor attendance, an evergreen arrangement on the breakfast table, a Christmas tree, nothing more. Katherine sank into the parlor couch as she watched the proceedings out of boredom. Bessie was trying to make a difference. Don didn't seem to realize anything was wrong. Little Margaret fiddled with one thing after another, making her mother nervous. Carrie tried to help Bessie raise holiday spirits while their mother became almost an attached appendage to Mrs. Davenport. Dr. Sligh was invited by Major Davenport into his smoking room along with Don, and so they removed themselves from the ladies until tree time. Katherine's thoughts returned to the evening before.

"You must really be in love to drift into daydreams here," Carrie commented as she sat down next to her sister.

"What else is there to do," Katherine asked.

"Climb the walls," Carrie responded quietly with a nervous chuckle. "How did two renegades like us become part of this family?"

"Bessie," Katherine replied, "and mother. They value things differently than we do, I guess."

"A lot differently," Carrie agreed. "So tell me about last night. Did Tom give you those pearls?"

Katherine made it through the tedious long morning only by sheer endurance. Her daydreams were her sole relief. By the time the Slighs actually left, the morning had become afternoon with just a couple of hours of light left. Katherine longed to be with Tom. If Lilly had been alive, she would have made sure they were together, finding an excuse to go sleighing or something, always in a group, always acceptable to her parents.

"The snow looks wonderful," Carrie commented. "Are there any sleds around?"

"I think there are a couple in the furnace room we could borrow," Charles offered.

"Really?" Carrie responded. "What do you think, Katie? Should we be wicked, and go sledding?"

"Yes," Katherine replied, "anything to get outside."

Carrie, Katherine, and Charles went sledding that afternoon, experiencing for themselves the thrill of the Lawrence Street hill. The fresh cold air, the speed of the sleds, and the laughter that sprung spontaneously from their lips as they glided out of control – all this did much to revive the life blood within them. By the time they got home for supper, their cheeks were red, their fingers numb, and smiles prevailed on their tired faces. Mrs. Sligh served hot soup to her children as conversation flowed natural and free between them.

The following afternoon, Dr. Sligh invited Katherine to accompany him to Montana National Bank where he would replenish his billfold from the holiday extravagances. She readily accepted.

"I won't be long if you want to see if Tom's in," Dr. Sligh offered as he got in line at the counter.

Katherine headed back to the offices.

"Miss Sligh, hello," Mr. Smith greeted with a smile. "I'm afraid Mr. Marlow hasn't returned from lunch. Is there anything I can do for you?"

"Just tell him I came by," Katherine requested.

"I will do that," Mr. Smith responded warmly.

By the time Katherine returned to her father, he was replacing his billfold in his suit jacket. "Tom wasn't in?" he asked.

"No."

"Maybe he took a late lunch," Dr. Sligh suggested as they walked out. At the street they nearly collided into Ella Hauser.

"Katherine, oh Katherine, I'm so glad I bumped into you," she cried as she pulled an invitation out of her handbag. "We're having a small dance party at the Kennetts tomorrow night, and I was really hoping you would come." Her eyes shifted to Dr. Sligh. "It's good to see you, sir."

"A dance party," Katherine repeated as she accepted the invitation. Her eyes drifted beyond Ella. Tom Marlow was returning to the bank.

"Please come, Katherine. I know it's short notice," Ella begged as she produced another envelope, "but I also have an invitation for..." Her voice fell off as Tom paused beside Katherine. "...for Mr. Marlow." She smiled, and handed it to Tom. "Will you bring Katherine?"

"I would like nothing better," he replied with a smile. "Thank you."

"Oh good," Ella responded as she turned again to Katherine. "I'll see you both tomorrow night then?"

"Yes," Katherine responded.

Ella turned momentarily to Dr. Sligh, and then hurried away.

"You've been to the bank?" Tom asked Katherine and her father.

"Yes," Katherine replied.

"Did you get everything taken care of Dr. Sligh?" Tom asked.

"Yes, but unfortunately I'm now running a bit late," he responded. "I'm afraid we have to be going."

Tom's eyes shifted to Katherine. "I'll pick you up tomorrow about seven."

Warm lights and Christmas decorations welcomed Katherine and Tom as they climbed the steps of the Kennett's stone porch. The house was a large, comfortable one, with granite block engulfing the basement and first floor, and wood shingles rising to protect the second and attic floors. The smell of Douglas fir and pine greeted the guests as they entered the house to mingle with their friends. Garlands festively draped the archways, mantels, and stairs as several adults scurried to join the company on the second floor. Miss Carpenter wandered over to Katherine and Tom.

"What's upstairs?" Katherine asked.

"Oh, it's a whist party for Miss Bonner's parents." She smiled. "The Bonners are from Missoula, you know, and the party is being given in their honor."

"Norm, it's good to see you," Tom responded as his friend also joined them. "How's Ed doing at Columbia?"

"Working hard," he responded with a smile. He turned to Miss Carpenter. "Would you like to dance?"

She accepted, and Tom Marlow and Katherine followed suit. The evening was passed enjoyably among friends. But as the hour grew late, Ella Hauser appeared at Katherine's side.

"Katherine, we have to talk," Ella pleaded as she drew Katherine out into the vacant kitchen. "I need your help," she continued. "I haven't seen Grace since the King reception, and we barely got to talk there. For a whole month I've been trying to figure out a way to see her, but she doesn't go out, and I can't go there. Please, you've got to talk to her for me. You've got to give her this letter." Ella pulled an envelope from her pocket.

"What do you want me to tell her?" Katherine asked as she accepted the envelope.

"Not to blame me, not to hate me for something I didn't do. Grace and I were best friends. I don't want to loose that. My father did everything in his power to help Lilly. Yes it went bad, but it wasn't our fault."

"They don't hate you," Katherine replied quietly.

"It feels like it," Ella retorted. "It feels like everyone does. I walk into a room and suddenly all the conversation dies. Everyone looks at me like I took out a gun and shot Lilly. I didn't. We didn't. We only tried to help."

Chapter Thirty-Four

"They don't hate you," Katherine repeated. "Mrs. Cullen told me so. It's just that their hurt is so deep. I think seeing you or your family brings everything back, makes the pain worse."

"What am I going to do?" Ella implored. "Grace is my best friend."

"I'm afraid there's probably not much you can do," Katherine replied quietly. "But I will give Grace your letter, and I will try and talk to her. I just wouldn't expect miracles."

"Thank you, Katherine. Thank you for trying."

Katherine showed up on the Cullen porch the following day. Puss opened the door as a large smile emerged on her face.

"Katherine," she exclaimed, "come in."

"Is Grace home?"

"Sure, upstairs. She's with mother," Puss replied.

Katherine glanced around her. "Where is everyone?"

"Daddy is down at the office," Puss explained.

"And I'm working in the library," Ernest offered as he appeared in the hall. "Hi."

"How is your mother?" Katherine asked.

"Sad. She's always sad any more," Puss replied.

"It's been four or five months," Katherine noted.

"I know," Ernest replied, "but I think mom blames herself. She thinks she should have been more devoted to her family."

"Is that why she no longer plays whist?" Katherine asked softly.

"You know about that," Ernest responded with a wane smile. He took Katherine's coat. "Yes, I suppose it is, but mom is wrong. If she were any more devoted to us, we wouldn't have lives, we'd just be an extension of hers."

"And Grace?"

"Grace blames herself for being in Europe when Lilly died," Puss replied. "She sits with mother for hours and hours."

"So what does your father think about it all," Katherine asked.

Ernest smiled softly. "He's concerned, really concerned. I think he'd like to take mom away, but with all the bills... I don't know. I think he's just coping the best way he can for now."

"Shall I go up to see Grace?" Katherine asked.

"No, we'll tell her you're down here," Ernest decided. "It will be good for Grace to get out of that room." He turned to Puss. "Come on, it may take both of us to pry her loose."

Brother and sister headed up, leaving Katherine alone. She wandered into the parlor as she took Ella's letter from her pocketbook. She sat down and waited, wishing there was something she could say or do to ease things in the house.

"Katherine." The voice was soft as Grace entered the parlor. She sat down opposite her friend.

"I was asked to give this to you," Katherine offered.

"What is it?" Grace asked.

"It's from Ella," Katherine answered.

"Ella?"

"She's afraid she's lost her best friend," Katherine responded quietly.

"She has," Grace replied.

"But why?"

"You know why," Grace responded.

"No, I don't."

"Katherine..." Grace's voice fell off as she stared at the envelope in her hand.

"Lilly wouldn't want this," Katherine stated.

"Lilly isn't here."

"But you are," Katherine objected. "You don't have to treat your best friend like this."

"My best friend... My best friend and her family promised to make Lilly well. She traveled across two whole states for that promise, and it wasn't easy for Lilly to travel as sick as she was, but she did...and for what?" Grace demanded. "The doctor wouldn't even see her, Katherine. Mom and dad had to take her across the Canadian border to find help. They had to leave the United States. What was wrong with the doctors in Tacoma? What was wrong with the doctors in Seattle, or Portland, or even San Francisco? No, they had to go clear to Victoria, B.C. Katherine, don't you understand? Sam Hauser has connections all over the country, but no one cared about Lilly."

"The Hausers must have, otherwise they wouldn't have gone to Victoria, they wouldn't have tried to get Lilly the best help they could," Katherine replied.

"But they failed, they made things worse," Grace retorted.

"Ella is your best friend," Katherine responded.

"It doesn't matter," Grace replied. "It doesn't matter what any of them were. Mother won't see them. It hurts her to see them. I won't hurt her. She's suffered enough."

"What about Ella?"

"Ella will just have to find a new best friend. I can't be that for her any more. Things have changed."

"Read the letter, Grace," Katherine coaxed.

Grace's eyes dropped to the envelope.

Katherine watched her friend. It was with dread Grace opened the letter and began reading it, and then slowly her expression softened, her eyes watered. Then suddenly Grace rose and threw the whole thing into the fire. Katherine's heart skipped a beat as she watched the flames lick the paper, turning more and more of the pages black.

"Why?" Katherine breathed. "Why can't you be her friend? Your mother wouldn't have to know."

"I would know," Grace replied. "I don't hate Ella. I just can't be her friend, not now, not any longer."

"Did you throw Lilly's letter into the fire too?" Katherine suddenly demanded.

Grace turned, her eyes piercing into Katherine. "How do you know about that?"

"She told me."

"Lilly told you she was writing me a letter?" Grace demanded.

"Yes."

Suddenly tears began flooding down Grace's face as she turned back to the fireplace, grabbing a fire iron, raking at Ella's letter, trying to pull it out. All she got were ashes. Sobs now broke from her.

"What did Lilly write?" Katherine asked gently as she knelt beside her.

"Just that she was going to die," Grace choked.

"Yes, she knew," Katherine confirmed. "Lilly knew that Sam Hauser and all his doctors held no miracles for her. She didn't blame them. Why should you?"

Grace's tear streaked face lifted, her eyes staring at Katherine. "I don't."

"Then why can't you be friends with Ella?"

"Because of mother," she answered.

"Don't tell her."

"Don't tell her?"

"She didn't forbid you to see the Hausers, did she?" Katherine asked.

"No."

"Then don't tell her. Just see Ella. Explain things. You've been too good of friends not to," Katherine pleaded.

"When?"

"Tonight," Katherine replied, "or now. Will you come?"

"Now?" Grace asked doubtfully.

"Yes." Katherine glanced up. Ernest had just returned downstairs, and was on his way to the library. Katherine rose to her feet. "Get your coat, Grace. We're going for a walk."

Together they headed outside. Five minutes brought them to the Hauser residence. Grace hesitated.

"Come on," Katherine encouraged as she took hold of Grace's arm. Grace followed Katherine meekly up the steps.

Tom Hauser answered the door. "Grace," he exclaimed, and instantly opened the door wider, "come in."

"Is Ella home?" Katherine asked.

"Yes, she's upstairs," the young man responded.

Mrs. Hauser appeared from the music room. "Grace, it's so good to see you. Hello, Katherine," she greeted with a hopeful smile. "Tom, get your sister."

Within moments, Ella was running down the stairs to them. She flashed a brief smile at Katherine, and then led Grace upstairs to her room.

Mrs. Hauser turned to Katherine. "Ella said she talked to you. Thank you, Katherine. At least you got those two to talk."

"I hope it goes all right," Katherine worried.

"What happens, happens," Mrs. Hauser responded. "At least you gave them a chance to straighten things out. That's more than I will ever have."

"I'm sorry," Katherine responded.

"I am too, dear," Mrs. Hauser replied quietly.

On Monday Mr. and Mrs. Will Wallace hosted a skating party at the Broadwater. The guests were taken out by streetcar in the early evening to find smooth ice and an exhilarating breeze. Electric lights illuminated the lake, and there was a warm cottage close at hand for warming up, or fixing a skate.

Tom finished strapping Katherine's skates on, and led her onto the ice. Every movement he made was graceful, never faltering, never looking awkward. It was such a contrast to the man's demeanor the first day Katherine met him at the bank. Then Tom had seemed so blunt, so ill at ease, so unsure of himself. But then he had just tripped over a child's toy, and been publicly humiliated by the child's mother. It could have happened to any one of the bank's customers. Men walked through the lobby all the time preoccupied by a newspaper or even their thoughts. Though in most cases, Katherine was reasonably sure the public humiliation would have gone the other way. Tom did have a soft heart when it came to children.

Katherine skated closer to her fiancé. She loved being with him, the way he held her hand, the way he smelled of vanilla. She would gladly follow him to the ends of the earth if that was what he wanted, but Tom Marlow loved Helena. He constantly spoke of the city's future and the city's potential. Katherine looked up. Ernest Cullen was skating straight for them.

"Katherine, Tom," Ernest greeted as he skid to a stop in front of them. His eyes focused on Katherine. "I don't know what you said to Grace on that walk of yours, but thank you. It really helped. Even dad has noticed."

A smile broke across Katherine's face. "I'm so glad."

"Even mom seems a little cheerier," Ernest offered.

"How is she these days?" Tom asked.

"Lonely, I think," Ernest responded. "She has all of us, but she always comments on how empty the house is." He smiled wanly. "Lilly was always around in one corner or another, usually with some book. I think mom half expects her to walk out of the shadows, and pick up life as it was before. I know I do."

"It must be hard," Tom noted.

"It is, especially for mom and Grace. I think they feel responsible somehow. I know it seems unlikely, but I think they do." Then he shrugged.

"I've dampened your spirits enough. You two have skating to enjoy. I just wanted to thank you, Kathcrine." With that, he skated off.

"So what did you say to Grace," Tom asked as they skated

"I took her to see Ella," Katherine answered quietly.

Tom slowed to a stop. "You did?"

"Yes."

"They've patched things up then?"

"From what Ernest says, it would seem that way," she responded. "I don't actually know. I wasn't in on the conversation."

The two began to skate again.

"You should probably know, Katherine," Tom began softly, "that the Cullens may not be with us much longer."

"What do you mean?" Katherine demanded as her pace slowed.

"The judge does a lot of work for the railroads, and that work is moving west. And with everything else that's happened... I just wouldn't be surprised if they moved."

"No," Katherine exclaimed, "no." She drew to a stop as she stared angrily at Tom. Then suddenly she skated off, away from him, along the edge of the bank as she circled the lake. She could hear him calling. She ignored him. It had been hard enough loosing Lilly, but now to loose the whole family... Katherine thoughts turned to Ella. She knew exactly how she felt.

Ernest was ahead of her, skating in a nonchalant manner, enjoying the freedom of being outdoors. Katherine spun in front of him, skidding to a stop, almost loosing her balance.

Ernest looked startled as he caught her.

"You can't move away from Helena," Katherine exclaimed. "I won't let you."

"Move? What are you talking about?" Ernest cried.

"Your law firm works for the railroads, don't they?"

"Yes, we always have," Ernest answered.

"And they're moving west. I don't want you to go with them," Katherine protested.

"We're not," Ernest responded.

"You're not?" Katherine repeated.

"No, not that I know of," he replied. "Dad would like to take mom away, I think, but that's not something we can do right now. We're still trying to get out from under the medical bills."

Relief flooded Katherine, and she suddenly embraced Ernest as his eyes lifted to Tom. He stood a short distance away, watching.

Then Katherine pulled back, and without a word, skated off. Tom Marlow fell in behind her as Ernest retreated to a nearby bench. He sat down in a state of confusion, watching as Katherine's pace began to slow. Tom eventually caught up with her, and then the two were in each other's arms. Ernest bent down, and took off his skates.

The Ball that was held at Electric Hall Thursday night was hosted by some of Helena's most prominent ladies in celebration of the leap year, and in the time honored custom of "the ladies' prerogative". The grand rout was not taken to so kindly, however, by various male individuals as they chafed against being deposited in some chair until rescued by another lady friend. A few made spasmodic efforts to usurp their old places, but were promptly frowned down; while others of meeker disposition were never left sitting long in their chairs. There was little doubt that the ladies enjoyed their wanton freedom from conventional bonds, tripping merrily across the floor unattended by escorts.

Katherine danced with Tom as she glanced at her mother. She was watching the activity with Mrs. Word. Both had been strong proponents in the creation of the event, but neither seemed to be too eager to approach any dance partner other than their own husbands. Katherine smiled to herself as Bessie went up to Judge DeWitt and asked him to dance. The judge accepted. Katherine glanced back at her mother. Mrs. Sligh was standing alone now, and looking toward Don Davenport. Katherine wondered if she would ask him to dance.

"Your mother's ball seems to be a success," Tom Marlow commented. "The turn out is large."

"Yes," Katherine agreed. Mrs. Sligh didn't ask Don to dance after all, but left him sitting. It wasn't until Carrie noticed that she went to her brother-in-law's rescue.

If her mother didn't feel comfortable asking men to dance, Katherine wondered, why had she supported the event? Mrs. Word didn't seem very fond of the whole idea, and Mrs. Power was nowhere to be seen. Why then? Katherine puzzled over the thought for some minutes, until one of the pink shaded light bulbs blinked momentarily over them. The electricity had fluctuated momentarily. It often did at Electric Hall. Tom was often employed downstairs during the dances the Board of Trade sponsored, making adjustments, checking fuses. But tonight wasn't his responsibility, it wasn't his dance. It was her mother's. Katherine glanced quickly at the woman. Was her mother competing with Tom Marlow?

The write up in Sunday's newspaper credited Thursday night's ball as a perfect success and a social glory, and Mrs. Sligh was pleased. It gave her ample conversation at her whist clubs the following week where she won two first place prizes; a silver knife, and a china cup and saucer. Her competitive spirit soared as she tried to get Katherine more involved in the game. Katherine was invited to Miss McConnell's card party on the evening of the thirteenth. But as this was the game of hearts, and not whist, Katherine found little relief from her mother's prodding until she attended the Foster Whist Club with Bessie on Thursday.

January became a month of whist parties, evening ice skating at the Broadwater, and regular visits from Tom as Katherine found diversion from her normal household routine. Then with the first of February, Tom Marlow's attentions turned exclusively to business. His partner C.J. McNamara was down from Big Sandy with his father. Two of C.J.'s nieces were at school at St. Vincent's, and their grandfather wanted to see them before he left for St. Paul. The girls were delighted to see members of their family, and spent two evenings with them. During the days, however, the McNamara men spent their working time with Tom. Katherine often joined them at dinner. She found Mr. McNamara, senior, to be a very forthright person.

"We leave for St. Paul on Thursday," the elder McNamara noted as he glanced at Tom.

"Your son is going with you?" Katherine asked.

"No, Tom is accompanying me to St. Paul," Mr. McNamara informed her. His eyes shifted to Marlow. "You haven't told her yet?"

"I told her I had a trip coming up," Tom responded as he turned to his fiancée. "I'll be gone about a month."

"A month?" Katherine exclaimed.

"Tom has a number of meetings scheduled," C.J. McNamara explained, "all the way from St. Paul to New York. He makes this trip regularly."

Katherine turned to Tom. Dread was quickly descending over her. "I thought you put the trip off until after the wedding."

"I considered it," he replied, "but the meetings were already scheduled, and Mr. McNamara has considerable sway in St. Paul. It's an opportunity I can't afford to miss. It could mean life or death to growth in Helena. We leave Thursday."

"Excuse me," Katherine quietly faltered as she rose from her chair. She left the table.

"Katherine..." Tom also rose from his chair, instantly loosing his air of command as he floundered in confusion.

"Go to her, son," Mr. McNamara, senior, encouraged.

Marlow glanced quickly from his elder to his partner, and then left the table. He caught up with Katherine at the cloak room.

"Katherine, be reasonable. I have to go," Tom Marlow pleaded.

She turned. "You said you were going to wait. How special do you think our wedding trip will be if you've just been to New York the month before? Did you really think I would just accept this because Mr. McNamara told me? Did you think I would be happy?"

"No, Katherine, I just didn't see how anything could change. I have to do this."

"And I have to leave," she replied as she acquired her cloak.

Chapter Thirty-Five

"Katherine, no, wait," Tom protested as he caught hold of her arm.

"I will not make a scene in the lobby of the Broadwater," Katherine stated quietly. Tom's hand slid off. "When you decide where you're taking me on our wedding trip, you let me know. I will not go to New York, not now."

Katherine walked briskly out as she wrapped her cloak around her. The ground was wet with melting snow, but the air felt balmy in comparison to the cold of the previous week. The streetcar siding was empty as Katherine sat down on a bench to wait. Her heart beat loudly in her breast. Her eyes kept clouding over with moisture. She pulled her hanky from her pocket.

"Katherine." Tom's voice was gentle as he sat down beside her. "I'm sorry."

Silence reigned for several moments.

"I should have talked it over with you, I guess. I just didn't see how it would change anything."

Katherine turned, her wet eyes glaring. "Anything and everything could have changed," she stated. "We could have been married yesterday."

"Yesterday," Tom gasped. "How?"

"By just doing it."

"No, your mother..."

"You're more worried about how my mother feels than me?" Katherine cried.

Tom stared at her.

"Maybe you should marry my mother," Katherine retorted in disdain.

"No, I want you," Tom replied quietly.

"Not enough," Katherine responded.

"Katherine, what do you want me to do," Tom suddenly exclaimed. "Tell me."

"I don't want you to leave me," Katherine replied as tears rose in her eyes.

Tom took her in his arms. "It's only for a month."

"A whole month of eternities," Katherine moaned.

"I know, love," Tom responded softly as he kissed the back of her head. "I know."

"Then why?" Katherine cried. "Why couldn't we marry so I could go with? Why?"

"Frankly, I didn't think it was an option," Tom admitted.

"Frankly, you didn't think to even ask me," Katherine retorted in tears.

"I'm sorry."

Again silence reigned.

"What do you want me to do?" Tom asked. "Mr. McNamara is counting on me."

"I don't know that there is anything that you can do now," Katherine responded miserably. "Reverend Love is out of town."

A heavy sigh escaped Tom. "I really have to go on this trip. It's good for the bank, and it's good for the city."

"Then I guess you will," Katherine responded as new tears flooded her eyes.

For ten minutes Tom held his sobbing fiancée in his arms. Then slowly the tears expired, and her eyes dried. The streetcar arrived shortly thereafter, and the two rode it back into town in near silence.

Thursday Tom Marlow and Mr. McNamara Sr. left for St. Paul. Katherine did not see them off. She was afraid she would make a scene. Instead, she climbed Mount Helena in the thawing February weather, and watched the train leave from there. It looked so small as it wound its way out of town and out of her life. It almost didn't seem possible that Tom could be on it.

But as Katherine hiked back into town, she knew it was true. She had thirty odd days to survive, and only twenty minutes had passed. She headed home. She had another whist club to attend that afternoon. She might as well. There was nothing else she wanted to do.

Sunday morning Katherine accompanied her family to church. Reverend Love was back from his short recess. Katherine smiled wanly to herself. The irony of his absence seemed like a melodramatic comment on life. Her eyes dropped from the pastor to Lilly's Bible. Katherine carried it regularly to church anymore, reading it throughout the service. It annoyed her mother to no end, but nothing was said. Mrs. Sligh didn't like to talk about anything that had to do with the dead.

The service finally concluded as everyone rose to leave. Katherine didn't join them. She had finally found a little diversion from her loneliness, and she wasn't going to give it up to wait for her family to finish with all their greetings. Katherine's attention returned to her reading.

The Cullens now filed down the aisle. Judge Cullen paused momentarily at Katherine's pew, and then proceeded on without a word. Katherine didn't notice. Grace sat down in the pew ahead. "Katherine," she called softly.

Katherine's concentration broke, and she looked up.

"I understand Tom is out of town. Why don't you come over? You could spend the day with us."

"I'd like that," Katherine responded as she finally closed Lilly's Bible. She rose, and joined the Cullens.

Katherine did not attend any whist parties that week, but spent her time with Grace, often staying overnight as they found their own distractions. Their families said little. Both had their own reasons for giving the young women a bit of freedom. Katherine and Grace attended the Sousa Concert on Monday evening, and then dared to visit Chinatown and walk through the colorful red remains of firecrackers that were left from the Chinese celebration. In some places they were two inches deep. Katherine and Grace even played a game or two of tennis with Ella Hauser during the week. The weather was nice.

Friday night Judge Cullen came home, and announced an upcoming trip to Spokane. His whole family was invited, and excitement ignited at the supper table. Katherine watched it all with increasing dread. Mrs. Cullen perked up at the news, Puss bubbled with excitement, Grace's eyes took on a twinkle, and only Ernest remained calm. His attention was on her.

Katherine shifted uncomfortably as Tom's warning came to mind.

"I'll stay here," Ernest decided aloud. "Someone has to look after things while you're gone."

"And Puss, don't you have tests next week at school?" her mother asked.

Judge Cullen's attention immediately shifted to his youngest daughter. "You haven't done as well this term. I think maybe you should stay home this trip."

"But daddy," Puss exclaimed, "I want to go."

"Maybe next time," Judge Cullen replied, "if your marks improve."

"But Lulu Bach has been helping me study during lunch, and my grades are improving."

"Maybe Puss can stay with the Bachs," Mrs. Cullen suggested. "Then they could study together more."

"Good idea," Judge Cullen agreed.

"Are you going to have many trips to Spokane," Katherine asked carefully.

"It's very possible," the judge smiled. "We leave Sunday night."

Katherine's heart sunk. Her eyes shifted to Ernest. Only he seemed to sense her dread.

As the others left the table in their excitement, Ernest remained. He now turned to Katherine. "How did you know?" he asked softly.

"Tom told me your father's been catering to his Spokane clients."

"Yes, he has," Ernest suddenly realized, "and by the looks of the family..." His eyes swung to her in shock. "I never dreamed... Tom's probably right. We will move."

Ernest's face paled, dread rising in his expression. Then his eyes returned to Katherine, and he saw her misery. Slowly a smile forced its way to his lips. "You'll hardly even miss us. You'll be too busy getting married, and having kids."

"I will miss your family," Katherine responded softly. "It won't be the same."

"Nothing in life ever stays the same," Ernest replied, "except love. I won't move if you don't want me to."

Katherine stared at him.

"I know you love Tom," Ernest confessed softly, "but I won't move if you don't want me to."

"I..." Katherine's voice fell off. She didn't know what to say.

"It's okay," Ernest responded quickly. "You don't have to say anything." He got up and left the room.

When Katherine got home that evening, her mother handed her eight letters. "You've been gone so much this week, I haven't had a chance to give these to you," she commented. "I suppose Tom's wondering why you haven't written back."

Katherine thumbed through her mail. The return address had chanced three times. "You could have left them where I would see them," Katherine responded.

"I never thought of that," Mrs. Sligh replied, and disappeared into the kitchen.

Katherine headed for her room, and closed the door. With trembling fingers, she ripped the top envelope open and read the letter; and then the next one; and the next. By the time she had read all eight, it was getting late. She pulled out her stationery anyway, and started to write. She had wanted to all week, but she didn't have an address. Tom told her he would mail it to her. Katherine wrote a lengthy letter, and signed off just as the kerosene in her lamp gave out. She would have to address the letter in the morning.

The following day Katherine found another surprise waiting. Her mother had set aside the whole day to start planning her upcoming wedding. By dinner they had traipsed the streets of Helena, talking to people and learning what exactly was involved in staging a stupendous affair. Mrs. Sligh wanted Katherine's wedding to be the social event of the year.

By the time they got home, Katherine had more to write to Tom. Her mother was as much the subject as the wedding plans. How could she endure it all, Katherine wondered. There were so many decisions to make, so many details to look after, so many people to invite. Suddenly Katherine broke into a tired chuckle. Lilly would have thought the whole thing was silly.

For the next week, Katherine and her mother planned the wedding, choosing bridesmaids, picking out colors and ribbons and flowers and food, and consulting with Reverend Love. Katherine viewed the man a little differently now. He could have saved her from all this folderol. She could be in New York with Tom at this very moment. But no one knew, no one suspected what she would have done, given the chance. So she played the kind, obliging, gracious role everyone expected. At least all the preparations were for her wedding with Tom. She hardly noticed that the season of Lent had begun on Lilly's birthday.

"What are you giving up for Lent," Bessie asked as she ate lunch with Katherine and their mother.

"We've been so busy, I doubt she's even given it a thought," Mrs. Sligh responded pleasantly.

"I'm giving up chocolate," Bessie decided.

"That sounds like a good idea, Katherine," Mrs. Sligh replied.

"What about it, Katie," Bessie asked. "Would you like to give up chocolate too? We could be miserable together."

"All right," Katherine replied. Her thoughts were elsewhere. Lilly had given up sweet things the year before. She couldn't believe that an entire year had already gone by.

Wedding arrangements ran Katherine's life as she wondered what to get Tom for his birthday. March 9th was approaching, and he would be home soon. Katherine couldn't wait. In the meantime, though, she wanted to get his birthday present and a gift for their wedding. This she had to accomplish in and around her mother's demanding schedule.

Katherine broke away early Monday afternoon, and headed downtown alone. She was in a quandary over Tom's birthday present. She really didn't know what to get him, and she was worried about the expense. The typewriter at Christmas had been expensive, and she didn't want to skimp on his wedding gift. That made the choice of his birthday present that much more difficult. Whatever she chose had to be quality and economically priced, a challenge in any situation.

Katherine haunted the streets of Helena, searching for ideas. She stopped at three different jewelry stores and priced possible wedding gifts, but this was only possible if she bought a very reasonably priced birthday present. Katherine turned in at the Sands Brothers and wandered about in her dilemma. They had a table of sweaters on a clearance sale. Katherine stopped. The price and the quality was good. She picked out a dark lambs wool as she considered the size. It looked like it would fit Tom comfortably. She hesitated. Sweaters made excellent winter gifts, but this was spring. Still there would be plenty of occasions to wear a sweater as coats were stowed away for the warmer weather. Katherine took the sweater to the sales counter.

Nearly everyday Katherine received a letter from Tom, and every evening she wrote back, posting it in the morning. However once her fiancé was finally on his way home, she stopped writing. She again had no address to send to. He had stopped writing as well, but Katherine was still receiving the letters he'd sent before his departure. Then the last one came on Thursday, and he told Katherine he would be on the four-thirty train.

A squeal of delight exploded from the young woman as she danced merrily out and announced the news to her mother.

"Settle down, Katherine," her mother scolded. "We have a lot to get done before then. Have you decided on the flowers for your wedding bouquet?"

"I don't care," Katherine responded in total bliss. "It doesn't matter."

"Of course it matters," Mrs. Sligh retorted. "Do you think you can get your head out of the clouds for a couple more hours at least? We have an appointment with the dressmaker to go over the gowns she's making up. You know Carrie hates anything too tight."

"Of course, mother," Katherine responded cheerfully.

At four o'clock Katherine was at the depot, waiting for Tom's train. At four thirty she was impatiently waiting. At five o'clock she was pacing the floor. At five minutes after five, a train finally arrived, but it was not Tom's. Five minutes later another train pulled in, but no Tom. Then at twenty minutes past the hour the right train pulled into the depot.

Katherine was instantly outside, waiting, searching for her fiancé. She spotted him emerging from a door, three cars down. She broke into a run, dodging the flow of passengers disembarking from the train until she was suddenly in his arms.

"Katherine," he responded happily.

She made no response as her throat choked within her, and tears welled in her eyes. She would not let go.

"Katherine, it's all right. I'm home," he responded. He pulled her back so he could look into her face. Tears of joy were streaming down her face. He smiled happily as he kissed her wet cheeks.

"I brought you something," he offered as he now put his arm around her shoulder and started inside.

"I don't want it. I just want you," she responded. "Never, never leave me behind again."

As they walked through the doors, Tom pulled his fiancée over behind a loaded baggage cart. There he kissed Katherine with all the passion that had built up over the past month. She responded in total bliss.

Tom pulled away as the squeaky wheels of the baggage cart began to move. His finger rose into the air, warning Katherine not to follow her passion. Then he smiled, and wrapped his arm around her again.

"Let me get my luggage, and then we'll get out of here," he promised. "Where are your folks?"

"Mother's probably at the dressmaker's, and daddy is down in Philipsburg. He left Helena as soon as the legislature closed for the term."

"Like last year," Tom noted. "Only last year your mother went with."

"She says she doesn't like pulling Charles out of school, but she likes Helena."

"More than your father, evidentially," Tom replied.

"Tom, be good," Katherine laughed as she hit him lightly with her hand.

Tom pulled his bags from the claim area, and made arrangements to have them dropped off at his rooms. Then he and Katherine walked outside. But instead of catching the streetcar for home, Tom caught a cab and had it drive them out to a location a few blocks west of the Esler house. There they got out, and the cab drove away.

"What are we doing here," Katherine asked, puzzled.

"This is the new addition to town," Tom responded. "I've just secured the necessary capitol to underwrite the whole thing. It's going to be the 'new' neighborhood." He smiled proudly, and pointed out the boundaries as they walked. "So where would you like your house, Mrs. Marlow," Tom asked.

"Anywhere," Katherine responded. "It doesn't matter."

"Doesn't matter?" Tom repeated.

"Everything is changing. You were right. The Cullens are moving."

"They are?" he responded as he slowed to a stop. "It's settled then?"

"They haven't said anything, but it doesn't matter. They're moving."

"How do you know?" Tom asked.

"They made a trip to Spokane while you were gone. The judge announced it at dinner. I was there. I saw their faces. They're moving."

"I'm sorry," Tom responded as he took her into his arms.

"So am I," Katherine replied as she buried her face in his coat.

For nearly a week, Tom and Katherine were nearly in-separable, parted only by the demands of the bank. During these times, Mrs. Sligh claimed as much of her daughter's attention as possible, but Katherine would escape at the earliest opportunity.

Tom Marlow's birthday was held at the Ashbys on Monday evening. The Sligh and the Broadwaters were in attendance. Tom liked his sweater, more for the giver than the gift. He received various other gifts as well, but nothing surprising or notable.

Wednesday evening Tom took Katherine to the Concordia Band concert at the Opera House. It was the fourth in a series of concerts, and was credited with steady improvement. Tom and Katherine hardly noticed. All their attention was on each other. Afterwards, Tom showed Katherine through the non-public areas of the theater, finding ample opportunities for stolen kisses. They simply could not get enough of each other.

By the time Katherine got home from the theater, her mother was waiting up. Katherine ignored the woman until Mrs. Sligh blocked her path. "Katherine Sinclair Sligh, I want some answers. You've been running around all week like you haven't a care in the world. You're never here for meals. You don't care about the appointments I've made for you. It's embarrassing. ...and you've gained weight. You probably won't even fit into that wedding dress you made, even with all the corsets in the world. Are you even regular?"

"I don't care," Katherine responded.

"Well, I do," her mother retorted. "Either you come to time, or I'll send a wire to your father. Do you understand me, girl?"

"Yes, mother," Katherine responded slowly.

"All right then, you can start by purging your body and your mind of all this silliness. Then go to bed. I want you up at a decent hour in the morning."

"Yes, mother," Katherine replied.

As the elder woman left the room, Katherine stared after her, her bliss fading rapidly. Her mother was angry, angrier than she had seen her in years. Katherine took off her cloak as she thought about her transgressions. She hadn't given much thought to her health lately, and she had gained weight.

She opened the closet door, and fingered her wedding dress.   Maybe irregularity was the problem.

    Katherine rose bright and early the following morning, and devoted her attention to her mother's demands. She couldn't see Tom until the lunch hour, so Katherine was free to concentrate on alleviating her mother's mood. They spent the morning at Bessie's as they tied ribbons for the wedding.

    "Katherine, you're awfully quiet," Bessie noted as she passed a dish of pastries to her sister.

    "Don't do that," Mrs. Sligh objected. "She's barely going to fit into her gown the way it is."

    "Don't worry, mother," Katherine replied. "I'm not hungry."

    "Well that's a switch," Mrs. Sligh responded.

    "You look a little pale," Bessie noted. "Are you feeling all right?"

    "My stomach is a bit queasy," Katherine answered. "It's probably nothing."

    "You're probably coming down with la grippe or maybe a case of influenza," her mother decided. "I told you that you've been running around too wild. You haven't even been wearing your coat half the time."

    At twelve o'clock, Katherine showed up at Montana National and sat outside Tom's office as she waited for him to finish with a meeting. Her stomach had not improved, and as she waited it gnawed at her. Then suddenly Tom emerged. His attention shifted immediately to her as his customer was re-directed to another member of the bank.

    "Katherine, you look pale. What's wrong?" Tom asked.

Chapter Thirty-Six

"I think I must be coming down with the flu," she responded. "I think I would like to skip lunch. Mother doesn't think I'll fit into my wedding dress anyway."

Tom smiled. "We have been living a bit high on the town. How about if I see you home?"

"I would appreciate it," Katherine replied.

To Mrs. Sligh consternation, Tom and Katherine did not see any less of each other despite Katherine's growing discomfort. He spent the evening with her, and came by on his way to the bank the following morning. Katherine's stomach ache was progressing into a real illness. She now carried a mild fever, and was constantly nauseous with occasional sharp, colic-like pains.

Then after a bad afternoon on Friday, Katherine's symptoms suddenly faded. In addition, she no longer had to worry about fitting into her wedding dress. She had lost more weight than she had gained.

Tom again spent the evening with Katherine as Mrs. Sligh occupied herself in the kitchen. Young Charles left to participate in a sports event at school.

"Where are we going on our honeymoon?" Katherine asked as she set her plate aside. She still didn't have much appetite.

A smile grew on Tom's face. "How about San Diego? It's warm there. Would you like to visit California?"

"California... Would we see the Pacific Ocean?" Katherine asked.

"The Hotel del Coronado sits on the beach across the bay from the port."

"I love the beach," Katherine responded. "We could hunt for shells."

"And get wet," Tom laughed.

"And maybe even build a sand castle, or at least get the stuff between our toes," she added. "The beaches are sandy, aren't they?"

"I think so," he replied.

A smile grew in Katherine's face as she stared into Tom's dark, loving eyes. His hand reached to caress her cheek, and then they kissed as dishes rattled in the kitchen. Their passion grew. Deeper and deeper the kiss became as their desire exploded. Suddenly Katherine pulled back in pain. Tom's surprise was mixed with concern.

"What's wrong?" he demanded.

"It hurts," Katherine replied as her eyes watered. "My stomach..."

"Shall I get your mother?"

"No... No, it's all right now," she replied, a little shaken.

"Perhaps you'd better rest," he advised quietly.

The next day when Tom arrived to see Katherine, he expected to find her feeling better, but her fever had returned along with a general state of misery.

She wasn't feeling well, and she looked it. Repeatedly, Tom asked Mrs. Sligh if he should wire her husband. Repeatedly she discouraged it. She and the doctor had had words before he left for Granite County, and Katherine's condition was nothing more than a stubborn little flu bug.

Tom never left Katherine's side as she progressively got worse. With all the illnesses Katherine had endured in her life, this one worried her. It was no longer just her stomach that felt sick. It was her whole abdomen. She felt like Lilly had looked. Her torso muscles were rigid and prone to spasm. It hurt to touch her stomach. – and with ghastly horror, Katherine suddenly realized she had had an enema.

"What is it, Katherine?" Tom asked as Katherine's eyes opened wide.

"Appendicitis," she breathed, "Lilly's appendicitis. I've got the same symptoms."

"Appendicitis isn't contagious," he replied. "Besides, it's been too long. You've just got a bad flu."

Katherine's attention left Tom as her mind went over and over her memories of Lilly's suffering. There were differences, but there were similarities too. "I need my father," Katherine stated.

"I've already offered to wire him. Your mother doesn't think it's necessary," Tom replied. "Do you want me to send for him anyway?"

"No, wait," Katherine replied as she now threw back her covers. With determination she began probing over her appendix like Dr. Dean had shown her once. Her expression became extremely taunt and her eyes filled with tears, but she continued. Then she suddenly fell back against the bed in relief.

"Katherine?" Tom inquired anxiously.

"It's all right. My appendix is not swollen," she replied quietly. A weak smile rose to her lips. "It probably is just a nasty flu."

She curled up to get some rest as Tom watched anxiously.

The following morning Mrs. Sligh checked on her daughter as she commented about Katherine's carelessness during the past week. Tom said nothing as he sat with his fiancée. He had fallen asleep in the chair, and spent the night. Mrs. Sligh departed for church, leaving her son behind. Katherine spent most the time sleeping, occasionally asking for a bite to eat, or a drink of water. The quantity was always extremely small. Concern was rising in Tom Marlow. Katherine's color did not look good; and he decided that just as soon as Mrs. Sligh got home from church, he was going to wire Dr. Sligh.

Katherine woke to the ringing of church bells. It was followed by the long blast of a train whistle. Her memory reverted to Lilly. She had mentioned these things. Katherine turned her head. Tom Marlow sat with her. Katherine, at least, was not alone.

A sharp pain now stabbed her left arm as Katherine suddenly winced. She tried to sit up as breathlessness nearly suffocated her. Tom was in front of her now, but his image was a blur, his shouting inarticulate. Katherine gasped for air as she fell limp against the bed.

"Katherine... What's happening?" Mrs. Sligh cried frantically as she pushed Tom out of the way. Katherine's brother stood hesitant in the door.

"It looks like a heart attack," Tom decided.

Mrs. Sligh suddenly turned to him. Her face was pale. "Wire Dr. Sligh." Tom ran from the room.

When Katherine came to she felt exhausted and weak. Both her mother and her brother, Charles, were bent over her in concern. "What happened?" Katherine asked weakly.

"We think you had a heart attack," Mrs. Sligh worried.

"Is daddy coming?" Katherine asked.

"Yes, dear. He's on his way," her mother answered.

Katherine smiled slightly, and closed her eyes again. Sleep set in.

When she woke again, Tom and her mother both sat in her room. Heavy concern rested in their faces. But Katherine didn't notice, she felt awful. Turning her head away, her thoughts drifted slowly and aimlessly. Her father was too far away. He wouldn't get there until the following day.

Within the hour Bessie arrived with her mother-in- law and their doctor. Forced to submit to the man's examination, Katherine asked what was wrong with her. The doctor smiled and claimed she was suffering from a bad case of indigestion. Anger swept her. She knew when she was being patronized.

When the doctor noticed her agitation, he promptly withdrew. A discussion followed in the next room, and Katherine could only guess at what was said.

Then after a few minutes Tom returned alone to her bedside. He smiled as he sat down. "How are you feeling? Any worse?"

"No," Katherine replied. "What's going on?"

"Oh Mrs. Davenport's doctor is trying to prescribe some medicine for you, but a telegraph just came in from your father recommending something else. I think the Davenports are leaving."

"Good," Katherine sighed in relief.

By evening, Katherine felt a little better. The medicine had helped. Now Tom and her mother both sat with her.

"Bessie said she'd come back by and see how you're doing in the morning," Mrs. Sligh offered as she noticed Katherine's wakefulness.

"What about Carrie?" Katherine asked.

"We've already wired her," Tom replied.

"Then the attack was serious," Katherine responded.

"Heart attacks are always serious," her mother stated.

"But if you're over the worst of your flu," Tom offered encouragingly, "your heart should have progressively less to complain about." He smiled.

"I don't have the flu," Katherine replied quietly. "I don't think I ever did."

"Of course you do," her mother retorted. "What else could it be?"

Katherine's eyes swung to Tom.

"Well yes, I suppose you could have gotten some bad food along the way," Mrs. Sligh decided. "It's not like you were ever home for meals last week."

"Katherine and I ate the same things," Tom replied. "I'm not sick."

Mrs. Sligh just rolled her eyes, and turned her attention back to her fancy work.

"Lilly Cullen had some of the same symptoms I do," Katherine stated now with a calculated coolness.

Her mother's attention flashed momentarily to her daughter, and then she rose to her feet. "I need some other thread," she decided, and left the room.

Katherine smiled to herself. Her mother hated talking about the dead girl.

"Lilly never had a heart attack," Tom responded softly.

"Maybe she never had diphtheria, or at least not as hard as I did," Katherine replied as her eyes returned to him.

Tom fell gravely silent. Lilly never got well. The thought frightened him.

"Would you keep Lilly's Bible for me?" Katherine asked now. "Mother hates it. I don't want her to throw it out in some fit of temper." She pointed to where it rested on the shelf.

Tom rose to his feet, and thoughtfully retrieved the Bible, fondly adjusting the slightly protruding picture. "She was always the last one out of the pews Sunday mornings," he noted softly as he put it with his coat.

Tom returned to Katherine. "You've got to get well."

"I am trying," she responded softly.

"We have our whole lives to look forward to," Tom told her. "You have to fight this, Katherine."

"And will you hate me if in the end I don't prove strong enough?" she asked.

"I could never hate you," he responded in surprise. "I love you."

"I love you too. I want to be your wife, and have your children, and grow old with you," Katherine told him. "But it might not happen. Life is so unpredictable. I could die."

"No," he declared, "no."

"Open your eyes, Tom. I'm getting worse, not better. Unless daddy has some miracle up his sleeve, it doesn't look good. ...and I don't want to linger like Lilly."

Tom stared at her in profound silence.

"I'm sorry, Tom," Katherine stated softly. "I never intended... I always thought..."

"Shh," he told her as he took her gently in his arms. "You're going to get well."

"No," she replied quietly, "not this time. Tom, you have to know. You have to understand that I'm not just giving up. You have to understand that sometimes death won't be refused."

Tom stared down into her eyes, his expression heavy with worry.

"Tom, it's not the end, you know. It's just change. ...and whatever heaven is like, Lilly is better off there, as I will be, as you will be...someday. Then we will all be together again."

"Shh, Katherine," he muttered softly. "I don't want you to change, just to get well."

During the night and into the following day, Katherine's misery increased. Her fever rose, her pulse quickened, and nausea and pain became her constant companions. She would not eat; she moved only in agony; and she suffered.

Tom was beside himself, cradling her head in his lap while Mrs. Sligh fussed and fumed over her husband's absence. Bessie was in and out most of the day until finally she had a long and serious discussion with her mother late in afternoon. Crying broke out. Bessie had evidently learned the truth from Mrs. Davenport's doctor, and Mrs. Sligh could no longer deny the facts.

Dr. Sligh arrived home, took one look at the women's tears, and headed for Katherine's bedroom. He found his daughter curled against her fiancé, her head laying in his lap. Her face was pale; her shoulders trembled; her breathing was shallow.

Tom Marlow looked up. "Help her, please," he begged.

Dr. Sligh took his stethoscope from his medical bag, and began examining his daughter. As he did, his concern only deepened.

"Katie, have you eaten any fish lately?" he asked. "Could you have accidentally swallowed a bone?"

Katherine's eyes rose, but she made no reply.

"No fish," Tom answered for her.

"Did she eat anything that might have been sharp? Maybe something with seeds," Dr. Sligh pleaded.

"No," Tom answered. "She ate mostly meat and potatoes, and a few pastries."

"It's appendicitis, isn't it?" Katherine asked quietly.

Her father's eyes fell to her. "No, it appears to be peritonitis."

"What is that?" Katherine asked.

He hesitated.

"I am not a patient. I'm your daughter," Katherine asserted with effort. "I want the facts."

Dr. Sligh pulled the chair over to the bed, and sat down. "Peritonitis is the inflammation of the membrane that holds your internal organs in place."

"How does it get infected," she demanded.

"You had a stomach ache?" her father inquired.

"Yes."

"Where?" he asked.

"Near my right hip," Katherine replied as her pulse raced." She paused breathlessly. "I'm right, aren't I? It is appendicitis."

"We don't know that," Dr. Sligh responded.

"Can you cure peritonitis?" Tom asked.

Dr. Sligh's attention shifted. Profound dread rested in his expression. Katherine's father made no attempt to answer.

"What about surgery?" Tom asked.

"It's of no use in peritonitis," Dr. Sligh responded.

"But..." Tom's voice fell off. Dr. Sligh held no miracles.

Dr. Sligh's attention returned to his daughter. She looked exhausted as she endured the misery. Dr. Sligh took some medicine from his bag, and helped Katherine take it. She promptly began to relax, and then fell asleep.

"How long does she have?" Tom asked.

"Maybe twenty-four hours," Dr. Sligh replied in a still voice.

As Katherine slept, Dr. Sligh left the room, closing the door quietly behind him. He was met by Bessie and his wife.

"Well?" Mrs. Sligh demanded.

Doctor Sligh just shook his head sadly.

"No," Katherine's mother shrieked as her hands rose to cover her face. Tears sprung from her eyes, and she ran from the room.

"I tried to tell her," Bessie replied miserably. "Mother Davenport had our physician examine Katie yesterday."

"How much time did he give her?" Dr. Sligh asked.

"With her heart condition, only a day or so," Bessie answered quietly.

"Has anyone notified Carrie and Lila?" Katherine's father asked.

"We sent a telegram. I hope Carrie makes it in time."

Tom Marlow tenderly stroked Katherine's hair as his eyes watered. She was sleeping peacefully now, almost as if her illness wasn't real. He longed for her health, for the days they had shared, regretting his trip east, regretting the loss of that month's time he could have shared with her. He bit his lip as he thought over what she had said to him the previous day. She, like Lilly, already knew the truth. Katherine was dying. The thought cut him like a knife. Tom could even taste the blood, and then he realized his lip was bleeding. He wiped it carelessly with the back of his hand as his eyes burned with tears.

Katherine's condition worsened, her consciousness impaired by the laudanum her father gave her. Katherine drifted in and out of a dream-like sleep. When she came to, Tom and one family member or another was always sitting with her. Occasionally Katherine's breath choked within her as she fought to maintain consciousness. Each time she managed to rally, but only as more and more of her strength was depleted.

"Tom," Katherine whispered. Her father rose from his chair and left the room. His daughter didn't have much time left, and Katherine would want some private words with her fiancé.

"I'm here," Tom offered with a gentle kiss.

"Tom, what day is it?" Katherine asked groggily.

"Tuesday. It's nearly five o'clock."

"Tuesday," she repeated quietly, "not even a week." She swallowed hard. "Tom, you have to do something for me."

"Anything," he responded.

"Make sure Lilly gets her stone. Make sure she gets her white marble," Katherine begged. "The name block is not enough." Her voice fell off as she gasped for breath. "I can't imagine going through this if she hadn't... She tried to tell me, Tom. She tried."

"I'll see she gets her white marble," Tom responded.

Katherine reached for his hand, pressing it trembling to her lips. "Lilly's gone ahead. Now it's my turn." She smiled bravely up at him; and then her eyes fell shut, her hand fell softly away.

"No," Tom screamed as panic swept him. He took Katherine forcibly into his arms, clutching her to him as he sought some sign of life. Over and over he kissed her, desperately looking, searching for some spark of life. But Katherine did not respond. She did not breath.

"Don't go," Tom whispered hoarsely as tears flooded his desperate eyes. "I love you."

Profound stillness answered him.

Katherine Sinclair Sligh was laid to rest in a pale lavender coffin covered with flowers. Some said she looked like a creature fresh from the hand of God, not one that had lived and suffered death. She appeared rather to be calmly sleeping, Tom's picture clutched to her heart. Bishop Brewer and Reverend Love paid high tribute to her many virtues and sterling qualities at the burial service provided by St. Peter's Episcopal Church. Katherine was buried in Forestvale Cemetery on Friday, the twentieth of March, 1896. She was twenty years old.

Epilogue

For over a hundred years Katherine and Lilly have laid buried in Forestvale Cemetery. Each has a white marble statue at their head. Katherine sits in calm repose holding a garland of flowers while Lilly stands upon her granite base a discreet distance away, within sight and with book in hand. Lilly's grandmother has a sandstone tree trunk at the head of her grave. Behind Katherine, Tom Marlow's remains lie near his wife, Louise. It took him ten years to marry.

The Slighs went home to Granite County where Dr. Sligh resumed the medical practice he was building in Philipsburg. He did not return to the state legislature the following session. Judge and Mrs. Cullen left town with Grace four days after Katherine's funeral, and by 1899 had moved to Spokane, Washington. Ernest lingered behind, not making the move until 1907. Norman Holter traveled to New York in June, sailing for Europe with his brother, Ed. Norm did not return to Helena until September. Edwin Holter graduated from Columbia Law School in 1897, and volunteered in 1898 for the Spanish American War where he was appointed aide de camp for Brigadier General Aimes. Thereafter, he took up residence in New York, marrying Sarah Sage in 1903. Norman Holter married Florence Jefferies of Helena.

Pictures of the following people may be
seen in the Montana Historical Society's
Photographic Archives:

Dr. James Sligh
Judge W.E. Cullen
Mrs. W.E. Cullen
Violet Cullen
Ernest Cullen
Major and Mrs. William Davenport
Albert, Norman, & Edwin Holter
Mrs. Broadwater, Wilder & Charles
Mrs. S.T. Hauser
Tom Hauser
Charles Benton Power